WHISPER
to the
BLOOD

WHISPER
to the
BLOOD

DANA STABENOW

Minotaur Books

New York

This is a work of fiction. All of the characters, organizations, and events portrayed in this novel are either products of the author's imagination or are used fictitiously.

www.minotaurbooks.com

Library of Congress Cataloging-in-Publication Data

Stabenow, Dana.
    Whisper to the blood : a Kate Shugak novel / Dana Stabenow.—1st ed.
        p.   cm
    ISBN-13: 978-0-312-36974-3
    ISBN-10: 0-312-36974-3
    1. Shugak, Kate (Fictitious character)—Fiction.   2. Women private investigators—Alaska—Fiction.   3. Murder—Investigation—Fiction.   4. Alaska—Fiction.
I. Title.

PS3569.T1249 W48 2009
813'.54—dc22   2008033959

First Edition: February 2009

10   9   8   7   6   5   4   3   2   1

This one is for my editor,
Kelley Ragland,
and long overdue.

And if she doesn't mind sharing,
it's also for Andy Martin
and the rest of the Minotaur gang, too.
My heartfelt thanks for the great editor, the great
covers, and all the great wine.

ACKNOWLEDGMENTS

My thanks to Irene Rowan,
whose wonderful and sometimes heartbreaking stories
inspired the plot of this novel.

My thanks to Talia Ross,
for the loan of her way-cool name.

And last but by no means least,
my thanks to Pat and Cliff Lunneborg,
who once said to me, "Do what you love. The money will come."
I've been waiting to say that in a book ever since.

. . . enemies that whisper to the blood. . .

—THEODORE ROETHKE, "PROGNOSIS"

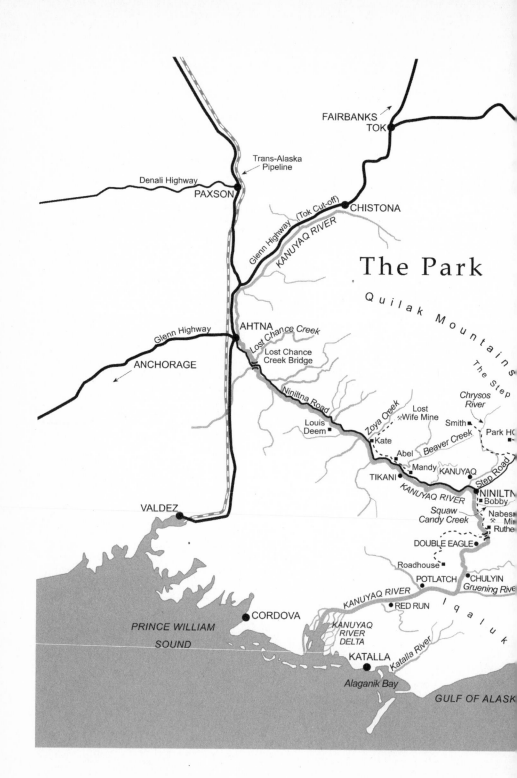

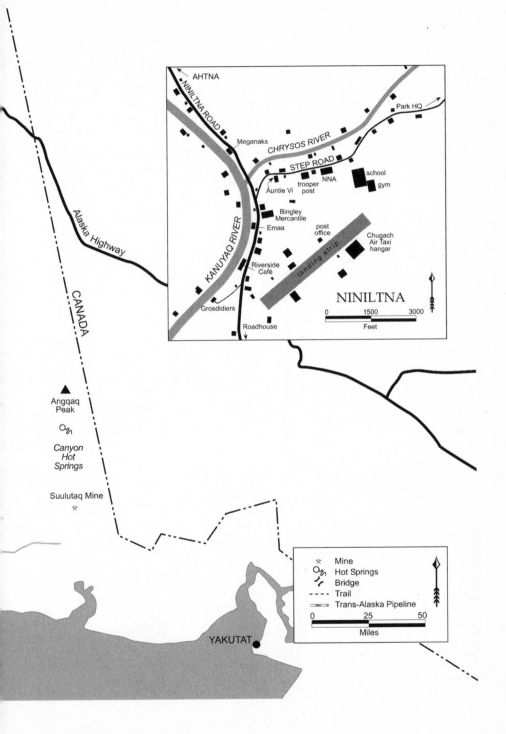

WHISPER
to the
BLOOD

SIX MONTHS AGO

VANCOUVER, BC (AP): A Canadian-based mining firm, Global Harvest Resources Inc. (GHRI), yesterday announced the discovery of a gold, copper and molybdenum deposit on state-leased land in Alaska's Iqaluk Wildlife Refuge. At a press conference at the company's headquarters in Vancouver, British Columbia, GHRI said preliminary estimates put the recoverable gold at 42 million ounces.

"That's more than seven times the total amount of gold mined during the Klondike Gold Rush," said GHRI chief executive officer Bruce O'Malley.

It's not only gold in them thar hills, according to O'Malley. "There are also 24 billion pounds of copper and 1.5 million pounds of molybdenum," a hard metal used to strengthen steel, in what GHRI has named the Suulutaq Mine. *Suulutaq* is the Aleut word for "gold."

At current prices, the gold alone in the Suulutaq Mine is worth over $38 billion.

The governor's office in Juneau issued a press release that said, in part, "The people of Alaska applaud Global Harvest Resources' entrepreneurial efforts in making this discovery, and look forward to a long and profitable relationship with them."

State senator Pete Heiman (R), representing District 41, appeared optimistic when asked about the proposed mine. "Global Harvest has already committed to hiring locally, two thousand employees during construction and a thousand for operation afterward, for as long as the ore holds out," he said. "Anything that puts my constituents to work is a good thing."

Calls to the Niniltna Native Association's headquarters in Niniltna, the community located nearest the prospective mine, were not returned as of press time. The village of Niniltna itself is unincorporated and has no elected officials.

ONE

SEPTEMBER

G rin bought out Mac Devlin."

Kate looked up from the dining room table, where she was wrestling with a time sheet for her last job. It had required extensive surveillance, some of which she had subbed out to Kurt Pletnikoff in Anchorage. Kurt was turning into quite the one-man Continental Op, and while Kate was glad to see the erstwhile Park screwup make good, and while she begrudged none of the hefty percentage of her fee he was earning, the bookkeeping strained her negligible mathematical skills to the red shift limit. It took her a moment to focus on Jim's news. "Grin?"

"Global Harvest Resources Inc. GHRIn. That's what we're calling them around the Park, hadn't you heard?"

"No. Appropriate, though. They have to be grinning from ear to ear."

"To be fair, everyone is—fed, state, local."

"Not everyone local is," Kate said.

"Yeah." Jim slung his jacket around a chair and pulled off the ball cap with the Alaska State Trooper insignia, running a hand through his thatch of dark blond hair. Jim was ever vigilant against hat hair. "And not Mac Devlin anymore, either. He's been operating on a shoestring for years, waiting on the big strike that never came. Last fall he had to sell off all his heavy equipment to pay his outstanding bills. Well, just to gild the lily, whoever his bank is got hit hard in the subprime mortgage mess, so they called in a lot of debt, including what they had on the land his mine sits on."

"And the Nabesna Mine also just happens to sit right on the route to the valley where Global Harvest has its leases," Kate said.

Jim nodded. "Owning the Nabesna Mine will give them easy access."

"Hell," Kate said, "Mac's road into the Nabesna Mine gets them partway there. And give the devil his due, it's a pretty good road."

"Better than the state road into the Park."

"No kidding. Although that's not saying much." She pointed with her chin. "The coffee's fresh. And there's gingerbread."

"Outstanding." He busied himself in the kitchen. "Mac's pretty pissed about the whole deal. You know how he was such a rah-rah boy for the Suulutaq from the get-go? Now he's saying Global Harvest and his bank must have been in cahoots, that they conspired to force him to sell for pennies on the dollar."

"Where's he saying this?"

"At the Roadhouse."

"What were you doing out at Bernie's?"

"Your cousin Martin was making a nuisance of himself again, so I went out to lay down a little law."

Kate sighed. "What'd he do this time?"

"Got stumblebum drunk, tripped over a chair, and spilled a beer on the current quilt."

"Holy shit," Kate said, looking up. "Is he still living?"

Jim regarded the quarter section of gingerbread he had cut with satisfaction, and not a little drool. "The aunties were pissed."

"Imagine my surprise. And Martin?"

Jim looked up and grinned. It was wide and white and predatory. "I think Bernie called me out more to get Martin into protective custody than because Martin was misbehaving in his bar."

"Martin being one of his better customers," Kate said. "Any other news from the front?"

Howie Katelnikof, boon companion to the late and unlamented Louis Deem, had been at the Roadhouse, too, hanging around the outskirts of the aunties' quilting bee, but Howie's life was hanging by a thread where Kate was concerned. Jim thought, on the whole, better not to mention Howie's presence.

It wasn't that Jim, a fair-minded man, didn't understand and to a certain extent didn't even approve of Kate's homicidal intentions toward Howie. He was as certain as he could be, lacking direct, concrete evidence, that Howie was responsible for the attack that had put Kate's truck in the ditch with Kate and Johnny in it, an attack which had also put Mutt in the hospital with a very nearly fatal bullet wound. There would be justice done at some point, no doubt, probably when Howie and the eagerly awaiting Park rats least expected it. Kate knew well the value of patience.

"The usual suspects," he said, in answer to Kate's question. "Pretty quiet on the northern front." He frowned down at the gingerbread, which didn't deserve it. "I have to say, it's been an odd summer all around, though."

Between the case and deckhanding for Old Sam on the *Freya* during the salmon season, Kate was a little out of touch on current Park happenings. "How so?"

He meditated for a moment. "Well, I guess I could sum it up by saying people haven't been calling me."

She looked up at that, amused. "What, are you bored? Suffering from a deficiency of mayhem?"

He smiled briefly and without much humor. "I guess what I mean is I'm getting called out a lot, but only after the fact."

She was puzzled. "I'm sorry? You're always called out after the fact. A crime is committed, victim calls the cops. That's the way it works."

"That's the way things are supposed to work." He put the Saran Wrap back over the cake and leaned on the kitchen counter. "I'll give you an example. Just today, Bonnie had to call me down to the post office to break up a fight between Demetri and Father Smith."

"What happened?"

"Smith dug up a section of Beaver Creek."

Kate thought for a moment. "Demetri has a trapline on a Beaver Creek."

"This would be the same creek. Demetri was seriously pissed off, big surprise, but instead of getting me, or maybe Dan O'Brien, chief ranger of this here Park, to call Smith to account, Demetri tracks him down on his own and proceeds to beat the living crap out of him."

The Smiths were a large family of cheechakos who had bought a homestead from Vinnie Huckabee the year before and had come close to federal indictment for the liberties they had taken with the Park land across their borders, principally with a Caterpillar tractor they had rented from the aforesaid Mac Devlin. "Really," Kate said. "What a shame."

"Yeah, I know, that's why I didn't toss the both of them in the clink. Anyway, I only meant the story as kind of an example of what's been going on."

"A lot of people been messing around on Park lands?"

"No, a lot of people taking the law into their own hands. Demetri alone wouldn't make me think, but when Arliss Kalifonsky shoots Mickey the next time he raises a hand to her, when Bonnie Jeppsen tracks down the kid who put the rotting salmon in the mailbox and keys his truck, and when the aforementioned Dan O'Brien kicks a poacher's ass all over downtown Niniltna when said poacher tries to sell Dan a bear bladder, then I think we can say we might maybe got something of a trend going on."

"Sounds like breakup, only the wrong time of year."

"God, I hope not. One breakup per year is my limit."

He brought cake and coffee to the table and just as he was sitting down she said, "While you're up . . . ," and pushed her mug in his direction. He heaved a martyred sigh and brought her back a full cup well doctored with cream and sugar.

"They're really moving," Kate said. "Global Harvest. Buying out Mac this quick. When did they buy those Suulutaq leases?"

Jim thought back. "When was the final disposition made on the distribution of lands in Iqaluk?"

Iqaluk was fifty thousand acres of prime Alaskan real estate tucked between the Kanuyaq River and Prince William Sound, in the southeast corner of the Park. It boasted one of the last unexploited old-growth forests left in the state, although the spruce had been pretty well decimated by the spruce bark beetle. There were substantial salmon runs in the dozens of creeks draining into the Kanuyaq, and there wasn't a village on the river that didn't run a subsistence fish wheel. With several small caribou herds that migrated between feeding grounds in Canada and breeding grounds on the delta, Iqaluk had been aboriginal hunting grounds for local Alaska Natives for ten thousand years.

It was equally rich in natural resources. Seventy-five years ago oil had been discovered on the coast near Katalla and had been produced until it ran dry. A hundred years ago, the world's largest copper mine had been discovered in Kanuyaq. All that was left of the mine was a group of deserted, dilapidated buildings. Niniltna, the surviving village four miles down the road, had as its origins the Kanuyaq miners' go-to place for a good time. It was a productive mine for thirty-six years, until World War II came along and gave the owners an excuse to close down the then depleted mine and rip up the railroad tracks behind them as they skedaddled Outside with their profits.

With a history like that, it was no wonder that ownership of Iqaluk had been fiercely contested for nearly a century before title was settled, which settlement had satisfied no one. Dan O'Brien, chief ranger, had wanted Iqaluk's total acreage incorporated into the existing Park. The state of Alaska wanted Iqaluk deeded over wholly either to Alaska's Department of Natural Resources or, failing that, to the U.S. Forest Service, famed for its aid and comfort to timber and minerals management companies. The Niniltna Native Association wanted it as a resource for hunting and fishing, if possible solely for its own shareholders and if not, at least for Alaska residents only, managed by a strict permitting process that gave preference to local residents.

Land ownership in Alaska was, in fact, a mess, and had been since Aleksandr Baranov stepped ashore in Kodiak in 1791. Until then Alaska Natives had been under the impression that land couldn't be owned, of which notion Baranov speedily disillusioned them. After the Russians came the Americans, with their gold rushes, Outside fish processors, and world wars, which brought a whole bunch more new people into the territory, including Kate's Aleut relatives, resettled in the Park after the Japanese invaded the Aleutian Islands.

Statehood came, due mostly to political machinations involving Hawaii becoming a state at the same time and Eisenhower wanting to field three Republicans to Congress to balance out the expected three Democrats from the Aloha State. After statehood came the discovery of oil, first in Cook Inlet and then a super-giant oil field at Prudhoe Bay. The new rush was on, to build the Trans-Alaska

Pipeline to bring the crude to market, which project came to a screeching halt when Alaska Natives cleared their collective throats and said, "Excuse me? A forty-eight-inch pipeline across eight hundred miles of aboriginal hunting grounds? That's going to cost you," and made it stick. Passage of the Alaska Native Claims Settlement Act, and later, the Alaska National Interest Lands Conservation Act, pulled a bunch more acreage off the table, which left less than ten percent of Alaska in private hands. Wildlife refuges, national parks, state parks, yes. Farms, ranches, corporate preserves, no.

Of course, a lot of people had made their way to Alaska long before the wherefores and whyases of said acts were a twinkle in Congress's eye, many under the auspices of the Homestead Act, others who came north with the gold rush and stayed, who came north with the army and the air force and returned after mustering out, who came north as crew on fishing boats or canneries, married locally, and settled in for the duration. Their holdings were grandfathered in and the parks and refuges created around them. Which was why Dan O'Brien's map of the Park, on the wall of his office in Park HQ on the Step, had all those minuscule yellow dots on it, each one signifying private ownership.

Land in Alaska, who owned it, and who could do what on it where was in fact a subject that preoccupied an embarrassing amount of everyone's time and attention—public official, corporate officer, and private citizen. Any discussion of the subject was generally preceded by all combatants producing driver's licenses and comparing numbers. The lower the number, the longer they'd been in the state, and the longer they'd been in the state, the louder and longer they got to talk.

"Land ownership in Alaska is like time travel in science fiction," Kate said out loud.

"How so?"

"Just thinking about it makes me dizzy. Where's Martin now?"

9

"Sleeping it off in the lockup. I'll let him out in the morning." He thought for a moment, and added, "If the aunties have calmed down by then. The quilt was for Auntie Edna's granddaughter."

"Yeah, I know. Elly. She's ready to pop any time."

"Who's the dad?"

"She won't say."

Jim took a long look at Kate's closed expression. There had been some muttering about a priest at the private school Elly had attended in Ahtna. No doubt he'd hear all about it in time from Ahtna police chief Kenny Hazen, whether he wanted to or not. He just hoped that if the rumor was true, Auntie Edna wouldn't follow the current trend and settle accounts with the man herself. He shuddered to think of the damage the four aunties could inflict if they put their minds to it. "Any luck on a vehicle for the kid?"

Johnny Morgan, son of Kate's dead lover Jack Morgan and Kate's foster son, had achieved the ripe old age of sixteen, and was now in the market for a vehicle of his very own.

Kate's face cleared. "Bobby's putting it out on Park Air this afternoon. I imagine somebody's got a junker they want to unload."

"You care if it runs?"

She made a face. "I'd rather it didn't."

He laughed out loud this time, and she was forced into a chuckle herself. "I didn't mean it that way," she said. "Or mostly not. I'd just rather he spent some time under the hood before he started driving himself. He should know how to change the oil and a flat and the points and plugs. You know."

"No," he said.

She looked at him, amazed and a little scornful. "You don't know how to change a flat?"

"In theory, I do," he said. "Never had to, though. And I would rather I never had to."

"You will," Kate said with certainty and perhaps with some

smugness mixed in. "Probably in winter. Probably January. The middle of the night. You'll be barreling down the road and one of your tires will pick up an old railroad spike and that'll be it, you'll have to stop and get your hands dirty."

"Or I could call you for help," he said. "You do know how to change a tire."

"That I do," she said.

"I'd expect there to be a price," he said.

"You'd expect correctly," she said.

"And I'd expect to pay it," he said, "in full," and he grinned at her.

The combination of wide grin, crinkled blue eyes, and rumpled dark blond hair was enough to make a grown woman sigh, but if Kate did sigh she kept it to herself. No point in giving Chopper Jim any leverage. Six-foot-four to her five feet, he outweighed her by seventy pounds and was as white as she was Native. Not to mention that he was a serial womanizer and she was strictly a one-man woman. He'd never expressed any interest in having children and here she was, a foster mother, and the kid was the son of Jim's ex-rival for Kate's affections, no less. Plus Jim was a cop and she was a PI.

By any sane standard of measurement, they shouldn't be here. Wherever here was. It's not like either one of them knew.

He ate the last bite of cake and washed it down with the rest of his coffee. "So, where is the kid?"

"At Annie's, splitting wood for her winter supply."

He snorted. "Sure he is."

Annie Mike was the guardian of one Vanessa Cox, Johnny's best bud ever since he'd arrived in the Park. Vanessa had been a gawky and awkward child who was growing into a very attractive young woman. Neither Jim nor Kate held out much hope that Johnny hadn't noticed. "That's my story and I'm sticking to it," Kate said.

"You two have the talk?"

"About seventeen times. I even gave him a box of condoms." She smiled at the memory. "He nearly died."

He laughed. "I bet." He stood up and pulled her to her feet, stepping in close. "Did we have the talk?"

His teeth nibbled at her ear. Her eyes drooped, her nipples hardened, her thighs loosened. 'Twas ever thus with Jim, and it would have annoyed her if she hadn't seen the pulse beating frantically at the base of his throat. "We did," she said, her voice the merest thread of sound.

"Thank god for that," he said, and led her upstairs.

Mutt returned from an extended lope around the homestead, her daily constitutional, nosed the lever handle on the door open, and bounded inside. She had been alerted to the presence of her favorite trooper by his truck in the clearing outside and was impatient to demonstrate her affection upon his person.

Instead, she paused just inside the door to cock a sapient ear at the ceiling. She listened for a moment, and then, displaying a tact it was a shame no one was there to see, quietly let herself out again.

TWO

The following weekend Kate and Johnny were under the hood of a 1981 Ford F-150 short-bed pickup truck, acquired from the son of one of Auntie Balasha's childhood friends, who had died in Ahtna at the age of ninety-seven after a life spent smoking like a chimney, drinking like a fish, and marrying seven times, which, as the son told Kate, "should be a lesson to us all." The truck had less than 75,000 miles on it and the son had sold it to Johnny for $2,500. It was dark blue, the bed offered up only a few rust spots after the most minute inspection, and Kate had thought on the day of purchase and thought now that it was a steal. She had even made a half-hearted attempt to offer the seller more money, an offer the son, an affable man in spite of being named Zebulon Porkryfki, had waved off. "I think Gramps'd like to see it go to a young man all full of juice and go. No, $2,500'll do."

Kate shrugged. "Okay," she said, and Johnny had whooped for joy. He passed his driving test at the Ahtna DMV that afternoon and she let him drive the whole way home. It was his first time behind the wheel over the Lost Chance Creek Bridge, seven hundred feet long, three hundred feet high, the width of one vehicle—barely—and no railings. He made it across, very slowly and very carefully, his knuckles white on the steering wheel. His father had been afraid of heights, too. "He puked on me once when we were at the top of a mine shaft," she told Johnny when they were safely on the other side, and Johnny had laughed so hard he stalled out the truck.

Today they were looking at the engine, a superfluous activity because in operation the pickup sounded like a contented tiger. Kate had had Rachel in Anchorage send up a Chilton's manual for Ford pickups from 1965 to 1986, which had immediately replaced Jim Butcher as Johnny's preferred recreational reading.

Mutt was pacing the perimeter, nose to the ground, picking up a scent for lunch. She was first to hear the vehicle coming down the track from the road. She raised her head and gave Kate a heads-up by way of an advisory yip.

Kate recognized the sound of it almost immediately, and swore beneath her breath. Next to her Johnny went still, frowning at the distributor cap. He said tentatively, "Auntie Vi?"

"Sounds like." She ducked out from under the hood of the pickup and beheld the powder blue Ford Explorer as it emerged from the trees. It drew to an impatient halt, and Auntie Vi, a round, brown little woman of indeterminate age and defiantly black hair, bounced out and stormed in their direction. "Katya!"

Kate recognized the signs. "Have I screwed up anything lately?" she said out of the corner of her mouth.

"Not that I've noticed," Johnny said. "Hi, Auntie Vi!"

"Hi, Johnny! Almost tall like your father now. Stop that."

Johnny grinned. "Yes, ma'am."

Mutt trotted over and paid her respects. Other than Kate, females of any species were usually beneath the notice of the 140-pound wolf/husky mix but Auntie Vi was accorded the respect of a sister sovereign, coequal in power and authority. "This the new truck then?" Auntie Vi said, patting Mutt's head absently as she looked it over with a critical eye. "Those tires need rotate, Katya."

"We'll get right on that, Auntie," Kate said, while Johnny dived cravenly back beneath the hood.

The tires were, in fact, new—bought, mounted, and balanced the day of purchase.

Auntie Vi dismissed the subject of the truck. "You hear, Katya?"

"Hear what, Auntie?"

"About dock."

"What dock?"

"That Katalla dock."

"What Katalla dock?" Kate said. "There's barely a dozen pilings left of the old dock there, and they're rotting and covered with barnacles."

Auntie Vi clicked her tongue, looking impatient. "The state say they starting survey to build new dock."

"What for?" Kate said, and then she said, "Oh. What kind of a dock? Deepwater?"

Auntie Vi was thrown off her stride. "How you know?" she said, suspicion darkening her face.

"If it's a deepwater dock, they're doing it for the bulk carriers that will be coming in to ship the ore out from the Suulutaq Mine."

"There," Auntie Vi said, pointing at Kate. "That! What they do!"

Kate, skewered by the finger, perceived that she was at fault, and found herself at something of a loss. "It only makes sense, Auntie," she said placatingly. "They have to ship the ore to market once they pull it out of the ground. That is the object of the exercise." She stripped the gloves from her hands and started toward the house. "Come inside. It's about time for lunch anyway."

"Grilled cheese!"

Kate grinned without turning around. "In your dreams, kid. Moose liver paté if you're lucky."

Johnny made gagging noises beneath the hood. Mutt departed in search of her own lunch. Auntie Vi followed Kate up the stairs to the deck and into the house. It was still hard for Kate to accept that she had a deck, never mind a house. Both had been a gift of the Park, a product of a Park rat house raising, what, almost two years ago now. She and Johnny each had their own bathroom and bedroom, and what was most amazing of all, she had a refrigerator. And electricity. And a whole bunch of other stuff that even if she thought about it for too long didn't weigh her down as much as she thought it ought to.

Comfort could be corrupting, she thought darkly. What she didn't have was the log cabin her father had built on that same site, the one he had brought her mother home to nearly forty years before, the one she'd been conceived in, had been born in, had grown up in. That cabin had been burned to the ground by someone who had thought to solve all his problems by burning Kate alive. That Johnny had also been living there by then appeared not to have concerned him. He was now a guest of the state in a maximum security prison in Arizona, where Kate cordially hoped he was rotting slowly away, one putrefying limb at a time.

She made coffee and seated Auntie Vi at the table with a mug and cream and sugar, and busied herself with the makings for lunch. "Why are you so upset about this dock, Auntie?"

"Not dock." Auntie Vi looked up from her coffee and said with bitter emphasis, "Mine."

"The Suulutaq Mine?" One grilled cheese for her, half of one for Auntie Vi, and three for Johnny. "That's past praying for, Auntie. Global Harvest bought the leases fair and square from the state, and that's state land."

"We hunt there," Auntie Vi said fiercely. "We fish there." She surged to her feet and thumped her breast with one fist. "We live there!"

"They gave us most of Iqaluk in the settlement, Auntie. Just not that part."

"And you think they don't know that gold there when they did!"

"Well," Kate said. "This is the state of Alaska we're talking about here."

Auntie Vi took in a visible gulp of air, became aware that she was on her feet, and sat down again. "You see plans for this mine?"

Every Park rat with a post office box had gotten the flyer, and just in case they hadn't Global Harvest had blanketed every public place in every town and village in the Park as well, from the Club Bar in Cordova to the Niniltna School gym to the Costco in Ahtna. It was a glossy production, color pictures of salmon spawning in streams, moose browsing in lakes, and caribou calves frolicking in the foothills. There was a map of the proposed mine, fifteen miles square, a tiny gold-colored splotch crowded between grids and graphs of different colors denoting the borders of three federal parks, one state park, two national forests, three marine wildlife refuges, and four separate Native land allotments belonging to four different Native tribes. Towns and villages were dots on the landscape and the map's scale was too small to distinguish the minimal amounts of private property. It was an excellent way to illustrate just how small the acreage in question was.

On the flip side of the flyer, an attractive man displaying a perfect set of teeth in a friendly smile was identified as Global Harvest CEO Bruce O'Malley. Next to his head a conversational balloon quoted O'Malley as saying, "Global Harvest is fully committed to ensuring the healthy stocks of fish and wildlife and all the natural resources of the Iqaluk region so essential to the lives of the people who live there. The Suulutaq Mine can only succeed if Global Harvest Resources becomes a working partner with the people who live next door. We will apply the best available science and technology to ensure an environmentally friendly operation that will coexist with and within the community. Our employees will be drawn as much as possible from that community, and since most estimates have the Suulutaq Mine in operation for a minimum of twenty years, at minimum an entire generation, we expect the relationship to be long and profitable for everyone concerned."

"Yeah, I saw the flyer, Auntie," Kate said. She poured a dollop of olive oil into a hot frying pan and tossed in a chunk of butter after it, and assembled sandwiches made of homemade white bread buttered on both sides, slices of Tillamook Extra Sharp, and green chilies. When the butter melted, the first two hit the pan with a loud and aromatic sizzle. She went to the door, opened it, and yelled, "Lunch!"

"I don't like mine," Auntie Vi said.

She sat there, a round dumpling of rage and, Kate thought, some bewilderment. Auntie Vi had seen a lot of change in her eighty-plus years, and now more of it was bearing down on her like a freight train.

Other Alaskan villages had tribal councils. Some even had mayors and city assemblies. The Park had the four aunties. They were its backbone, its moral center, its royalty. They were all widows, Auntie Vi serially, four or, if Kate's suspicions were correct, possibly five times. They had all been born in the Park, and Auntie Vi was the only one who had ever been farther away from it than Anchorage. This was due to her third husband, an enthusiastic gambler who had introduced her to the illicit joys of one-armed bandits in Vegas before he keeled over of a heart attack after a successful run at the craps table.

The aunties knew the Park and they knew everyone in it chapter and verse, birth to death, white, black, Aleut, Athabascan, or Tlingit, male or female, old or young, married or single, gay or straight, atheist, agnostic, or born-again Christian. They could be found most nights at the Roadhouse, working on the most recent quilt and knocking back Bernie's Irish coffee in quantities that would have had anyone else facedown on the floor. They called it a quilting bee, but everyone else called it holding court. If a kid was a serial misbehaver, he or she was hauled before the aunties when the parents and the schoolteachers threw up their hands. If a husband was beating on his wife, as a last resort before calling in the trooper the wife could complain to the aunties, who would deputize the four Grosdidier brothers to haul him up in front of them. Since the four Grosdidier brothers were also Niniltna village's first responder EMT team, this solved the punishment and the 911 call afterward with neatness and dispatch. If someone let his dog team run wild, to the detriment of another neighbor's ptarmigan patch, and upon protest refused to restrain said team, the neighbor could complain to the aunties, one of whom was always related to the offender's mother and all four of whom had probably babysat him at one time or another.

A summons before the aunties was something no Park rat could ignore. As each individual case demanded, Auntie Joy would look sorrowful, Auntie Balasha would cry, Auntie Edna would glare, and Auntie Vi would fix the offender with a basilisk stare that, combined with the other three aunties' disapproval, generally reduced the Park rat with even the stiffest spine to a gibbering, knee-knocking wreck, sobbing their contrition and swearing on his or her negligible honor never, ever to do it again.

Most of the time it was enough for the offender to slink off beneath the stern admonition to go and sin no more. The aunties were remarkably evenhanded in their dispensation of Park justice, dealing fairly and with very little favoritism with all who came—or were forcibly hauled—before them. Jim Chopin, while taking no official notice of this ad hoc court of civil justice, had been heard to say that the four aunties halved his caseload.

Although even the aunties had their blind spots. Willard Shugak was one. And to Kate's considerable surprise, Howie Katelnikof was another, or had become one lately. Perhaps they had decided that now that he was out from under the influence of Louis Deem, Howie deserved their best redemptive effort. If so, Kate didn't think turning a blind eye to Howie's repeat offender status was quite the right tack.

Kate had her own issues with Howie Katelnikof. However, she knew that Howie wasn't smart enough to stay out of trouble for long. She could wait.

"I don't like mine, Katya," Auntie Vi said again, and Kate was recalled to the present.

"I don't, either, Auntie," Kate said, "but you can't stop it."

Auntie Vi's expression became, naturally, even more obdurate. "Why not?"

Johnny clattered in the door and headed for the kitchen with the single-minded voracity of the average adolescent. "Fuggedaboutit!" Kate said. "Wash those hands or you go hungry."

Johnny rolled his eyes and muttered something about Kate's anal attention to personal hygiene and stamped into the bathroom. Kate served the sandwiches cut in halves with a bowl of tortilla chips and another of salsa. Johnny dived in like he hadn't eaten in a month, and Kate, a notorious feeder, tucked in with only marginally less appreciation, while Auntie Vi nibbled around the edges of her half of a sandwich with the air of someone who seldom ventured beyond the realm of PBJ on pilot bread, and who liked it that way just fine, thank you. An occasional desecration of mac and cheese by diced ham was about as far into the culinary wilderness as any of the four aunties cared to go.

Afterward Johnny cleared the table and washed up and Kate walked Auntie Vi to her car. "Look at it this way, Auntie," Kate said. "We're Alaskan citizens. We'll get royalties. More, as citizens of the region, we'll get jobs. If there's steady work, maybe some of the kids will move home from Anchorage. Maybe some of them won't leave in the first place."

Auntie Vi closed the driver-side door and Kate thought she might have gotten away clean, until Auntie Vi rolled down her window. "That what you say at meeting?"

Kate's heart sank. "The board meeting?"

Auntie Vi gave her an impatient look. "What other meeting there is?"

The board of directors of the Niniltna Native Association met quarterly, in January, April, July, and October. Last year, board president and NNA CEO Billy Mike had died, leaving a vacancy. Without even running, indeed over her strong objections, Kate had been nominated to fill out the rest of his term, largely at the instigation of the diminutive woman at present fixing her with the beady eye through the car window.

Kate had missed her first NNA board meeting in July by virtue of the fact that she had been deckhanding for Old Sam Dementieff during the salmon season. Disapproval of her dereliction of duty was ameliorated by the fact that three other board members, Demetri Totemoff, Harvey Meganack, and Old Sam himself, were also fishing. Impossible to argue with the fact that everyone needed to make a living, and that in Alaska much of the time that meant working through the summer. So it was with a reasonable certainty that she would not be scolded, at least not for that, that Kate felt she could say, "I'm not Emaa, Auntie."

"Nobody say so," Auntie Vi said.

"Like hell," Kate said.

Auntie Vi looked away, scowling to hide what Kate knew was a beginning smile. Kate was the only one who dared to lip off to Auntie Vi, and though she'd never admit it, Auntie Vi enjoyed the fight.

"I'm not Emaa," Kate said again. "Don't make the mistake of

thinking I am. Running the Niniltna Native Association for the rest of my life is not on my agenda. I've got a life, I have a job that pays pretty well, I have Johnny to provide for, and I have a home to look after. Don't say it!" She held up a hand, palm out.

Auntie Vi did her best to look wounded. "Not say nothing."

"Yeah, but you were thinking it." They both looked at the house, a virtual palace by Park standards, built in three days and change by a volunteer army of Park rats. "I'm grateful, I always will be, but not to the point of indentured servitude."

"You not coming to meeting?" Auntie Vi said sharply.

Kate sighed. The next meeting was October 15th, a month away. "Of course I'm coming. I said I would, and I don't make promises I'm not going to keep."

"So you saying what, then?"

"I'm saying I'm not Emaa," Kate said, meeting Auntie Vi's eyes without flinching. "I am not my grandmother. Don't think I'm going to lead an effort against the Suulutaq Mine. I'm not against progress. I'm not against change. I'm not against industry coming into the Park, especially if it's going to bring jobs with it."

Auntie Vi was staring at her with a stony expression, and Kate smiled, a little grimly. "Kinda sorry you forced me onto the board now, aren't you, Auntie?"

Auntie Vi snorted, and thereby avoided a direct answer to a simple question, a skill all the aunties were famous for. "You say mine bring jobs. Hah! Jobs for Outsiders, maybe. No jobs for us."

"Auntie," Kate said. "The mine workers are going to need a place to wash their clothes. They're going to want to buy potato chips. They're going to want to mail packages. Sometimes they're just going to want a night away from camp, out on the town, even if that town is dry. They can buy a burger and a latte at the Riverside, cookies at one of the basketball team's bake sales. They could even have a beer at Bernie's if they can score a ride that far. Two thousand workers during construction, Auntie. Niniltna will be the closest community to them." Kate shrugged. "We've even got a road out. Well. For half the year anyway."

Auntie Vi leveled an admonitory finger. "What about road, Katya? Not good enough for big trucks. They pave it, then what?"

The thought of semi-tractor trailers running in and out of the Park a quarter of a mile from her doorstep did not please Kate at all. "Hah!" Auntie Vi said, triumphant. "Everything change with mine, Katya. Everything! Not just digging big hole in some land away far from here." She started the engine. "You be at that meeting."

"I said I would be, Auntie."

"October fifteenth!"

"Yes, Auntie."

"That on a Wednesday!"

"Yes, Auntie."

"Ten A.M.!"

"Yes, Auntie."

Auntie Vi nodded, a sharp, valedictory movement. "You be there."

"Yes, Auntie."

Auntie Vi held up a finger. "Forgot." She jerked a thumb backward. "I bring something to you."

Kate opened the rear passenger-side door and found a small U-Haul box. "What's this?"

"Association stuff. You take."

"I've got the newsletter, Auntie, I don't need—"

"You take!"

Kate took, and without further ado or admonition Auntie Vi stepped on the gas. The Explorer wheeled around in something approaching a brody, narrowly missing Mutt emerging incautiously from the brush. She yelped and affected a kind of reverse vertical insertion, levitating up and back so that Auntie Vi's tires just missed her toes. She looked at Kate, ears straight up and yellow eyes wide.

"You got off lucky," Kate said. She turned to see Johnny had come out on the railing of the deck.

"So," he said, "you going to that meeting next month?"

Her eyes narrowed.

He leaned on the railing and grinned. "You know. The one on Wednesday?"

She dumped the box in the back of his truck and started for the house.

"On the fifteenth?" He started to back up. "You know, the one at ten A.M.?"

She hit the bottom stair and he ran for his life.

THREE

Johnny sat very straight behind the wheel of his pickup as he made his first solo journey into Niniltna the next morning. He drove with sobriety and caution, and pulled into Annie Mike's driveway with nary a flourish.

This sedate impression of middle age disintegrated when the front door opened and Van stepped out onto the porch.

Vanessa Cox's posture was so good that she would always seem taller than she was. Her dark hair was thick, fine, and straight, cut bluntly to brush her shoulders, with a spiky fringe to frame her dark eyes. She had a slim, straight nose, a full, firm mouth, and a delicately pointed chin.

For years her attire had consisted of bibbed denim overalls with a marsupial front pocket and buckled shoulder straps, worn over a T-shirt in summer and a turtleneck in winter, usually accessorized with Xtra Tuffs and a down jacket. Recently, her wardrobe had expanded to include low-rider jeans, cropped T-shirts, and Uggs. She wore thin gold hoops in her ears and her lips shone with gloss.

Johnny didn't notice any of this in detail, of course. All he knew was that his best buddy Van had suddenly and inexplicably turned into a girl. "You look good," he said.

Her answering smile revealed a surprising set of dimples, a crooked left incisor, and a sparkle in her eyes that was as unsettling as it was exhilarating. "Thank you," she said demurely.

"Want a ride?"

She hopped in without answering. He may have put little more English on his departure than he had on his arrival, and who can blame him?

It was a beautiful day, barely a wisp of cloud to obstruct the view of the Quilak Mountains scratching a harsh line into the eastern sky. The Kanuyaq was as yet ice-free, and running low after a dry spring and a warm summer had pushed all the snowmelt down to the Gulf. The days were crisp, the nights cool but not yet cold. Canada geese practiced their V formations overhead, browsing moose cows were waiting for the siren call of moose bulls in rut, and two yearling griz- zly cubs shot across the road inches in front of the blue pickup's bumper. Johnny took his foot off the gas but retained enough wit not to stamp on the brakes, and the cubs' hindquarters disappeared into the brush on the other side of the road. A second later and he would have clipped their hindquarters.

Johnny pulled to a halt at the corner, where Annie's driveway met the road to the Niniltna School, and paused. He looked at Van and suddenly driving up to school in his very own vehicle in front of all the kids seemed less appealing. On impulse, he turned left.

"This isn't the way to school," Van said. She had her window down and the cab was filled with the sound of dry leaves and fallen spruce needles crinkling beneath the truck's tires.

"I was thinking we could skip."

"Skip school?" she said.

"Just once," he said. He patted the steering wheel and gave her a sidelong grin. "We don't have to make a habit out of it, but today's kind of a special day."

She considered. "Where do you want to go?"

There weren't a lot of places to hang out in the Park, and that was a fact. "We could go watch the bears at the dump," he said.

She smiled. "Been there, done that."

"It's a nice day. We could hike up to the Lost Wife Mine."

She shook her head. "I don't feel like sweating."

"Riverside Café and the espresso drink of your choice?"

She raised one shoulder and let it fall. She turned her head and opened her eyes. One eyebrow might have raised, ever so slightly.

"Want to go to Ahtna?" he said.

Technically, he had his driver's license. He had his own truck in his own name, bought and paid for with his own money, earned in a dozen odd jobs. He had deckhanded with Kate for Old Sam Dementieff the previous summer. He'd hauled, cut, and stacked wood for Auntie Balasha, Auntie Joy, Auntie Vi, and Annie Mike. He'd swabbed floors at the Roadhouse and canned salmon for Demetri Totemoff. He'd even helped Matt Grosdidier smoke silver salmon the month before, although for that job he'd gotten paid in fish, not that he was complaining. Neither was Kate. He'd even filed paperwork for Ranger Dan and Chopper Jim.

And it wasn't like Kate had told him he couldn't go to Ahtna if he wanted to. Of course, he hadn't asked her. Mostly because he had had a pretty good idea of what her answer would be, especially if he was cutting school the second week of the year, and using his brand-new truck to do it. And then of course there was the little matter of his license being provisional until he was eighteen. He could drive himself but he wasn't supposed to drive anyone else underage. But who bothered with that in the Bush?

He had a niggling feeling that Kate and Jim both might have an answer for that. What they would like even less was their destination. Ahtna was a big town, over three thousand in the town proper. Every student in Park schools had been weaned on stories about the kids at Peratrovich High.

Ahtna was the biggest town closest to the Park, bigger even than Cordova, and you had to fly or take a boat to Cordova. Ahtna had a movie theater, a courthouse, a DMV, a Safeway, and a Costco, making it the market town for the Park. It had bars, and two liquor stores. The Park had Bernie's Roadhouse, where owner, proprietor, and bartender Bernie Koslowski by virtue of also being the Niniltna basketball coach knew the birthday of every kid in the Park. There was no buying a drink at the Roadhouse if you were underage.

Ahtna was a different story. It was easy, so they said, to get lost in the crowd in Ahtna. It was easy to pass for legal. All you needed was a fake ID, and sometimes you didn't even need that. The very mention of Ahtna's name brought an intoxicating whiff of sin to any Niniltnan in his or her teens, and a corresponding shiver of fear to their parents.

But "Sure," Van said, before he could think better of his invitation, and smiled at him again.

They went to Ahtna forthwith.

It wasn't an easy drive, a battered gravel road that had begun life as a remnant of the railroad roadbed for the Kanuyaq River & Northern Railroad, built to haul copper ore from the Kanuyaq copper mine to the seaport in Cordova, there to be loaded onto bulk carriers and shipped to foundries Outside. The copper ran out after thirty years and the mining company left, pulling up the railroad tracks behind it. Unfortunately, they weren't quite as conscientious about the railroad spikes that had held the tracks together.

The road had not improved in the interim. Maintained by a state grader twice a year, once in the spring after breakup and once in the fall before the first snow, it was ridged and potholed, with shoulders crumbling to narrow a road that was barely wide enough for one car to begin with. Overgrown in some places with alder and stands of rusty brown spruce killed from the spruce bark beetle, and with cottonwoods where it crossed creeks, the road of necessity to its original purpose followed the most level possible ground, which meant it followed the twisting, winding course of one river and creek after another, which did not make for good visibility. Head-on collisions were frequent occurrences, as were sideswipes and rollovers, as the only places to pull over were the trailheads into cabins, homesteads, mining claims, and fish camps.

Johnny negotiated all these hazards more or less successfully, and even managed to cross the bridge at Lost Chance Creek without incident. It was a relief when they hit pavement just outside of Ahtna. When he'd driven that road the last time, he'd had Kate with him. Kate was the grown-up, his legal guardian, and as such responsible for him. This time, he was with Vanessa. It was his truck, and it had been his idea to go to Ahtna. Plus, she had that whole girl thing going on.

Not that he ever thought of women as the weaker sex, in need of protection from the big strong he-man. Not with Kate Shugak an in-his-face example every day, he didn't. It was just . . . well, he wasn't sure what just it was. All he knew was that this trip was his responsibility and he didn't want it ending in a ditch somewhere between Ahtna and Niniltna.

Van gave a little wriggle of delight when the ride smoothed out and all seven thousand parts of the pickup stopped banging against each other, which noise was replaced by the hiss of vulcanized rubber on asphalt. "I love paved roads," she said.

He grinned at her. "Me, too. So, where do you want to go first?"

"Costco," she said instantly.

He pretended to groan. "Shopping. I shoulda known. Do you have a card?"

She nodded enthusiastically. "I'm on Annie's family card."

So they spent a solid hour in the hangar-sized big box, Van trying on every item of clothing, male and female, there was on offer, Johnny mooning up and down the tools and auto parts aisles, and both of them drifting inexorably to the book table.

"That was fun," she said as they were leaving.

He gave her a quizzical look. "We didn't buy anything."

She gave him a sunny smile. "So what? Someday we will."

He laughed. "Okay. Where next? You hungry?"

"Starving!"

He could have taken her to McDonald's—Ahtna had one of those, too—but Johnny was determined to be cooler than that. "Can we afford this?" she said, wide-eyed, as they pulled into the parking lot of the Ahtna Lodge.

He grinned at her. "I didn't spend all my money on Old Blue, here," he said, patting the dashboard. He opened the door and said over his shoulder, "Most of it, but not all of it." His grin widened when he heard her laugh behind him. She'd had the same laugh since he'd first met her, a loud, brash blare of no-holds-barred amusement that sounded like it came right out of one of the songs of those old blues singers Kate listened to sometimes, raunchy, rough-edged, knowing, sad. He'd seen adults startled and sometimes alarmed by that laugh, as if they hadn't expected it to come out of the mouth of someone so quiet, or so young.

He didn't see the man in the parking lot turn his head at the sound of that laugh, gaze at Van for a moment, and then look at Johnny. He didn't see the man's eyes widen. Johnny held out his hand and Van came around the front of the pickup and took it as if it was the most natural thing in the world, as if they'd been holding hands for years.

They walked up the steps and through the restaurant doors. A slender, dark-haired man with a gold hoop earring in one ear and a white apron wrapped twice around his slim waist spotted Johnny at once. "Hey, kid," he said, shifting the tray of dirty dishes he was holding from one shoulder to the other so he could shake Johnny's hand. "How you been? How's Kate?"

Mercifully, he did not comment on its being a school day, which Johnny was belatedly realizing could be a question raised by everyone who knew who he was and who he lived with. "Good," Johnny said, "we're both good. Tony, this is my friend Vanessa."

Vanessa looked startled. It was the first time Johnny had called her anything but Van. Johnny pretended not to notice, too busy pretending to be a grown-up.

"Hey, Vanessa," Tony said, giving her an appraising look as he shook her hand. He winked at Johnny. "You hungry?"

"Stan cooking?" Stan being Tony's partner in life and in the Ahtna Lodge and the genius behind the steak sandwiches that were a magnet for everyone within a hundred miles.

"That he is."

"Then we're starving. Can we get a table by the window?"

Tony looked over his shoulder. "Give me five minutes, and it's yours."

"Thanks, Tony."

They were seated and they both ordered the specialty of the house. In the interval, two virgin daiquiris arrived, ice and syrup and strawberries whipped to a froth and swirled into glasses the size of hubcaps.

A delighted smile spread across Van's face.

"Uh," Johnny said, loath to see the smile go away. "We didn't order these, Tony."

Tony nodded at the bar. "Courtesy of your friend."

Uh-oh. Johnny turned his head, hoping against hope it wasn't anybody like Ahtna police chief Kenny Hazen, who would be sure to mention that he'd seen Johnny in Ahtna on a school day the next time he saw Jim.

It wasn't Chief Hazen. It was instead someone almost as tall, but with a rangier build and a broad face that smiled at Johnny from beneath the bill of a Colorado Rockies ball cap.

"Who is that?" Vanessa said.

"I don't—" Johnny stopped. "Doyle?" He half rose from his chair, his voice uncertain. "Doyle Greenbaugh?"

Greenbaugh's laugh was hearty. He walked to their table and smacked Johnny's hand in an enthusiastic grip. "For a minute I thought you didn't recognize me. How you doing, Johnny?"

"For a minute I didn't," Johnny said, returning Greenbaugh's handshake. "What are you doing in Alaska, Doyle?"

Greenbaugh shrugged, still grinning. "It's your fault. You made it sound pretty good. I figured I'd come up and see how much you were bullshitting me." He nodded over Johnny's shoulder. "Who's your friend?"

Johnny, on his first date with his first—he was pretty sure—his first real girlfriend, could not resist the urge to show off a little. "Doyle," he said proudly, "this is Vanessa Cox." He'd even remembered to introduce the girl first. "Van, this is Doyle Greenbaugh." He hesitated, and then said, "I know him from Outside."

"How do, ma'am," Greenbaugh said. He actually removed his cap and even gave a nod that was halfway to a bow.

Vanessa, as yet unaccustomed to male deference to the fairer sex, tried for a regal inclination of the head in reply. Her pinkened cheeks gave her away, though.

"We drove in for lunch," Johnny said, adding manfully, "Would you like to join us?"

Greenbaugh waved a hand. "No, no, I don't want to intrude." He turned his head so Vanessa couldn't see and winked. *I won't horn in on your action.*

Johnny felt his ears get hot, and mumbled something in reply.

"We should get together and catch up, though," Greenbaugh

said. "You live in Ahtna? I thought it was another town, can't remember the name of it. Ninilchik?" He mispronounced it "NIN-il-chik." You could always tell when someone was new to the state by how badly they mangled the place names.

"Actually, it was Anchorage," Johnny said, "but it's Niniltna now."

"How's that?"

"Nuh-NILT-nuh."

"Niniltna," Greenbaugh said. "That close to here?"

"East, up a gravel road a hundred miles or so."

"It the size of this place?"

Johnny laughed. "Not hardly. Only a couple hundred people."

Greenbaugh made a face. "That small, probably no jobs."

"You looking for work?"

Greenbaugh shrugged. "Gotta eat."

"There's an outfit starting up a gold mine in the Park," Johnny said impulsively. Van, sitting with her eyes downcast, looked at Johnny briefly and then down again. "They say there are going to be a lot of jobs in it."

Greenbaugh brightened. "A gold mine?"

"I could maybe talk to somebody for you."

"Man, I'd appreciate that."

"Well, it's not like I don't owe you," Johnny said. Van looked up again, dark eyes on his face. "You staying here in Ahtna?"

"Yeah, I got a room here."

"Got transportation?"

"Got a little Nissan pickup, packed with all my worldly belongings. Which ain't much."

"What happened to your rig?"

Greenbaugh grimaced. "One deadhead too many. Bank repossessed her."

"Damn. I'm sorry, Doyle."

"Luck of the draw. Why I came north, start over."

"Lot of people do that," Johnny said. "Lot of people drop their past life at the Beaver Creek border crossing."

Greenbaugh grinned. "You seen a lot of that in your long life, have you?"

Johnny felt his ears get red again. "It's just something Kate says."

"Who's Kate? Vanessa's competition?" He grinned at Vanessa, who didn't grin back.

For a moment Johnny was stumped for a reply. "Kate's who I live with. She's my legal guardian. You probably forgot, but my dad's dead, and my mom's . . . well, my mom's out of the picture."

Greenbaugh gave a thoughtful nod. "I remember now. Your mom's the one stuck you with your grandparents in Arizona. You didn't like it, so you left. This Kate was who you were headed for when we met?"

"Yeah."

"What's she do?"

Johnny shrugged. "Whatever she can do to make a buck."

Greenbaugh raised an eyebrow.

Johnny flushed beet red. "Not that!" he said. "Jeez! What I mean is she's like any other Park rat, she hunts, fishes, traps sometimes." Johnny felt Vanessa look at him again, and avoided looking back. He didn't know why he didn't tell Greenbaugh what Kate did for a living. It wasn't like Greenbaugh wouldn't know five minutes after he stepped into the Park. Or even if he stuck around Ahtna long enough.

"Park rat?" Greenbaugh said.

Johnny laughed a little too loudly, relieved at the change of subject. "It's what we call ourselves."

" 'Ourselves'?"

"I'm a Park rat now, too," Johnny said, betraying his youth with his pride.

Greenbaugh shrugged. "Okay. Any place decent for a man to stay in Niniltna?"

"Nuh-NILT-nuh," Johnny said again. Again, he hesitated, and then said, "Sure, just ask the way to Auntie Vi's, she runs a B and B in town. I'll tell her you're coming."

"Sounds good. Thanks, kid."

"Thanks for the drinks."

"Be seeing you." Greenbaugh sketched a wave and was gone. Johnny sat back down.

"How do you know him?" Vanessa said.

At that moment Stanislav himself brought out their steak sandwiches, a platter upon which red meat sizzled with a heavenly aroma, and everything else was put on hold.

But Vanessa hadn't forgotten, and on their way home and safely past the Lost Chance Creek Bridge she said, "How do you know that Greenbaugh guy?"

Johnny negotiated a turn with care. "It's just somebody I met on the way home from Arizona. You heard him."

"Hey, look, another moose," Vanessa said. "What's that make, the tenth or twelfth one we've seen today? Annie says when they come down out of the mountains this early it means a long cold winter." She turned to him again. "Come on, Johnny. Who is that guy?"

Johnny sighed. "Okay. Remember I told you my mom sent me to Arizona when my dad died?"

"Yes. You told me the two of you didn't get along."

That was an understatement. "No. We don't." In a burst of candor he added, "I don't think she even liked me that much. Mostly she just used me to piss off Dad."

Van said nothing, and Johnny appreciated her tact. "So when he died, she didn't need me around anymore, so she sent me to her folks in Arizona."

"And you didn't like it there."

"No," he said, very definitely. "So I hitchhiked home. Doyle Greenbaugh was one of the guys who picked me up. He was driving a semi. He picked me up outside Phoenix and took me all the way to Seattle."

"Oh." She digested this in silence for a moment. "So he followed you up here? That's kinda creepy."

Johnny shrugged. "It was a long drive. We talked a lot. He asked me where I was going, and I told him I was going home. He'd never been to Alaska, and he wanted to know what it was like." And he hadn't asked Johnny any uncomfortable questions, like why somebody Johnny's age was standing with his thumb out on an interstate in the middle of the night. "He was a good guy, and he didn't try anything."

She knew a faint chill. "Did someone else? Johnny?"

He shifted in his seat. "Maybe. Yeah." He risked a look at her. "Don't worry, I figured out what was going on in time and I bailed before anything happened."

She swallowed. "That's . . . that's awful, Johnny."

"Woulda been," he said. "Wasn't. I was careful."

"And lucky."

"And lucky," he said, nodding. He hadn't thought about it at the time, but he'd thought about it after, or he had when Kate had finally stopped yelling at him. He had been very lucky.

Van said, "How come your mom lets you live with Kate?"

"I'm sixteen now, so it's my choice. But before, when I got here? I think Kate blackmailed her."

Van turned her head to stare at him, eyes wide, and grabbed for the dash when the truck jounced through a pothole. "You're kidding."

"Nope."

"What did she blackmail her with?"

"I don't know. I don't want to know. All I cared about was staying with Kate, and Kate made it happen. She made Jane give her custody." He smiled at her. "And here I am."

She drew a deep breath. "Yeah. Yes, you are. Did I say thank you for today? It's been fun."

"Yeah," he said, happily. "It has, hasn't it?"

"Pull over," she said impulsively.

"Huh?"

"Pull over. There, at that trailhead."

"How come?" Johnny said, obediently pulling over and putting the pickup into park.

"So I can do this." She slid across the bench seat and put her arms around his neck. She smiled at him, a little shyly, and kissed him. Her lips were warm and soft, and she smelled faintly of flowers, and maybe a little bit of wood smoke.

"Wow," he said, dazed, when she raised her head.

Her cheeks were pink. "There," she said. "Our first kiss. Now we don't have to fumble around worrying about if you want to, or if I want you to."

"I want to," he said fervently. "I've wanted to for a long time."

"I know," she said. "I wasn't ready."

"It's okay," he said, anxious that she wouldn't take his comment as a rebuke.

"Yes, it is," she said smartly, and he had to laugh.

They drove home in a glow of delicious contentment. They got back to Niniltna at about three thirty, safely past the hour school let out, and they stopped by Auntie Vi's. They found her in her net loft, a length of salmon net draped in front of her, thin green monofilament in a spool at her feet, the needle a blur as she mended the holes put in it by last summer's salmon catch. "Hey, girl," she said as they came up the stairs. "You want job?"

"I've never mended nets before, Auntie," Vanessa said.

Auntie Vi waved a hand. "No problem, I teach. Tomorrow morning, you come." She eyed Johnny. "What you want?"

Wise in the ways of Auntie Vi, Johnny was not put off by this brusque inquiry, and told her she might have a paying guest shortly.

She grunted. "Maybe I got room, maybe I don't."

"Maybe he'll come and maybe he won't," Johnny said promptly.

"You watch that mouth before your elders!" Auntie Vi said, but he saw the corners of her mouth twitch irrepressibly upward as they left.

When he drew up outside Annie Mike's, he made as if to kiss her. She warded him off. "Not where people can see us," she said. "That kind of thing should be private, and personal. Besides, we'd have to answer a bunch of questions, and then Annie'd want to have the talk again, and she'd tell Kate—"

He held up a hand in pretend despair. "Got the picture. I am convinced." He smiled at her. "But you want to."

She laughed, and hesitated. "Listen, Johnny. This Greenbaugh guy?"

"Yeah?"

Her brow creased, and she looked down at her clasped hands. He waited. She looked up and said simply, "He has eyes like a calculator."

There was a brief, startled silence.

"I don't know what that means," Johnny said tentatively. "I'm guessing you don't like him?"

She chose not to answer him, or to answer only obliquely. "He gave you a ride when you needed one, and he didn't try to mess with you. Those are good things."

"But?"

She looked up to give him a grave smile. "I don't know, exactly. I just get the feeling there is a lot more going on there than he lets on."

It was one thing for him to second-guess Greenbaugh's sudden appearance. It was another to fall in with Van's doubts. Johnny snorted. "Him and every second Park rat we know."

"Yeah." She slid out of the pickup. "Thanks again for today. I had a good time."

"Me, too. Tomorrow?"

She shook her head. "I'd love to, but I'm working for Auntie Vi tomorrow."

"Oh yeah, that's right."

"What do we say if they find out we skipped school?"

"Don't lie," he said.

"Will Kate ground you?"

He grinned and patted the steering wheel, chock-full of sixteen years' worth of bravado. "She can try."

FOUR

OCTOBER 15

W hat?" Kate said.

Auntie Joy beamed at her. "You chairman of board, Katya." She applauded, and was joined in that action immediately and with attitude by Old Sam Dementieff, more moderately by Demetri Totemoff, and belatedly and without enthusiasm by Harvey Meganack. Harvey was sitting on Kate's right and she could almost warm her hands on his resentment. He was dressed in gray slacks and a white button-down shirt. He hadn't actually put on a tie but there was the sense that he would have if he knew the effort wouldn't have been wasted on the rest of them, not to mention ridiculed by every Park rat who saw him that day.

Demetri sat on Harvey's other side in jeans, blue flannel shirt, and dark blue fleece vest. Next to him and across from Kate was Auntie Joy, a plump little brown bird with bright eyes and long graying hair tucked into a neat bun skewered with lacquered red chopsticks. The red matched her blouse, long-sleeved and loose over the elastic waistband of black polyester slacks. Auntie Joy always matched and was always comfortable.

Old Sam, dressed in Carhartt bib overalls and a faded black and red plaid shirt worn bare at the elbows, sat exactly midway between Auntie Joy and Kate, smelling aggressively of the summer's fishing season and not about to apologize for it.

"Wait a minute," Kate said. At Auntie Joy's words, any outward calmness of demeanor she had assumed before arriving at the Niniltna Native Association building that morning had deserted her. Now something close to panic was crawling over her skin with delicate spider feet. "I said I'd be on the board. I didn't say I'd be chairman."

"You're the only one who could be, girl." Old Sam looked at Harvey, who scowled at the top of the round table occupying center stage in the Association board room. "The only other candidate failed to gather a majority."

In spite of herself Kate's voice rose. "We didn't even vote yet."

"The board had an ad hoc meeting last night."

"Nobody told me."

Old Sam gave Harvey a sardonic look from beneath bristly brows. "Can't understand that."

"Anyway," Kate said, feeling desperate and not working real hard to conceal it, "I thought the shareholders vote on who's chairman. The same way we vote on board members."

Demetri, a short, stocky man with dark hair, steady eyes, and a stubborn jaw, said, "In the event of the death of a current member of the board, the bylaws allow the board to name a replacement. The candidate must be a shareholder and must be of legal age. The bylaws also allow the board to name a new chair. Both are interim appointments until the next annual shareholder meeting, when the entire membership votes to accept or reject the slate of officers."

41

"In January," Auntie Joy said helpfully, still beaming.

January, Kate thought numbly. January 15th. Three very long months from now. "I wasn't here," she said. "I didn't get to vote."

"Wouldna mattered," Old Sam said, "you weren't on the board yet, so you didn't have a vote anyway. And even if you were, the vote was three to one," and he smiled, not at all amiably, at Harvey, whose grinding of teeth was audible.

"But—" Kate was beginning to feel like she was lost in the middle of a Joseph Heller novel.

"It's done, girl," Old Sam said, and slid a piece of paper down the table. "Let's get on with it. I've got other things to do today."

The piece of paper proved to be the agenda for the meeting, embossed with the Niniltna Native Association logo.

The Association logo had been the subject of a great deal of controversy when the Association was first formed over thirty years before. One group of shareholders had held out for art, another for commerce, a third for culture, a fourth for history, and a fifth for the artist of their choice, usually a near relation. The divergent opinion resulted in a verbal fight at the first shareholders meeting that very nearly ended in a riot which, legend had it, Emaa quelled by sheer force of personality. The resulting logo, designed by committee, was a jumbled ball of black silhouette images, a leaping salmon, a browsing moose, a Sitka spruce, a jagged mountain with what might have been a tiny mine entrance halfway up it, a dogsled with the musher snapping his whip over the dogs' heads, a dancer with a drum, a seiner with its nets out, a gold pan. That many images were, of necessity if there were to be anything written on the rest of the page, minuscule, and as such difficult to identify. At first glance the whole thing looked like a Rorschach inkblot. This had of course pleased no one, but Ekaterina Shugak, Kate's grandmother and the first board chair, had been impatient to move on to more important topics and had pushed it through.

Kate said the first thing that came into her head. "God, that's ugly."

Old Sam gave out with a stentorian guffaw. Auntie Joy's radiance dimmed a trifle. Harvey and Demetri said nothing. Belatedly, Kate realized that all four of them would have had their own opinions on the NNA logo long before Kate was old enough to vote as a shareholder. She looked around, casting about desperately for a less incendiary topic.

The Niniltna Native Association headquarters was a modest, rectangular building two stories high. It had asphalt shingles, vinyl siding, vinyl windows, and an arctic entryway, and was painted brown with white trim. It sat on the side of a hill in back of the village, next to the state trooper's post on the road to the airstrip.

The board met in a corner room upstairs, with windows in two walls, large sliders equipped with screens. Through them could be seen the washed-out blue sky and the thin sunlight of an arctic fall day, with the gathering edge of an ominous bank of dark cloud. Snow was late this year, and the temperature was dropping fast, putting pipes at risk of freezing all over the Park.

The room held a table, and like almost every project involving shareholder funds, it was made from spruce bark beetle kill harvested from Association lands. The blight had swept through spruce forests across southeastern and southcentral Alaska over the last ten years the way the bubonic plague had swept over the world in 1350. Sensibly, the board had reasoned that if the spruce trees were going to fall over dead anyway, they might as well put them to good use. There were spruce bark beetle kill countertops, cupboards, floors, paneling, sleigh beds, rocking chairs, and farmhouse tables in every public and private building in the Park.

This table had been made by Demetri to Ekaterina's specific instructions, round in shape, because Ekaterina didn't think there ought to be a head to a table where sat equals, and modest in size, because Ekaterina disapproved of large governing boards. Privately, Kate thought it was because Emaa knew that smaller groups were more easily manipulated.

The table was sanded and polished to a satin gloss, although the individual boards did have a tendency to bow occasionally. Annie Mike had been in the room once when one of the boards, imperfectly dried, had split open with a crack like a .30–06 going off. Demetri had mended it with epoxy but it could still be seen, a narrow lightning bolt of rich dark brown running almost all the way from Auntie Joy to Kate.

Annie, Association secretary-treasurer and its only full-time employee, was there today, too, sitting at a small desk in the corner, taking notes on a laptop. Annie's husband, Billy Mike, previous chair of the Niniltna Native Association, had died last year of a massive coronary. They'd lost their son Dandy the year before and after a double whammy like that everyone would have understood if Annie had retreated into a life centered around her last two children left at home. Both were orphans, both adopted. The baby boy, half Korean, half African-American, was named Alexei for Annie's grandfather. Vanessa Cox, who had lost first her parents to an automobile accident Outside and then her last surviving relatives here in the Park, one to murder and the other to jail, had been acquired the following year.

Contrary to conventional wisdom, Annie had not retreated. Instead, she had soldiered on, doing her duty by Association as secretary-treasurer and by Park as an upstanding Park rat, first in line to offer aid and comfort to those in need. She was pretty much an auntie in waiting, Kate thought. She looked up now from her computer, and the sympathy in her expression made Kate realize that the four board members were sitting in various states of impatience, waiting for Kate to start the meeting.

She looked down at the agenda. Reading and approval of minutes.

Reports. Unfinished business. New business. How hard could this be? She sat up straight and cleared her throat. "Okay. Somebody read the minutes so we can approve them."

There was silence. Kate looked up. "What?"

There was a look of dawning realization in Harvey's eyes, along with a growing and malicious amusement. "You have to call the meeting to order first."

"Oh. Uh, okay then. I call the meeting to order. Who reads the minutes?" She looked at Annie. "You're the secretary, right, Annie? You take the minutes, right? So you probably read them, too. So go ahead."

Another uncomfortable silence. Harvey settled back in his chair, folded his arms, and looked like someone sitting in the front row of a Steve Martin concert, with balloons.

Harvey, fifty-three, born in Niniltna but raised in Anchorage, was a commercial fisherman like Old Sam and a professional hunting guide like Demetri. Active in local politics, a crony of district senator Pete Heiman, his past term on the state board of fish and game had been notable for his vocal and vociferous and often incendiary support of increasing the length of the hunting and fishing seasons and upping the legal limits on anything with fur or fins. Ekaterina had backed Harvey's ascension to the NNA board as a sop to pro-development voices in the Association, and had lived to regret it when he openly supported development in Iqaluk. While he had his adherents, there were among NNA shareholders people still suffering the effects of the RPetCo Juneau oil spill who as vociferously disagreed.

Annie looked at Auntie Joy and the two women communed in silence for a moment.

"What?" Kate said.

"You not read your minutes, Katya?" Auntie Joy said.

"What minutes?" Kate said.

Auntie Joy's radiance dimmed still further. "Viola bring you the minutes, Katya."

"No, she didn't," Kate said indignantly.

Auntie Joy nodded. She wasn't enjoying herself. "Last month, Katya. One U-Haul box."

"Auntie, I—" Kate remembered Auntie Vi's visit the previous month. "Cardboard? Brown?" she said without much hope.

"Auntie Vi bring."

Kate slumped a little. "Auntie Vi bring." Where had she left that box? She had a vague memory of putting it in the back of Johnny's truck. It couldn't still be there, could it?

"And Katya not read," Auntie Joy said sorrowfully.

"No." Then Kate rallied. "So what? The agenda says for them to be read and approved. So somebody read them, for crying out loud."

Next to her Harvey chuckled, a little louder than was perhaps strictly necessary. "The rest of us already have, Kate."

"So what?" Kate said again. "The agenda says read them, we read them."

"You see, Kate," Harvey said, enjoying himself hugely, "Annie sends out the draft minutes of the last meeting to all the board members. Board members read them in advance, so we don't have to waste our time reading them during the meeting. Then we approve them."

"Oh."

Auntie Joy said anxiously, "But we read now. Is okay. Okay?" She looked around the table.

Joyce Shugak, eighty-something, was a subsistence fisher, retiring each summer to a fish camp on Amartuq Creek, upstream from Alaganik Bay where all the commercial fishers in the Park got their nets wet. She had been married once, long ago, and the great tragedy of her life was that she had had no children. The result of this child-hunger led her to adopt every soul in the Park from one to a hundred as her very own. She was a plump, cheerful person, easy to please, ready to praise, and if not quite capable of being blind to faults in others, at least nurtured a determined nearsightedness that worked just as well.

Like the other aunties, she spoke a truncated, rhythmic form of English that came from speaking it as a second language, as all the aunties grew up speaking Aluutiq, Eyak, and Athabascan. Kate suspected that they could all of them have spoken flawless English if they had chosen to do so, but by now it was a matter of pride to speak in their self-invented patois. It branded them as Alaska Natives, born and bred and living the life. They were proud of it, and they didn't mind reminding people of that fact every time they opened their mouths, which obviated the necessity of their having to actually say so.

Old Sam shrugged. "Sure," Demetri said. Harvey heaved a sigh and said wearily, "Sure, why not? I've only got six other things that need doing today."

"Yeah," said Old Sam with his patented nasty grin, "but this one you get paid for."

Kate looked at him. "We get paid?"

There was a moment of silence. Annie Mike cleared her throat. "If the board please," she murmured to her laptop, "the secretary will now read the minutes of the last meeting, dated April fifteenth."

"April?" Kate said, still reeling from the information that she would draw a paycheck for this. How much? Did they get paid per meeting or was it all in one check at the end of the year? Or maybe the beginning of the year? She wondered if it would be enough to cover the cost of a new four-wheeler. She could use a new—

"Wait a minute," she said.

Annie paused. "Yes, Kate?"

"April? I thought the last meeting was in July."

Harvey rolled his eyes. "It was cancelled, Kate. You and Old Sam were fishing. Demetri was upriver running his lodge, and the aunties were downriver at fish camp. We didn't have a quorum."

Kate was pretty sure she knew what the word *quorum* meant from the context but she resolved to look it up in her tattered copy of *Webster's Unabridged* at the earliest opportunity, just to be sure. "Sorry," she said shortly. "I forgot."

Annie finished reading the minutes. There was silence. "Oh," Kate said. "Am I supposed to say something?"

"Ask if there are any corrections," Harvey said briskly. He even smiled at Kate.

Enjoy yourself while it lasts, asshole, Kate thought. Out loud she said, "Are there any corrections to the minutes?" There weren't, the minutes were approved, and it was with distinct relief that Kate said, "Reports?"

Annie gave the treasurer's report. NNA sounded fiscally healthy to Kate, but then she wasn't the best person ever with numbers, so she resolved to ask Auntie Joy privately.

"Unfinished business?" Kate said.

"I move we table all unfinished business for the moment," Harvey said.

"Second," Demetri said.

"Huh?" Kate said.

Auntie Joy leaned across the table and said, "Motion moved and seconded. In favor say aye. Opposed, say nay."

"Oh. Okay. All in favor say—"

"All in favor of tabling unfinished business," Auntie Joy said.

"Okay, all in favor of tabling unfinished business say aye."

"Aye," Harvey said.

"Aye," Demetri said.

Old Sam gave Harvey an appraising glance. "What's this about, Harvey?"

Harvey glared. "Out of order!"

Auntie Joy patted the air with pacific hands. "I say aye, too, Old Sam. No fighting, now."

"Oh, all right," Old Sam said, giving in, but he fixed Harvey with a cold and untrusting eye.

Auntie Joy said encouragingly, "Okay, Katya, motion carried."

"The motion is carried," Kate said obediently.

"No, you say what motion is."

"Oh. Okay. The motion to table unfinished business is carried. By majority vote!"

She couldn't help the note of triumph, and Harvey's laugh was immediate and unkind, and Kate's hackles rose. She looked down at the agenda. "All right, then I guess we go to new business. Anybody have any new business to discuss?"

"I do," Harvey said, promptly and predictably. "With the board's permission, I'd like to introduce Global Harvest Resources Inc.'s personal representative to the Niniltna Native Association, and to the Park." Before anyone could say anything, he got up and went to the door. "Talia?" He ushered a woman into the room.

"Katya!" Auntie Joy said urgently. "Point of order, Katya!"

"Point of what?" Kate said.

"Question!" Old Sam said.

"What was the question?" Kate said.

"Everyone, meet Talia Macleod," Harvey said. "Talia, this is the Niniltna Native Association board of directors. Starting on your left, Sam Dementieff, Joy Shugak, Demetri Totemoff, myself, and our recently named interim chair, Kate Shugak. In the corner, that's Annie Mike, our secretary and treasurer."

The name was instantly recognizable to them all, as was the dazzling smile she sent round the room, which had graced the front page of every newspaper in Alaska, as well as the cover of *Alaska* magazine, *Outside* magazine, and *Sports Illustrated*, twice. True, one of those had been a group shot of the whole Olympic team, but still.

Talia Macleod was an Alaskan athlete of international renown, a member of the American biathlon team, finishing six times in the top ten nationally, taking first once, and going to the world championship five times and the Olympics twice. Her hair was a white blond mane, her eyes cerulean blue and widely spaced, and she had a lithe figure that looked equally well in ski pants and bathing suits, this latter attested to by the most recent *Sports Illustrated* swimsuit issue, her second appearance in that periodical.

And then, there was that smile. Full-lipped, white-toothed, dimpled even at rest, it had been described as incandescent by one besotted journalist, and it lit up the newspapers, the magazine covers, and any room she walked into.

Including the Niniltna Native Association board room. She didn't suffer from shyness, either. "How nice to meet you," she said, walking around the table to shake hands. Either Harvey had rehearsed her or she was very good with names, because she addressed them all faultlessly and without hesitation.

"I hear they call you Old Sam," she said with an up-from-under flutter of eyelashes. "I can't think why."

"Mrs. Shugak," she said, holding one of Auntie Joy's hands in both of hers. "It's an honor to meet one of Ekaterina Shugak's closest friends, and one of the founding members of the Niniltna Native Association. I'm looking forward to working with you."

"Demetri," she said, pulling Demetri to his feet and giving him a warm hug. "Great to see you again."

"You, too." Demetri hugged her back and sat down again, avoiding everyone's eyes.

"Demetri took me and a bunch of friends of mine from Outside hunting up in the Quilak foothills a couple of years back." She smiled down at him. "My, that was a good time."

Demetri Totemoff, fifty-five, had been born in Anchorage to Park rats who had moved away. He had moved to the Park after two tours in Vietnam. Married with three children, he was a big game guide with a high-end lodge back in the Quilaks on a salmon- and trout-rich stream, in close proximity to bears black and brown and within an easy hike of all the moose and caribou a great white hunter could possibly want. The lodge, a rustic affair with hot and cold running water, one-bedroom suites, a full bar, maid service, and a live-in gourmet chef during the fishing and hunting seasons, had become so well known among business executives, the Hollywood elite, and the jet set that nowadays it ran full on word of mouth alone. While not as pro-development as Harvey, unlike Auntie Joy Demetri was not averse to commerce, especially when it might make him a buck or two. On the other hand, he wouldn't take kindly to any development that might affect the raw, rough, wilderness experience of his guests, either. Of everyone on the board, Demetri had the best grasp of numbers. If it looked like the mine would make him more money, bottom line, than his lodge, he'd be for it. The opposite, the opposite. Self-interest was a wonderful thing, and at least it made him predictable.

Macleod walked around Demetri, trailing a hand across his shoulders, and increased the wattage of her smile to where it was almost blinding. "And of course the legendary Kate Shugak."

Old Sam's responding smile had been wicked and appraising, Auntie Joy's handshake had been brief, the tips of Demetri's ears were red, and Harvey looked like a proud, lecherous parent. Kate found herself very much on her guard. She leaned forward as if to get to her feet, caught sight of Auntie Joy's stony visage, and only just stopped herself in time. She hated being loomed over but since Macleod was at least five ten in her stockings and the heels of her boots added two inches more, and Kate was only five feet nothing, she would have had to look up anyway. She accepted Macleod's hand from a seated position and said, "I don't know about legendary."

"I do," Macleod said. Her grip was firm and strong and lasted just long enough. "Mandy says hi, by the way."

"And you know Mandy," Kate said. Mandy Baker, expatriate Boston Brahmin and champion dog musher, lived on the second homestead over from Kate's, and was one of Kate's closest friends.

Macleod grinned. "I think everybody in Alaska has cheered her out of the chute on Fourth Avenue at least once."

"Talia," Harvey said, reasserting his control of the situation, "joined us today at my invitation to tell us a little bit about the Suulutaq Mine."

There was instant attitude from around the table, beginning with Auntie Joy's continued imitation of Washington on Mount Rushmore. Hard for an old Native woman to look like a dead white guy, but Auntie Joy managed it. Old Sam leaned back in his chair, propping his knee on the edge of the table, and linked his hands behind his head, but the carefree pose couldn't hide his attentiveness or his tension. Demetri closed his eyes and shook his head very slightly.

"Really," Kate said. There was a lot going on here that she didn't understand. Kate never enjoyed feeling ignorant, unsure, and out of control. "Listen, Ms. Macleod—"

"Talia, please."

"Okay, Talia," Kate said. "No offense, but while I'm prepared to acknowledge that you can ski and shoot my ass off, what do you know about gold mines?"

There was the barest perceptible glimmer of emotion from Auntie Joy. Old Sam laughed outright. Demetri pretended to be invisible. Harvey sucked in his breath but before he could protest Macleod said, "Maybe a little more than you do, but only because I've been boning up on them since Global Harvest hired me."

Kate thought about it, and nodded. "What's your interest here?"

Macleod gestured at Harvey. "Like Harvey says, they hired me to liaise with the Park. It's a paycheck. Biathlons don't pay real well."

"Fair enough," Kate said. Auntie Joy had reverted to the Great Stone Face again, and Old Sam was maintaining a watching brief, so no help there. "Okay. Make your pitch."

Macleod shrugged. "I'm not going to bullshit you, Kate, or anyone else in the Park for that matter. Global Harvest is in the gold mining business because they can make money at it. They bid on the leases at Suulutaq because they had a good hunch as to what they'd find there." Macleod pulled a wry face. "I don't think they knew just how much was there, but now that they do, they're in for the long haul. Gold, last time I looked, was a little over nine hundred an ounce and rising. For that kind of money, they're willing to do things right from the get-go."

"Beginning with?"

"Well, just for starters, we'll be taking applications the first of next month for a hundred jobs, to Park residents only, entry level twenty dollars an hour, six-weeks-on, six-weeks-off rotation."

The front two legs of Old Sam's chair hit the floor. "Twenty dollars an hour?"

"A hundred?" Kate said. "That isn't a lot."

"During exploration and development, we expect the mine will employ a minimum of two thousand," Macleod said, and was obviously pleased with the expressions she saw around the table. "When we move into production, the payroll should be around a thousand."

"Twenty dollars an hour?" Old Sam said.

"Time and a half for overtime," Macleod said.

"What kind of jobs?" Kate said.

"So far, we've got one person on the payroll, as caretaker on the site. I'm looking for a second so they can work in rotation. As I'm sure you know, we've got a trailer out there already, a small one serving as a rudimentary office, lab, and bunkhouse. We'll be bringing in more housing shortly. Future jobs will be in drilling and analyzing core samples to define the extent of the mine, and in support of same. Some people will be working with microscopes and test tubes, others will be washing dishes and making beds."

"Twenty dollars an hour?" Old Sam said.

"Anything over eight hours a day, anything over forty hours a week is overtime," Macleod said.

"You'll train them?" Kate said.

Macleod nodded. "On the job. And they get paid for it, at the full rate, starting their first day."

"Twenty dollars an hour?" Old Sam said.

"Double time for state and federal holidays," Macleod said.

"Where will they live?" Kate said.

"They live where they work, on site. Right now, there are four trailers sitting in Ahtna, three fifty-man sleepers and one for offices. And that's just the beginning."

"Twenty dollars an hour?" Old Sam said.

Old Sam Dementieff, a contemporary of Auntie Joy's and someone who knew where all the bodies were buried, was ancient, vigorous, practical, and irascible. He had no time for fools and he considered everyone who wasn't him or Mary Balashoff, his main squeeze, a fool. That included Kate, who deckhanded for him on the *Freya*, his fish tender, during the salmon season. All that being said, he was loyal through and through, although to whom and to what could be changeable. Most of the time he was loyal to the Association, by which he meant the tribe. He was loyal to the Park and to the Park rats who lived in it, whether they were shareholders or not. Or he was to the ones who'd survived at least one full winter without turning tail and making tracks south. After the Park rat in waiting passed that first crucial test, Old Sam was known to say, "Weeeellll, you're showing me something. Let's see you make it through another." He was Everyfart, the quintessential Alaskan Old Fart, and not only did he know better than anyone else, he said so, early and often. The hell of it was that he was right most of the time.

Macleod smiled at him. She even looked amused when he didn't visibly wilt from the heat in that smile. "When we really get started, it's going to go twenty-four seven, two twelve-hour shifts. With overtime, one employee could pull down as much as nine thousand dollars a month."

"How are you going to get the trailers out to the mine?" Kate said.

"Same way we got this one out there. Airlift. We've leased a helicopter, a Sikorsky, I think they told me, until we get the airstrip in."

"Airstrip?" Kate said. "Where will you be flying your employees in from? Ahtna? Anchorage?"

"Wherever we hire them from," Macleod said. "Park people will be flown in from Niniltna, until we get the road in. But, yes, other employees will fly in from Ahtna, Fairbanks, Anchorage."

"Outside," Kate said.

Macleod spread her hands. "Some of the expertise necessary to exploration and development isn't available to us here in Alaska."

Auntie Joy cleared her throat deliberately. All eyes turned toward her. She was red-faced and sweating. Kate knew how much she loathed speaking aloud in front of strangers, so she appreciated the courage it took today for Auntie Joy to say what she had to say. "Fish? Caribou? Moose? Bear? All wildlife? This mine bad for those things."

"Mrs. Shugak," Macleod said, "Global Harvest Resources knows that we have to be good neighbors to the people who live in the Park. That includes respecting the fish, the wildlife and the environment, and the subsistence lifestyle practiced by everyone who lives here. We're going to use the very best science available to us to run an operation that has the lowest possible impact on the Park, and on the lifestyle of the people who live in it."

Fine words, Kate thought. They would have been more convincing if they hadn't sounded so well rehearsed. "You're going to have to get a lot more specific than that," she said.

"We know," Macleod said. "And we will. We're just getting started here, Kate. We're not naïve enough to think there won't be problems. Of course there will be. But every step of the way we expect a Park—what is it you call yourselves?—a Park rat at our elbow, telling us what we're doing wrong. We'll be listening for that advice, and we'll be acting on it."

"You better be listening for it," Old Sam said, "because you'll be getting it. A lot of it."

"Thanks for dropping by, Talia," Harvey said with an enthusiastic handshake.

"My pleasure," Macleod said. "Ask me back any time." With a wave and a smile she was gone.

"Anything else?" Kate said. "Great, we're outta here."

The last thing she heard as she escaped through the door was Auntie Joy's faint, despairing, "No, Katya, no further business, meeting adjourned!"

FIVE

Auntie Vi opened the door before he had to knock twice. "What," she said inhospitably, but Johnny knew better. "Is that fry bread I smell, Auntie?"

Auntie Vi grumbled and opened the door wide enough for him to enter. "Got a nose on you like that Katya," she said, shooing him up the hallway to the kitchen. "I start bread, she show up on doorstep. Better than a bear at sniffing out food, that girl."

He grinned down at the heavy cast-iron skillet on top of the stove. Half a dozen flat, gently puffed circles of dough were already turning a golden brown in sizzling oil. On the counter next to it sat a bowl of bread dough.

Auntie Vi poked him in the side. "You want fry bread, you make."

He gaped at her. "I don't know how, Auntie."

"Best you learn, then." Briskly, she showed him how to pull off a handful of dough, flatten it and stretch it into a circle, and hang it over the side of the bowl to wait its turn in the frying pan. She handed him a spatula and he got the pieces in the pan onto a cookie sheet lined with paper towels. When he put the spatula down and reached for one of them, she smacked his hand.

"But, Auntie, I'm hungry, I—"

"You eat when you finish," she said.

"But they'll all be cold by then!"

She cast her eyes up to the heavens. "Fine, then. One. One!"

"Where's the powdered sugar? Oh. Thanks, Auntie." He tossed the fry bread from hand to hand, and when it had cooled a little sprinkled the sugar over it generously. The first bite was a little crunchy, a little chewy, a little greasy, and a lot sweet. He closed his eyes. "Auntie, this is . . . this is just one of the best things I ever want to put in my mouth."

She gave a skeptical grunt but he could see that she was pleased.

They finished frying the batch—Johnny managed to talk her out of another piece before they were done, and three more after that—and then he made her sit down at the table, poured her a mug of coffee, and cleaned up the kitchen. She put down two pieces herself, along with three cups of coffee, while maintaining a running criticism of his kitchen skills. There was also a lesson in the proper cleaning of a cast-iron skillet, involving warm water, no soap, and drying it over a hot burner.

As he was folding the dish towel and hanging it on the oven door handle, he said, "Auntie, did that guy I told you about last month ever show up?"

She eyed him as he sat down across from her. "He come a week ago. He stay here. You know him."

He nodded. "Yeah, from when I was Outside. Is he okay for money?"

She shrugged and picked up a deck of cards and began to shuffle them. "All right, I guess. He pay his rent on time."

"Good. Is he looking for work?"

"He look," she said. "Don't know if he find."

"I was wondering if maybe he could get on at the mine," he said.

She looked at him. "They hiring?"

His turn to shrug. "It was all over the school at lunch. Global Harvest is going to start hiring the first of next month, with preference given to Park rats."

Her lips pressed together.

"What, Auntie?" he said.

She glared at him, but there might have been a lurking twinkle in the back of her eyes. "I just hear this myself from Auntie Joy. Who tell school?"

"A lady came from the mining company. She's the skier, they hired her to be their representative. She talked to us at lunch, told us about the mine and how they were going to start taking applications right away and hiring next month. It's a big deal. Twenty bucks an hour, Auntie."

Auntie Vi shuffled cards in silence. "Your friend got job at Bernie's. Temporary, while Amy gets teeth fixed in Anchorage." She swept the cards up with an air of finality, and he took that as a hint to leave.

As he got up, she said, eyes on the cards as she shuffled them, "That mine lady rent room here, too."

"Oh," he said, taken aback. "Okay. That's good, I guess." He couldn't help ending the sentence on an interrogatory note.

"Of course good," she said briskly, tapping the cards on the table and sliding them back into their box. "All money in the bank for me. Mine a different story. Good for me maybe, but maybe bad for the Park. Now shoo you!"

Outside, he climbed back on the snowmobile and looked at the sky while he was waiting for the engine to warm up. It was almost three thirty, and it was cold and getting colder. It would be dark soon. He really ought to head for the barn.

But he wanted to see Doyle Greenbaugh, make sure he was all right.

It had been a long drive, almost twenty-five hours from the outskirts of Phoenix where Greenbaugh had picked him up to the warehouse in the International District in Seattle, where he'd got off. When they'd both got tired of listening to golden oldies on a series of radio stations, they'd started talking. Greenbaugh had never been to Alaska, but like everyone else in the known universe said he'd always wanted to go. Partly because he was homesick, and partly because he wanted to make sure Greenbaugh didn't fall asleep at the wheel, Johnny had told him all about his home state, and then he'd told him all about himself.

He wouldn't have done it today, but he'd been a lot younger then, and a lot less wary of casual friendship, and he'd been so very grateful for the ride that he had been willing to pay his way with conversation. In one ride, he'd traveled almost a thousand miles, well out of his mother's reach. He knew his grandparents weren't coming after him. He wondered if they'd bothered to tell her he'd left. He hoped not, and on the whole, he thought not. They hadn't liked his father any more than their daughter had, and they hadn't liked him much, either. By the time Jane knew he was gone, he'd be well out of reach, and by the time she caught up with him, he'd have Kate on his side.

And Greenbaugh had been so very interested, and not in a bad way, either. He'd bought Johnny a huge and sorely needed meal in a diner at a truck stop in Idaho and between mouthfuls of chicken fried steak and mashed potatoes and gravy he'd urged Johnny to keep talking. He'd listened uncomplaining to Johnny talking about his dad and had laughed at all the best stories and sympathized in all the right places. He'd come across as good-hearted, with an occasional flash of temper that faded as quickly as it sparked. He hadn't much education but he was sharp enough to own his own rig, which was admirable, even if he had lost it in the end.

No, not a bosom buddy, but someone to whom Johnny owed a debt of gratitude, so instead of turning right for the road to home he turned left and went out to Bernie's, a fifty-mile trip that had his nose bright red and his cheeks numb by the end of it. A helmet with a face shield would have cut down on the frostbite but nobody ever wore a helmet in the Bush.

The Roadhouse parking lot was crowded but it was easy enough to find a spot for the snowmobile. He went up the steps and opened the door. Inside, the belly dancers—one in full diaphanous regalia, one in bra and blue jeans, and a third in what looked like an Indian sari—beat on tambourines and clanged on finger cymbals and shook their hips at an adoring crowd consisting of the four Grosdidier brothers and Martin Shugak and a couple other guys he didn't recognize. Johnny watched the dancers himself for a few minutes, just to make sure they had the steps down. He wondered if Van had ever wanted to learn to belly dance.

Old Sam Dementieff and the usual crowd of old farts sat around a table watching football on ESPN on the enormous television hanging from another corner. Leaning against the bar, Mac Devlin stood, red-faced and angry, holding a bottle of beer. Someone else was sitting on the stool next to him, shoulders hunched, but he had his back turned and Johnny couldn't tell who it was. At a table in the back, Pastor Bill, his congregation a little smaller than in years past, exhorted the righteous to be faithful, to which everyone replied with a hearty "Amen!" and drinks were ordered all round, some of them not sodas. It looked like the no alcohol in church rule had been waived, which once the news got around might go far to increase the size of the congregation.

In the center of the room stood Talia Macleod, who he recognized from the lunchroom at school earlier that day. She was the focus of a group of Park rats who stood in a circle facing her with a communal expression that made him feel a little uncomfortable. Most of them were staring at her chest, currently displayed in a soft turtleneck sweater the color of which matched her hair and looked as inviting to the touch.

"In the past year alone the price of gold has gone up eighty-one percent," she said, although it sounded more like a purr, "silver a hundred and twenty-three percent, and zinc a hundred and thirty-two percent." She smiled at her admirers, and a collective quiver ran over the group. "I've heard all the naysaying and the doom and gloom, but when has Alaska ever gone the way of the South forty-eight when it comes to the economy? Whenever there is a recession Outside, we get a boom."

Howie Katelnikof, visiting with Auntie Edna and Auntie Balasha at their corner table, scurried over to stand a step behind Macleod. "She's right," he said, punctuating his words with a portentous nod.

Everyone wasn't buying into it, though. "And whenever Outside gets a boom, we go bust," Mac Devlin said loudly from the bar.

Without looking around, Macleod said, "True, but with gold on the way up to a thousand an ounce for the first time in history, even if we do get a little bust it'll never fall back to what it was. Guys, I'm telling you, Global Harvest is in it for the long haul. We won't be ripping out any railroad tracks on our way out of the Park."

"We sure won't," Howie said.

"You will when the gold runs out," Mac Devlin said. His contempt felt a little over the top, a little manufactured, and no one was listening to him anyway.

Doyle Greenbaugh came to Macleod's elbow with a tray of drinks, and Johnny saw her hand him a credit card that was as gold as the nuggets Global Harvest was prepared to pull out of the ground in Iqaluk, along with a brilliant smile. Howie smacked him genially on the back and made sure he snagged the first drink on his return.

"It'll be twenty years minimum before the gold runs out," she said, "and by then Global Harvest will have found something else worth harvesting. It's a big fucking Park, in case you hadn't noticed."

They laughed at that, Howie loudest of all, titillated by her use of profanity.

"You!" Bernie said, pointing at Johnny. "Get out, and don't come back for another five years!"

His voice was loud and meant to carry, so naturally all activity came to a halt while everyone turned to look where he was pointing. It was a technique that Bernie had perfected over the years in ridding the Roadhouse of wannabe underage drinkers.

Johnny felt his face redden. "I'm not looking for a drink, Bernie."

Any other time an underage entered the bar Bernie wouldn't let up until the door hit him in the ass. But then Bernie had not been the same since a year before, when Louis Deem had robbed his house of a greater part of Bernie's gold nugget collection and in the act of escaping had killed Bernie's wife and eldest son, Fitz. Fitz had been a friend of Johnny's, and he could not look at Bernie now without pain and sympathy. Bernie, unable to face it head on, turned his back abruptly and said in a hard voice, "Then get the hell on outta here."

Johnny caught Doyle Greenbaugh's eye, and nodded at the door. Greenbaugh nodded and said, "Take five, boss?"

Bernie nodded without looking around, and Greenbaugh snagged his coat and followed Johnny out on the porch. "Man, that Koslowski is one cranky old bastard."

Johnny stiffened. "He's a good guy, Doyle. He just lost his wife and son last year, and he's not over it yet."

"I heard. Helluva thing." Greenbaugh blew on his hands and shoved them into his pockets. His coat wasn't down and wasn't a parka, and he started to shiver almost at once. "How you doing, Johnny?"

"I'm fine. I dropped by Auntie Vi's to see if you'd shown up, and she said you were working here."

"Yeah, I remembered your stories about the place. I didn't believe the half of it when you told me." Greenbaugh grinned. "Especially the belly dancers."

Johnny laughed, appeased. "Now you know better."

"No kidding. Anyway, I told Bernie I was looking for work, so he put me on temporary while his regular barmaid is off."

Johnny remembered his dad saying that the Salvation Army was the best place to go for a bed and a meal when you were down to your last dime. It was the one charity Jack had been willing to write a check to, but there was no Sally's in the Park. A little shyly Johnny said, "Are you okay for cash?"

Greenbaugh shrugged. "I'm okay for now, but thanks for asking."

"Did you hear about the mine?"

Greenbaugh jerked his head at the bar. "Hard to miss, with the babe going full steam. She's been here for a couple hours now, talking it up to everyone who walks in."

"Did she talk to you?"

"She did." Greenbaugh grinned. "She says she thinks she might be able to find something for me. There are some real opportunities in this mine. Get in on the ground floor and a person can just coin the money, you know?" He winked at Johnny. "I'm hoping it ain't only a job, if you catch my drift." He nudged Johnny with a jocular elbow. "We're staying in the same boardinghouse, after all."

Johnny felt uncomfortable at sexual badinage with someone so much older than he was—the guy had to be in his thirties—so he pretended not to understand. "That's great, Doyle, I'm really glad to hear it. She told everybody up to the school that they were going to start taking applications immediately and that they'd start putting people to work on the first."

"Barely two weeks from now, I know. Howie Katelnikof was talking to me about it."

"What's Howie know about it?"

"He was the first guy she hired, caretaker out on the claim. He says he'll try to get me on next. He's a good guy."

"You're kidding."

Greenbaugh looked surprised. "No. Why would I be?"

Because, Johnny thought, every Park rat worthy of the name knew that Howie Katelnikof was the best excuse for preventive homicide the Park had ever seen. Because whenever a cabin was burgled, a snow machine stolen, a truck stripped for parts, Howie Katelnikof was the guy voted most likely to. Because Howie Katelnikof was always going to be the go-to guy in the Park to fence stolen property, buy a lid of dope or a hit of coke, and Jim Chopin was certain he was cooking up batches of crystal meth and selling it retail out of the homestead he and Willard Shugak had been squatting on since the death of Louis Deem.

But mostly because Howie Katelnikof had tried to kill him last year, and Kate, and he had almost killed Mutt. Johnny thought of himself as a pretty easygoing guy, but once he got pissed off he stayed pissed off, and he was pissed off at Howie for life. He opened his mouth to issue a warning of some kind, but he'd hesitated too long. Greenbaugh had something else on his mind. "Listen, kid, do me a favor?"

"Sure," Johnny said. "Not like I don't owe you about a hundred."

"I'm going by the name of Gallagher here. Dick Gallagher. Richard, if you want to get technical on me." He grinned again, but he was watching Johnny with a sharp eye.

"Oh," Johnny said inadequately. He rallied. "Um, I guess it's none of my business why."

Greenbaugh—Gallagher—shrugged. "I don't mind saying. There's stuff left over from my life I'd as soon be shut of." He grinned again. "Women, mostly. I want to start fresh, new life, new name, new job. Remember how you told me that day in Ahtna that a lot of people do that at the border crossing?"

Johnny had said that. "Yeah."

"Well, that's me, to the life. I'm starting over here, clean slate. So Dick Gallagher from now on, okay?"

Johnny thought back to earlier that day and making fry bread with Auntie Vi. Had Greenbaugh's—Gallagher's—name been mentioned? "Is that the name you're registered under at Auntie Vi's?"

"Yep. Started the way I mean to go on. So what do you say? Forget that loser Greenbaugh?"

It seemed ungrateful and unreasonable to refuse. What did it matter, anyway? A new name to go with a new life. Wouldn't be the first time that had happened in Alaska. He remembered the stories Kate had told him of her time in Prudhoe Bay, when the news cameras would come into the mess hall and half a dozen guys would get up and walk out, leaving their dinner on the table, before the deserted wife or the parole officer they'd left Outside caught them on film at eleven. "Okay," he said, "sure. Why not?" He was proud that Greenbaugh—Gallagher—trusted him enough to ask the favor. How many times does a sixteen-year-old kid get asked to help somebody hide out from his past? It was right out of Zane Grey. It made Johnny feel like a card-carrying member of the Last Frontier.

Greenbaugh—Gallagher!—thumped his shoulder and grinned at him again. "I'm sure glad I picked you up on the road, Johnny. You're my lucky charm!" He laughed heartily, gave Johnny's shoulder another thump. "Oh," he said, pausing with one hand on the door, "and maybe you could tell that little girlfriend of yours, too. Make sure she knows my new right name, and tell her why?"

"Sure," Johnny said. "Van's cool. She'll be happy to."

"Great," Gallagher said, and disappeared back inside.

Without knowing how, Johnny had the distinct feeling that there was a joke he was missing, but it was getting darker and colder and later by the minute, so he shrugged it off, climbed back on his snow machine, and headed for home.

SIX

"K ate?"

She heard Jim's voice from downstairs. She didn't move. His footsteps sounded on the stairs. "Kate?"

"Go away," she said, her voice muffled by the comforter she'd pulled over her head.

"Kate? Where are you?" The overhead light clicked on. "Oh. Hey, Mutt." The bed moved as Mutt lifted her head and whined, a single, plaintive note.

"Kate, what's wrong?" Jim said in a different tone. "Are you sick?"

"No. Go away."

The side of the bed sank beneath his weight and she felt the comforter pulling away. "Don't," she said, grabbing for it, but by then it was too late. She blinked up at Jim and Mutt, two pairs of eyes, one blue, one yellow, staring down at her with equal concern.

"What's going on?" Jim said. "You're never in bed during the day."

"None of your business. Leave me alone." She pulled the cover back over her head.

The weight of him on the bed didn't move. Neither did Mutt's.

"Oh. Has this got something to do with the board meeting this morning?"

"I don't want to talk about it."

"I take it it didn't go well."

"I don't want to talk about it!"

"Okay." The bed heaved and she heard footsteps go downstairs. The bed heaved again as Mutt jumped down and followed, the ticky-tack of her claws sounding on the floor.

"Traitor," Kate said, her voice muffled by the comforter. Given Jim's come-hither presence downstairs, and given Kate's present mood, it was doubtful that Mutt would have returned even if she had heard Kate call her name.

Kate was, in fact, sulking. Nobody loved her. Everyone thought she was stupid. In fact, she was stupid, didn't even know what a quorum was. She'd looked it up in *Webster's* when she came home and it was the minimum number of members of the group meeting required to take a vote. She'd had the vague idea that it had had something to do with books, and how they were put together, but no. Thank christ she hadn't said that during the meeting.

The aroma of frying bacon crept beneath the covers, a sinuous and seductive smell.

Although she'd said plenty else that Harvey Meganack would be happy to repeat over the bar at Bernie's for months to come. If not years. She still couldn't believe they got paid for sitting on the board. And what the hell was a point of order, anyway?

Johnny's truck drove up and a few minutes later she heard the sound of his feet on the stairs. The door slammed. He said something to Jim. Jim replied, and both of them laughed. Probably laughing at her.

She'd looked for the U-Haul box when she got home. It wasn't in the back of Johnny's truck. It wasn't in the garage. It wasn't even in the woodshed. She wondered if maybe she'd tossed it onto the slash pile from the beetle kill the three of them had cleared at intervals this summer. The slash pile was a mile from the house and she didn't have the energy to navigate the three-foot layer of snow between, especially not in the cold and the dark.

There was more banging around in the kitchen, and other interesting smells began to waft upstairs.

Kate's stomach growled. It was getting very hot and humid beneath the comforter. She swore a ripe oath, extricated herself from the tangle of bedclothes, and stamped down the stairs.

"Hey, Kate," Johnny said with a grin.

"What's that supposed to mean?" she said. Maybe she snarled.

Startled, he actually backed up a step. "I . . . I . . ."

Jim, pouring a bottle of red wine into a pot, said, "It means hello." He gave her a look from beneath lowered brows. "At least it does in most of the cultures I run in."

"What's with the wine?" she said.

"Relax, the alcohol will boil off."

She knew that, he'd cooked with wine before and on occasion she'd been known to pour a dollop or two into a soup or a stew, but it left her with nothing to argue about. She stamped over to the couch and flung herself down and glared out the window.

Johnny withdrew stealthily backward, sidled into his room, and closed the door very gently behind him. He'd meant to introduce the subject of Greenbaugh—Gallagher!—into the conversation at the first opportunity, let Kate and Jim know the Park had acquired a good guy, but it could wait.

Meanwhile, back on the couch, Kate glowered at the view. It was clear and cold that evening, a dark sky glittering with stars and a waxing moon on the rise, a luminous, reflected glory in the snow-covered landscape beneath. The Quilaks bulked up on the eastern horizon, igneous bullies flexing their sedimentary and metamorphic muscles to intimidate the lesser beings cowering in their shadow. Angqaq towered above them all, the jagged, homicidal peak a reckless gaunt-let flung down to every mountaineer worthy of the name. From the heights, the mountains and glaciers fell precipitously, interrupted only by an irregular shelf of land called locally the Step, before rolling out into a vast plateau seamed with rivers and carpeted with spruce and cedar and willow and hemlock and birch and cottonwood. Bordered on the south by the Gulf of Alaska, on the west by the Alaska Railroad and the Trans-Alaska Pipeline, on the north by the Glenn Highway, and on the east by the Quilaks and the border of the Yukon Territory, the Park was twenty million acres in size, several steps out of the mainstream of Alaska life and a light-year away from the rest of the world. They got their news from satellite television, the state was bringing at least one Internet connection into every village with a school, and every adult and not a few children had a Costco card, but that didn't necessarily make them members of the global community. It frequently wasn't enough to make them Americans.

Alaskans had attitude, no doubt about that. They loved their land with a fierceness that bordered on mania, while freely admitting insanity was a prerequisite for living there. This might have been a partial explanation as to why, as a community, they voted Republican with an enthusiasm that continually overwhelmed Democrats at elections, disavowing anything that smacked of big government subsidies. At the same time they paid no state income taxes, instead accepting a check every year from the state in per capita payment of the gross annual taxes on oil produced in Prudhoe Bay.

And that, Kate thought, was why Global Harvest Resources Inc. was going to get the red carpet treatment from everyone involved, governor's office on down to the lowliest Park rat. Alaskans had grown accustomed to handouts. A whole generation of kids had been raised to believe it was the natural order of things, the permanent fund dividend, earmarks to congressional budget bills for big budget construction projects like schools in villages and bridges to nowhere, government subsidies at federal, state, and local levels to actually run the government. The federal government was Alaska's biggest employer.

The Niniltna Native Association wasn't blameless in this, either. It handed out a quarterly dividend, one to every shareholder, representing half the Association's annual profits, the rest of the profits going back into the Association's operating capital account. The payments were legitimate, earnings from leases sold to companies like Global Harvest, though heretofore much smaller in scale, to exploit natural resources on Native land.

But it bothered Kate. It had been a bone of contention between Emaa and herself. "All this money coming at us, Emaa," she had said, "and we don't do anything to earn it. The state grades the road into the Park. Who pays for that? Not us. The village has running water and electricity. Who pays for that? Not us."

"You want to send money to the state, Katya," her grandmother had said dryly, "you go right ahead," and that was the end of that conversation.

"Supper's on," Jim said, and Kate looked up to see the table set and a pot of stew steaming on a trivet in the middle of the table.

She seated herself and Jim ladled out stew all around.

"Smells great," Johnny said. "What is it?"

"Coq au vin."

"Huh?"

"Chicken stew with bacon and mushrooms, you little cretin."

"Yum," Johnny said after the first taste, and for a while was heard from no more.

Kate took a bite. Johnny was right. The bread was store bought, but she knew what Jim would have said if she'd remarked on it. She'd been in no shape to bake any when she'd gotten home, so she didn't. She ate, silent while the men exchanged news. Jim had responded to an accident out at the Sheldons', a bad one. "They were digging a hole for a new septic tank."

"Now? In October?"

"They did leave it a little late, which might have something to do with why the Cat broke a tread on a slope and rolled over. Maybe, I don't know. The Cat used to belong to Mac Devlin—I could see where the Nabesna Mine logo had been on the side before it got painted over—and it didn't look real well cared for. At any rate, it killed the driver. Messy. The driver? The son. Yeah, just the one kid. Bad news all the way around."

Most of the news featured Talia Macleod's arrival in the Park, the community's reaction to her, and what the mine was going to mean in the long run.

"More work for me," Jim said, "is all I see."

"Why?" Johnny said.

Jim helped himself to more stew. "They'll mostly be hiring young men, and when you put young men together with a lot of money, trouble comes."

"You mean like drugs?"

"Drugs, booze, women, bigger and better and more dangerous toys, and people who will be selling all of the above." Jim gave his head a gloomy shake. "Not to mention all the hucksters hanging around the fringe offering the newly rich wonderful investment opportunities, most of them scams. I've heard about some of the stuff the Slopers have been sucked into, apple and pistachio farms in Arizona, oil wells in Colorado, real estate deals in Seattle. All of them fail, everybody takes a bath, and the losers start looking for somebody to blame, which always ends well. It won't be pretty."

"But there'll be jobs," Johnny said tentatively. "Macleod says there will be as many as two thousand jobs during construction, and a thousand after, when the mine is operating. A thousand steady jobs, Jim, where there were zero before. That's gotta be good. Doesn't it?"

"Sure," Jim said, reaching for more bread. "But there's a price for everything, Johnny."

"I was thinking. . . ." Johnny looked at Kate and hesitated, but she wasn't listening. "Macleod said there were certain professions that would be especially attractive to Global Harvest, like engineers and geologists."

"And?"

"I graduate in two years. I figured I might check out the degree programs at UA, see if any of them fit."

"I thought you were interested in biology, in wildlife management."

Johnny grimaced. "I've been talking to Dan O'Brien, and he says those kinds of jobs are almost always government. He says they're hard to come by, and that they don't pay very well, and you don't get to pick where you work."

"Do you have to make a lot of money?" Jim said.

Johnny looked uncertain. "I thought that was what everybody wanted."

"Do what you love," Jim said. "The money will come."

Johnny was unconvinced, but he let the subject slide for now.

He looked over at Kate. She'd finished and now sat frowning at her empty bowl.

"Something wrong with the stew?" Jim said.

"What?" She came to herself with a start. "No. No, it was great." She saw his eyebrow go up and said with forced warmth, "It was terrific. You can make that again any old time."

"What, then?"

Kate's spoon clattered into her bowl. "She didn't say hi to Annie."

Jim exchanged a glance with Johnny. "Who didn't?"

"Talia Macleod. When Harvey brought her into the board meeting. She glad-handed everyone on the board, called us all by name, knew something personal about each and every one of us. But she didn't even say hi to Annie."

"She's hired a caretaker for the mine site," Johnny said.

"Who?" Jim said.

Johnny looked at Kate with some caution. "Howie Katelnikof."

Jim paused in the act of running his finger around the edge of his bowl. "You're kidding," he and Kate said at the same time.

"That's what I said," Johnny said.

"Who the hell told her that putting Howie on the payroll was a good idea?" Jim said. "Didn't she ask around first, get some names?"

Kate got up and headed for her coat and boots. "Where you going?" Jim said.

"To see Mandy," Kate said.

Mandy Baker's place was down the road toward Niniltna, at the end of a rutted track a little narrower than a pickup. It was a rambling, ramshackle collection of buildings that had once housed a wilderness lodge whose original owner had bankrupted himself in a failed attempt to attract big game hunters, most of whom were already clients of Demetri Totemoff's. The lodge was threatened on all sides by a dense forest of willow, black and white spruce, black cottonwood, and white paper birch, which had been allowed to grow unhindered save for half a dozen trails the width of a dogsled. The trees on the south side closest to the house had been trimmed to stumps and were used as posts to restrain Mandy's dogs from heading to Nome on their own. When Kate pulled up in the clearing, they set up a collective howl that could have been heard from the moon.

Kate winced and put her fingers in her ears. Mutt trotted out into the middle of the pack, sat down, raised her nose, and gave one loud, minatory bark, showing a little teeth while she was at it. There was an instantaneous silence, and Mutt stared around her with narrowed yellow eyes, just to make sure the point had been taken. It had.

"Man, I wish they'd do that for me," said a voice from the door, and Kate looked up to see Mandy standing in it.

"Why do you mush dogs if their howling drives you crazy?" Kate said, threading her way through the pack.

"Why do you think I took up mushing?" Mandy said. "They don't howl when they're hitched up and running."

"There's a problem with that reasoning but I'm just going to let it go," Kate said. She paused on the doorstep. "You doing some late culling? Doesn't seem to be quite the teeming mass of caninity that it usually is."

"Caninity?" Mandy said.

"Caninity," Kate said. "If Shakespeare can make up words so can I."

"Coffee?" Mandy said, standing back and holding the door wide.

"Sure." Kate shed parka and boots and went inside.

The door opened into a large room that served Mandy as kitchen, dining room, living room, and harness shed. There was an enormous old-fashioned woodstove in one corner with a fireplace in the corner opposite, and a higgledy-piggledy jumble of tables, chairs, couches, refrigerator-freezers, sinks, counters, and cupboards in between. On this dark, cold October night the room glowed with the muted light of half a dozen Coleman lanterns, hissing gently from hooks screwed into overhead beams. Mandy preferred them to electric light and had never installed a generator. Pots and pans, traps and ganglines hung from more hooks, making the entire area a hazard to navigation.

Mandy was a tall, rangy woman with a face full of good, strong bones, hair cut a la Prince Valiant, and a latent twinkle in her gray eyes. The scion of a wealthy Bostonian family, she had abandoned crinoline petticoats and charity balls for down parkas and dog mushing as soon as she was of legal age. This had distressed her proper, conservative family no end, although her parents had come around after an eventful visit to the Park three years before. Since then, relations had been cordial, punctuated frequently by care packages featuring L.L.Bean, a telling switch from the usual Neiman Marcus.

"Chick around?" Kate said, accepting a steaming mug and adding a generous helping of canned milk.

She looked up in time to see the twinkle vanish. "Not lately."

Kate groaned. "Not again."

Mandy sat opposite and added three spoonfuls of sugar to her own mug. "To tell the truth, I don't know. I suppose it's possible he's not on a bender. All I know is he went to Anchorage last week to visit his mom, and I haven't heard from him since."

Chick was Chick Noyukpuk, Mandy's lover and mushing mentor. He was also a chronic alcoholic. A short, rotund little man with a cheerful disposition when sober, when drunk he turned maudlin and suicidal. Mandy had bought her first dogs from him. Then he had had his own kennel. Then he had been a world champion distance musher in his own right, earning the nickname the Billiken Bullet, much beloved of sports reporters for his evenhanded way with a bar tab. Now, he worked for Mandy, overseeing the breeding and training of the teams and as a tactical advisor on the trail, with the result that Mandy had been finishing in the money since her third Iditarod.

"His mom okay?" Kate said.

"She's in assisted living. She's pretty much all there mentally, she just needs help with the physical stuff. He's a good son, he goes in a lot. He just doesn't usually stay this long without calling. Unless he's on a bender."

"Um." Kate, knowing sympathy would be unwelcome, didn't offer any. "I met a friend of yours today."

"Oh, yeah? Who?"

"Woman by the name of Talia Macleod."

Mandy's face lit with pleasure. "Talia? No kidding? What's she doing in the Park?"

Kate told her.

"Not a bad gig," Mandy said. "An outfit like Global Harvest would pay for a face like that to put on a project this size. Lay a lot of Alaskan hackles, too, her being a local hero and all. And she is very smart and very personable."

Kate, about to refute this, recognized the justice of it in time. "Yes, she is," she said ruefully.

"How'd you meet her?"

Kate described that morning's board meeting, and when Mandy stopped laughing, she said, wiping tears away, "I would have paid real money for a ticket to that show."

Kate could smile about it, too. Now. "I'd have been all right if they hadn't sandbagged me with being chairman. Probably. Anyway. Is this Macleod the real deal, Mandy? Or is she just bought and paid for?"

"A little of both, probably," Mandy said thoughtfully. She looked at Kate. "The thing you have to understand, Kate, is that no one in her position makes any money to speak of. She's not Brett Favre or Kevin Garnett."

Kate recognized neither name but she understood what Mandy was saying. "That's hard to believe. She's got all kinds of endorsements, doesn't she?"

"Sure, in Alaska. But Outside, or internationally?" Mandy shook her head. "As attractive and as personable as she is, she is a biathloner. She skis and shoots and skis. It doesn't make for riveting television, so it's not gonna be what sells Nikes. My guess is she took this job for the paycheck."

"That's what she said. But she talks like a true believer."

Mandy raised an eyebrow. "That's what they're paying her for. She's got a good heart, Kate."

"Then how come the first person she hired was Howie Katelnikof?"

Mandy stared. "You're kidding."

"I wish I was."

"Oh, crap." Mandy closed her eyes.

"She didn't run names by you?"

Mandy glared at Kate.

"Of course she didn't," Kate said. "Sorry." She started to say something else, and stopped.

"What?"

Kate shrugged. "She didn't say hi to Annie. When Harvey brought her into the board room, she greeted every board member by name and had something to say to each of us to show us how well she'd done her homework. But she ignored Annie. Like the secretary-treasurer was beneath her notice. It pissed me off."

Mandy frowned. "Doesn't sound like her. Still, Annie doesn't have a vote on the board, and Talia didn't have much time."

"Doesn't mean she can get away with rudeness. Not on my watch."

Mandy rolled her eyes. "Look at you, de chair o' de board. Wasn't even a job you wanted and now you're the Emily Post of the Niniltna Native Association. My mother, the queen of Beacon Hill, would be so proud."

Kate had the grace to flush, and held up a hand. "Okay, ya got me. But," she said stubbornly, "she should have said hi." She hesitated, turning the mug around in her hands. "Mandy, what do you think of this mine?"

Mandy shrugged. "I think at nine hundred dollars an ounce and climbing every day, Global Harvest is gonna build it no matter what anyone in the Park says. Might as well close our eyes and think of England. What do you think?"

Kate sighed and drained her mug. "The same. At least it's far enough away that it won't impact you."

"Don't you believe it," Mandy said. "Don't you believe it, Kate, it's going to seriously impact both of us." She pointed. "It'll start with that road, traffic, heavy equipment, pretty soon it'll start falling apart even worse than it already is and the state will come in and repair it and probably pave it, and then we'll get every retired insurance salesman who drives up the Alcan in an RV stopping by to have their picture taken with one of the famous Park rats."

Kate stared at Mandy, the memory of an incident in Russell Gillespie's yard in Chistona a couple of years before floating up out of the ether that occupied the back of her brain. They'd caught a tourist who had been rooting around for artifacts in back of the abandoned store in the ghost town. The only problem was, Chistona wasn't a ghost town and Russell's store wasn't abandoned. Apprised of this fact, the tourist had then insisted on taking a photograph of Kate and Russell so she'd have a picture of real Alaskan Natives in her vacation album. She said, a little weakly, "But we're not famous."

"We will be," Mandy said grimly. "Our privacy will be the first thing to go, Kate, I promise you."

"So you hate the very thought of the mine," Kate said, a little startled by Mandy's vehemence.

"Don't hate it. Don't love it, either. I'm just counting the cost." Mandy shrugged. "And way before we have to pay. Best to wait and see. Only thing we can do, really."

They brooded together in silence. "How are the dogs looking?" Kate said, changing the subject.

"Healthy, ready to go." Mandy spoke with little enthusiasm.

"Problem?" Kate said.

"I don't know if global warming could be defined as a problem,"

Mandy said with a twisted smile. "Snow gets later every year, Kate, and thinner on the ground when it does finally come down. Last couple of years we've been running the dogs on frozen grass after Rainy Pass. Beats the hell out of sled, musher, and dogs." She shook her head and sighed. "I don't know how much longer I can keep it up."

Kate sustained another shock. "You thinking of quitting?"

"I barely finished in the money last year, Kate. The mushing has to pay for itself, or I can't afford to keep doing it."

"What about your trust fund?"

"It never paid for everything," Mandy said. "It'll be enough for me to retire on here."

Now that Kate was looking for it, she could see the fatigue in the lines of Mandy's face and the hollows beneath her eyes. "What will you do with your dogs?"

"Sell them. Won't be a problem."

Mandy's current team of dogs were the result of going on two decades of careful breeding and training. "Mandy—"

Mandy stood up. "Let me refill your mug, Kate, and you can tell me how you and Jim are getting on with the whole cohabitation thing."

Kate bowed to defeat and held out her mug.

SEVEN

The next day, five minutes after Jim sat down at his desk, the phone rang. It was Cindy Bingley. "Jim," she said without preamble, "you've got to do something about Willard."

Jim felt the hair prick up at the back of his neck. "What about Willard?" he said.

"He keeps stealing stuff out of the store. Yesterday he walked out with a gallon jug of white vinegar."

Jim couldn't help it. He laughed.

"It's not funny, Jim," Cindy said. She paused, hearing her voice rise. "Well, okay, maybe it is a little. When I caught him on the steps I asked him what in the world he was going to do with that much vinegar and he said he brushed his teeth a lot."

Jim closed his eyes in momentary supplication of some heavenly entity to intercede on behalf of all fools and children, of which Willard was both.

Willard Shugak, a cousin a couple of times removed from Kate, and Auntie Balasha's grandson, was in his early forties. It was a blessing that he was even still around, if a mixed one. Most people with fetal alcohol syndrome died young.

"And then," Cindy said in despair, "he started to cry. You know how he does."

"Yes," Jim said, sober now, "I know. Do you want to press charges, Cindy?"

"No! Of course I don't! Aside from the fact that Auntie Balasha would probably boycott the store, along with the other three aunties and shortly thereafter most of the rest of the Park, Willard's just a baby. A kleptomaniac baby. Sometimes I wish I could just turn him over my knee. Could you just, I don't know, put the fear of god into him or something? Lock him up overnight?"

Jim sighed. "I can probably do that." It wouldn't be the first time.

"He's in here every day right after we open," Cindy said promptly.

It was a gray day not expected to get out of the teens, with the winds sweeping down out of the Quilaks at fifteen miles an hour and bringing a fine, white snow with them that immediately frosted anything stationary, including Jim's windshield. The forecast called for three to six inches more. Combined with the layer of black ice beneath it made for hazardous movement, either by foot or by vehicle. Not that that would stop anyone from climbing into their Ford Explorer or their Subaru Forester and barreling up and down the roads, such as they were. Jim resigned himself to a day spent responding to ditch-diving daredevils. He just hoped none of them involved fatalities. The sooner the Park was snowed in and everyone switched to all snow machines all the time, the better.

He also hoped nothing happened anywhere else in the Park that required him to get in the air. The troopers gave first preference to any applicant with a private pilot's license, and Jim was licensed for both fixed wing and helicopters. The state of Alaska had kindly provided him with a Cessna 206, parked on the Niniltna airstrip in a rented space in George Perry's hangar.

The helicopter had been pulled when they opened the Niniltna post, the reasoning behind that decision being he was closer to the action and didn't need two methods of transportation, plus the Cessna could carry more weight. Jim had disapproved of the decision, as the Bell Jet Ranger could get into a lot more places than the Cessna could, but he understood the economics behind the decision and held his peace. Most outposts in the Park had their own airstrips, and those that didn't would simply go longer unserved by the law. That was life off the road in Alaska.

"The first response on the last frontier," so ran the state troopers' latest recruiting slogan, but the state was 586,412 square miles large, and those miles contained some of the most challenging terrain the planet had on offer, with some of the worst weather the atmosphere could manufacture. The Alaska State Troopers, a mere 240 officers strong, hadn't a hope in hell of responding to every outrage perpetrated by or against Alaskan citizens, or even most of them, no matter how many airplanes they spotted their officers.

There was, nevertheless, the expectation that they would try to do so. Jim, like every other Alaska Bush pilot, was well acquainted with the aviation axiom: There are old pilots, and there are bold pilots, but there are no old, bold pilots. If the weather was going to be bad, he wanted it awful, as in below minimums.

For the moment, all that was required was the Blazer. Bingley Mercantile was a solid, square building about twenty-five feet on a side, six hundred and twenty-five feet of retail space crammed with shelves, a wall of refers, and a small row of bins for produce. Their stock-in-trade was Lay's Potato Chips, Cherry Coke, and EPT tests, but they made a praiseworthy attempt to bring in small amounts of oddball—for the Park—items like jasmine rice and tamari almonds, these last, after the freight was factored in, worth about the same amount per ounce as the gold Global Harvest would be taking out of Suulutaq. It was clean, well lit, and when the apples got spotty they threw them out. Park rats really couldn't ask for more than that.

Cindy and Ben Bingley had started the little store eighteen months ago with money from the Niniltna Native Association's nascent small business loan program. They'd spent most of it on the building and the rest on stock and Jim understood and appreciated Cindy's concern over some of that stock walking out the door under Willard's arm. A grocery store had at best a marginal profit line.

He could also appreciate Cindy's reluctance to lodge a formal complaint over Willard's pilferage.

He himself was reluctant to arrest Willard Shugak for murder.

Willard's rusty old International pickup was already in the store's parking lot, the engine running, the cab empty. Jim swore a round oath and got out, killing his own engine and taking the keys. He didn't care if the Blazer froze up while he was in the store in the subzero temperatures. Rather that than a drunk Martin Shugak driving off in it, siren blaring and Christmas tree flashing. It had happened before in the Bush, though not to him, and he was going to make sure it never did.

The top of the door hit the little silver bell and it tinkled softly as he entered, a pleasant sound. What wasn't pleasant was the expression on Cindy Bingley's face when he spotted her standing at the end of one of the aisles.

What was distinctly unpleasant was the gun Cindy was waving around. Crap. Jim craned his head.

Willard was crouched down in front of the candy shelves, a half-empty box of Reese's Peanut Butter Cups clutched to his chest and a lot of empty wrappings scattered on the floor around him. He had chocolate smeared around his mouth, although the flood of tears down his face was making inroads into it. His eyes were squinched shut and snot bubbled out of his nose with every sob.

Cindy, meanwhile, had lost it. "You lousy little weasel, I ought to shoot you right now! Look at this mess! How many of those candy bars have you had? How many did you steal this time?" She hauled back a foot and kicked him, not gently, in the leg.

Willard gave a high, thin, pitiful shriek. Even Cindy seemed momentarily paralyzed by it.

Into that brief silence, Jim said quietly, "Cindy?"

She whipped around, a dumpy, doughty little woman of faded prettiness, pouchy eyes, blond hair graying fast, a triple chin threatening the line of her neck. Her blue eyes were large and slightly protuberant and veined with red. She looked ever so slightly insane, especially when she fixed Jim with a hard look and said, "Yes? Something you wanted? Something you couldn't get here in time to take care of yourself? Goddamn fucking trooper?" There was special emphasis on the last word.

"Cindy," he said, dropping his voice even further, letting it fall to a soothing murmur she had to lean toward him and away from Willard to hear clearly, "you know you're not going to shoot Willard over a candy bar."

"It wasn't just a candy bar!" she shouted.

Behind her Willard whimpered. Jim was grateful when Cindy didn't round on him. "What was it?" he said, still in that calming, sympathetic murmur.

"Look at this!" She stormed toward the checkout counter and rifled around on the top. The gun got in her way and she tossed it to one side. It slid off the edge of the counter and fell behind the cash register. Jim flinched, but it didn't go off, and he relaxed again.

"Here!" she said, waving a piece of paper. "Right here! Look at this!" The paper was shoved beneath his nose. He tried to pull back far enough to bring it into focus but she shoved it up at him again. "I knew he was stealing, and then after I called you I started making a list. Look at it! It's almost a thousand dollars' worth of goods! And I had to beg you to come down here and do something about it?"

85

She looked as if she was going to spit in his face. For a moment he was afraid she was going to kick him, too. Fortunately, the moment passed. She marched back to Willard, hands on her hips, and glared down at him. "You don't ever come back in this store, Willard, you understand me?"

Willard, still crouched beneath the candy shelf, cowered. "Nuh no," he said. "No, no, no, Cindy, I won't, I promise."

She grabbed hold of his ear and he gave another of those pitiful little shrieks. She ignored it and hauled him to his feet. Since she was a foot shorter than he was he had to bend over to let it happen, and bend over he did. "Get out of my way," she said to Jim.

He got out of the way, using the opportunity to step behind the counter and filch the gun, a 9mm automatic. He checked. Loaded, with a round in the chamber. He wanted to fall on his knees and give thanks.

The building shook as Willard stumbled down the steps. Jim made sure the safety was on and tucked the gun into the back of his pants beneath his jacket, just in time to return to his previous position and assume an innocent expression when Cindy slammed back inside.

"There," she said, not at all appeased.

"There, indeed," Jim said. "I took your gun, Cindy. I think it's best."

For a moment she looked ready to erupt again, and he braced himself, but she settled back on her heels. "Fine," she said. "Did you want to buy something?"

"No," he said.

"Then get your ass out of here."

She didn't add, "You useless piece of crap," but he could hear the words hovering on the tip of her tongue. He got.

Outside, Willard was standing at the bottom of the steps, shivering.

Willard Shugak was a tall man and big with it, handsome until you looked close and saw the vacant look in the wide-set eyes beneath the fey brows, the slackness in his mouth. His clothes looked better than normal today, clean and neat and whole, which was a pleasant surprise. Howie Katelnikof, his roommate, must have taken over the wardrobe that morning. Jim only wished he'd do it every morning. At the same time he was suspicious, because it was unlike Howie to do anything that didn't provide an immediate return. Maybe Howie had a yen for some Reese's Peanut Butter Cups?

Willard, not content with neat and clean, had gilded the lily. Draped around his waist and over his shoulder, kind of like a toga, was a large and most colorful quilt, made for him by the aunties. It was a departure for them in two respects, in that until then quilts had been made only for new mothers, and that this one didn't feature a traditional pattern. Instead, it was made up of squares featuring embroidered portraits of *Star Wars* characters. In the center was one of Anakin Skywalker, which likeness bore an uncanny resemblance to Willard.

This, from four women who prided themselves on following the traditions set down by colonial American women slowly going blind in ill-lit pre–Revolutionary War log cabins on lonely and dangerous frontiers as they pieced together intricate patterns from leftover scraps of fabric. It was an action akin to Nathan Jackson carving a totem pole out of Disney characters. It just wasn't done. Nevertheless, the aunties had. It was a nine-day wonder all over the Park.

Willard hadn't been seen in a coat since the aunties had given him the quilt. Jim didn't know what the aunties were going to say when they saw the chocolate smeared down the front of it.

"Hey, Willard," Jim said.

Willard spun around as if he'd been shot. His face was red and liberally adorned with chocolate, tears, and snot. "Uh, hi, Jim." He sniffed and gulped and wiped his face on his sleeve, which didn't improve matters. "I didn't see you there. How are you? Anakin, say hi to Jim." He pulled the quilt down.

"Hey, Anakin," Jim said to the *Star Wars* action figure peeping out of Willard's shirt pocket. "Willard, you going to share that candy bar in your pocket with Anakin?"

Willard's eyes darted to left and right, and he ducked his head. "What candy bar? I ain't got no candy bar."

"Sure you do." He reached into Willard's pocket and pulled it out. Sure enough, one last Reese's Peanut Butter Cup. Willard made a frantic and belated grab at stopping him, but came up only with a handful of air. He looked indescribably guilty.

"Willard, we've talked about this," Jim said. "You can't just take things from the store without paying for them."

Willard hung his head. "I know, Jim. I'm sorry, Jim."

"I know you know, and I know you're sorry." He held up the candy bar. "You got the money to buy this?"

Willard shook his head without looking up.

"Oh, for heaven's sake," a voice said behind Jim. "I'll buy him the damn candy bar."

Jim turned and beheld a vision.

Well, perhaps not quite a vision, but certainly one of the more attractive women he'd ever met. Blond, blue-eyed, a lean figure with enough curve to offset the muscle, a rosy complexion, a smile that was as charming as it was inviting.

He knew instantly who she was, of course. "Talia Macleod," he said involuntarily.

She looked delighted, her face framed by a white fur ruff on her parka hood, her breath making little clouds in the cold air of the parking lot. "How did you know?"

"I've heard."

"Of course," she said. "You would have. Chopper Jim."

"How did you know?" he said.

She dimpled. "I've heard."

He laughed, and then caught Willard's arm as he tried to sidle away. "Excuse me," he said to Macleod, and walked Willard to his truck. He opened the door and helped him inside.

"Thanks, Jim," Willard said, sniffling. With a hungry glance fixed on the candy bar in Jim's hand, he said, "You going to eat that, Jim?"

"Willard," Jim said, holding the door open, "a store is where people buy things. They pay for them with money they bring with them." He spoke slowly and carefully. "I know we've never had a store in the Park before, but it works just like all the other stores you've ever been in."

Willard was following this carefully. "Like Costco?" he said, his brow knit in labored thought.

"Just like Costco."

"Do I need a card before I take things out?"

Jim repressed a sigh. "No. Willard, unless you have money to buy stuff, stay away from Cindy's store, okay?"

"Okay, Jim," Willard said, happy enough to promise anything if it'd keep him out of jail this time.

Jim closed the door, and Willard started the engine and backed carefully out into the road and drove off.

Jim stood there, watching Willard's truck move down the road.

There wasn't a Park rat breathing who didn't think that Louis Deem had robbed Bernie Koslowski's home last spring, and that in his panicked rush to escape had shot and killed Bernie's wife, Enid, and Bernie's son, Fitz.

The celebration that followed Louis's own murder had quite drowned out Jim's subsequent inability to bring anyone to justice for it, investigate he never so thoroughly. Park rats were unanimous in feeling that Louis, a career criminal who had preyed on them for years with impunity, beating every charge brought against him including the murder of all three of his wives, with a record that was a veritable monument to his lawyer's genius in the courtroom, had finally got what had long been coming to him. Nobody cared who killed him, only that he was dead and in the ground and they never had to worry about him around their sisters, daughters, and wives ever again.

In the meantime, only Jim knew who was really guilty of the Koslowski murders, and he was watching him drive away. He couldn't prove it. Other than his own personal understanding of Louis's and Willard's respective characters and a photograph of the crime scene, he had no evidence. Willard himself, his brain destroyed in the womb, didn't remember it. No one else knew, only Jim.

For that matter, no one else cared. And no day passed without him thinking about it, worrying at it, the knowledge gnawing away at him until he felt like he was bleeding internally. Louis Deem's legacy. Sometimes he thought he could hear Louis laughing.

"Is he simple?" Macleod's voice said from next to him.

Recalled to the present, he said, "FAS. His mom was a drunk."

"I'm surprised he's allowed to drive a car."

"He manages to pass his driving test," Jim said. "Every time. And I have to say he's one of the better drivers in the Park. And certainly the best mechanic. But, yes, it surprises me, too."

She held out her free hand. "It's nice to meet you. I was meaning to drop by the trooper post and introduce myself." She grinned, and it was a great grin, with a wattage that could have powered a small city. "My company is going to be responsible for bringing a packet of trouble your way."

"I've heard," he said dryly, and she laughed, a husky, intimate sound. She had moved in kind of close, and she was tall enough that he could feel the exhale of her breath warm on his cheek. It smelled of cinnamon. "How about a cup of coffee at the Riverside Café? My treat."

"Why, Ms. Macleod," he said, drawling out the words. "Are you attempting to bribe me?"

"If coffee at the Riverside Café will get the job done, you bet," she said promptly. "Global Harvest would probably give me a bonus for getting it done so cheap."

This time he laughed. "Sure, I've got time for coffee."

She fluttered her eyelashes. "I might even have time for lunch."

Mac Devlin was at the Riverside Café when they walked in the door, sitting at the counter nursing a cup of coffee and a grudge. The way Jim could tell was that Mac was mouthing off against the proposed Suulutaq Mine, with an occasional slap at the proposed deepwater dock in Katalla. An equal opportunity trasher, that was Mac Devlin these days.

He had an attentive audience, which Jim found interesting. Mac was generally regarded as a blowhard, and as such not necessarily anyone to be taken seriously. Of course, it could be a case of hearing what you want to hear that kept most of them in their seats. They were mostly fishermen—including Eknaty Kvasnikof, who had recently inherited his father's drift permit for Alaganik Bay, Mary Balashoff, who had a set net site there, and assorted Shugaks (including Martin, who gave Jim a wary glance)—and various other Park rats and ratettes.

There was a brief pause when he and Macleod came in.

Mac gave Jim a belligerent look. "What, the cops in bed with the mine now?"

Macleod fluttered her eyelashes again. "Not yet," she said, drawling out the words. Everyone laughed.

Mac reddened to the point where it looked like the skin on his face might ignite.

Mac Devlin was a mining engineer, born in Butte, Montana, of another mining engineer who had booted him out of the house when he was eighteen years of age and told him to go find his own mine. He put himself through school digging copper out of the Kennecott Copper Mine in Utah, the world's largest open-pit mine. Upon graduation he'd gone to work for British Petroleum and had literally seen the world on their dime, or at least that portion of it that was a good prospect for oil. He transferred to Prudhoe Bay on the northern Alaska coast just in time for the discovery well to come in on the super-giant Sadlerochit oil field.

When construction of the Trans-Alaska Pipeline was complete and all the good jobs were moving on to the next big oil field, he sank his savings into the Nabesna Mine in the Park, a small gold dredging concern on Miqlluni Creek that included a bunkhouse, offices, and a selection of heavy equipment, and settled into a marginal existence, producing just enough gold to pay for his attempts to increase and extend his lease. Anybody he hired was called a MacMiner. Rowdy, raunchy roughnecks to a man, they were the inspiration for the baseball bat behind the bar at the Roadhouse.

Mac, in fact, had never been popular in the Park. He wouldn't hire Park rats, he brought his supplies in from Seattle, and he was such an unattractive little shit to boot, a short, heavyset man with the same general build as a culvert, with a red, thinning brush cut, small, mean blue eyes, and a wet mouth that was always flapping. Jim didn't think he'd gotten laid once since he'd moved to the Park, which could account for his cantankerous attitude.

Mac turned pointedly back to his audience. "We're talking three miles wide, five miles long, and two thousand feet deep. That's bigger than the Kennecott Mine in Utah, and that sucker's big enough to be seen from space."

"How big is the Park, Mr. Devlin?" Macleod said.

Mac affected not to hear.

"It's about twenty million acres, isn't it?" Macleod said, raising her voice. "Twenty million?" She emphasized the last word. "Global

Harvest's leases are on less than sixty thousand." She distributed her charming smile with perceptible effect and predictably the crowd warmed to her. She was a lot prettier than Mac. "I've always been lousy at numbers. What is that as a percentage of the total acreage of the Park? Three percent? Four percent? You'll barely know we're there." She smiled again. "Until you start cashing our paychecks."

She took all the honors, and Jim followed in her triumphant wake to a booth in the corner as a muted buzz of conversation rose behind them. "Nicely done," he said as they seated themselves.

She gave a slight shrug, looking over the rudimentary menu with a meditative frown. "Mr. Devlin is unhappy at the price Global Harvest paid for his mine holdings, especially after we announced our find. He is determined to make a nuisance of himself until we buy him off."

"And will you?"

"The longer we ignore him, the lower his price will go." She put down her menu and smiled at Laurel Meganack, a very pretty thirty-something who arrived pen and pad in hand to take their order.

"Whose call is that?" Jim said.

She turned the smile on him, but this time he could see just how sharp all those beautiful teeth were, and he wasn't surprised at her answer. "Mine."

EIGHT

NOVEMBER

Snow had came late to the Park that year, but winter had come early, three weeks of consistent below-zero temperatures in early October. The Kanuyaq froze solid practically overnight, and when it snowed twenty inches in twelve hours the first week of November the river promptly took up its winter role of Park Route 1, carrying dog teams, snowmobiles, and pickup trucks between Ahtna and the villages downriver, also known as the 'Burbs. The ice got a little mushy nearer the river's mouth on the Gulf of Alaska, but farther north and certainly as far as Niniltna it made for a fine highway, better, many said, than the actual road into the Park. It was certainly wider, with room for many more vehicles, as well as the occasional race, and its reach was much farther.

Early on the morning after Thanksgiving Johnny hitched the sled to his snow machine and packed it with tent, sleeping bag, two different sets of five layers of clothes, and everything on Bingley Mercantile's shelves with a high percentage of fat content, including two large jars of Skippy peanut butter and two more of strawberry jam.

"If you get in trouble and can't build a fire," Kate said, "you can always use a spoon. Do you have your GPS?"

"For the third time, yes," Johnny said.

Kate tucked in some more fire starters and a second large box of waterproof matches. "Have you got your PLB?"

"For the fifth time, yes," Johnny said.

"You checked the batteries?"

"And I have spares," Johnny said.

"You've got them in an inside pocket."

"Where they'll stay toasty warm and ready to use if I need them."

"Rifle?"

"Cleaned and loaded and strapped to the snow machine."

His patience was monumental and meant to be noticed, but she couldn't help herself. "Extra shells?"

"Two boxes, Kate."

"Good." She prowled around the snow machine. "Have you got that tool kit I put together?"

"In the sled."

"Extra gas?"

"In the sled."

"And Van's riding with you?"

"Yes, Kate."

"And Ruthe's got her own machine."

"Yes, Kate."

"Maybe I'll just ride to Ruthe's with you."

"Maybe you won't," Johnny said. "Maybe I've been driving the snow machine back and forth to Ruthe's cabin for going on three winters now. Maybe I know the way."

He was right. Still, Kate fretted. "You're not going to deviate from your route, are you?"

"No, Kate. We'll be following the Kanuyaq a lot of the way. It's kind of hard to miss." Sheesh. By contrast, Jim this morning had tossed him a casual wave and said only, "Have fun, kid. Yell for help if you need it," before clattering down the steps and heading off to work.

"You can take Mutt," Kate said.

"I really can't," Johnny said. "Van's riding with me. I'd have to unload the sled to make room for Mutt. Then we'd have Mutt and nothing to eat. Oh, wait, we could eat Mutt."

"Very funny. Ruthe could take her."

"Then Ruthe'd have to unload her own sled. We'll be fine, Kate."

"I know you will be," Kate said, not believing a word of it. "Just, you know, just be careful, okay?"

"I always am."

"Ruthe's no spring chicken. Look out for her."

It was Johnny's considered opinion that Ruthe Bauman could outthink, outshoot, and outsurvive better than any other sentient being in the Park, with the possible exception of the woman standing in front of him, but he wasn't suicidal enough to say so. "I will," he said instead, and climbed on the snow machine.

"You're back Sunday evening before eight, or I call out the National Guard!" she said, raising her voice to be heard over the engine.

"You got it!" He put the machine in gear and slid smoothly out of the clearing, keeping the speed down to just short of flight. He received a Mutt escort for a quarter of a mile, all the way to where the track to the homestead met the road to Niniltna.

"See you in a couple a days, girl!" he yelled, and opened up the throttle.

She barked until he was out of sight, and then trotted back down the trail to find Kate shivering in the clearing. She butted Kate's thigh with her head, more purposeful than affectionate, and with the full force of a hundred and forty pounds of half wolf, half husky behind it it did not fail of effect. Kate stumbled in the direction of the house, Mutt shepherding her with repeated bumps and nudges and the occasional nip at the hem of her jeans, all the way up the deck and inside.

"I hate being a mom," Kate told her.

Mutt went to curl up on her quilt in front of the fireplace. Kate went to the kitchen to clean up after yesterday's turkey dinner. After that, she made bread, measuring out flour and yeast and salt and water with a ferocious attention to detail. Yesterday she'd made rolls, but there had to be bread for turkey sandwiches.

Bobby, Dinah, Katya, Ethan Int-Hout (Margaret had walked out on him, again), Dan O'Brien, and Ruthe had all been invited to Thanksgiving dinner at Kate's house. Ethan had pled a prior invitation to Christie Calhoun's, whose spouse had just walked out on her, and who was home alone with three daughters who would do as well as any to stand in for Ethan's own. Jim, who didn't like Ethan living even as close as the next homestead over, heaved a private sigh of relief. Kate didn't notice, or pretended she didn't.

Ruthe had also declined, on the excuse of having to get ready for the expedition. Johnny was carrying a tinfoil package of turkey and dressing with him to Ruthe's.

Jim had been called out to a domestic disturbance, endemic over the holidays and in the Park frequently fatal if some calming, uniformed presence was not applied. This had turned out to make for a more enjoyable dinner, because Dan had been wound up tighter than a bedspring when he walked in. The moment Jim walked out the door he relaxed, leaning back suddenly against his chair as if the wires holding him up had been cut.

Later, after everyone had gone and Jim had returned, Kate said, "What's with you and Dan?"

Something stirred at the back of his eyes, but he said, "What do you mean?"

She shook her head and got up from the couch. "Don't tell me if you can't or if you just don't want to, but don't tell me nothing's going on." She went upstairs, brushed her teeth, stripped, and got into bed.

He followed, climbing in next to her without speaking. They went to sleep on their sides facing away from each other, but she woke up in the middle of the night to find him parting her legs with his knee and sliding inside her in one bold stroke. Something got off the chain then, and she rolled, forcing him to his back. She nipped at his ear, his belly, the sensitive curve of his thigh, and when she rose again he was red-faced and straining, his body one long pleading arch. She mounted him this time, pinning his hands to the mattress, and rode him furiously to an explosive culmination that left them both sweat-soaked and gasping for breath.

There was more rutting than making love about it but it made for a solid and dreamless sleep, and she woke the next morning if not with a song in her heart then at least with a sense of well-being and renewal, which had lasted until Johnny began packing to leave on his camping trip.

"If you find out that the herd has decreased," Kate had asked Ruthe when informed of the trip, "and if you find out that wolf predation is the cause, you're going to tell Dan about it, right?"

Ruthe didn't answer, but then Kate hadn't expected her to. Ruthe was perfectly capable of effecting some predator control all by herself, thank you. With twenty-ten vision and an upper body strength honed by decades of backwoods life, she was one of the best shots in the Park. Certainly she was better than Kate.

Kate kneaded the dough until it was smooth and elastic, covered the bowl with Saran Wrap, and set it to one side to rise. She washed her hands and got out her USGS map of the Park. Three of the four corners were missing and it was coming apart at every crease. She really must order a new one.

She unfolded it on the dining table and located Niniltna and the approximate location of Ruthe's cabin, about halfway between Niniltna and the Roadhouse. Ruthe had told her that they were planning on following the Kanuyaq for ten or twelve miles and then cutting overland on a heading east-southeast.

After some searching, Kate found the Gruening River, its source in the Quilaks south of the Big Bump, running by tortuous twists and turns south by southwest to drain into the Kanuyaq River just above the delta where the Kanuyaq itself drained into Prince William Sound. She traced an imaginary line from Ruthe's cabin to the Gruening River basin, and sat back with an air of having all her worst suspicions confirmed.

What no one had said but what was perfectly obvious to anyone with even rudimentary map reading skills was that Ruthe's suggested route was going to take them right over Global Harvest's Suulutaq Mine leases.

Jim had to fly to Cordova that morning to put Margaret Kvasnikof and Hallelujah Smith on a plane to Anchorage. They would be taking up residency in the Hiland Mountain Correctional Facility, there to begin serving a four-year sentence for defrauding the Alaska Permanent Fund of almost a quarter of a million dollars, by way of false dividend applications in the names of forty-three imaginary children over a period of five years. It was the biggest single PFD bust in state history and Kate's biggest paying case to date, and every Alaskan loved to hate people who ripped off the PFD. There had been significant airtime devoted to the conviction, which hadn't done Kate's business any harm.

He handed the two felons over to their escort at Mudhole Smith Airport and waited till the Alaska Airlines 737 was wheels up before hitching a ride into town with a local fisherman just back from a visit to the dentist in Anchorage. He could drive his truck but he couldn't talk, so it was a quiet ride, which suited Jim. He had a lot on his mind.

He knew why he'd been pissy lately. He was keeping secrets from Kate. Only one secret, actually, but it was a whopper. He couldn't prove it in court, and Willard didn't even remember it, but Jim was certain that Louis Deem had loaded Willard like a gun and shot him off in the direction of the Koslowskis' house that night with the intention of burgling the gold in the display case in the living room.

He knew that the longer he went without telling Kate, the worse it would be when he did tell her. Worse still would be if she found out on her own, but since he was equally certain that he was the only one who knew, he wasn't afraid of that. Much.

The thing was, she'd been a little pissy lately, too. No reason had surfaced as to why. He wondered if he'd even have noticed it if they hadn't been all but living together. He still rented his room at Auntie Vi's, but it was more an overnight flop for when he had to work late than separate living quarters, and the step increase he got for working in the Bush more than covered the expense.

No, he thought grimly, he was living with Kate, all right. All he kept at Auntie Vi's was a change of clothes and a spare toothbrush.

It didn't frighten him as much as it once had. There was still passion, and laughter, a shared sense of the ridiculous. They had a lot in common in work and in play. He was a trooper, she was a PI. They both read recreationally, anything and everything, and that was a bond right there. Kate, he knew, thought better of people who read. He sometimes thought it was what had pushed her over the top as far as he was concerned. Okay by him. They both liked to talk about any and every topic under the sun, nothing sacred, everything fair game from abortion to gay marriage to states' rights to Alaska seceding from the union and forming its own country with Siberia and the western provinces of Canada.

They both loathed recreational exercise. Jim had been a little surprised by that. Kate would think nothing of strapping on cross-country skis to go over to Mandy's if the snow machine wouldn't start, but ask her to go skiing just for the fun of it and she'd look at you like you'd grown a second head. He supposed it was natural for someone born to a Bush lifestyle, though. Anyone who could fix a hole in a roof that had been punctured by parts falling off a Boeing 747 was bound to be in good enough shape for anything else that came along.

She was beautiful. Or maybe not beautiful, exactly. He didn't know anymore. He knew he liked looking at her, waking, sleeping, laughing, loving, happy, even pissed off, even if it was at him. He liked watching her work, that innate curiosity that demanded satisfaction, that would brook no distraction until all the questions had been answered.

It surprised him that she still believed in justice. She'd been lied to, beat up, shot at, her house had been burned down, her truck had been run off the road, her dog had almost been killed, she herself had been in the hospital more times than Evel Knievel, and left not in the best of shape even when she managed to stay out of it. Only too well did he remember finding her bruised and covered with blood, driving a stolen truck with the exaggerated care of a drunk down what was little more than a goat track out of the back range of the mountains north of Anchorage. She put herself at risk too often, and all for a lousy paycheck.

He smiled to himself.

It wasn't the paycheck, and no one knew that better than he did.

His smile faded. Still, she had been getting a little pissy lately. Thinking, he dated it back to the Louis Deem murder the year before. Amazing first, that he'd noticed. Amazing second, that he wanted to know why.

The fisherman let him off in front of the Cordova cop shop, and he went in to meet and greet and compare notes on several of the Park's most stupid, most drunk, most likely to, and most wanted. Afterward he walked down to the Club Bar for a burger and a Coke.

The first person he saw when he walked in was the ubiquitous Talia Macleod, holding forth to a table of Cordovan movers and shakers, all with drinks at their elbows for which Jim was willing to bet large Macleod had paid. They were all sprouting GHRI ball caps, too, the ones with the golden sunburst peeping over a line of mountains, recognizable as the Quilaks if you looked close.

She saw him at once and raised a hand in greeting without missing a word of what she was saying. He sat at the bar and ordered, and as he was finishing his meal her meeting broke up and she joined him there. "Cheese it, the fuzz," she said.

He grinned. "How you doing?"

She grimaced. "Sometimes I feel like I've taken a vow. And that I get paid by the convert." She looked over her shoulder and waved someone over.

Jim looked and saw a burly man of medium height, late thirties, dark hair and wary eyes. He patted the air and shook his head, nodding at the group he was talking to. She insisted, and he trailed over, obviously reluctant and equally obviously trying not to show it.

"Jim Chopin, meet Dick Gallagher," she said.

"How do," Jim said.

"Hey," Gallagher said. His handshake was brief and a little clammy. "So," he said, his eyes taking in the blue and gold, "you a cop?"

"Trooper," Jim said. He'd been one too long not to recognize the reluctance, and ran a quick interior scan of the most recent wants and warrants. None of them sported Gallagher's name or his description, and few people liked cops anyway, so mentally he stood down, for now.

"You need me for anything else?" Gallagher said to Macleod. He half turned from Jim as he spoke, focusing his attention on Macleod. Crowded in close, too, and touched her knee.

"No, I think our work here is done," Macleod said, composed. "For today, anyway. You can head for the barn if you want."

Jim watched the tension in Gallagher's jawline increase. "A couple of the gentlemen want to shoot some pool down to the Cordova House. Figured I'd tag along."

"You lose your own money, not Global Harvest's," Macleod said, unperturbed.

Gallagher laughed, but it rang false. "What time do we leave tomorrow?"

"Ten A.M., George picks us up at the airport."

"See you then," he said. He gave Jim a distant nod without meeting his eyes and left with the other men.

"I've been duly warned off," Jim said lightly.

"No need to be," she said, as lightly, and smiled at him.

Jim felt an unwilling sympathy for Gallagher, so easily discarded, and Macleod must have somehow intuited it because she added, "He's like every other boomer who ever came into the state, his hand out for any and everything he can get before he hauls ass south."

The bartender came over and she ordered a glass of chardonnay.

"Women always order chardonnay," Jim said.

She made play with her eyelashes over the rim of her glass. "Sometimes we order pinot grigio." She sipped. "But most of the time they don't have it. Besides, men always wear blue."

He looked down at himself. It was true. "In my own defense, it is the color of my uniform."

"What are you doing in town?" she said.

"Prisoner escort, and I had to reach out to the local cops on a few things. Routine. I don't have to ask you what you've been doing. How long have you been here?"

"Two days. Got a suite at the Reluctant, or what passes for a

suite, which is two rooms with a connecting door. I have had breakfast with the Chamber of Commerce, lunch with the school board,
attended a meeting of the library advisory board, played pinochle at
the Elks Club and Bingo with the retired folks at Sunset Arms."

Jim smiled. "Whatever they're paying you, it isn't worth it."

"I don't know." She shrugged. "I had a lesson in beading from a
nice lady, name of Pat, retired from the school administration. Or I
did until her granddaughter Annie showed up. She told me to go
find my own beading teacher."

"Gotta watch out for them granddaughters," Jim said. "Where
do you go next?"

She brightened perceptibly. "I'm spreading the word to the villages on the river, by snow machine."

"No kidding," he said, impressed. "You're heading out to the
'Burbs, are you?"

"Yeah, I've been waiting until the river froze up enough for
traffic."

"You want to be careful when you get close to the mouth. It
starts to get a little slushy."

She laughed. "I'm told that it's fish camps the last twenty-five
miles before the Sound, summers only, so I should be all right. I'm
going to take my skis, see if I can get in some snow time while I'm
out there."

"Your rifle, too?"

She looked mock shocked. "Of course."

Her enthusiasm was contagious, and he warmed to her. "Should
be a great trip, so long as the weather holds."

She shrugged. "I've been snowed in in Bush Alaska before. I'll
bring a deck of cards."

He ate another french fry. "I have to say that snow machining
down the Kanuyaq sounds like a lot more fun than eating bacon and
eggs with the Cordova Chamber of Commerce."

"Tell me about it." She hesitated. "Actually. Tell me about something else."

"What?"

"You know Howie Katelnikof?"

"Everybody knows Howie," he said casually, suddenly on the alert.

"What do you know about him?"

He shook salt onto his plate and started mopping it up one fry at a time. "A lot more than I can prove."

"Shit," she said. It was a long, drawn-out expression of annoyance and frustration, and it was heartfelt.

"What'd he do?"

"I think he's been stealing stuff from the trailer out on the leases."

"You think?"

"I know stuff is gone, a computer monitor, a telephone, some other office supplies. I don't know that Howie took them, but he was the guy out there when they went missing. It was his shift."

"His shift?"

"Yeah, I hired Dick Gallagher to work a week on, a week off with Howie."

"Guy just here."

"That's him."

"You don't think Gallagher is responsible?"

"Wrong weeks."

Jim thought of the wariness in Dick Gallagher's eyes. He and Howie could be ripping off the place together. "Those snow machines don't work only on the river."

"You got something against Dick?"

"Just met the guy. Don't like to jump to assumptions, is all." He ate another french fry. Salty goodness. "Howie never was the brightest dog on the gangline. Come to think of it, that was probably an

105

insult to any dog on a gangline. Actually, maybe anything on four feet."

"I guess I should have talked to somebody before I hired him," she said moodily.

"That would have been good," he said.

She smacked him halfheartedly on his arm. "What's more, he's decided he's in love with me."

"Only a matter of time," Jim said.

"Why, thank you, Sergeant Chopin."

"Howie falls in love pretty easily," Jim said. "A working pulse is pretty much all it takes for him."

She smacked him again, less halfheartedly this time, and they both laughed. "Well, I'm not all that hard to please, but I'm a lot harder to please than that," she said. "How mad at me are the Park rats going to be if I fire him?"

"Not very. You might even get some more converts on the strength of it."

"Oh, well, then I'll fire him the next time I see him."

"Where is he?"

She made a face. "Out at the lease site. It's his week on."

The bartender came with the check. "Anything else?"

"I'll get that," Macleod said.

Jim managed to snag it a second before she did. "I'm here on business. I'll expense it."

The bartender stood there, waiting. "I'll have another glass," Talia said. "Jim? Want a beer?"

Jim shook his head. "Can't. I'm flying home this afternoon. Can't drink and fly. I might hurt myself. Not to mention that three-hundred-thousand-dollar plane they gave me."

She put a hand on his arm. "Simple. Don't fly."

He took a deep breath, and let it out before turning his head to meet her eyes. They were large and very blue, and the lashes were long and thick and heavy. They weighed her eyelids down, giving her a slumberous, sexy look. Her face was flushed and her lips were shiny with gloss and half parted, and as he watched her tongue came out to tease delicately at one corner.

He swallowed hard. "You know I'm with somebody now."

She didn't look away, and the smile didn't falter. "I've heard. So?"

She was making it clear she knew the score. An evening spent enjoying each other's company, and then parting the next morning with no promises on either side.

How uncomplicated that sounded, how downright relaxing.

How tempting.

She slid from her stool and leaned close to whisper in his ear. "Room 204. Come up the back stairs. I'll leave the door unlocked."

She walked away and he watched her attentively, because he was a trained investigator and there might be a clue in the way her well-toned muscles moved together as they went away from him.

He waited until she was out of the door and then turned and flagged down the bartender. "Could I have a receipt, please?"

NINE

It was always a bad idea to sit around brooding, so when the bread came out of the oven Kate went outside to split kindling until her nose and her toes were numb. She came back inside to thaw out beneath a steaming shower and dress. She called to Mutt and the two of them went into town to check the mail. She hadn't checked it since before the holiday so her mailbox was jammed and there was an overflow notice. She took it to the window and Bonnie gave her a hurt look and came staggering back with a plastic tub full to the brim. Kate detoured to the Niniltna dump and tossed nine-tenths of it into the ever-growing pile presided over by a flock of sleek, fat ravens and another of cranky-looking eagles, all of whom went silent as the tomb when they saw Mutt.

There were only a few people at the Riverside Café that morning, and Kate got the best table by the window. Through it she could keep an eye on Mutt, who was sitting on the seat of the snow machine, surveying the passersby with a lofty air and accepting tentative greetings with a regal condescension and, when someone dared to take liberties, a baring of teeth.

"Americano double tall, with lots of half-and-half," Kate told Laurel, and added two packs of sugar when it arrived.

"Damn, girl, how can you do that to an innocent little espresso? Sorta defeats the purpose of caffeine, you know?"

She looked up to see Pete Heiman standing next to her table, a grin on his face.

"Ah," Kate said, "Pete, hello. Still unindicted, I see."

His grin didn't falter. "I remain free on my own recognizance. Isn't that how you cop types put it?"

"Not quite," Kate said dryly, "but it'll do for going on with."

He indicated the seat across from her. "You mind?"

Kate shrugged. "Suit yourself."

"Just coffee, honey," he told Laurel, and sighed when Laurel winked at him and put extra into her hips as she departed their table. There was a reason the Riverside Café was so popular with men.

Kate sipped her Americano and schooled her face into an expression of cool neutrality as she regarded Pete over the rim of her mug.

Pete Heiman was a third-generation Alaskan with an irreproachable Alaskan family tree that included a stampeder, a Bush pilot, and one of Castner's Cutthroats. Grainy newspaper photographs going back a hundred years showed a succession of Heiman men who looked like they'd been cloned, the same coarse dark hair clipped short, the same merry eyes in the same narrow face, the same shovel-shaped jaw, and the same grin somewhere between ingratiating and shit-eating. The president and CEO of Heiman Transportation, a trucking firm that was responsible for a minimum of twenty percent of all goods moved between Fairbanks and the Prudhoe Bay oil fields, and a lifelong resident of Ahtna, Pete was also in his third term as the Republican senator for District 41, which included the Park.

Laurel brought his coffee and swished away again. "How you faring this winter?" he said.

"Like always," Kate said. "Fuel bills are killing me, but they're killing all of us. I'll get by."

"Heard about that PFD fraud ring you broke up." Pete gave an approving nod. "Good work there. Hate people who rip off the PFD."

"Everybody does," Kate said. "Helps that everybody gets one. Makes them feel real proprietary about the fund. If their lawyer had wanted them to get a fair trial, he should have petitioned for a change of venue, to a courtroom out of state."

"Uh-huh," Pete said, clearly not attending.

"Something you wanted, Pete?"

He did his best to look wounded. "Can't I just sit down and have a friendly cup of coffee?"

"No," Kate said.

To his credit, Pete laughed. "Yeah, okay, you never were one for the bullshit, Katie. Okay." He faced her squarely. "I hear you're the new chair of the Niniltna Association board of directors."

"Interim," Kate said. "Interim chair. The membership may decide differently when they vote in January." As she devoutly hoped they would.

"Yeah, okay, interim. But you're chair now."

"I am. What do you want, Pete?"

He cocked an eye. "Word is it was a pretty interesting first meeting."

Kate stiffened. "That wouldn't be any of your business, now, Pete, would it?"

"No," he said hastily. "None at all."

His thoughts were pretty plain on his face. Kate Shugak had once had a pretty robust sense of humor, and instead of squashing his interest in the board meeting she had only ratcheted it up a notch. He wouldn't rest until he got all the gory details, and he'd probably be telling the story for years to come, too. Him and

Harvey, it would be like getting it in stereo. Wonderful. "So?" she said.

He shrugged, but the tension in his shoulders gave him away. "Well, as the new NNA chair, a lot of us are wondering what kind of stand you're going to take on the Suulutaq Mine."

Her eyebrows raised. "That would be my business," she said blandly. "And the board's, and the shareholders'. Why do you ask?"

He snorted. "Ah, Jesus, Katie, you know damn well why I'm asking. Global Harvest is going to bring a lot of jobs into my district."

"And a three-by-five-mile open pit mine into my backyard," Kate said.

"Ah, shit," he said, half in distaste, half in dismay. "You ain't gonna fight them on it, are you?"

"I don't know what I'm going to do yet, Pete," Kate said. She drained her mug and rose to her feet. "And even if I did, I wouldn't tell you before I told the board and my fellow shareholders."

He snatched up her check as she was reaching for it. "I'll get that."

"No." The receipt tore a little as she pulled it from his hand. "I'll get it."

His hurt feelings were well simulated, she had to give him that much. "Shit, Katie, I've bought you coffee before."

"I wasn't chair of the board, before," she said.

She paid for her espresso and left.

Outside Auntie Balasha was making obeisance to Mutt, who was accepting it with a gracious air. "Hey, Auntie," Kate said, giving her a hug.

"Katya," Auntie Balasha said. "The dog, she look good. Nothing bad left over from last year?"

Last year Mutt had been shot and almost killed, requiring surgery and a week's recovery at the vet's in Ahtna, a traumatic period that Kate even now had difficulty reliving. "She's fine, Auntie." Kate looked up and down the narrow little street to see if anyone was in listening distance. There wasn't, but she lowered her voice anyway. "Listen, Auntie, have any of you seen anything of the Smith girls?"

Auntie Balasha's face darkened. "Vi keeping watch. She go out to Smith place once a week. She even get parents to say okay for the girls to come to her house after school sometime. When they come, they talk to Desiree."

Desiree was the school's nurse practitioner, and Auntie Balasha's granddaughter. "What does Desiree say?"

Auntie Balasha's lips tightened and she said sternly, "Desiree never talk about patients."

"Auntie."

Auntie Balasha sighed. "Desiree say they don't talk much, but they do talk some. She say this is little bit of good. Maybe better later."

Kate felt a tightness in her chest ease. "Good. That's good, Auntie. I was keeping tabs last winter but this summer I was fishing and then I was working and—" She stopped making excuses. "I'm glad you and Desiree and Auntie Vi are keeping tabs on them." She hesitated. "Do they still refuse to tell their parents about what Louis did to them?"

"They don't tell parents nothing," Auntie Balasha said succinctly.

There were twenty-one kids in the Smith family. Kate wondered if it was harder or easier to keep secrets in a family that size. Easier to hide them in the noise, or harder to hide because of all the noses standing by to sniff them out? She hoped for Chloe and Hannah's sakes that when their parents did find out the girls got all the love and support they needed, but she'd seen the family in action and she doubted it. She had Father Smith pegged as a greedy opportunist, and Mother Smith as someone who had perfected the art of going along. "How about you, Auntie?" she said out loud. "Everything okay?"

"All well."

But Auntie Balasha seemed preoccupied. Kate looked at her, standing there in her homemade calico kuspuk, lavishly trimmed with gaudy gold rickrack and lustrous marten that she had probably trapped and tanned herself. Like all the aunties she was comfortably plump, with long graying hair she kept bundled out of her face, round cheeks a pleasing walnut brown, clad in skin that was by now wrinkled like a walnut, too. She was missing a tooth, and there was a faint scar on her left check, remnants of her marriage. It had ended when he had gone down the boat ramp in Cordova, drunk as a skunk, tripped over his own feet, and drowned in the harbor, leaving her with three children to feed and clothe and shepherd into adulthood. She had succeeded, partly because she'd had the love and support of the extended family of Park rats, and partly because she would have sold herself on the streets of Spenard before she let her children go cold or hungry. What Kate considered most remarkable was that she'd never heard Auntie Balasha whine or complain. She just kept on keeping on, and when her own children were grown and gone like Auntie Joy she had progressed to an enthusiastic and indiscriminate adoption of every stray that wandered across her path, strays like Martin, and Willard, and evidently now Howie, who of course lost no time in exploiting the situation.

That thought roused Kate's protective spirit like nothing else. If Willard and Howie were stealing fuel from Auntie Balasha again, this time she wouldn't just beat Willard to the ground, she would eviscerate him. "What is it, Auntie? Is there a problem? Something I can help you with?"

Auntie Balasha raised her enormous brown eyes, liquid with love and concern. "I worry about you, Katya."

Kate was taken aback. "Worry about me?" She even laughed a little. "Why? I'm fine."

"You live so far out of town." Auntie Balasha gestured vaguely in the general direction of Kate's homestead. "If you get in trouble, who help you? Who come when you call? You should live in town. I live here. Vi live here. Joy, Edna live here. You get in trouble, we help you. We drop by more often, check up on you, see if you okay."

The prospect of the aunties dropping in at any hour of the day or night to check up on her froze the blood in Kate's veins. Trying to speak amiably, she said, "That's a nice thought, Auntie, and I thank you for it, but you know I've got Johnny with me now." Driven to it, she added, "And Jim Chopin stops by now and then."

This artless addition got the skeptical look it deserved. "But you chair of Association now, Katya."

Kate stiffened. "Yes."

Balasha, ignoring the warning signs, carried on. "Position of responsibility. People need to talk to you about something, where you are? Far away! Can't walk there, have to drive truck or snowgo. If shareholders need you, if emergency happens, long time it takes to come get you. You should move to town."

"Auntie," Kate said, "I've got to go, I've got some business down the road. I'll see you later, okay? Mutt. Up."

It came out as more of an order than a request and a startled Mutt scrambled to her feet. Kate climbed on in front of her and pressed the starter. The roar of the engine drowned out Auntie Balasha's further remonstrances. Kate smiled tightly, tossed her a cheerful wave, and got the hell out of town.

But not out of Dodge, as it turned out. One step into the Roadhouse she walked slap into Martin Shugak, who smirked at her. "Madam Chair. Got a motion I'd like to run by you. Or do I mean over you?"

She told him what to do with his motion and marched up to the bar, ears burning from the snickering that came from Martin's knot of misfits, malcontents, and misdemeanors in waiting, a group that encouraged Martin to temporarily forget all the ways she could hurt him if she put her mind to it.

"Kate," Bernie said. He'd undoubtedly heard the story, too, but he was a little wiser in the ways of Kate Shugak than Martin was and he refrained from comment. With her usual insouciance Mutt reared up, paws on the bar, and panted at Bernie, who snagged the usual package of beef jerky and tossed it her way. He put a can of Diet 7UP and a glass full of ice in front of Kate and moved down to the end of the bar, where Nick Waterbury sat, arms around what appeared to be not his first beer of the day. She frowned and checked the clock on the wall. Not even three o'clock. Nick was a lot of things but he wasn't a boozer. "Hey, Nick," she said. "How you doing."

"Fine, Kate. No worries." He didn't look up and his dreary voice contradicted his words.

"How's Eve?"

"She's fine. We're just fine."

Since they'd lost their daughter Mary two years before at the hands of Louis Deem, who had walked on the charge, Kate doubted the veracity of that statement. "Tell her I'll be out in a couple of days. I'm jonesing for her coffee cake."

"Sure," Nick said. "Whatever."

Now that it seemed safe Bernie slid back down the bar. "How are you holding up?" she said.

He didn't blow her off and he didn't sugarcoat it. "I'm maintaining."

"Just maintaining?"

"It'll do. For now, it'll have to."

"The kids?"

He thought about his answer for a moment or two. "Quieter," he said finally.

"That doesn't sound good."

"It isn't," he said without rancor. He raised a hand, palm up, and let it drop. "But what can we expect. Their mother and brother were murdered last year. And they don't even get to spit in the eye of the asshole who did it."

"At least he's dead," Kate said.

Bernie met her eyes, his own empty of expression. "That he is."

God, it was cold. The frigid air bit through the windshield of the snow machine and all five layers of his clothing with the ferocity of a wolverine biting into flesh, and it felt just that hungry, that angry, and that voracious. He wore a balaclava and a knit cap inside his hood and his face was still cold. Beneath his down parka with the wolf-trimmed hood and a down bib overall guaranteed to twenty below, he wore a Gore-Tex Pro Shell and a pair of ski pants, and beneath them Patagonia Capilene, the ne plus ultra in long underwear. His boots were Sorel Caribous rated to forty below, and inside his winter mitts he wore heated gloves powered by a D battery guaranteed to keep his hands warm for five hours, minimum.

Nevertheless, the only truly warm part of his body was in fact his back, and that was because Van was snuggled against it, her arms wrapped tightly around his waist. "You okay?" he yelled over the noise of the engine.

"Great!" she yelled back. "Isn't it gorgeous?"

She could talk, she was all warm and comfy back there with him as her wind foil, but she did have a point.

The white swath of snow-covered ice wound through a landscape of low banks and rounded foothills. Thick stands of willow flashed by, leaving Johnny with retinal after-impressions of enormous brown lumps, moose in groups of four and five, curled up in the snow, conserving energy, waiting out the cold snap before they got up to feed again. High overhead, a bald eagle soared, looking for the unwary rabbit or that foolish pika who had been improvident in preparing for winter and whom hunger had forced out to feed. Eagles mostly ate fish, Johnny knew, but with the Kanuyaq frozen solid and the salmon out to sea anyway the eagles made do with what was on the ground. Or in the garbage dump. Maybe Benjamin Franklin was right, maybe the turkey should have been the national bird.

It was a clear, cold, calm day, the sky a pale, sere blue. The sun was up after ten and in bed before four, and in the few brief hours that it traveled above the horizon its reflection off the snow felt sharp enough to draw blood. They all wore goggles with polarized lenses to guard against snow blindness.

Ahead of them Ruthe goosed her Arctic Cat with the verve and enthusiasm of a woman half her age, following truck trails when there were any, breaking new trail where the wind had blown the snow into sculptured drifts that were so beautiful and otherworldly that it seemed a shame to Johnny to destroy them. Ruthe skimmed their tops or plowed through their bases without a backward glance, resulting in explosions of snow that momentarily obliterated the trail. When now and then he managed to pull even with her he could see the grin beneath her goggles. "She's loving this," Van shouted.

He felt an answering grin spread over his face. "Yes, she is!"

There was traffic on the river that day, other snow machines as well as pickups and four-wheelers and one guy on cross-country skis towing a sled. When asked, he said he was from Anchorage, just out for a weekend wilderness experience. He seemed rational, which was unexpected, and shared with them some homemade fudge that even frozen solid melted in the mouth like chocolate silk. It could have been a highway anywhere north of the fifty-three, if there wasn't the occasional guy fishing through a hole he'd chopped in the ice, hoping for a mess of whitefish for dinner.

The others were inhabitants of the villages they passed, isolated clusters of log cabins and small prefabricated buildings brought up- or downriver at great expense, for most of whom their airstrip doubled as main street. Usually downtown consisted of a tiny store with inflated prices and an even tinier post office in someone's front room. Most had a government building that might also house the rare village public safety officer and whatever air taxi flew there. They all had schools, in spite of steadily dwindling school populations as more and more people moved to where the jobs were. Johnny had heard that topic discussed by the four aunties more than once. He wondered if the mine would help, if it would stop the drift of Alaskans from the rural to the urban world. He knew Kate didn't think so. "How do you keep them down on the farm," she had said once in his hearing, "after they've seen what's out there on satellite television?"

They didn't stop to talk, though, so he couldn't ask the people who lived there how they felt about it. One group of three, all wearing helmets, circled around and came back by them, and then circled again and roared by a third time. A pickup came into view, and the three jumped a low section of riverbank and disappeared into a stand of spindly spruce trees.

"Who was that?" Van said.

"Dunno," Johnny said, "but they sure know how to drive snow-gos." He was nagged by the feeling that there was something he should have made notice of. He faced forward to see Ruthe going up the bank on the opposite side of the river. "Hold on, Van!"

He followed Ruthe's tracks off the river and over the bank and found her waiting at the top. "Still good?" she said.

"Still good," he said. He might be cold but he wasn't frozen, and he was enjoying the feel of Van's arms around him. He could keep going all day.

"Okay," Ruthe said, and off she hared again, he and Van faint but pursuing. They climbed for almost a mile, Ruthe perforce slowing down for safe passage through giant and mostly dying spruce trees crowded by thickly growing birches, all on the south-facing slope of what resolved into a high valley. Once in it, mountains rose up on either side to give it a wide, exaggerated U shape edged with sharp peaks, notched peaks, double peaks four and five and six thousand feet high. They were in the foothills of the Quilaks.

Ruthe halted and Johnny pulled up beside her. Ruthe killed her engine and Johnny did likewise, and everyone pulled their hoods back and pushed their goggles up, eyes narrowed against the brilliant sunlight. The sudden and immediate silence fell like a blow. The scene before them was like a painting, richly textured in the subtle hues of an Arctic winter day, hushed, serene, and achingly beautiful.

"Wow," Van said, and dismounted.

"Don't!" Ruthe and Johnny said simultaneously, but before they could stop her Van had stepped off the machine and almost immediately sank into the snow up to her waist. She blinked up at them, astonished.

Ruthe threw back her head and laughed, the explosive cackle frightening a ptarmigan from beneath a bush, wings as white as the snow, a blur of motion. After a moment's inner struggle, Johnny started to laugh, too.

Van couldn't help it, she joined in, followed by a quick yelp of distress. "Oh no, I can't laugh, it makes me go in deeper!"

At that Ruthe lay back on the seat of her snow machine and simply dissolved. Johnny pulled himself together and by dint of superior upper body strength, which he did not neglect to point out to both of them, managed to lever Vanessa up on her belly, like a seal, across the seat in back of him. She banged her boots together to get the snow out of her laces, and pulled herself up and back in the saddle. "That's me, ladies and gentlemen, the light relief for the day. Well, how was I to know? I've never ridden out in the backcountry before, just on roads and trails."

Ruthe grinned at her, deep laugh lines creasing her lean cheeks. "What's called throwing you in at the deep end."

Johnny and Van were accompanying Ruthe Bauman, the Park's self-styled naturalist, on an expedition to check on the Gruening River caribou herd. It wasn't much of a herd, less than two thousand strong, but it was part of the Park ecosystem, and Ruthe was the self-appointed patron saint of all Park wildlife, flora and fauna. She tolerated the presence of Dan O'Brien's Park rangers, even if they did tend to get in the way when they were least wanted. They meant well, and she was even on occasion pleased to approve of this or that action taken, but she'd watched almost forty seasons come and go from her front porch, and the rhythm of the life of the Park was as natural to her as her own. It was a byword in the Park that Ruthe could step outside the door of the cabin perched on the hill-side with the southern view, look at the sky, take a sniff or two of the wind, and give anyone who asked a forecast that would be more timely and more accurate than any National Weather Service weather report. When Ruthe said to put the snow tires on the truck, Park rats put them on their trucks. When she said it was safe to take them off, they took them off. She was a handy neighbor.

Lean as a tough steak, brown eyes still clear beneath a mop of soft white gold curls, Ruthe Bauman was an ex-WASP who had towed targets for WWII fighter pilots doing target practice over the Atlantic. After the war she'd come north hoping for a job in aviation in Alaska when they weren't on offer to women Outside. She and her friend, Dina Willner, dead three years now, had joined forces with an enterprising travel agent out of Fairbanks that specialized in big game hunts. They bought him out in 1949, acquiring two de Havilland Beavers in the deal, and added air taxi services to remote sites to their business model. In the 50s they bought a cabin and eighty acres twenty-five miles south of Niniltna, added another ten cabins, and took out an ad in *Alaska* magazine. In that hour one of the world's first eco-resorts, Camp Teddy, was born. So was the Park's conservation movement, which came as something of a shock to the Park rats.

Ruthe and Dina had been close friends of Ekaterina Shugak and were mentors, teachers, and friends to her granddaughter. When Kate acquired Johnny, Ruthe naturally extended that relationship to include him, and he spent a great deal of time literally as well as metaphorically sitting at her feet, learning everything she cared to teach him about the Park and every creature in it.

This winter, Ruthe had been doing some public worrying over the notion that the Gruening River caribou herd might have suffered some serious depredations due to the increase in population of the resident wolf pack. Dan had organized a couple of overflights on Chugach Air, but the budget didn't really allow for an on-the-ground look, too. Ruthe volunteered. "She didn't actually volunteer," Dan told Kate, "she just told me she was going." Ruthe had asked Johnny if he wanted to go. He had in turn invited Van along.

"Sorry you came?" Johnny said, knowing the answer.

Van just laughed.

But Ruthe's attention had shifted, one hand shading her eyes as she looked up the valley. "There it is," she said, and pointed.

The sun was behind the mountains now, and the reflected light less brilliant and hurtful to the eyes. Johnny squinted and could just make out a lone trailer a long way up the valley. It was white, so it was hard to distinguish it from the surrounding countryside, but it had a gold stripe around the top, which was what he found first. "Yeah," he said, "I see it. So that's where they'll dig the Suulutaq Mine."

"That's it," she said. "Can you imagine a pit three miles wide, five miles long, and two thousand feet deep, right there?"

"How tall is two thousand feet?" Van said.

"Two hundred stories," Johnny said.

"Yeah, but what's that mean? Compare it to something."

"I don't know." Johnny thought. "You could put four Washington Monuments in it, one on top of the other."

Van had only ever seen the Washington Monument in pictures. "Oh."

Inspired, Johnny said, "Those mountains, right here at the opening of the valley? I looked on the map before we came, and those first ones are about two thousand feet high. Which means you could put them down in the mine and you wouldn't even see the tops of them."

Van digested this, looking from the mountains to the valley and back again. "Wow," she said, impressed. "That's pretty deep."

Ruthe, unheeding, pointed. "See there? All the way up the end of the valley, on the right, that edge of that mountain?"

They sort of did. "Yeah?"

"The source of the Gruening River is right there, in those hills, and there's a pass just the other side of that edge that the river follows."

"Where does it go?"

"Right into the Kanuyaq, boy. Right into the Kanuyaq."

Johnny had read the flyers that came in the mail, and the handouts that Talia Macleod had given out at the school the month before, too. So had Van. "You're thinking about the salmon runs, right?" Van said. "I thought they were going to build a lake to contain the effluent, and two dams, not just one, to hold it all in."

"Who says the dams will hold?"

"They're going to be pretty big dams, Ruthe," Van said.

"Maybe," Ruthe said. "And maybe there aren't going to be any dams. Come on, let's go say howdy."

Johnny leaned over and grabbed Ruthe's hand before it could push the start button. "I thought we were supposed to go looking for the Gruening River caribou herd."

She smiled at him kindly, or that's what he thought she meant to do. On the receiving end she looked more like a feral fox, all sharp teeth and attitude. "We'll get to them, don't worry. But we're so close, it'd be impolite not to drop in and say hello. I'm sure whoever's stuck all the way out here alone in that little trailer would be glad of some company."

The loud roar of her snow machine's engine split the sky and she was off, going fast enough to send up a faint rooster tail of snow in her wake. Johnny regarded Ruthe's profession of altruism with extreme skepticism, but he hit the start button. "Hang on, Van!" They set off in pursuit, him pushing his snowgo as hard as he dared.

It was futile and he knew it. Ruthe's Arctic Cat was brand new that winter, a green Jaguar Z1, with an 1100 4-stroke engine, the ACT Diamond Direct Drive, twin spar chassis, and slide-action rear suspension. She could hit a hundred miles an hour without breaking a sweat. It had cost a cool ten large, and the first time he'd seen it Johnny had been struck dumb with envy, completely forgetting that he was the proud owner of his very own pickup truck. Trucks didn't count in the winter, not out in the Bush.

He, too, was driving an Arctic Cat, Kate's spare, but it was practically an antique, being all of seven, almost eight years old. It wheezed long before it got to a hundred, and even though the speedometer was broken Johnny knew because he'd tried to keep up with Ruthe before and failed just as abjectly. It was a lot farther to the isolated little trailer than it had looked from the top of the pass, which gave him a perspective on how big the valley was. Now that they were down in the middle of it, he could see it was more of a high plateau, mostly flat, or so it seemed filled up with snow. "What do you think?" he yelled at Van. "Five miles wide?"

"More!" she yelled back. "And at least twelve miles long!"

"Probably more like fifteen!"

With the sun behind the mountains not only was the light fading but the temperature was dropping, too. He hunched down behind the windshield and was grateful for Van's warm weight at his back.

Ruthe had stopped on a little rise a hundred yards short of the cabin, and was waiting for them when they pulled up. "Took your time," she said smugly.

"Yeah, yeah," Johnny said.

Her grin flashed. She stood up on her machine, leaning a knee on the seat, and yelled, "Hello, the trailer!"

They waited. There was no response.

It was a peaceful enough scene, smoke wisping up through the chimney, a path shoveled to a woodpile, a rusty oil tank on a cross-bar stand at one end of the trailer, a large metal put-together shed big enough to house a snow machine and a standing toolbox. There was an orange wind sock on a pole stuck in the snow some distance away. It hung limp in the still air, and blowing snow had long since filled in the tracks of any skis an airplane might have left behind.

It seemed somehow forlorn to Johnny, as if the trailer and its accessories had been plunked down here and forgotten. "I thought there'd be a drill rig," he said.

Ruthe shook her head. "They moved it into storage for the winter."

"It's beautiful," Van said, "but it sure would get lonely if you were out here for very long."

Ruthe tried again. "Hello, the trailer! Don't shoot, we're friendlies, and we're coming down to say hi! Put the coffee on!"

When there was no answer to her second hail, Ruthe led the way to the little group of buildings, still perched with one knee on the seat, one foot on a running board, nose up, almost sniffing the air.

They pulled up in front of the door of the trailer. Ruthe shut off her engine and tried again. "Hello, the trailer! Wake up in there, you got company!"

Still, nothing. "I don't like this," Van said, her voice very soft.

"Probably out walking a trapline," Ruthe said, dismounting. She saw Van looking at her and laughed. "It's packed down here, girl, you can get off and walk around safely."

Van put out one foot gingerly to feel the snow, and then got off with more confidence. Johnny followed, standing uncertainly for a moment, and then he went to the door and knocked. "Hello? Is anybody in there?"

No answer. Ruthe clicked her tongue against her teeth and brushed by him to grab the knob and pull the door open.

The smell hit them first. It was strong enough to stop Johnny in his tracks, and behind him Van actually backed up a step. Ruthe froze in place for one long second, and then with a set face climbed the two steps into the room.

There was a brief pause, and then they heard her say, "For crissake! What the hell were you doing out here?"

Johnny steeled himself and followed her inside, Van at his shoulder.

The door opened into the office area of the trailer. There was a desk, a four-drawer filing cabinet, a whiteboard, and a map of the Park on a scale so large it covered one wall floor to ceiling and corner to corner, including the two windows in that wall that showed up as light rectangles through the map. Flyers, brochures, and statistical handouts, all sporting the GHRI cheery sunrise logo, were piled all over the room.

The desk was large and metal and gray. Across it lay the body of Mac Devlin, his chest a torn mass of flesh and blood and bone, his square, red face gaping at the ceiling in astonishment. He was starting to bloat.

Behind Johnny, Van made a sound and the warm of her at his shoulder vanished, followed by quick footsteps going down the stairs and the crunch of her knees on the snow. He heard her retch. He wasn't far off it himself.

125

Ruthe surveyed the scene, her face grim. "How long ago, do you reckon?"

Johnny swallowed hard and steeled himself to step forward and grasp Mac's hand. It was cold. He tried to move it. It wouldn't. "Rigor has set in," he said.

"What does that mean?"

Oddly, he seemed to have adapted to the smell, and was able to speak more easily. "Rigor mortis starts setting in about three hours after death. It takes about twelve hours to reach maximum stiffness, depending on conditions." He looked around and saw a small Monitor stove, probably fueled by the tank outside. "It's warm in here." He tried to move Mac's hand again, and succeeded in shifting it just a little. "I'd say he's been here longer than three hours but less than twelve." He looked at Ruthe. "It'll go off again in about seventy-two hours. If someone trained is there to observe it, they can get a good idea of time of death." He took a deep, shaky breath. "For now, we need to get out of here."

"What? Why?"

"It's a crime scene, Ruthe. We shouldn't be in here, and we need to leave now and go get Jim." He walked out of the trailer. Van was on her feet, washing her face with a handful of snow. "Are you okay?"

She nodded and tried to smile with stiff lips. "I'm okay. Was that . . . was that Mac Devlin? The MacMiner guy?"

"Yeah, it was."

"What happened? What are you doing?"

He had bent over to look in the snow around the stairs. There was hardly any light left to the day and he couldn't see anything. "It looks like he was shot from a long way away, in the back, with a rifle, but a lot of times a killer can't resist taking a closer look. It's how we catch them."

"'We'?"

"It's how my dad used to, anyway." He straightened.

"You learned a lot from him."

"Yeah." He shrugged, trying to be casual. It wasn't easy, with the memory of Mac's gruesome remains fifteen feet away. "It was interesting." He swallowed. "Well, you know. When it wasn't gross."

"He's dressed like he just walked in the door," Ruthe said from the doorway. Something clicked and a light came on over the doorway. "Parka, snow pants, boots, and all."

"I think maybe he was shot in the act of stepping inside," Johnny said, standing straight and looking up at Ruthe. He pointed two fingers at her. "He'd probably already opened the door, and was standing on the threshold." She turned around, standing in the open doorway and looking at Johnny over her shoulder. "The bullet hit him and the impact spun him around—" Ruthe's hands flew up and she staggered two steps forward, turning to face him. "—and then he fell on the desk."

Ruthe looked over her shoulder again, at Mac's corpse this time, and came back to the door and frowned at him. "But the door was closed when we got here."

Johnny frowned, too. "The killer could have closed it if he came up to take a look. Or maybe Mac could have pulled it shut when he fell." Johnny gestured at his feet. "I can't see anything other than our tracks, Ruthe, but that doesn't mean Jim won't be able to. You should close the door. And lock it, if you can."

She reached behind the knob, felt around, and nodded her head. Pulling the door to, she tried the knob and nodded again when it held. "Okay. Time to go for help. Like you said, Jim needs to know about this, pronto."

"Wait." Johnny fumbled with one of his pockets. "Here. We can trigger this."

It was an orange electronic device the size of a pack of cigarettes. Ruthe took it. "What's that?"

"A PLB, a personal locator beacon. Kate insisted on getting one for me to carry in case I got into trouble in the Park. If I trigger it, it'll send our coordinates and a 911 call via satellite to the local police. That's Jim."

"Clever. And smart of Kate." She shook her head and handed it back to Johnny. "No can do."

"But he could fly out here, and land. There's a wind sock, I saw it on our way in."

"So did I," Ruthe said, "but he's not flying out here in the dark and landing in a place he's never landed before, also in the dark. If you trigger that thing, they'll think we're in trouble. We aren't. No. We go get him."

Johnny hesitated. "One of us should stay here. Make sure no one contaminates the crime scene."

"No," Ruthe said definitely. "I'm not leaving either one of you around here with some nut on the loose with a gun." Impossibly, she grinned, and jerked a thumb at the trailer.

"Besides, I just locked the door to the only warm place to wait."

TEN

The journey back down the side of the hill to the valley seemed a lot shorter, but it was well past dark by the time they got to the river. They stopped to gas up the snow machines and wolf down steaming bowls of ramen that Ruthe insisted they take the time to cook on her single-burner Coleman stove. "It's been a long day and we're all tired. We need fuel to get us home. Drink lots of water, too, and keep a bottle handy, tucked in somewhere it won't freeze."

She had them stuff peppermints into their outer pockets. "A sugar hit for the road," she said, "when we start to run out of steam."

"We could stop at one of the villages," Johnny said.

"We could," Ruthe said. "I don't think we should. Once the word gets out, there's going to be a stream of rubberneckers up there, and some of them won't stop with looking."

She looked at Johnny. He nodded. "You're right. Best to get the word to Jim as fast as we can. He can fly in tomorrow at first light." He looked at Van. "You want to drive awhile?"

A smile broke through the strained look on her face. "Sure!"

Behind her back Ruthe gave him an approving nod, and he felt good because he knew he'd done something smart.

They packed up and headed out.

The dark fabric of the night sky was textured with stars and constellations and globular clusters, the North Star directly overhead as the Little Dipper's handle started a slow and steady revolution around it. There would soon be a waning moon rising in the eastern sky, more than enough to light their way home. The frozen river was wide and flat and smooth and a good clean trail had been broken by the day's traffic. So long as they didn't drive into an open lead and freeze to death before they drowned, it should be a quick trip.

Or even if they did.

"Keep it at a steady fifty," Ruthe shouted. "No point in blowing out an engine if we don't have to."

Van gave her a thumbs-up, and she hit the gas. Johnny's arms tightened around Van's waist, and she wriggled a little farther back into the vee of his legs, her body warm and firm against his. There was an occasional snow machine, and one truck going in the opposite direction. For the rest, they were alone on the river. In any other circumstances, this would have been an enchanted evening.

The snow machines ate up the miles with a steady, reassuring roar, the lights of tiny Red Run passing on the left, and later the lights of the even tinier Potlatch. There was a long stretch of nothing before Chulyin. Here the trail hugged the right bank and the scraggly white spruce made insubstantial shadows on the snow that wavered as they passed by.

"Are you okay?" Johnny said.

"Fine!" she said. "Can I keep going?"

"Absolutely!" he said, and then he frowned. His engine sounded suddenly louder, and then louder than that. He looked at Ruthe ahead of them. She didn't look around, so evidently she wasn't noticing anything odd.

"What—," he started to say, and then the first of them launched itself from the riverbank, soaring over their heads so close one of the skids glanced off the windshield, inches in front of Van's face. It cracked with a sound like a gun going off and Van screamed and involuntarily took her thumb off the throttle. They slowed fast enough to throw him against her.

"No!" Johnny said. "Keep going! Keep going!" he yelled at Ruthe, who had paused to look over her shoulder, and was starting to turn. He saw another snow machine cut in front of her. The driver had something in his hand and he was raising it as he came at her.

"Christ!" Johnny said. "Ruthe, watch out!" He got a confused impression of a third snowgo behind them and fumbled for the rifle in the scabbard strapped to the seat.

Something hit his shoulders, hard, jerking his arms free of Van's waist and tumbling him off of the snow machine. In the very short space of time between launch and impact he felt as if he were floating, the stars passing dizzily overhead in slow motion.

And then he hit with a force that drove the breath from his body, and everything went black.

He woke up to the steadily increasing feeling of cold seeping into every part of his body. After a moment he realized that he was face-down in the snow. He made a tremendous effort and managed to raise his head an inch.

All was silent and still. There was a faint radiance from the east, the moon announcing its imminent entrance, ready to light up the frozen length of the Kanuyaq River like a phosphorescent ribbon, leading the way home.

He put his head back down and thought about this. That's right, they were on the river. He frowned, and the movement rubbed the ice into his cheek. It stung, and seemed to stimulate his brain cells.

Ruthe. The Gruening River caribou herd. The Suulutaq trailer. Mac. The rush to tell Jim. The attack.

Van.

Vanessa.

He pulled himself inch by painful inch to his knees and looked around.

His snow machine sat twenty feet away. The sled was gone. The sled with all their supplies in it. Memory returned in a terrifying rush.

"Van," he tried to say. "Ruthe." He staggered to his feet. "Van! Ruthe!"

He thought he heard a low moan from one direction and staggered toward it, almost falling over a dark, huddled lump. It was Ruthe. "Ruthe!" he said. He shook her, possibly a little less gently than he should have. "Ruthe!"

She groaned again. In the steadily increasing light of the rising moon her face looked bleached of all color, like a death mask. "Johnny?"

"Yes," he said, almost sobbing. "It's me. Are you okay? Here, squeeze my hands. Good, now push your feet. Good. Good."

"Where's the girl?" she said, raising her head.

He staggered to his feet. "Van! Vanessa! Where are you, Van?"

He found her beneath the lip of the riverbank. She didn't answer his call, she didn't move, and he was shaking so badly from fright and the cold that he could barely pull down her collar to check the pulse in her throat. It beat strongly against his fingers, warming it. "Oh, Van," he said, his head drooping. "Oh, Van."

Her voice was a thready whisper. "Johnny. What happened?"

Her voice, the sense of her words was like an on switch for a fury he hadn't known was there. He surged to his feet and very nearly howled at the sky. "Those assholes jumped us!"

"What assholes?"

"Those assholes on the snow machines!"

She raised herself painfully to one elbow. "I know you're mad, but don't yell, okay?"

Her pitiful little smile melted his heart. "Okay," he said, mastering his anger, not without effort, at least for the present, and dropping again to his knees. "Sorry."

"It's okay. I understand, believe me." Van tried to rise and faltered, putting a hand to her head. "Oh," she said, and then leaned over and vomited in the snow. He tried to help her, to hold her hair out of the way, and then brought her handfuls of clean snow so she could rinse out and off.

She looked up at him and smiled again, this time a little less tentative. "Tell me you don't know how to show a girl a good time," she said.

He surprised himself by laughing. It was a pale effort but it was real.

He got back to Ruthe to find her on her feet. She was wheezing slightly. "Are you okay?"

"Think I busted a rib," she said.

"I think that asshole busted it for you," he said, his anger coming back to a simmer. "Fucker was using a two-by-four."

"I see they took your sled. Why didn't they take the snowgo, too?"

"Not enough drivers, probably. I don't remember really well, but I think there were only three of them, one for each machine."

"Where's mine, then?"

They found it a thousand yards up the river, nose buried in a drift beneath the lip of the riverbank and miraculously still with the sled attached. "I pushed the throttle all the way up, last thing before I fell off," Ruthe said. "It must have got away from them and they were scared they'd get caught if they wasted time looking for it."

"Not as scared as they're going to be when I catch up with them," Johnny said fiercely. The thought of beating on the guy with his own two-by-four was as warming as the fire Van had started next to his snow machine.

He fumbled for the pocket that held the PLB and pulled it out. He held it up and said to Ruthe, "Are we in trouble now?"

Her sleep was made restless that night by dreams of Johnny heading off over the horizon on a snow machine, laughing over his shoulder at her just before the machine carried him over the edge of a cliff. And dreams of Jim, too, although these dreams were less story and more snapshot, Jim kissing her much against her will—really and truly, against her will—the day Roger McAniff went on a killing spree in the Park, Jim crouched behind the bar after getting his Smokey hat shot off during the most recent shoot-out between the Jeppsens and the Kreugers, Jim bleeding all over the floor of Ruthe and Dina's cabin after she'd beaned him with the file box. And bleeding all over her afterward.

She was jerked awake before she got to the really good part, by Mutt's full-throated bark and vehicle lights flashing across the interior of the house. She got up, pulled on sweats, and trotted downstairs. She reached for the .30-06 at the same time she switched on the porch light, which revealed Bobby's snow machine stopped in the yard, engine running, one person dismounting and running to the stairs. A frisson of nameless fear shivered up her spine. She put the rifle back and opened the door. "What's wrong?" she said before Dinah had her foot on the bottom step.

Dinah looked up and without preamble said, "Johnny triggered his PLB. Jim got the word and the location and he's on his way there with Bobby."

Kate ran upstairs and found clothes, ran back downstairs, pulled on bibs, parka, and boots, grabbed her gloves, goggles, and rifle, and ran outside. Dinah had pulled Kate's snow machine out of the garage and Mutt was already waiting next to it. The engine started without fuss, Mutt hopped up behind, and Kate slid the rifle into its scabbard and followed Dinah up the trail, swung wide onto the road, where both women opened up the throttles.

The miles sped by as Kate tried very hard not to think of all the different ways Johnny could have gotten hurt going down the river. A pickup could have run into them. A snow machine pileup. Some drunk in one of the villages could have been shooting at hallucinations and they got in between him and his target. The river could have opened up one of its inexplicable leads and they could have fallen in, and Johnny's last conscious act before the water closed over his head was to trigger the PLB.

She could feel the beginnings of hysteria, a coldness seeping over her from the inside that was worse than the windchill without. No, she thought, very firmly. You don't know anything. Don't speculate, don't borrow trouble. It'll be as bad as it is and you'll deal. Right now all you're doing is going from your house to Bobby's. All you have to do is hold on until you get there.

The trees lining the road blurred, the stars overhead were a silver smear against the black sky. They met no traffic along the way, and in Niniltna Dinah slowed down just enough to take the turn for the road leading downriver that led to the Roadhouse and then opened up the throttle again. Kate stuck to her tail like a burr, Mutt holding the shoulder of Kate's parka in her teeth to maintain her balance. The two miles between the village and the turnoff at Squaw Candy Creek passed in a blink and then Dinah was negotiating the trail that led to her and Bobby's house. Kate saw with dismay that Bobby's truck wasn't outside.

They killed the engines and went into the house, shedding outerwear as they went.

"I'm freezing, let me make some coffee," Dinah said.

"Talk while you do," Kate said. At her side stood Mutt, tense and ready to rip a new one in whatever had Kate so upset. She looked up and Kate rested a hand on her head. Mutt's ears flattened and she gave an interrogatory whine.

"It's okay, girl," Kate said with more confidence than she felt. "Everything's going to be fine." She hooked the rung of a stool with her foot and sat down. Mutt, not entirely convinced, allowed herself to be persuaded to sit, too, but she wouldn't move from Kate's side, leaning against her thigh, a solid, anxious presence. When Dinah gave her a strip of moose jerky, she took it politely, gave it a gnaw or two, and then set it down, which had to be a first.

"Where's my goddaughter?" Kate asked belatedly.

"With Bobby. We figured it was better Katya was in the truck with him."

"What happened?"

"At about—" Dinah glanced at the clock on the wall and calculated. "—I guess it would have been about one A.M. . . . maybe one thirty, everything happened so fast I wasn't paying attention to the time . . . Jim banged on the door. He said that Johnny's PLB— Your idea?"

"Yes."

"I think I'll have one welded to Katya's ankle. The Park equivalent of a LoJack. Anyway, Jim said Johnny's PLB went off and wherever the alarm is received alerted Kenny Hazen, who called Jim. Who evidently was in Niniltna?" A raised eyebrow.

Kate raised her shoulders. "I don't know, work, I guess. He didn't make it out to the house last night."

"We need cell towers in the Park and we need them now," Dinah said. "Jim was going out after them. Bobby said he'd ride shotgun. Jim said no, he didn't know what the situation was, if anyone was hurt or how badly, be better if Bobby brought his truck, and the snow machine trailer, too."

Kate drew in a sharp breath.

Dinah held up one stern hand, like a traffic cop, and repeated

Kate's own admonitions to herself almost word for word. "Don't, Kate, don't borrow trouble. They'll bring them back and then we'll see. We can handle whatever happens. Just keep calm."

But Kate noticed that her hands were a little unsteady with the teakettle.

They drank in silence. The minutes crawled by, the drag of every second like a fingernail on a blackboard. It was twenty-plus miles from Bobby's house to where Jim said the PLB was transmitting from. Bobby and Jim would have taken the road to a mile or so past the turnoff to Camp Theodore, Ruthe's eco-lodge. There they would have left the road to Bernie's and taken to the river.

Kate walked to the window and looked out. It was a clear, cold night, and it was early enough that there shouldn't be any traffic on the river and less on the road. She stared at the track that led from Bobby's yard to the little bridge that crossed Squaw Candy Creek and disappeared into the trees, willing the nose of the white Blazer with the trooper seal on the side to appear.

It didn't. By a sheer act of will she turned her back on the window and walked away.

Bobby's house was one large, open A-frame room, except for the bathroom in one corner—bedroom, kitchen, living room surrounding the central work station in one continuous space. At the work station, a doughnut-shaped desk supported a whole bunch of electronic equipment, which was connected to a snake's nest of wires writhing up a central pole to disappear through the roof. Outside, they were connected to antennas and microwave shots and who knew what else hanging off the 112-foot tower that stood out back.

Bobby Clark had lost both legs below the knee in Vietnam. After too long in a vet hospital, he spent the intervening years making a lot of money in endeavors that no one was so impolite as to inquire into before he arrived in the Park, flush in the pocket and with a mind to buy land and build. The A-frame and the tower went up the first year and shortly thereafter Bobby became the NOAA weather observer for the Park. It was gainful employment that gave him a vague aura of respectability and more important, a verifiable income. If said income didn't come close to equaling his expenditures at least its existence laid the hackles of law enforcement personnel who might be otherwise inclined to inquire as to the provenance of his additional funding.

Bobby broadcast Park Air from that same console, a pirate radio station featuring pre-seventies rock and blues, with occasional forays into post-acoustic Jimmy Buffett, and irregularly scheduled public service programs featuring swap and shops, talk radio, and broadcasts for messages on the Bush telegraph. He flew a Super Cub specially altered to accommodate his disability, drove a pickup and a snow machine ditto, and he was Dinah's husband and the father of a three-year-old imp named for Kate. She'd delivered the imp and done duty as best man and maid of honor both at Bobby and Dinah's wedding, all three on the same day, the memory of which never failed to give everyone involved the heebie-jeebies.

She looked around the room, noting the distance between Katya's crib and the California King not that far away, and her eyes came to rest on Dinah, who was watching her with a worried expression. "You're going to need to add on," Kate said. "Katya's getting to be an age where she could seriously interfere with your love life."

Dinah actually smiled. "Tell me about it. She's already interrupted us a couple of times. There is nothing more, um, deflating, than a three-year-old kid saying, 'Daddy, get off, you're squishing her!'"

Kate laughed dutifully.

"We've already talked about building another room," Dinah said.

"Where will you put it?"

Appreciating Kate's determination to act as normally as possible, Dinah fell into discussing the proposed addition. It would be built on the east side of the existing house, cutting a hole in that wall, extending the foundation, and building the room on top of it. "She's almost too big for the crib now anyway, she's been climbing in and out of it for almost a year. We think—"

Mutt's ears pricked up and she padded forward. "Listen," Kate said sharply, running to the window.

The white Blazer bumped into the clearing, followed by the brand-new black Ford Ranger Bobby had bought Dinah for her birthday that year. The motion detector lights on the outside of the A-frame lit up the two snow machines lashed to the trailer it pulled, both of them looking worse for wear.

Kate gave something like a sob. "Kate—," Dinah started to say, but by then Kate was out the door and halfway down the steps.

Jim popped his door and stuck his head out. "They're okay, Kate," he said. "They're all okay."

By then Johnny was out of the cab and on the ground, looking tired and beat up, and Kate had her arms around him and her face buried in his bib overalls. She wasn't crying, she never cried, but she didn't want anyone to see whatever it was on her face. His arms came around her, hugging her back just as fiercely.

She might have sniffled, just a little, and then she forced herself to let him go. "You're okay, then," she said, a little gruffly.

"Yeah," he said, with a long sigh.

She looked past him, at Ruthe and Van, Ruthe angry, Van exhausted. "All of you?"

"Yeah. All of us. Kate?"

"What?"

He suddenly looked older than his years. "Mac Devlin has been murdered."

ELEVEN

Jim was in the air at first light, on his way to Suulutaq. Kate was with him. "You'll need help loading the body," she said. "And if some nut is running around out there with a gun, you could use the backup, preferably backup that knows enough not to mess with your crime scene."

No point arguing with that, and Jim didn't waste his breath. She had her snow machine. If he hadn't let her come with him, she would have been on the river by sunrise.

Bobby had fetched the Grosdidier brothers, who patched up the walking wounded and made sure everyone saw two fingers, after which Bobby drove them and Van home. Ruthe put away a gargantuan breakfast, eggs and bacon and potatoes and the better part of a loaf of bread, toasted and slathered with butter, and departed for home on the Jag, resisting Dinah's entreaties to rest up on one of the couches before making the journey. "Gal's almost psychic, she'll know something's wrong and she'll be anxious after me," she said, adding, not unaffectionately, "Damn cat."

On the doorstep she paused. "I never liked Mac Devlin much," she said after a moment, appearing to chew on the words. "But he was a Park rat, and a neighbor. We lent him one of our cabins the year his burned. He stayed there for two months while he rebuilt. After that, whenever we needed some dirt work done, he was there with his D6 or his front-end loader. Never had to ask more than once. Never had to ask, really, just had to say what needed doing and he was there, usually the next day."

She looked at Kate. "You'll find out who did this, and why, and you'll make sure they get what's coming to them."

"Yes," Kate said.

Ruthe nodded, still in that ruminant way, and took herself off.

Katya attached herself to Johnny like a barnacle and refused all attempts to remove her, until she finally fell asleep, drooling into his shoulder. Dinah detached her and put her to bed. In turn, Johnny passed out on one of the couches. Kate covered him with a blanket and stood looking down at him.

"Little fucker like to give his momma a heart attack?" Bobby said fondly, rolling his chair up next to her.

"Shh," she said, "you'll wake him."

"Couldn't wake that boy with a goddamn air horn," Bobby said. "Wanna try?" Without waiting for an answer he rolled to the table and tucked into his own breakfast. "When's my next fare?" he said between bites.

"Me to the airstrip," Kate said. "I'm flying out to Suulutaq with Jim as soon as it's light."

Bobby chewed and swallowed. Mutt was sitting next to him, gazing at him with an adoration that had very little to do with the strip of bacon he was eating. He fed it to her anyway, still eyeing Kate. "Mac Devlin," he said. "The Park's least favorite miner. At least until Global Harvest came along. You know Global Harvest bought him out for about ten cents on the dollar?"

"Yeah."

"He wasn't happy about that."

"No," Kate said, "he wasn't."

"He's been popping up everywhere in the Park that Macleod broad has shown up talking about the mine—Bernie's, the Riverside Café, up the store. I heard he was at the Chamber of Commerce meeting she spoke at in Ahtna, even. You could almost say he was stalking her."

"You could," Kate said.

"What the hell was he doing out there, Kate? Trying to burn it down? Even Mac Devlin had to know what a futile gesture that would be."

"You'd think," she said. "I don't know anything about it yet, Bobby. All I know is he's been shot, and that he's dead, and that it happened in the Global Harvest trailer at Suulutaq."

"Interesting to speculate, though," he said. "There'll be a lot of that going on in the Park."

"Yes," she said grimly. "There surely will."

The high over the Park was holding and according to Bobby was supposed to keep holding at least through the weekend. It was another clear, calm day when they rose into the air off the end of the forty-eight-hundred-foot gravel airstrip that ran behind the village of Niniltna.

"I love CAVU," Jim said over the headset.

Ceiling and visibility unlimited. "I heard that," Kate said with feeling. "Have you talked to Macleod yet?"

His voice came back over her earphones, sounding tinny and devoid of its usual resonant assurance. "Yeah."

"Where is she? I kind of thought she might insist on accompanying us."

"She probably would have, but she's in Cordova."

"You talk to her on the phone?"

"Yeah. She'll be back in the Park this evening."

"She say what Mac Devlin was doing out there?"

"No, but she said he was really unhappy over what Global Harvest paid him for the Nabesna Mine, and he didn't mind saying so every time he saw her."

"Bobby said he was stalking her."

"Pretty much. She told me that she figured he was going to make enough of a nuisance of himself that Global Harvest would buy him off. And that Global Harvest knew that the longer they waited the lower Mac's price would be."

"Whoa."

She could hear the shrug in his voice. "That's business. It's all about the bottom line for those people, Kate."

The Quilaks rose up on their left, the land falling gradually and inevitably to sea level in a series of lesser mountains, foothills, knolls, buttes, plateaus, and valleys, hedged about by glaciers large and small, creviced by rivulets, streams, and creeks, all frozen now, a hundred, no, a thousand wrinkled cracks in the face of the Park smoothed to a crisp white finish by a thick layer of snow. The sky was a pale, icy blue, the Gulf of Alaska a hint of deeper blue on the southern horizon, and the sun a small, bright ball of pale yellow on the rising half of its tiny winter arc. It'd be below the horizon again in five hours. They didn't have a lot of time.

Fortunately, the Suulutaq wasn't far by air, and shortly Jim was banking left and losing altitude to glide the length of a wide, majestic valley, one end open to the southwest, curving up and right to the other, northeastern end in a roughly half-moon shape, the top end much narrower and steeper, and hemmed about by nervous mountains afraid to give up their jealously held treasures.

Too late, Kate thought.

Jim brought the Cessna down to fifty feet off the deck and passed over the isolated little trailer. The wind sock hung limply from its pole, and the snow looked smooth and settled enough to land on without sinking out of sight. He pulled up, came around, and let down the skis. They set down with a hiss of metal on snow, rolling out to a stop about ten feet from the cleared area between trailer, woodpile, and shed.

"Show-off," Kate said.

The smug grin beneath his sunglasses was answer enough.

They got out and walked carefully to the trailer, and any lingering amusement vanished when Jim popped the lock on the handle of the door and they went inside.

The odor that the others had described was even stronger now, but rigor had yet to wear off. Jim took photographs of the scene as Kate prowled around outside.

"No shells," she said. "Guy was careful." She walked a few steps away from the trailer and turned. "If it was Mac specifically he was shooting at, then he must have followed him out here."

He nodded, waiting.

"If it was Everynut with a gun, shooting at anything that moved because the hairy pink enchiladas were after him, then it could have been the same thing. Or the nutcase was already here and Mac could have just been a target of opportunity. Or." She took a deep breath and let it out and looked at Jim soberly. "It could have been someone who doesn't like the idea of the Suulutaq Mine, and figured anyone who was out here was fair game. Mac. Howie."

"Talia."

"Who?"

"Talia Macleod," Jim said.

"Oh. Yeah."

Mutt, who had been conducting her own investigation by trotting to and fro with her nose to the ground, raised her muzzle in the direction from which they had come and barked sharply, once. Kate looked over her shoulder. "That's George's Cub. I heard she put him on retainer, so that's probably her now."

"Who?"

"Macleod. Your new girlfriend."

"She's not my new girlfriend."

She looked at him, startled by the bite in his voice. She couldn't see his eyes behind his sunglasses, but after a moment he smiled. "Well, she isn't."

"Good to know," she said. "Kinda hoping I had dibs there."

His smile broadened. "Good to know."

"Want to get Mac bagged up?"

"Might as well." They trudged back to the trailer, neither of them in a hurry to face the task ahead. It helped that rigor had not worn off. There was nothing worse than trying to stuff the body of a human being into an elongated plastic bag. It tended to flop around a lot. Stiff with rigor, you were just dealing with mass, much easier to handle.

It wasn't the first time for either of them and they were bringing him out of the trailer by the time George and Macleod had gotten to the door. They stood back, George stoic, Macleod pale. They deposited Mac in a snowbank for the moment.

"Is it okay to go inside?" Talia said. Her face was pinched and she looked cold.

"Sure," Jim said.

They went inside and stood around the office. "Talia, I'd like you to take a look around, see if anything's missing."

She made a helpless gesture. "There isn't anything out here to steal, really. There's a television in the living quarters, with a bunch of DVDs and a player."

"All still there," Kate said.

"Anything in the way of papers or information about the mine that someone might want to take a look at?"

She gave Jim an incredulous look. "Certainly nothing that I can imagine anyone killing for, Jim." She pointed. "There's the map, but it's the same map that's been reproduced in every one of the handouts, brochures, and flyers." She picked up a flyer and waved it, and then tossed it back on its pile. "We knew there would be rubberneckers, especially after the first snow. The caretakers are instructed to let no one leave here without a fistful of Global propaganda."

"Where's Gallagher?" he said. Kate looked at him, frowning a little.

"Who?" Macleod said vaguely. "Oh. I sent him back to Niniltna with someone else. George didn't want to bring in anything bigger than his Cub, so only room for one passenger." She turned to face him. "There is one thing I don't understand."

"What?"

"Where's Howie Katelnikof?"

"Howie?" Kate said. "Why would Howie be out here?"

"It was his week," Macleod said. "I hired him to sit out here every other week, in rotation with Dick Gallagher. This is Howie's week. He should have been here. He should be here now."

"Ah hell, I knew that," Jim said, disgusted. "But I didn't connect the dots." He looked at Kate.

While it was a truth generally acknowledged that Mac Devlin had not been the most beloved of Park rats, neither of them had been able to come up with a good reason for anyone to kill him. Beat on him a little, sure, maybe, but not shoot him. He wasn't married, and if he had had a girlfriend Jim hadn't heard of it. So far as anyone knew he had no children. On the face of it the list of suspects in Mac's case wasn't just short, it was virtually nonexistent.

Howie Katelnikof, on the other hand, while he was also single and childless, had over the course of a long and prolific criminal career lied to, cheated, and stolen from anyone who had ever set foot in the Park who wasn't smart enough to see Howie coming. He had also done a lot of Louis Deem's wet work, especially when it came to intimidating juries. Kate herself had a very good reason to wish Howie dead. In fact, she had three.

The list of suspects in an investigation into the murder of Howie Katelnikof would have been so long Jim would have had to take numbers. Hell, if somebody shot Howie, the Park rats would have taken up a collection to reward the shooter.

That was a thought far too close to home for Jim.

Kate and Jim flew the body to Cordova to put it on the jet to Anchorage, and returned to Niniltna, landing at twilight. They walked into the trooper post and dispatcher Maggie Montgomery's face lit up. "Thank god! Here, take 'em!"

He looked down at the fistful of messages with resignation. "What, a crime wave?"

"They're all about the snow machine attack on the river. Jim?"

He paused in the door of his office. "What?"

She looked at him with wide eyes. "It's not the only one."

TWELVE

Jim didn't make it home until the next evening. "How come you didn't know about this?" he said, walking in the door.

"I don't know," Kate said, honestly bewildered, and not a little aggrieved. It wasn't often she was this out of the loop in Park affairs. In fact, she couldn't remember a time when she'd been out of the loop at all. It was the Association board meeting in October all over again, leaving her swamped in an ignorance so complete she felt like she was going down for the third time. "I haven't been into town longer than it takes to check the mail and grab a cup of coffee since I got back. Maybe that's why I hadn't heard anything."

"I thought Auntie Vi was the town crier when it came to bad news, and what Auntie Vi knows, you know."

"I can't explain it," she said again. Mutt leaned her head on Kate's knee and looked up at her with sympathetic yellow eyes. "I haven't heard a word about it, Jim. Nothing. I would have told you."

"Bet your ass," he said, still smarting. He didn't like it when shit was dumped in his own backyard and he didn't smell it. He went to the map of the Park Kate had recently attached to a piece of cork and framed with colonial molding left over from the house raising.

It was smaller than the one in the Global Harvest trailer, and in much worse shape, but it was adequate to the purpose. He traced the course of the Kanuyaq River with his forefinger.

"Attack the first," he said. "Ken and Janice Kaltak on November sixth, headed home to Double Eagle from a trip to Ahtna, doctors' appointments and shopping. Stopped in Niniltna for a mugup at the Riverside Café. There was some light snow but no wind so visibility okay and not cold enough not to keep going. About a mile from home, three snow machines barreled out of a willow thicket, one of the drivers coming straight at them like he's playing chicken with them, while another one, this one with a two-by-four, comes up from behind and hits Ken across the side hard enough to knock him off his sled. Janice is riding behind and she rolls off with him. It all happens too fast for Ken to get to his rifle. The third snow machine roars around them in circles, loud, distracting, scary, while the first two guys disconnect the trailer, loaded with groceries from Safeway and Costco, and they're gone. Lucky they left them the snowgo, they woulda been dead otherwise and it would have been murder along with assault and robbery." He paused. "What amazes me is they didn't take the rifle."

"Was it registered, maybe?" she said.

He looked at her.

She closed her eyes and held up a hand. "Sorry, I wasn't thinking."

"Attack the second. On November ninth, three days later—" He moved his finger downriver. "—just outside Chulyin, maybe a mile from their house, Ike Jefferson and his kid, Laverne, are hauling home a fifty-five-gallon drum of diesel fuel when what sounds like the same three assholes on snow machines show up, whack Ike with the two-by-four, terrorize the kid, and take off with the diesel."

"Did they hurt her?" Kate said.

He shook his head. "She's only eight and they laid her dad out in front of her a mile from home. She got him back on the sled and

home all right. She was pissed by the time I got there yesterday."
He gave a reluctant smile. "Told me I had a shiny new gun but it
didn't look like I used it much."

Kate smiled, too. "Good for her."

"Yeah, she's a feisty little pup. I can see why Ike is so proud of
her. And I'll tell you, Kate, if I'd had one of the bastards at point-
blank when her dad was telling me the story, I might have pulled
the trigger on my shiny new gun then and there."

"You said there were three incidents."

"Yeah, attack the third." He looked back at the map and slid his
finger farther down. "November fifteenth. They waited a week this
time, by which time they had upgraded their arsenal." He held up a
small, innocuous-looking black cylinder. "Don't move," he said,
and gave his hand a casual flick. A telescoping rod cracked out with
astonishing speed and Kate jerked back instinctively.

"It's weighted on the end," he said.

A chill went up Kate's spine. "I know," she said quietly. "It's a
collapsing baton, isn't it? I've heard about them but I've never seen
one before."

"It's lethal force, Kate. You whack someone with this, you can
hurt them badly, you can even kill them. And you can order them
off Amazon for twenty bucks apiece." Another wrist flick and the
baton collapsed in on itself again. "They used it on Christine and
Art Riley of Red Run when they were on their way home from a trip
to Niniltna to bring Art's mother home. Grandma Riley has been
feeling poorly lately, and wanted to go downriver once more before
she died."

Kate closed her eyes briefly. "Grandma Riley is something like
ninety years old, isn't she?"

"Ninety-three. Evidently these assholes are no respecters of elders. They jumped the Rileys halfway between Potlatch and Red
Run. Christine managed to get their rifle out of the scabbard but

this thing knocked it out of her hands. The good news is, it knocked this out of the attacker's hands, too. Christine picked it up and brought it home. I had to talk her into giving it to me. I think she was planning on using it on them if the Rileys ever ran into them again. Can't say I blame her." He ran a hand over his face. "I'm figuring that's why they went back to the two-by-four for the attack on Johnny and Ruthe and Van thirteen days later. Attack the fourth."

"Although they've probably already ordered another of those batons."

"They've probably already ordered another dozen," he said. "Fifty-five gallons of diesel fuel at, what's the most recent Bush price, four sixty a gallon? That's almost two hundred and fifty-five bucks. They could sell that off a couple of gallons at a time, buy a dozen of these fuckers, and have enough left over for a case of Windsor Canadian." He tossed the baton into the glove and hat box behind the door and scrubbed his face with his hands. "Art Riley says it was the Johansens."

The spatula paused in the act of flipping a steak. "He identified them?"

"They were wearing helmets. But he says it was them." He scrubbed his face again. "God, I'm tired."

Kate decided it was time to relax, regroup, and reassess, and for her that always began with food. "The question is, are you hungry?"

He gave her a tired smile. "Is the answer to that question ever no?"

She smiled back at him. "I just started a fire. You want something to drink?"

"I'd love some Scotch, but I better not. I've alerted all the village councils about the attacks, up and down the river, and I've called Kenny Hazen and got him excited about it, too. I better be sober if any of them call back."

"Grab a shower, then. You've just about got time."

Demonstrating the innate ability of the adolescent to arrive just as dinner was put on the table, Johnny walked in the door as Kate served up a large and redolent offering of country fried caribou steak and gravy, mashed potatoes, and canned green beans drained and stirred into caramelized onions and crispy bacon bits. Served with bread baked fresh that morning, everyone dug in with a will, and everyone felt better afterward.

"You do groceries well," Jim said to Kate.

"Yes, I do," she said, and looked at Johnny. "Things okay at school today?"

He hunched a shoulder. "Yeah, fine."

They both looked at him, Jim pausing in the act of loading up dishes for a trip to the sink. "What?" Kate said.

"It's all anyone is talking about," Johnny said. "I'm a hero for getting beat up coming up the river. Poor old Mac gets shot and hardly gets a mention."

Jim started stacking dishes again. "It's a matter of setting priorities, Johnny. Folks are on the river every day, going hunting, buying fuel and supplies, visiting relatives, going to basketball games. Safe passage on the river is essential to the life of the 'Burbs."

"And what's one miner more or less?" Kate said.

"Oh man, Kate," Johnny said in dismay. "That's kind of harsh."

"Pretty harsh, yeah," she said. "Also true. And, you know, it's life. Or at least it is around here." She looked at Jim. "Have you tracked Howie down yet?"

Jim let out a long, heartfelt sigh. "Oh, yeah," he said. "Howie. No. No, I haven't. He isn't at home, and Willard claims he hasn't seen him. Of course we all know that Willard can't remember today what happened yesterday, unless yesterday was Darth Vader's birthday. Howie hasn't been to the Roadhouse for the last five days, according to Bernie, which fits because he was supposed to start his shift at the trailer on Monday. You'll remember that storm we had just before Thanksgiving?"

"No tracks?" Kate said.

Jim gave a gloomy nod. "No tracks."

"Who's out there now?"

"At the trailer? FNG name of Gallagher."

"What?" Johnny said, looking up from his trig homework.

Jim looked at him. "Talia Macleod hired Howie and a new guy, a Dick Gallagher, to babysit her trailer a week on, a week off. This was supposed to be Howie's week."

Johnny opened his mouth and Kate said, "Is he armed?"

"I didn't ask. He's a fool if he isn't. And Macleod would probably insist." He hesitated.

"What?" she said. "You want me to find Howie for you?"

He gave an irritated wave of his hand. "No, I'll find Howie. I always find Howie whether I want to or not."

"Uh . . . ," Johnny said.

"No," Jim said, "I want you to go talk to the villagers for me."

"But you already have."

"Come on, Kate. They'll say things to you that they won't say to me."

"Oh. You think the highwaymen have to be the Johansens because that's who Art Riley said they were. Even if he couldn't identify them."

He winced. "Please don't call them that. People'll start romanticizing them, think they wear cocked hats and carry swords and fall in love with the landlord's daughter, and the next thing you know there'll be stories about them robbing from the rich to give to the poor."

"Okay," she said obligingly, "you think Art's right about who the assholes on the snow machines are."

He nodded. "If not know, then suspect. Hell, don't you? Maybe

153

the Kaltaks or Ike saw something. Find me an eyewitness and I'll lock up those sonsabitches and throw away the key."

"Usual rates?"

He grumbled. "Yeah, fine. You're getting to be my single biggest budget item, Shugak."

She batted her eyelashes. "But you know I'm worth it."

Johnny opened his mouth for the third time and Jim said, "You got a mouth on you, Shugak, I'll give you that. A disease for which there is only one known cure." He leaned forward and kissed her.

Johnny made the obligatory gagging noises and departed for less saccharine climes, otherwise known as his room.

It was furnished in a style Kate called Late American Adolescent, which is to say that the original of no horizontal or vertical surface showed through the clutter of clothes, shoes, boots, books, toys, posters, gadgets, CDs, DVDs, truck parts, snow machine parts, four-wheeler parts, notebooks, *X-Men* comic books, but only the ones written by Joss Whedon, used bowls containing leftovers in a communicable state of congealment, and many different varieties of shampoo, deodorant, shaving cream, pimple unguent, and cologne, all of which had been used once before being tossed aside in favor of the next new thing.

Not on view was the pile of *Penthouse* and *Playboy* magazines that both he and Kate pretended she didn't know were under the head of his bed. Not that she ever came in here anyway. "Your room, your mess," she had said cheerfully when they moved in. "My prime request, which I do last pronounce, is that anything that breeds in there? Stays in there."

He cleared his bed by the simple expedient of lifting one corner of the tangled spread and shaking it. Everything on it fell, slid, or crashed to the floor, and he flopped down on his back to stare at the ceiling.

So Doyle—Dick—had scored a job with Talia Macleod. That was good. "It is good," he said to the ceiling.

He tried to remember some of the stuff they'd talked about over the night and day they'd spent in the cab of that semi, more than two years ago now. He'd been homesick and filled with longing for the clean, cold air, the lack of crowds, the empty roads, the silence. Yes, he'd raved about Alaska, he remembered that much, and evidently Doyle—Dick!—had believed every word. Well, why not? Johnny hadn't lied.

He was worried, though. Alaska wasn't easy. It was beautiful enough to break your heart, but there was a price. It didn't tolerate fools gladly. "Suicide by Alaska," Kate called it whenever a cheechako did something particularly stupid that got them killed, like planting a tent on a known bear trail, or moving into the backcountry with no experience in a subsistence lifestyle, or climbing Denali without a radio, or taking off in an overgrossed chartered floatplane for a fishing trip that ended with the people inside as bait.

Dick was tough, though. You didn't spend years driving an eighteen-wheeler across country without learning how to take care of yourself.

Johnny still hadn't told Kate about Dick being in the Park, much less about him changing his name. That was partly because she went into orbit every time he mentioned his hitchhiking home that August. But he'd had to do it, there was no other way to get home, and he'd had to get home.

If he'd still been living in Anchorage he could have tolerated living with his mother, too, but Jane had dumped him with his grandparents. He'd met them twice in his life before that, and they lived on a golf course, for crying out loud! Who lived on a golf course? Nobody under seventy-five, that was for sure. It might not have been so bad if he'd been old enough to drive, the country looked interesting farther out, but there he was, stuck between the golf course and school. He had nothing in common with the kids in his classes, he wasn't into sports or shopping. In the summer you couldn't even go outside or the heat would come down on you like a sledgehammer. You couldn't even breathe in heat like that.

It wasn't like he hadn't asked his mom, repeatedly, if he could come home. His appeals had gone unanswered, and his grandparents hardly spoke to him. The three of them never sat down to a meal together except when they went out to Denny's for the senior special. There had been a bunch of Stouffer's frozen dinners in the freezer, cereal and Top Ramen in the cupboard, milk in the refrigerator, and bananas in a bowl on the counter, and that was it. He'd felt like he was starving to death.

That August night he had left the house well after midnight, a daypack over his shoulder filled with clean underwear and every penny he had. It wasn't much, and, he was ashamed to remember, the sum had included two twenty-dollar bills he'd stolen out of his grandmother's purse. The first thing he'd done after Kate gained legal title to him and it was okay to tell them where he was was to borrow forty bucks from her and enclose it with a card, apologizing for the theft.

They hadn't answered. That was okay with him, because it indicated a reassuring lack of interest in having him back.

He got his first ride on a pickup full of Hispanic day laborers, heading up to Wickenburg looking for work. His second ride had been the drunken car salesman, and the less remembered about that brief ride the better. His third had been Doyle Greenbaugh—Dick Gallagher, dammit—at that truck stop just outside Phoenix on Interstate 10. They'd swung right through Utah, left and up through Idaho, cut across the northeastern corner of Oregon, and he'd gotten off in Seattle. There had been a lot of stops, it seemed as if Dick—that's right, Dick—couldn't see a truck stop without stopping to say hi to somebody. "Half a mo, kid," he'd say, shoving the semi into neutral with a grind of gears, yanking on the parking brake, and giving Johnny a broad wink. "I see a friend I hafta say hi to."

After that, it was easy. He'd taken a bus to the border, walked into Canada, and hitched a series of rides on RVs. Most of them were with older retired couples, which got tricky a couple of times when they'd ask where his parents were. It was lucky he was tall and looked older than he was. Mostly they believed him when he told them he was eighteen, although one woman had demanded to see some identification. He pleaded time in the john and skinnied over the KOA campground fence just in time to hitch a ride with another trucker, this one hauling building materials to Fairbanks. He was an incurious, middle-aged man who sang along to country-western music, which got tiresome after a while.

He walked into Alaska, avoiding the border crossing at Beaver Creek by sneaking around through the woods and catching a ride on the other side with a couple of moose hunters, who gave him a ride and a meal and let him sleep in the cab of their pickup in exchange for chopping wood for their campfire that night. In Ahtna, the fuel truck had been making its fall run into the Park, and he caught a ride on it to the turnoff to Kate's cabin.

And he'd been here ever since.

But it was that long ride Dick Gallagher—say it again, Dick Gallagher—had given him that had set the tone of his journey home. He owed Dick a great deal. They weren't best friends or anything but nevertheless Johnny felt the heavy responsibility of a debt unpaid.

He wasn't proud of thinking it, but he hoped the nut with the gun really had been aiming at Mac.

THIRTEEN

J im and Johnny left early the next morning, one for work, the other for school. Kate busied herself with packing up for the trip, extra clothing, food, tent. She didn't know how long she'd be gone, and while she expected the usual Bush welcome mat, if things got awkward she wanted to be able to survive a night or two out on her own.

Rifle, ammunition. A lot of ammunition.

Then she traded the rifle for the 12-gauge pump action. If the highwaymen—excuse her—if the assholes on snow machines wanted to rob her, they'd have to get close to do it. Nobody got close to the business end of a shotgun, not if they were sane.

She loaded everything into the trailer, hooked it to the sled, donned bib overalls, boots, parka, and gloves.

She stood in front of the map for a while, running the sequence of the attacks through her mind.

So far, all the attacks had been downriver, south of Niniltna, south of the Nabesna Mine turnoff, south even of where the road left the river to go to the Roadhouse.

First attack, a mile north of Double Eagle.

Second, three days later, six miles downriver from the first attack, just outside Chulyin.

Third, a little north of Red Run, six days later and twenty miles farther south, almost where the Gruening River met the Kanuyaq.

Fourth, thirteen days later, three miles north of Red Run.

Three of four of the attacks had been made on people coming home fat, trailers loaded with groceries, clothes, parts, fuel. Which made a case for Johnny and Van and Ruthe being a target of opportunity.

It also opened up the possibility that someone upriver was alerting the jackals as to potential pickings, at least for the first three attacks. Kate didn't like the thought of that, not one little bit.

"I think they cruised us on the way out," Johnny had said. "There were three guys on snow machines who kind of harassed us that morning. Didn't jump us, just did circles around us and then took off when they saw a truck coming. I knew there was something off about them, but it didn't hit me until later. They were wearing helmets, Kate."

"So you couldn't see who they were."

"And nobody wears helmets on the river, Kate." He'd managed a smile, even if it had looked a little worn around the edges. "Not even an old safety-first girl like you."

Ten minutes later she was moving down the road, Mutt on the seat in back of her, headlight illuminating the road in front of her.

Auntie Vi was up in her net loft mending nets, bone needle whipping in and out, gear swiftly and almost miraculously made whole again. "Ha, Katya," she said.

"Morning, Auntie." Before Auntie Vi could get started in Association business Kate got her oar in first. "You hear about the attacks on the river?"

Auntie Vi gave an emphatic nod. "Sure. Everybody hear."

"I didn't," Kate said.

Auntie Vi looked surprised. Kate, watching her closely, thought the surprise was exaggerated. "How not?" Auntie Vi said.

"Nobody told me. Why didn't you?"

Auntie Vi raised her eyebrows in a faint shrug and bent back over the gear. "You not interested enough in Association business to learn how to run board, you not interested enough in Park business to need to know all that goes on."

"I see," Kate said. Something very like rage rose up over her in a red wave and she fought an inner battle to keep her composure. Mutt, who read Kate better than most humans, looked longingly at the door. "Is this the way it's going to be, Auntie? You're going to shut me out unless I do what you want?"

Auntie Vi didn't answer.

"Well, I know about them now, and I'm going downriver to see what the hell's going on. I'm going to find out who's pulling this shit and I'm going to kick their collective ass. It's a darn shame I didn't know about it before, so I could have stopped it earlier, and Grandma Riley and little Laverne Jefferson and Ken and Janice Kaltak wouldn't have been terrorized and robbed."

Kate left before Auntie Vi could reply.

Her next stop was Auntie Edna's, a prefab home in a little ten-house subdivision at the south end of Niniltna, perched precariously on the edge of the river. This time she knocked, instead of walking in like she did at Auntie Vi's. Auntie Edna's face was stony when she came to the door, but then Auntie Edna's face was always stony. "Auntie Edna," Kate said without preamble, "you know about the attacks on the river?"

Auntie Edna shrugged. "I guess."

"You should have told me."

Auntie Edna raised her eyebrows in elaborate surprise. "You interested?"

Kate could feel her temper begin to rise again, and bit back her first retort. "I'm headed downriver. Do you know who they are?"

Another shrug. "Nobody say."

"Well, I'm going to find them, and I'm going to beat the crap out of them when I do. And after that I'm going to feed them to Mutt. You can put that out on the Bush telegraph if you've a mind to."

She turned to leave.

"Katya."

Kate was in no mood. "What?" The curt tone, the omission of the usual honorific, both were significant, and they both knew it.

"That man that live with you."

This was so out of left field that Kate was momentarily speechless. "There's no man— Oh. You mean Jim?"

Auntie Edna gave a curt nod.

"What about him?"

"White man."

Kate snorted out a laugh. "Unregenerately."

"Not right for Association chair, Native woman, to be sleeping with white man."

At that Kate turned completely around and said incredulously, "Are you kidding me, Auntie? You of all people dare to lecture me on my love life?"

In her youth, Auntie Edna had been married three times, and in between and sometimes during those marriages had enjoyed the company of many other men. She had more children than the other three aunties put together. Her romantic history probably ranked right up there with Chopper Jim's in number and variety.

Auntie Edna thrust out her jaw. "Don't change subject, Katya. You sleeping with that man don't look good. You boot him out, get you a nice Native man. That be better for everyone. Your kids be shareholders on both sides."

"Just for the sake of argument, Auntie, what nice Native man would you recommend?"

At this Auntie Edna looked momentarily at a loss, and then rallied. "Them Mike boys is all good men, Annie raised them right."

"And they all live in Anchorage," Kate said, and made a come-along motion with her hand. "Come on, Auntie. Serve 'em up. Who else is vying for my hand?"

"Martin Shugak, he—"

Kate's rage dissipated in an instant and she burst out laughing. "Martin! Oh, Auntie!"

"What wrong with him?" Auntie Edna said pugnaciously.

"What's wrong with him?" Kate rolled her eyes. "Well, first there's the little problem of his being my cousin—"

"Second! Second cousin!"

"—and so our children would all be born with two heads. Not to mention he's a drunk, so they'd all have FAS, and he's chronically unemployed, so they'd all be hungry, and—" Kate shook her head. "I'm headed downriver, Auntie. Do you know who's doing these attacks?" She waited, and when Auntie Edna said nothing she started down the steps.

"Not necessary, Katya," Auntie Edna said behind her.

Kate paused in the act of mounting the sled, and looked at Auntie Edna with a gathering frown. She didn't like what she heard in Auntie Edna's voice. "Why not, Auntie? Somebody has to stop them. And," she added with little satisfaction and less pride, "it's almost always been me."

"Maybe already somebody stop them," Auntie Edna said.

She gave Kate another long, hard stare, and then Auntie Edna turned and went back inside, the door closing firmly behind her.

Jim gassed up the Cessna and flew back to Suulutaq. There was a thin line of clouds on the southern horizon, the edge of a low front that had so far been held off by the high hanging in over the Park. Otherwise it was another clear, calm day, and this time he knew where he was going.

In half an hour he was over the trailer. He continued on up the valley, all the way to the end, as far as he could get without running into a cloud filled with rocks. Here the landscape closed in, a series of pocket basins that in spring were carpeted with grasses, interspersed with rocky crags clothed in lichen and kinnikinnick. There was one exit, a high, narrow pass where rose the spring that formed the headwaters of the Gruening River, which cricked and jigged and jagged down the other side, collecting the flows of errant streams and creeks to itself before its course smoothed out to join up with the Kanuyaq River at Red Run.

The Gruening River had a healthy run of red salmon, which was why the origins of the fish camp on the confluence of the two rivers went back a thousand years. The smoke fish from Red Run was prized above all others, and the lucky recipients of Red Run canned smoked salmon hoarded it more jealously than they did their wives and girlfriends.

But that was the other end of the river. At present Jim was circling cautiously over the river's beginnings, keeping a weather eye cocked toward the south. At the first hint of the shred of a cloud he would turn and skedaddle for home. It was amazing how crowded clouds could make a pilot feel, and Jim had not accumulated 2,722 accident-free single engine hours by letting weather jog his elbow.

The head of the valley was the winter grounds of the Gruening River caribou herd. He could see some of them now, groups of five and ten far below, scraping a meal out of the snow and ice with their small, sharp hooves. The big bulls had shed their antlers two months before but there were still racks on a few of the smaller bulls and most of the cows. They looked to be in pretty good shape. Of course this was still only November. Another couple of months and all the fat they had stored up over the summer and fall in those big old jiggly butts would be almost gone.

Like most but not all of the Alaska herds, the Gruening River herd migrated annually. When spring came, usually around mid to late May, they migrated over the narrow pass and down the Gruening River to where it met the Kanuyaq, about forty miles, where they calved and fed on willow and blueberry leaves, sedge grasses, tundra flowers, and mushrooms. In September, they moved back up the mountains, feeding on shrubs and lichen and kinnikinnick.

It was a small herd, never over five thousand on its best year, as there was a very healthy wolf population in the area, and then there were the bears. So far, the three species were holding fairly stable. For now, it was a matter of if it ain't broke, don't fix it. The state and the feds were less concerned about the Gruening River herd than they were about the Central Arctic herd that migrated through Prudhoe Bay, whose population had dropped precipitously in the last twenty years, or the Mulchatna herd that had increased so geometrically that they were letting hunters take five each, including cows, and one season going so far as to allow hunters to fly and shoot same day.

If the mine went in, of course, much more attention would be paid. The herd would be tagged and monitored to a fare-thee-well, as would the wolves, the bears, the eagles, geese, ducks, wolverines, foxes, marmots, porcupines, pika squirrels, voles, and mosquitoes. Jim wasn't saying the attention would be a bad thing, but it had been his experience that the more attention was paid to an ecosystem, the more alarm was raised when that ecosystem changed in even the smallest degree.

It didn't matter if the change was the natural order of things. Say the herd decreased after a die-off following a hard winter. There would always be someone to tie it to the mine. Someone, say, like Ruthe Bauman. She wouldn't necessarily be wrong, either, but it was true that wildlife in Alaska could be used by any side to bolster

whatever viewpoint was held to be most politically correct or eco-
nomically feasible by the group in question, corporate, legislative,
environmental, Native, whoever. The oil companies in Prudhoe
Bay claimed that the caribou liked the gravel pads built for the
roads and structures, where the wind kept the mosquitoes off them,
and that some small groups of cows and calves had wintered under
some of the structures.

Even the devil could quote scripture to his purpose.

Meantime, Jim drew a series of economical circles in the sky. He
didn't know what he was looking for, exactly, but his gut was telling
him that Howie was out here.

Howie Katelnikof was a liar and a thief and a bully and an all-
around waste of space, and he might even be a murderer, although
Jim wasn't sure he was the murderer of Mac Devlin. There was no
bad blood between Mac and Howie so far as Jim knew, and while
Mac might hate Global Harvest and all who sailed in her, he
wouldn't go out to Suulutaq with the intention of picking a fight
with Howie. Howie was little more than a gofer and, as Macleod
had discovered to her dismay, from the get-go had been ripping off
everything that wasn't nailed down. Far more likely Howie was
fencing the stuff he stole to Mac.

Which might be a thought worth pursuing, Jim thought, checking again for weather before easing into a lazy figure eight that gave
him a commanding view of the upper valley. Howie, ever on the
alert to make a buck, might have sold Mac a look at the trailer and
its contents. Mac might have paid for it on the off chance that he'd
find something to help him pressure Global Harvest, in hopes of
causing enough irritation that they would at long last buy him off.

That, Jim thought, seemed much more in character for both men.
Weasels once, weasels ever.

Then his attention was caught by something on the ground.
Color and movement, that's what Ranger Dan counseled when

looking for wildlife, and that's what Jim had been looking for when he spotted a flash of blue through a dense stand of dark green spruce tucked into one of the little pocket basins. He banked left and continued a tight spiral downward, until he was circling a hundred feet over the spot where he'd seen the color flash. The nearness of the mountains was uncomfortable to him, but the weather was still holding. He throttled back as far as he could without losing lift and stood the Cessna on its left wing for a good, long look.

There shouldn't be spruce up this high, but the little basin was south-facing and well protected, a tiny patch of microclimate the spruce had claimed for its own. They weren't very tall, almost dwarfs, and grew in such a tangled thicket, one on top of the other, each desperate to grab its own square foot of arable soil, that it was difficult to see under them.

"Well now," Jim said. Under them, as he saw now, was where all the action was. There were snow machine tracks going in and out, leading to the remnants of a large caribou slaughter, a pile of skins, another of racks, and an assortment of quarters, looking even at this distance frozen solid in the frigid November air. The hunters had taken care to do their butchering under the trees, and some of the trees had been encouraged to form a shelter by lopping off a lower layer of limbs. To one side there were a couple of dark green tents with two snow machines parked beside them, one blue, the other black. He thought he saw the shadow of a third but not distinctly enough to discern any identifying color or make.

A figure darted from a tree near the meat mound and ducked into one of the tents. They'd heard him. He climbed back to cruising altitude and resumed the lazy eight, the possessor of more facts than he'd had before he arrived.

Caribou hunting season in this game unit didn't begin until January first, over a month away.

The black snow machine was instantly recognizable as the

brand-new Ski-Doo Expedition TUV, a cherry little tricked-out sled that had emptied out the Roadhouse when Howie drove up in it the first time. It retailed for just under thirteen thousand dollars, and a lot of Park rats had wondered out loud how Howie, noticeably lacking in gainful employment, could afford it.

Jim had wondered, too. Howie dealt strictly in cash, having learned well from his mentor and master, the execrable Louis Deem, that checking accounts had an uncomfortable way of revealing your transactions at the most inconvenient possible time, and that credit card companies sold your information to everyone else. Now Jim wondered if perhaps Howie had been supplementing his income by retailing commercial quantities of caribou. Gas was expensive, with the price per gallon increasing every day, especially in the Park, where it had to be hauled in by the barrel after winter shut down the road in. It made hunting, even from a four-wheeler or a snow machine, that much more expensive, too.

He peered below again. Three snowgos meant three people. All three, displaying a prudence beyond what their current activity would suggest, remained inside the tents.

He decided that he'd tested the limits of aeronautical safety enough for one day. He put the Cessna's nose on three-one-five and let the ground fall away from him as he flew down the broad plateau of the valley.

He had a little time to think over what he should do next. It was vital to lay hands on Howie Katelnikof as soon as possible, but there was nowhere flat or long enough for him to sit down that was near enough to the camp for him to get to them before they took off, which they would do because they'd hear him land and because they had ground transportation and he didn't.

The trailer and its rudimentary airstrip sat in the middle of a very wide valley that he estimated was a minimum of four to six miles across. If he put her down there and waited, they'd just go around him. Aerial bombardment was pretty much all that a Cessna in the air could do to stop a snow machine on the ground, and Jim was fresh out of grenades.

The mouth of the valley widened to a slope that fell gradually down to the east bank of the Kanuyaq River, the southwest-facing hill well treed but nowhere impassable by snow machine. If he set down in one place, top or bottom, they'd simply go another way. They would have recognized the white Cessna with the gold stripes and the gold seal on the fuselage, so they would be doubly wary coming out.

There was no point, he decided, in trying to apprehend them from the air. Now that they knew he was looking for them, they'd probably leave the kill to the ravens and the wolves and the rest of the Park's carnivores. He couldn't swear it was Howie he saw running for the tent, and while he had recognized Howie's Ski-Doo, Howie could always ditch it and say it had been stolen. It wouldn't be the first time.

No. He had to think up some way to make Howie come to him.

Movement a thousand feet below caught the corner of his eye and he banked the Cessna a little to see George Perry's Cub take off from next to the GHRI trailer. Had he dropped someone off? Someone like Talia Macleod, perhaps? He changed channels. "Piper Super Cub at Suulutaq, that you, George?"

There was a burst of static. "Jim? Where you at?"

"On your six, a thousand feet."

A pause as George looked up and back. "Oh yeah, I gotcha. Where you coming from?"

"Up the valley. Sightseeing. Did you just drop somebody off at the Suulutaq trailer?"

"Yeah."

"Macleod?"

"I wish. No, one of her caretakers. Poor bastard. They're marooned out here for a week at a time, with only a bunch of *Debbie Does Dallas* DVDs for company."

"But I hear she pays well."

Jim could hear the smile in George's voice when he replied. "That she does."

"Think I'll go down and say hi."

"Guy makes lousy coffee."

"I have been warned. Cessna seven-nine Juliet, out."

"See you back at the ranch, Jim. Super Cub one-three Tango, out."

Jim dropped down to a hundred feet, buzzed the trailer to alert the occupant of his imminent arrival, and landed.

Gallagher was waiting in the open door. He didn't look happy when he saw Jim coming, but he was civil. "Sergeant Chopin, isn't it? Dick Gallagher."

"That's right, we met at the Club Bar in Cordova, didn't we?"

"That we did, sir. What can I do for you?"

Jim shrugged. "Just stopped by for a cup of coffee."

Gallagher didn't believe him, but he stepped back and let Jim inside.

George was right, the coffee was awful, but then Jim, who ordered his Tsunami Blend direct from Captain's Roast in Homer, was something of a coffee snob. He hid his wince and said, leaning against the counter, "Nice job you scored here."

"Pays well," Gallagher said, sitting behind the desk.

Jim nodded at the desk. "You heard what happened here, I guess. We always try to keep that kind of thing quiet while the investigation is ongoing, but . . ." He shrugged.

"Yeah," Gallagher said with feeling, "I heard, all right. I had to clean up the mess. Jesus." He seemed to grudge the mess more than the murder.

"You're new in the Park, aren't you?" Jim said.

Gallagher went wary again. "Yeah. Couple of months."

"New to Alaska, too, I take it."

Gallagher shrugged.

Now, it was a maxim of Alaskan etiquette never to ask where somebody was from, but Jim had a badge that said he could ask anyone anything anytime. "Where you from?"

"Arizona," Gallagher said promptly.

Jim smiled. "Jeez. It's a lot warmer there come this time of year. What brought you north?"

"Heard there were jobs here."

Jim gestured at the trailer. "You heard right."

"Yeah," Gallagher said. "It pays well."

"It must, you said that twice," Jim said. "Maybe I should quit troopering and hire on with Global Harvest."

Gallagher grinned, but it seemed forced. "Maybe you should. Although I hear state employees do okay in Alaska."

Jim laughed. "We do all right," he said. "Wonder if you could do me a favor."

Whatever Gallagher was expecting, it wasn't that. "Sure. I guess. If I can."

"Might be some guys driving snow machines down the valley later on. Two, maybe three of them. If they stop in, be helpful if I knew who they were."

"I don't know many people round these parts," Gallagher said, "not yet, anyway. But if they stop in, I can ask."

"Appreciate it," Jim said, and set the still full mug on the counter. "Thanks for the coffee."

"Anytime." Gallagher showed him out without haste. He even waited in the open doorway to wave as the Cessna rose into the air.

Jim circled the trailer as he gained altitude and waggled his wings in a friendly good-bye, but as he straightened out and put the nose back on three-one-five, he was sure of one thing, and maybe two.

Gallagher was nervous about something.

And he sure didn't like cops.

FOURTEEN

The weather held, granting an ephemeral warmth outside if you were bundled up in dark clothes and standing still, but Kate was almost constantly in motion, visiting the downriver villages of the 'Burbs, in order—Double Eagle, Chulyin, Potlatch, and Red Run.

Ken Kaltak had taken to carrying his rifle with him wherever he went. He listened with a stone face as Kate pleaded for time to find the robbers, but she could see he wasn't listening to a word she said. His wife Janice, the lone schoolteacher for the Double Eagle School, which had ten students in seven grades, sent her husband outside on the pretext of getting some moose out of the cache and said bluntly, "Times are tough, Kate. Ken says he's never seen so many fish go up the river, and he's never caught less. Fish and Game gives preference to sports and subsistence fishers and by the time the drifters are allowed to put a net in the water the fish are all up the river. We've got a fish wheel and we catch enough to eat most years, but we rely on what we catch driftnetting in Alaganik to pay for groceries and fuel. We had almost a thousand dollars' worth of food on that sled." Her eyes filled up. "How are we supposed to eat this winter?"

Ken saw Kate to her snow machine, where he exchanged cautious greetings with Mutt (they'd howdied but they hadn't shook), and said, "You know who did this, Kate. Why waste time? Why don't you just head straight for Tikani?"

Kate settled onto the seat. "Can you identify any of your attackers, Ken?"

His lips tightened. He didn't answer.

"Didn't think so," Kate said. "They were wearing helmets, is what I understand."

"Yes."

"So you didn't see their faces. And you didn't recognize the machines."

"No."

She pressed the starter. "When there is evidence that points toward Tikani, I'll go there."

In Chulyin Ike Jefferson was incandescent with rage and treated Kate with something that bordered on contempt. It would have hurt her feelings if she hadn't been so shocked. "Where the hell have you been?" he said. "These guys have pretty much turned the river into a free-fire zone, and you've been where? Because it sure as hell hasn't been anywhere around here!"

"I just found out about them yesterday," she started to say.

"And where's the trooper?" He directed a pointed look over her shoulder. "Sorta conspicuous by his absence, now, ain't he?"

Ike Jefferson was another fisherman, who supplemented his summer earnings by working construction in Anchorage during the winter. A finish carpenter, he was an artist and a craftsman and was better off financially than any of the other victims, but his wife had died giving birth to Laverne and he was raising her alone. "I moved us to Anchorage in the winter because of the work," he told Kate tightly, "but whenever we can, we spend the weekend on the river. It don't happen anywhere near as often as either one of us would like. All I was doing was hauling in some fuel so the place don't freeze up while we're gone. Who pulls this kind of shit, Kate? Since when do Park rats prey on their own? This used to be a good place to live, with good neighbors that'd look out for the place while we're gone, but I might as well live in Anchorage full time and let Laverne hang out at the Dimond Center for all the peace we're getting here."

The Dimond Center mall in Anchorage was a notorious hangout for gangbangers, with APD responding to shoot-outs there half a dozen times a year. No Park rat regarded Anchorage itself as anything more than a place to get your eyes checked, your teeth fixed, to buy food, clothing, and parts, eat fried chicken at the Lucky Wishbone and pizza at the Moose's Tooth, and maybe see a movie if enough things were blown up in it. That Ike had been reduced to winters there only added insult to this newest injury in his eyes.

Laverne, a chunky little girl with a self-possession that belied her years, calmly corroborated her father's description of the attack and the perpetrators, and added the interesting detail that all the snow machines were new.

"Did you recognize what kind?" Kate said.

The girl nodded. "They were all Ski-Doos, and they were all black."

Ike's lips were pressed into a thin line. "Somebody's making money doing this," he said. "Good money. Where you headed now?"

"Red Run," she said.

He snorted. "Why bother? We both know where you shoulda gone first."

She said the same thing to him that she had to Ken Kaltak. "Did you recognize your attackers, Ike?"

He let loose with a string of profanity and stamped off toward the outhouse. "'Bye, Kate," Laverne said, and went back in the cabin.

Dismissed, Kate pressed the starter, negotiated the steep trail over bank to river, idled for a few moments to give Mutt time to catch up and hop on, and headed south.

She got to Red Run that evening and spent the night in her sleeping bag on the floor of the school gym, courtesy of the new teacher who lived alone in a little cabin out back and who was so hungry for company three months into the school year that she insisted Kate join her for dinner and *Notting Hill* on DVD afterward. They both agreed they liked Hugh Grant's friends more than they liked Hugh Grant, and Kate went to sleep that night thinking Red Run School would be lucky if Alice Crawford lasted out the year.

Kate was at the Rileys' home at first light, a small, snug house that Art had built himself from the ground up over the past thirty years. It had begun life as a one-room log cabin, added on to as the children came, and then when Art's father died of lung cancer he built a mother-in-law apartment on the side facing the river. It had its own kitchen where she could make agutaq and fry bread for the granddaughter, the child of Art and Christine's eldest son, an Alaska National Guardsman stationed in Anchorage who was presently serving in Iraq. The mother had vanished shortly after the child's birth and the child had never lived with anyone else.

They welcomed Kate and invited her to share their breakfast. Art was a trapper who ran lines up a couple of creeks in the Quilak foothills, one of them in the Suulutaq Valley. "Best wolf run I've ever had, and last year the best prices I've ever got," he said. "Seems all the Hollywood types are trimming their coats with wolf nowadays, and where they go everybody follows. 'Course the mine'll put paid to all that."

"Doesn't have to," Kate said. "Not if we watch them."

He shook his head. "Don't kid yourself, Kate. It'll change everything."

"Only if we let it," she said, but she was put forcibly in mind of Mandy's certainty on the same subject. "About that attack, Art," she said. "I was wondering if you'd remembered anything else about them. For starters, do you have any idea who it was?"

"No," he said, "no idea."

His tone was oddly tranquil. The five of them were at the kitchen table surrounded by the remnants of bacon and eggs and fried potatoes and toast, the granddaughter absorbed in constructing a house from her potatoes. "You told Jim Chopin you thought the Johansen brothers were the people he ought to talk to."

"Did I?" He shook his head, and produced a sheepish grin. "Probably a hangover from them corking me last summer. The Johansen brothers are a waste of space, true, but I didn't have any reason to suspect them more than anybody else. Still don't."

She stared at him, puzzled.

The Riley kitchen was a warm, crowded, and friendly place, with a woodstove for heat and a propane stove for cooking. The table was homemade beetle kill spruce and big enough to seat eight comfortably, covered with a tacked-down sheet of blue-checked oilcloth. The cupboards were homemade beetle kill, too, like the table a little clunky but sanded and polished to a smooth finish that had been darkened by years of cooking oil and wood smoke. Faded linoleum covered the floor and the walls were a pale yellow, chipped and peeling, on which faded patches showed signs of photographs added and moved around over the years. Dishes were stacked in a wide porcelain farmer's sink that was rather the worse for wear. Underneath the table were two dogs of indeterminate breeding, still and wary but unafraid of Mutt, who was sitting next to Kate, her ears up as if she were listening to and understanding the conversation. She looked up at Kate, yellow eyes meeting hazel, and one ear went back inquisitively. Kate put a hand on her ruff, and looked back at the table.

Grandma Riley looked like one of the aunties, round, brown and wrinkled, a woman of spirit and substance. Like the aunties, she had time served in the Park, and was a repository of knowledge about all the rats who lived therein going back generations, extending to fourth cousins five times removed who now lived in Bowling Green, Kentucky. When a Park rat wanted to draw a family tree, Grandma Riley was everyone's first stop. She'd been failing lately, which was why the extended stay in the elder health care facility in Ahtna, and Kate had the feeling that this might be her last trip south.

Art was the grandson of a white stampeder, a handsome, reckless fellow with a slight limp, known in Dawson City as Riley the Gimp, from New York, who had met and married a local beauty from Tok. They'd moved to the Park to work at the Kanuyaq copper mine, and had stayed on after the mine had closed in 1936, to homestead on the river and raise a family. Grandma Riley had married their son, Arthur Sr., and their children, beginning with Art Jr., had inherited their share of their grandparents' looks.

Christine Riley had been an army brat, born in Anchorage. She had met Art at the University of Alaska and he had brought her home to the river the year they graduated. She was a woman of quiet beauty, still slim and with a full head of pure white hair that was always neatly dressed in a braid wound around her head like a crown. Kate didn't think it had been cut in Christine's lifetime. She worked in the tanning shed next to the house, curing the wolf and mink and beaver and lynx skins Jim brought home, preparing them for sale at fur auctions in Anchorage.

It was, in short, an almost idyllic life for the three of them, two born to it and one who had adopted it wholeheartedly. Kate would have thought that any threat to the life they had built so painstakingly over the years would have roused them to the same incendiary level as the Kaltaks and the Jeffersons.

Instead, she was surrounded by a calm so placid it was almost grating. She looked at each of them in turn and was met by an identical bland stare. "What's going on here?" she said.

Art made an elaborate show of perplexity. "Why, nothing, Kate. We're not happy about what happened, but we know you and Jim will catch whoever did this and make it right."

Christine and Grandma Riley nodded and chorused their agreement, though Grandma Riley wouldn't look up from her mug.

"What about the grandbaby?" Kate said. "You gonna let an attack on her slide, too?"

Art's eyes hardened momentarily, and then his face smoothed out. "We'd left her with a neighbor, as it happens," he said. "We wish we could help you, Kate, but you know how it is. It all happened so fast. I wouldn't worry." He glanced at his mother, smiling. "Grandma always says, what goes around comes around." He drank coffee and grinned. "I hear you had a high old time of it at your first board meeting."

"Jesus," Kate said, "did somebody take out an ad?"

Art laughed and rose to his feet.

Kate, caught by surprise, rose, too. Since when did folks in the Bush urge winter visitors out the door? Usually they were so glad to see anybody they insisted they stay for a week.

It was almost eleven when she hit the river, Mutt on the seat and the sled attached, hiding from the windchill created by her forward motion behind the windshield.

What the hell had that been all about? It was almost as if . . .

The snow machine slowed abruptly as her thumb relaxed on the throttle.

It was almost as if they hadn't wanted her to find the attackers.

No, she thought, that wasn't it, not exactly.

It was as if they were recommending that she not waste her time.

And the only reason for them to think that she was wasting her time was that the attackers had already been caught. And dealt with.

Maybe already somebody stop them.

"Oh, no," Kate said.

Mutt gave an interrogatory whine.

Kate hit the throttle.

But when she stopped at the Jeffersons' again, no trace of the fire-breathing dragon she'd left the day before remained. Ike was now smiling and affable. "No luck, Kate? That's a shame. Well, tomorrow's another day."

And when she got to the Kaltaks in Double Eagle, Ken was equally and eerily serene. He wasn't carrying his rifle anymore, either. "Well, sometimes there's just nothing to be done about a situation, Kate. I expect they were all from Anchorage. You know how those people are, no sense of private property. I'm guessing they'll get what's coming to them one day."

"Ken," she said with what she thought was pretty fair restraint, "when I was here yesterday you were breathing fire and smoke and threatening to shoot on sight. Now you're sounding like Mahatma Gandhi. What happened between then and now?"

He scratched his chin meditatively. "Maybe I got religion." He smiled, a slow stretch of his lips that was more a baring of his teeth than an expression of humor. "You know. Turn the other cheek?"

Frustrated, she took her leave, and Ken saw her out. "Hey," he said, "you still seeing Jim socially?"

She floundered for an answer. "I . . . I . . . sort of," she said. "Yeah."

"Oh. I just wondered."

"Why?"

He gave a vague shrug. "Hear tell he was getting all friendly with the mine woman in the Club Bar in Cordova a couple days back. Probably nothing. I expect they'll have a lot to do with each other once the mine gets going."

He smiled again. There was just the merest hint of pity about it, and it ruffled Kate's feathers. She made a brusque farewell and left.

That smile was before her eyes as she headed out on the river.

She thought about that smile for at least a mile, about what it might mean, along with the reception she had received at the Rileys' and the change in attitude at the Jeffersons' and the Kaltaks'.

Wait a minute, she thought. Wait just a damn minute here.

That remark about Jim and her. It had been more than the usual Park rat interest in the affairs of their fellows. It had been designed to distract her from the attacks.

And it had worked, too.

Distract her from what, though?

She thought about it for another mile, and then she turned around and headed south again, running slow and close to the west bank, seeing many sets of tracks. She followed it as far as Red Run before she turned again and headed north, this time hugging the east bank. Again, many sets of tracks, could be hunters, trappers, ice fishermen, kids out joyriding, people visiting village to village. Nothing that looked out of the ordinary or intrinsically suspicious. She did find a large section of snow in a willow thicket that looked beaten down, as if a lot of snow machines had rendezvoused there, or as if a few had been there more than once. There was an empty bottle of Yukon Jack frozen into the snow under a tree. Not your usual Park tipple, for one thing it was too expensive, but Kate took it anyway. "Anything?" she said to Mutt.

Mutt had been trotting back and forth, nose to the snow. She looked at Kate and sneezed.

When they got back out on the river Kate looked up and saw a line of dark, encroaching cloud. "That's why it felt warmer," she said, unzipping the throat of her parka just a little.

Mutt gave a soft whine and touched a cold nose to Kate's cheek.

She pointed the machine north and opened up the throttle, pausing only to gas up in Niniltna. People waved and called from their seats in pickups and on snow machines and four-wheelers. She waved but didn't stop to talk, just kept going north as fast as she could push it without blowing a track. She was airborne more than once where a crack had caused a bump in the ice and blowing snow had built up a hummock. Mutt found it very exhilarating, on occasion leaping from the back of the snow machine before she was thrown and galloping alongside with her tongue lolling out of her mouth, waiting for Kate to slow down so she could jump back on.

It was three o'clock in the afternoon, the sun getting low on the southeastern horizon, when she came to a tiny cluster of buildings perched between the Kanuyaq and a narrow, high-banked creek. Overgrown with brush and trees, the half-dozen houses were little more than tumbledown shacks, originally built of logs and over the years patched with whatever was handy—tar paper, pink fiberglass insulation, plywood, shingles fashioned from Blazo boxes, now and then a sheet of Tyvek. Some of it had been applied with duct tape. Someone in the village must have scored a pile of corrugated tin because it was on every roof, although it was stained and aging.

About twenty miles short of the halfway point between Ahtna and Niniltna, Tikani was a forlorn place, unkempt, unloved, a line in the Bush drawn decades before that had since blown away on the wind. It supported thirty souls in its peak years, most of them named Johansen for the Norwegian stampeder who settled there in 1906 with his Gwitchin bride. Isolated, insular, and xenophobic in the extreme, Tikani was the product of years of inbreeding and the blood feuds that result when close families fight over too small a piece of what is to begin with a very small pie. They had been too proud and too stubborn to sign on to ANCSA, relying instead on the ownership of their homes and on property being grandfathered in around them when Jimmy Carter signed the d-2 lands bill in 1980. As a result, the unincorporated village sat on the original hundred and sixty acres their great-grandfather had proved up on under the Homestead Act, and no more. They weren't one of the 220 recognized tribes of Alaska, and they received no federal funding as a group over and above what was funneled through the Bureau of Indian Affairs and the Indian Health Service. Refusing to sign off on ANCSA meant they hadn't shared in the billion dollars and the forty-four million acres that had been distributed by the federal government in the ANCSA settlement.

The rationale given by the senior surviving Johansen, Vidar, eldest son of Nils and Almira, was that signing on to ANCSA effaced any future rights signatory Native tribes had to Alaskan lands. He wasn't willing to do that, and he wasn't alone, as several other Alaskan Native villages had refused to go along with ANCSA as well. They had all suffered for it financially, but they still had their pride.

Pride didn't fill a belly.

They'd lost their school five years before due to low enrollment. The school, the largest building in the village, sat a little apart, its roof visible over the trees. There was no smoke coming out of the chimney, and it had that forlorn, defenseless air all abandoned buildings in the Arctic do just before the roof falls in. No one was in sight, in spite of the fact that the wind was calm and her engine had to be audible to anyone indoors.

"Off," Kate said, and Mutt hopped off to allow Kate to negotiate the rudimentary trail up the bank alone.

There weren't any streets per se, just a narrow track postholed through the snow. She parked the snow machine to one side and slipped the key into the pocket of her parka, the first time she had done so since she had bought the machine.

She waited. No one appeared. No curtain moved at a window. There was no chunk of an ax, no clank of tool, only a tiny breeze teasing at a strand of her hair. If there had been a sign hanging from the front of one of the cabins, it would have been creaking. Any second now a tumbleweed would come rolling down the street.

Her thighs were sore from straddling the snowgo seat for so long and it felt good to stretch. "Hey, girl, come here," she said in a loud voice. Mutt trotted over, looking a little quizzical, and Kate said, still in a voice raised to carry, "That's my good girl. Think there's a cup of coffee in this town with my name on it?"

Still no one came to greet her, and when enough time had passed for politeness' sake she walked to the largest house in the village, the only one showing smoke from its chimney, and knocked on the door. While she waited, she noticed that the woodpile at the side of the house didn't seem near high enough for November, not with six more months of cold weather to get through.

At last, a rustle of noise, a shuffle of feet. The door opened. A rheumy eye peered out at her and a cracked voice said, "What do you want?"

"Can I come in, Vidar?" Kate said. "It's cold as hell out here, and I sure could use some coffee."

He thought about it for long enough that Kate actually considered the possibility that she might be refused entrance, and then the door swung wide. "Get your ass in here, then, and be quick about it so I don't have to stand here all goddamn day with the goddamn door open letting the goddamn winter in."

"Nice to see you, too, Vidar," Kate said, and she and Mutt quickstepped inside.

Vidar glared down at Mutt. "Didn't say the goddamn dog could come in, too."

Mutt dropped her head a little and lifted her lip. There was no love lost between Mutt and Vidar.

Kate ignored both of them and said brightly, "I'm about froze solid. I sure could use that coffee, Vidar."

He grumbled something that probably would not measure up to the generally accepted standards of Bush hospitality and shuffled to the stove. "Siddown if you want."

The interior of the house was so cluttered with traps and magazines and tools and parts and dirty clothes and Louis L'Amour novels and caribou antlers and moose racks and bear skulls and pelts in various states of the curing process that it took a minute or two for a chair to coalesce out of the jumble. There was a table, almost invisible beneath a thicket of beaver skins hanging from the exposed trusses that formed the roof. She pulled the table out from under the beaver skins as far as there was room for it and displaced the wolf skins on the chair to a stack of four-wheeler tires. Mutt rumbled her disapproval of the wolf skins.

Kate sat down in the newly liberated chair. She did not remove her boots, as she would have as a matter of custom and courtesy in any other house in the Park, or Alaska for that matter. Mutt sat down next to her with an air, while not wishing to rush Kate through her business in any way, of nevertheless being ready to quit the premises at their earliest opportunity.

A very old woodstove, encrusted with years of soot and ash, was doing a poor job of heating the house, probably because Kate could see daylight through a crack here and there in the unfinished two-by-twelves that formed the walls. There was an old-fashioned blue tin coffeepot with a wire handle sitting on the back of the stove and from this Vidar produced two thick mugs full of liquid that put Kate persuasively in mind of Prudhoe Bay crude. It tasted like it, too, and Kate used fully a quarter of the can of evaporated milk on the table to thin it down. She didn't go light on the sugar, either, although that had mostly solidified in the cracked bowl it sat in.

Mutt wasn't offered anything. She did not take the snub in good part.

An upholstered rocking chair with stuffing leaking from various rips and tears sat at right angles to the woodstove and into this Vidar subsided, although it could be more properly said that he collapsed.

Vidar Johansen was in his nineties, the sole surviving child of the village's founders, who were the direct and indirect progenitors of anyone born there. He had his father's height, in his prime standing six feet six inches tall. He was bent with age now, with wispy gray hair that looked as if he cut it himself whenever it got in his eyes, and a beard that was mostly grizzle. He wore a plaid shirt so faded it was impossible to tell what the original color had been, and a pair of jeans whose seams looked ready to give at any moment. His feet were bundled into wool socks and homemade moccasins lined with fur gone threadbare. His cheekbones stood out in stark relief from the rest of his face, and the skin on the backs of his hands was so thin Kate imagined she could see the bone through it.

"What are you staring at?" he said belligerently, and she looked away, at the Blazo box shelves on the wall that were mostly bare, at the half-empty case of Campbell's Cream of Tomato soup that sat on the counter, at the oversize box of Ritz crackers sitting next to it. An empty trash can sat under a rough counter that supported the sink, which held a saucepan, a bowl, and a spoon crusted with red.

She looked down at her mug, and wished she hadn't used so much of Vidar's milk.

He rocked and slurped down some coffee and looked at her. She drank heroically and managed a smile. "Oh, that's great, Vidar, thanks," she said. "You're saving my life here."

He grunted. The wooden runners of his chair creaked. "What you want," he said.

Okay. "I was hoping your sons would be around."

He grunted again. The chair creaked some more. "Why?" He was avoiding her eye, but she couldn't decide if that was because he had something to hide or it was just Vidar being his usual antisocial self.

"Need to talk to them," she said.

Grunt. Creak. "What about?"

"Some people were attacked and robbed on the river by some other people on snow machines."

The chair stilled and Vidar was silent for a moment. "You think it was my boys."

"Their names have been mentioned, yes."

"Somebody see 'em?"

"Not to identify them, no."

He grunted and resumed rocking. "Probably was them."

"Yeah," Kate said. Vidar had as many illusions about his sons as she or any other Park rat did.

Icarus, Daedalus, and Gus Johansen were Vidar's sons by his only wife, Juanita, a Guatemalan woman who had waited on him at the Northern Lights Denny's in Anchorage while on a supply run to town. She wanted American citizenship and at fifty-five he wanted someone to cook and clean and warm his bed. Twenty-four hours after she'd brought him breakfast for the first time they were on the road to Ahtna with a truck full of groceries and a full set of brand-new winter gear for her.

There were many who said it wouldn't last, Juanita used to being a lot closer to the Equator and all, and Vidar not necessarily the sweetest-talking man in the Park, and nearly thirty years older besides, but she stuck it out until Gus was born. She vanished out of the hospital in Ahtna the next day. Vidar didn't waste time trying to find her, he just took Gus back to Tikani, where the other two boys were being looked after by a relative. "Your ma's gone off somewheres," he was reported to have said. "You boys'n me'll be batching it from now on."

He never spoke her name again, and there had never been money to waste on fripperies like photographs, so Gus never did know what his mother had looked like, and neither his father nor his brothers remembered or wanted to. There were no soft edges on Vidar. There weren't any on his sons, either. They'd brought women home and every time, when the romance of living in the wilderness wore off, they had in their turn been abandoned, too. There were children, no one knew how many. It looked like all of them had left with their mothers.

"So," Kate said. "The boys around?"

"Not lately."

Kate looked again at the can of milk, the cans of soup, the crackers. "When was the last time you saw them?"

He hawked and spat, missing the metal water dish on the floor by a good six inches. "Month. Maybe less. Maybe more."

"Don't they live here anymore?"

He glared at her from beneath thick, wiry eyebrows, one eye gone kind of white, the other a red-streaked brown. "Didn't say that. You asked had I seen them. Said no. Haven't. Heard their machines, though."

"So they are still living here."

He shrugged. "Far's I know. They haven't been up to the house for a while."

Kate felt a lick of anger. Vidar's house was maybe fifty feet max from the front door of the house in Tikani farthest away from his. "Anybody else seen them? That you've talked to lately?"

"Ain't talked to anyone lately," he said. "Everybody's gone."

"What?"

"Something wrong with your hearing? Said everybody's gone. Nobody left here 'cept us."

"Jesus Christ, Vidar," Kate said, her worst suspicions confirmed. "You mean you're here all by yourself?"

He grunted. The chair creaked. "Ick's new girl was the last one out. At least she stopped in to let the young uns say good-bye to their grandpa. More'n I can say for the rest of those losers the boys brought home."

"I'm sorry," Kate said. "I didn't know."

Grunt. Creak.

"Do the kids know?"

Grunt. Creak.

"You want to come back to Niniltna with me?" she said.

The chair stopped and he glared at her. "Hell no. No towns for me, not any longer'n it takes to buy a new set a spark plugs. I'm fine out here."

"What if you run out of fuel? Food? What if you get hurt and there's no one here to help? Come on, come back with me. We'll get you a room with Auntie Vi and then figure something out for the long term."

Grunt. Hawk. Spit. Creak. "Told you. Don't do towns. Like it here fine. Man can hear himself think."

"Is it because you're worried that the boys'll come back and find you gone? We can leave them a note."

"Ain't going nowhere," he said with a finality that denied opposition. "Tell the boys you was here when I see 'em again."

"Vidar . . ."

"You had your coffee, got yourself warmed up. Time for you and that hound to go, if you wanna get home safe."

He stared at her with his one good eye. "Like you said. Bad things happening on the river lately."

FIFTEEN

Dinah met Jim at the door, finger to her lips, and stepped back to let him enter.

Bobby was right where Jim wanted him, broadcasting on Park Air, the pirate radio station that had been changing channels one step ahead of the FCC for a dozen years now. This morning featured an interview with one Talia Macleod of Global Harvest Resources Inc. Bobby was sitting knee to knee with her in front of a microphone and appeared spellbound. Nothing loath, she was flirting hard right back, but that didn't stop either one of them from getting what they wanted said out on the air.

"Open pit mining isn't known for having the environmental friendlies," Bobby said. "Don't you need a lot of water for the extraction process? Where you gonna pull all that water from?"

"Plenty of water in local feeder streams to get the job done," Talia said, her voice a low purr.

Anyone listening would think, with some justification, that they were listening to pillow talk, Jim thought. Talia looked up and saw him, and a smile spread across her face. Behind Jim, Dinah frowned.

"Yeah, but babe," Bobby said, his voice a correspondingly

caressing rumble, "those feeder streams are pretty much all of them salmon streams. You might miss the Gruening River, it being so far up the valley from the mine, but what about Keehler Creek, Jones Creek, the Stone River? They run straight down the valley. You're going to use toxic chemicals to extract the gold, which means you're going to have a lot of acid runoff. It gets into those salmon streams, the salmon are dead." He gave her a winsome smile, his caressing tone unchanging. "And so are a lot of the families who live off those salmon runs, from Ahtna to Alaganik Bay."

Talia returned a smile every bit as winning as his own. "If you'd look at our construction plans, Bobby, you'd see that we have designed a 4,700-acre drainage lake to capture all the acid runoff, protected by a dam." Her smile widened. "Two dams, in fact, just in case. Global Harvest is all about safety first."

"Earthen dams, as I understand it," Bobby said without missing a beat. "Made out of dirt. Which, as we all know, turns to mud in the rain." He chuckled. "And then there are, um, what do you call those things? Earthquakes, that's it. A whole lotta shakin' goin' on. What does that do to the stability of a dam that's going to be bigger than the Hoover Dam? Sounds like a Superfund site in the making to me."

"Why, Bobby," she said, "if I didn't know better I'd say you were against the Suulutaq Mine."

"You would?" Bobby said innocently.

They laughed together. Jim looked at Dinah, who rolled her eyes and went to admire Katya's efforts at a dangerously tilting block castle.

"No reason for you to be against it," Talia murmured, "and plenty of them for you to be for it. Didn't I mention? We're going to be bringing jobs into the Park in numbers that haven't been seen since the old days of the Kanuyaq Mine. Two thousand, maybe more, during construction, and a thousand to keep it running after, and did I also mention how long we expect to be here? Forty years,

189

minimum. That's forty years of jobs for Park rats, Bobby, and good-paying jobs, too."

"Yeah, Talia, but what kind of jobs we talking about here? Making beds, serving slop?" Bobby's smile slipped a little. "Not something I aspire to for the kid." He looked up at Jim and said, "Chopper Jim Chopin in the house, folks. Hey, Jim."

"Hey, Bobby," Jim said, walking forward so his voice was within reach of the mike.

Bobby watched him with a sapient eye. "You look like a man with a purpose. What's up?"

"I'm looking for Howie Katelnikof. Have you seen him?"

Bobby's eyebrow quirked up. "No, can't say's I have. What's Howie up to these days?"

"Well," Jim said apologetically, "he's in a little bit of trouble, and he's got some people looking for him. Not very nice people, I'm afraid."

"Really," Bobby said, his basso dropping to profundo. "Imagine my surprise."

"Yeah," Jim said, trying not to laugh, "and these people looking for him have put up a reward for whoever finds him."

"Really?" Bobby said. "How much?"

"Hear tell it's five figures."

Bobby gave an appreciative whistle, but he frowned a little. He disliked Howie as cordially as the next person but he didn't necessarily want to get the guy killed on Park Air. "Wow, he must have really pissed someone off this time."

"Well, as you know, a couple days ago somebody got shot out at the Suulutaq when Howie was supposed to be working there," Jim said. Talia frowned this time. "So I wanted to get the word out to folks. If they see Howie, tell him to come on in, okay? I'll keep him safe."

"Okaaaaay," Bobby said, drawing the word out, "you heard it here first, that's Park Air, today at nearly ninety-five on your FM dial, but we won't be here tomorrow! Thanks to the lovely and talented and babealicious Talia Macleod for being on our show today. That would be the same Talia Macleod who sold her soul to the devil, oh, I'm sorry, of course I meant to say Global Harvest Resources Inc., aka GHRIn, to convince us all that a fifteen-square-mile open pit mine in the Park is a goo-oood thing."

Talia, unoffended, laughed out loud, and Bobby grinned. "Hey, I'm convinced. Th-th-that's all, folks!"

He flicked a switch. On the console a green light went red and a red light went green and the sound of the Temptations singing "My Girl" soared out of the Bose speakers mounted in the four corners of the room. He turned his chair to Jim. "Okay, boyo, what the fuck was that all about? You think I'm rerunning episodes from *Wanted: Dead or Alive* on Park Air now?"

"I need to talk to Howie, ASAP," Jim said, "and either someone is going to bring him in for the reward, or what I'm hoping is he'll beat them in scared they're going to catch him."

A warm hand settled on his arm and he looked down to see Talia standing very close next to him. "Do you think Howie Katelnikof killed Mac Devlin?"

"I don't know," he said, and didn't mention what he'd seen at the head of the valley the previous morning. "But he was supposed to be there, and he's my best shot at a witness. So to speak."

She laughed, low down in her throat, and leaned in toward him a little more. He smiled back at her—she was pretty irresistible—and then felt a cold draft on his back as the door opened.

He looked up and beheld Kate, standing in the doorway with a face wiped clean of all expression.

It took less than twenty-four hours for Howie to present himself at the post. "In a place the size of the Park," Annie said appreciatively, "that's making pretty good time."

"Being scared shitless increases ground speed," Old Sam said. "Fact."

Demetri stared pensively out the window of the front office of the Niniltna Native Association, where many people had gathered to watch the fugitive give himself up. "I heard that even Martin was looking for him."

"Five zeros," Annie said. "That'd be enough to get any Park rat through the winter."

Old Sam snorted. "Always supposing that reward story was true, I'd a done it for ten bucks."

Howie arrived alone, on his cherry little Ski-Doo, the engine purring as seductively as Talia Macleod, but that, Jim figured, was only because Willard would have been assigned responsibility for tune-ups, repairs, and maintenance. Howie wasn't careful of machinery, because he knew he could always steal something else when whatever he was driving broke down.

He stumped up the steps of the post and walked into Jim's office, receding chin thrust out as far as it would go. "What's this I hear about some damn reward out on me? I ain't done nothing wrong, Jim, and I expect you to take care of me same as you would anybody else in the Park."

"Hey, Howie," Jim said, carelessly. In fact he'd spent the night at the post on the off chance that Howie would show up earlier and spook when he didn't find anyone there. He'd watched Howie arrive through his office window with quiet joy. There was nothing better than when a plan worked. It made up for all the ones that didn't. "Where you been?"

Howie's eyes slid away. "Around."

"Okay. So why weren't you at work?"

"Work?" Howie said the word like it was a concept foreign to his tongue, which it pretty much was.

"Yeah, Talia Macleod told me she hired you as one of two care-takers for the trailer Global Harvest's got up to the Suulutaq Mine."

"Oh yeah," Howie said. "Right. That work."

"You were supposed to be there all last week, Monday to Monday, until your relief came."

"I was there," Howie said. "I was there, you know, work. Working." Again, he stumbled over the word. He didn't even know the right verb to use with it.

"Well, I'm really glad to hear that, Howie," Jim said, smiling.

Wary now, Howie said, "Oh? Why would that be?"

Jim let his smile fade. "Because Mac Devlin's body was found at the Suulutaq trailer, and I was hoping you could tell us something about how it got there."

Howie's jaw dropped. "Huh?"

"Mac Devlin," Jim said, adding, since Howie seemed to need to hear it, "you know, the ex-owner of the Nabesna Mine. Someone killed him on the doorstep of the trailer and then went away, leaving him to rot where he fell. If you were there, you must have seen something that could help me find this someone." He raised polite eyebrows.

"Mac's dead?" Howie said.

"Murdered," Jim said.

"I didn't do it," Howie said.

"Really," Jim said.

"I wasn't there," Howie said.

"Really?" Jim said. "But you just said you were, Howie."

Howie's voice, naturally a nasal whine, started to rise. "I wasn't there! I didn't do anything! I'm innocent! Let me go, right now, I'm not doing any more time in one of your lousy cells!"

"If you weren't there," Jim said, "where were you?"

His eyes bored into Howie's. Howie stared back like a fright-ened rabbit. "If you weren't at the mine, where were you, Howie?"

Howie stared back, blinking, agonized, and for the moment blessedly mute.

Jim sighed. "Maggie!"

A head poked in. "Boss?"

"Get Howie's rifle off of his snow machine and bring it in, would you?"

"Sure thing, boss."

"No!" Howie said, making an abortive attempt to stop her, but the door shut smartly in his face.

"Have a seat, Howie," Jim said.

When Maggie got back with Howie's rifle, Howie was rigid in a chair in front of Jim's desk, tugging at the handcuff holding him to the left arm of the chair. It was still cold outside, although those clouds he'd seen over the Gulf earlier in the week had paid off in a thickening overcast. This morning smelled like snow. Nothing worse than chasing down a perp in a snowstorm. Actually, nothing worse than chasing down a perp, period. They never watched where they were going, for one thing, and for another, it was just plain exhausting. Jim much preferred to dispense with the possibil-ity altogether.

"Thanks, Mags," Jim said, reaching for the rifle. "Close the door on your way out, please."

Jim sat on the edge of his desk and examined the rifle. A .30-30 Winchester Trapper, well used and not well cared for. Jim looked up and allowed himself a personal comment. "You really are a worth-less piece of shit, Howie."

"I didn't do it! I didn't do anything! I'm innocent! I want a lawyer! Get me whathisname, Louis's lawyer! He'll fix it so I don't have to stay here, so I can go home!"

"Rickard?" Jim said.

"Yeah! Him! Get me Rickard! On the phone, right now!"

"Well, I could do that, Howie," Jim said. "Or you could just tell me what happened. If you weren't there, you don't have anything to worry about."

Something about the deep, inexorable tone in Jim's voice unlocked Howie's spine, and he slumped in his chair. "I wasn't at the trailer over half an hour that Monday. I just stopped to take a crap and grab some grub."

"Where'd you go?"

Howie mumbled something.

"Where'd you go, Howie?" Jim went around his desk and sat down.

"I was up the head of the valley," Howie said, studiously addressing the floor.

"What were you doing up there?" Jim said. "That's a ways to go just to sightsee, and it's been a damn cold stretch of weather lately."

"Might have been doing some hunting," Howie said defensively.

"Caribou?" Jim said.

"Maybe," Howie said.

"Out of season?" Jim said. "Howie, you astonish me. Anybody with you?"

Howie rolled his shoulders.

"Be a lot better if someone can corroborate your testimony, Howie. It can't do you any good if all you did was go on a joyride with nobody looking."

"Fuck," Howie said in a kind of furious mutter. "Martin was with me."

"Thought I recognized that old Yamaha," Jim said. "Anybody else?"

"We was just taking those caribou because we was hungry," Howie said, and then added, "we was taking the meat to the elders." He looked up, inspired. "Ask the aunties. They'll tell you."

There was a gloating kind of certainty in Howie's eyes that Jim didn't like. "Okay, I'll ask them. Where's Martin, Howie?"

"I don't know," Howie said. "We split up after we come down off the mountain."

"I see," Jim said. "Tell me, Howie, who have you pissed off lately?"

Howie stared at Jim, wounded. "Nobody," he said. "I didn't hurt nobody."

"Yeah," Jim said. "You need to think about this some, Howie. Somebody shot Mac Devlin in the back. I actually think you're telling me the truth, mostly because I saw you up there butchering out half the Gruening River caribou herd, so I don't think you did shoot him. I shudder to think what's going to happen to you when Ruthe Bauman finds out about your off-season slaughter, incidentally."

Howie looked aggrieved. Before he could say anything, Jim said, "But Mac wasn't supposed to be at Suulutaq. So far as I know, he didn't tell anyone he was going there, either. Which means that maybe whoever shot Mac didn't know they were shooting at Mac. Maybe whoever shot at Mac was thinking he was somebody else. Maybe whoever shot Mac was thinking he was shooting at somebody who was supposed to be there, whose job should have kept them there twenty-four seven, Monday to Monday."

Howie's head came up and he stared at Jim, his face sallow and starting to sweat.

Jim smiled at him. "Yeah, Howie," he said happily, "I'm thinking somebody tried to kill you and shot Mac Devlin by mistake." He shook his head sorrowfully. "Poor Mac."

"Poor Mac," Howie said mechanically, and seemed to revive. "What do you mean, poor Mac! What about me?"

"What about you? Lucky you, I'd say." Jim knotted his hands behind his head and leaned back in his chair to look at the ceiling. "Well. Unless they try again, of course."

"Unless they try again?" Howie said.

"Yeah, you know," Jim said, adding helpfully, "to kill you." He shook his head. "Seemed like a pretty serious effort to me. In my experience, anybody who's that determined is likely to give it another shot. So to speak." He stood and came around the desk. "Here, let me get that off you so you can get out of here."

"Wait," Howie said. "Wait, Jim, wait!" He hopped the chair backward, trying to get out of range of the handcuff key.

"Howie, come on now. You've got to sit still or I'll never get that cuff off you."

"I got something to tell you! Something you don't know about Louis!"

"Louis's dead, Howie," Jim said, grabbing him before he could hop any farther. He jammed the key in the cuff and twisted. The cuff came free but before he could stop him Howie slammed the cuff back around the arm of the chair and locked it, holding his hand over it so Jim couldn't get at it again.

"Howie," Jim said, starting to get a little irritated, "I've had a long couple of days. Knock it off."

"The aunties hired his killing, Jim! They hired it done!"

SIXTEEN

Jim bagged the rifle and took it out to the Niniltna airstrip, where he was lucky enough to catch George Perry on a flight to Anchorage. He gave him the rifle for delivery to the crime lab.

Howie he locked up, and told Maggie no one was to talk to Howie except him. "Okay, boss," she said.

Maggie Montgomery's chief qualification for the job of dispatcher/telephone answerer/clerk was her determined incuriosity. "My plan is to leave the job at the office when I go home every day," she'd told him during the interview, and he'd hired her on the spot. She might try to tell him what to do on occasion—as in attempting to discourage him from finding Louis Deem's killer last year—but that he could live with. Discretion in a cop shop was a rare and precious commodity, especially in a small town, and Jim was willing to put up with any amount of backtalk in private so long as he got a smiling, uncomplaining, and stolidly uncommunicative face in public. So far, Maggie, an Outsider who had married a Moonin she met on a fish processor in the Bering Sea, was holding up very well, both as his chief cook and bottle washer and as a Park rat. She might just stick.

He went down to the Riverside Café and got a hamburger and french fries to go and delivered it back to Howie. Howie actually thanked him. Jim wanted to open the door of the cell and beat him to death, and something in Jim's eyes must have indicated this because Howie dropped his eyes and became very, very still.

Jim went back to his office and closed the door, and then, for several minutes, he just stood there in the middle of the room, hands dangling uselessly at his sides. For the life of him he couldn't figure out what to do next.

He'd always figured Howie was the most likely suspect, but all this time he had thought Bernie had hired it done directly.

The year before, Bernie Koslowski's wife and son had been murdered in their own home. General consensus was that the killings had been committed by Park bad actor Louis Deem, whom it was supposed Enid and Fitz Koslowski had caught in the act of burglarizing the cabinet full of gold nuggets in the living room.

Shortly thereafter, Louis Deem had been shot and killed on the road to the Step. Bernie was the obvious suspect, so Jim had looked hard at Bernie, to the general disapprobation and not a little vocal abuse of the entire Park. The subsequent investigation had cleared Bernie of all suspicion of the crime.

Not least because his alibi was Sergeant Jim Chopin, with whom he'd been visiting over a latte at the Riverside Café at the time of the murder, in full view of café owner Laurel Meganack, Old Sam Dementieff, and half a dozen other Park rats, all with excellent memories.

"What is it you want me to do, Bernie?"

"Your job."

Well, he'd done his job. He'd maintained the peace and the public order.

One of the principal core values of the Alaska State Troopers was loyalty, first to the state of Alaska, then to the highest ideals of law enforcement, and, in third place, to the truth, although as stated "the truth, regardless of outcome."

Jim had been thinking a lot about that particular core value lately. The truth was he liked working in law enforcement. The truth was he didn't like the messes people got themselves into and he liked using what ability he had to step in and straighten those messes out. The truth was he was good at his job, and he knew it.

He'd opened the Alaska State Troopers' forty-fourth post in Niniltna going on three years ago, and if he had been a Park fixture before, by now he was a full-fledged Park rat. He was well aware of the dangers of being so dug in. A cop was always going to be a little bit on the outside looking in, or he should be if he was going to function effectively. If he was regarded as a member of his community, then it followed that other members in that community might feel comfortable enough with his presence to approach him with suggestions they wouldn't have dared to propose to the cop perceived to be Other.

"What is it you want me to do, Bernie?"

"Your job."

He had not allowed himself any preconceptions as to the identity of the killer of Louis Deem. He had conducted a by-the-book investigation into his death, reconstructing Deem's movements as minutely as was possible in an area as vast and as unpopulated as the Park, extensively interviewing the people closest to Louis as well as all the people who had last seen him alive, and, as near as he was able, keeping his prior knowledge of the character of the dead man from coloring his work.

He'd been thorough and conscientious enough to have discovered a missing piece of evidence and tracked it down to Park ranger Dan O'Brien. Dan had found the body and removed the piece of evidence before fetching Jim to the scene. Jim should have charged Dan with evidence tampering and obstruction of justice. He hadn't.

Since any list of Louis Deem's enemies included pretty much the entire population of the Park, all this had taken some time. Meanwhile, there had been pressure from his boss in Fairbanks to either close the case or move on. In the end, he'd come up empty, and obedient to authority, he'd moved on. Louis Deem's murder was a cold case now, and there wasn't a soul in the Park who would want it reopened.

Howie had not confessed to Louis's murder. It was the one thing he had stopped short of doing this morning, and though Jim had poked and prodded and tried to provoke him into admitting to it, he remained obdurate. He would only reiterate that the aunties had hired the job done on Louis, and he wasn't going to say any more until Jim gave him immunity, a fine word everyone in the Park with a television had picked up from goddamn *Law and Order* or goddamn *CSI*. Fictional crime fighters made life so much harder on the real ones.

Howie was obviously afraid that Jim was right, that whoever had shot and killed Mac Devlin had thought he was aiming at Howie.

Which led to another thought: Maybe that was why Howie had taken on his first gainful employment in years, and from what Jim had heard, possibly in Howie's life. Maybe the job was isolated enough for him to feel safe. Though, of course, being Howie, he had lost no time in turning the location to his advantage. That had been a caribou hunt of wholesale proportions.

The question remained. Who was Howie so afraid of that he'd ask to be taken into protective custody?

The aunties were at their corner table when he walked into the Roadhouse, and he went directly to them, pulling up a chair and straddling it. He put his arms across the back and leaned his chin on them and stared at the aunties in turn, calling out their names as he did so. "Auntie Vi. Auntie Joy. Auntie Balasha. Auntie Edna."

"Jim," Auntie Vi said, a little mystified by this formal greeting and a little suspicious because of it. "Where Kate?"

"She's doing a job for me downriver," he said.

Auntie Vi gave this statement her cautious approbation. "Always good to make some money."

Normally he would have talked to them individually. Some instinct had urged him to take this to the aunties head on. It might not have had as much to do with good police work as it did with self-preservation. No matter. Either he'd carry the barricades or they would repulse his attack, and he'd have to live with that.

He'd chosen here, in public, in a venue in which they felt comfortable and where they were in a position of authority, however unofficial it was. Out of the corner of his eye he saw Bernie coming toward him. He shook his head. Bernie altered course for the table around which the four Grosdidiers were celebrating something monumental, as evidenced by the number of dead soldiers on the table. Matt had a black eye, Luke a fat lip, and the knuckles of the hand Mark used to reach for his beer were swollen double, so probably a fight in which one or all were victorious. Or maybe just a fight. The Grosdidier boys were rabble-rousers of the first water. One of the smartest things the Niniltna Native Association had ever done was to harness all that energy in an EMT program and put it to good use.

Quit stalling, he told himself, and faced the aunties again and took a deep breath. "Aunties," he said, "I just talked to Howie. He told me that you hired him to kill Louis Deem."

It felt as if time stopped, which was ridiculous. He could still hear the clink of glasses, laughter, a heated argument over drift net regulations, the squeak of sneakers on wood on television. Life continued, of course it did. But here, at this moment, at this table, it was as if everyone was holding their breath, as if the intake of oxygen had been suspended, and depending on the answers he got here, as if the world might begin spinning backward when time resumed.

He looked at their faces again, one at a time. Tears gathered and fell down Auntie Balasha's face. Auntie Edna looked pissed off, but then she always did. Auntie Joy's needle froze halfway into the fabric square she was working on. She didn't meet his eyes.

Auntie Vi alone did not so much as blink, her needle flashing in and out steadily, rhythmically, a straight line of even stitches progressing steadily across the quilt. "Such nonsense, Jim," she said, in a chiding voice. "You smarter than that."

"So you didn't hire him to kill Louis?" Jim said.

She paused in her sewing to give him an impatient look. "Of course not. Silliness. Surprised I am that you would believe him enough to ask us. Howie!" She snorted. "Nobody believe a word that out of his mouth come. Why you now?"

"Auntie Balasha?"

Her smile was wavering. "Silliness," she said, echoing Auntie Vi.

"Auntie Edna?"

Auntie Edna snorted her reply and without moving gave the distinct impression of turning her back on him.

"Auntie Joy?"

Auntie Joy's hands trembled. She still wouldn't look up. "What Vi says, Jim. Silliness."

Auntie Vi jumped. "Aycheewah!" She put her finger in her mouth, and stared down at the perfect circle of bright red blood staining the cloth.

When he walked into the house that evening, Kate was frying moose liver rolled in flour, salt, and pepper in olive oil with a dab of butter and mashing potatoes with butter and cream in what looked like proportions equal to the potatoes. She was mashing the potatoes by hand, and she was mashing with vigor. She didn't look up when Jim came in. "Johnny," she said, "would you go out to the cache for me and find a package of peas and onions?"

"Sure," Johnny said, and got up from where he had been studying Alaska history at the dining room table. As he passed Jim in the doorway, he touched his arm and said in a low voice, "She's mad about something, Jim."

Jim looked at Kate. "As it happens, so am I."

Johnny stared at him in consternation and gathering indignation. "Oh, good," he said. "At least it'll be a fair fight." He grabbed his parka and the door closed behind him.

Jim looked to Mutt for succor. Mutt, a reliable barometer when it came to Kate and a loyal friend even in the face of Mutt's undeniable lust for Jim, was parked in front of the fireplace, nose under her tail. She hadn't even looked up at his entrance. It was not the kind of treatment he was accustomed to, and even more than Johnny's warning, it put him on full alert. A proponent of the best defense is a good offense, he divested himself of parka, boots, and especially his sidearm and said without preamble, "What's wrong?"

At least he could rely on her not to respond with a falsely bright, "Nothing!" but he wasn't expecting what did come out.

"Do you have something going on with Talia Macleod?"

It caught him so flat-footed that his response was a brilliantly articulate, "Huh?"

"I've been up and down the river and in and out of Niniltna the past two days, and everywhere I go I'm told about the Father of the Park's new target."

"Wait a minute—"

"You've been seen everywhere together, it seems." She gave the potatoes a savage mash, her already tight shoulder muscles bunching with the effort. "In Niniltna at the Riverside Café. At the Roadhouse. In Cordova at the Club Bar. At Bobby's. You've been seen everywhere together, getting on like a house on fire, and the general consensus seems to be that I'm out and she's in. Fine by me, you do what you want, but I'd appreciate knowing if that's the case."

She pushed the pot of potatoes to the back of the stove and started turning the strips of liver. Each move she made was accomplished with a delicate precision, centering the pot and the frying pan on the stove's burners, piercing each slice of liver precisely at a spot on one end that would counterbalance the weight so it wouldn't slide off the tine of the fork, setting it back into the pan at the correct distance so no slice would adhere to the slice next to it. Each strip was a perfect brown, no charring allowed, and the potatoes looked like a pot full of cumulus clouds, fluffy and creamy and mouthwateringly appealing. A dish full of browned onions sat next to it.

He said the first thing that came into his head. "Why the cache for the peas and onions? Why not the freezer?"

She paused, one strip of meat in the air, and gave him a look that would have turned a lesser man to stone. "Why spend the money on diesel to run the generator to run the freezer when winter will do the job just fine?"

"Makes sense," he said. He took in the rest of the kitchen. There were two loaves of white bread cooling on a rack, a loaf of date nut bread cooling in the pan, and coffee cake cooling in a cake tin. "You've been busy."

"It's cold, I'm hungry, answer the question."

"You're jealous," he said.

Such a wave of fury rolled over the counter in his direction that he almost instinctively ducked out of the way of the frying pan that—oil, liver, and all—he was certain would be coming in his direction next.

She struggled for control and won. He breathed easier. "I told you once," she said, her voice very tight, "I don't stand in line. You want to sleep with Talia Macleod, go sleep with Talia Macleod. Just don't come back here after you have."

She banged open a cupboard and slung a plate in the oven to warm with such vigor he was surprised it didn't shatter.

"I'm not sleeping with her," Jim said, and as the words came out of his mouth wondered at them. Had he ever had this particular conversation with a woman before?

"Uh-huh," she said.

He realized she was hurt, and knew a momentary flash of guilt, which corresponded almost exactly to a simultaneous lick of resentment. Since when did he feel guilty over how he treated women?

Since never. His women were supposed to know the score, they were carefully selected and the relationship structured on a rational basis where everyone had a good time and nobody got hurt when it was over. "I've never lied to you, Kate," he said, the words coming out maybe a little hotter and harder than he'd meant them to. "If it comes to that, I've never lied to any woman I've ever known. I'd appreciate it if you wouldn't automatically assume I was lying to you now."

She paused, a strip of liver dangled momentarily over the frying pan, and then set it carefully flour-side down in the sizzling oil. "All right," she said. "That's fair. I apologize." She set the fork to one side and looked him straight in the eye for the first time since he'd come into the room. "The day you were seen with her in the Club Bar? You didn't come home that night." At his expression, she heaved an impatient sigh. "I'm a trained investigator, Jim, not to mention which people tell me stuff." She added bleakly, "I don't know why, but they always do. Sometimes I think I should have been a priest, because I have to be the depository of more secrets than any other Park rat walking around on two legs."

She paused, but he could tell she wasn't done, so he waited.

"I hate this," she said with a heartfelt intensity. She picked the fork up again, evidently this time for the sole purpose of slamming it down.

"What?" he said.

"This!" she said, waving a hand that indicated the space between the two of them. "I hate it that I care this much! That I care for you more than either of us is comfortable with!" She glared at him. "If I could snap my fingers or wiggle my nose or click my heels three times together and make it all go away, I would!" She put a lid on the frying pan, removed it, and slammed it back on again.

"I'm not loving it a whole lot, either," he said, stung, and his voice rising with it. "You think this is easy for me? I've never had a relationship last this long. Hell, I've never had whatever the hell that word means before! But you're in my life, Kate, whether I like it or not, and there doesn't seem to be a whole hell of a lot I can do about it!"

"Well, I'm sorry it's such a trial to you!"

"I didn't say that!" He registered that he was almost shouting with a faint astonishment that failed to moderate his tone. "I'm okay with it! But I'll tell you something I'm not okay with!"

"What?"

He took a deep breath, mastering his anger with an effort, the anger and the effort both still a surprise. "I am not okay with you keeping evidence quiet that pertains to an ongoing investigation."

It was her turn to say, "Huh?"

He gave it to her bluntly, without trying to soften the words. Maybe he even meant to hurt her this time, and maybe that was because he was furious and frightened that he felt guilty and maybe even a little hurt himself that she had so immediately decided that the rumors were true, and he wanted to share the pain. "I've got Howie Katelnikof sitting in a cell at the post."

"You arrested Howie?"

"Not yet, although I've got a pretty good case for him hunting caribou out of season, in amounts that I can prove are commercial. No, Howie appears to think he needs protection from whoever it is who's trying to kill him."

She stared at him for a moment. "So, who does he think is trying to kill him?" And, Katelike, returning like a little homing pigeon to the original item under discussion, "And what does that have to do with me withholding evidence in an ongoing investigation? What investigation?"

"Louis Deem's murder."

She flushed and hung her head, looking undeniably guilty. "Oh," she said weakly.

Ruthlessly he pressed his advantage. "Howie says the four aunties hired the job done, Kate."

Her head snapped back up and she stared at him, obviously shocked. "What?"

"Just when were you going to let me in on that little tidbit of information?"

At this inopportune moment, Johnny returned with the peas and onions. "Here you go, Kate," he said with false cheer. "Sorry it took me so long, the veggie box is kinda buried in moosemeat."

She was still staring at Jim with her mouth open and no sound coming out. Jim was still glaring at her. Johnny looked from one to the other and said, "You know what? Van's having some trouble with the Alaska Native Claims Settlement Act, getting the movers and shakers straight, Willie Hensley, Tyonek, all those guys. We've got a test on it tomorrow in History of Alaska class. I think I'm going to drive over and help her out."

He fetched a daypack from his bedroom and swept the books and papers on the dining table into it with more efficiency than finesse. "Don't worry about me," he said, still cheery, "I'm sure Annie'll give me dinner and a bed for the night."

Still nothing from the tableau vivant at the kitchen counter.

Johnny looked at Mutt. "You want to come with?"

Mutt cocked one ear and bent a reflective gaze on Kate and Jim, but in the end decided she didn't want to be compared to a rat deserting a sinking ship, and sneezed a polite refusal.

"Yeah, well, just try to stay out of the line of fire," Johnny said, and left the building. A moment later the Arctic Cat started up, followed immediately by the sound of it moving up the track to the road and out of earshot. Truth to tell, he was a little surprised at getting away with it, the twenty-five-mile drive alone through a cold winter night. He was heartened at this apparent evidence of faith in his maturity.

Meanwhile, back in the house, Kate had barely registered his departure. "I—," she said. "I—"

He was suddenly and thoroughly fed up. "Yeah, you," he said, rounding the counter. She slapped off the burners and turned to face him. "You don't trust me not to be sleeping with anyone else. You don't trust me enough to inform me of crucial evidence in an open murder investigation."

"But I didn't—"

"What do you trust me for, Kate?" He looked down at her and the anger whipped itself into a white-hot flame. "Oh hell, we both know what you trust me for," and he picked her up off her feet and kissed her so hard she felt her lip split.

She squirmed, her feet dangling a good foot off the floor, pushing against his shoulders, bending herself backward so she could free herself enough to speak. "No, Jim, wait—"

This only inflamed him further. "Wait, my ass," he said, and started for the stairs to the loft.

Mutt came to her feet at that, her yellow eyes wide. "You stay right there," he told her. "This is between us."

Mutt looked uncharacteristically indecisive. Attack or stay? Was Kate in trouble or not?

Meanwhile Kate began struggling in earnest. "No, Jim, stop, you don't understand—"

"I understand plenty," he said, starting up the stairs.

She was strong and slippery but he had more muscle mass than she did, as well as a longer reach, and he managed to hold on until he got them upstairs. He didn't so much drop her to the bed as throw her at it. She bounced once and tried to scramble to the floor.

"Oh no you don't," he said, and 220 pounds of outraged male dropped full on her, driving all the breath out of her body.

"Jim—," she said, her voice a squeak of sound.

"Shut up," he said, kneeing her legs apart. He was fully aroused, hard against her. "Just shut the hell up."

She fought him, she really did, but he ripped the white T-shirt over her head and left it to tangle her hands before he went for the buttons on the fly of her jeans.

"Jim, don't," she said frantically, "not like this."

"Just like this," he said, ripping open her jeans and shoving them down. He kissed her again, not so much a caress as a claiming, rough and demanding.

This time she kissed him back, biting at his lips, his jaw, setting her teeth into his throat almost hard enough to draw blood. He growled and bit back and he wasn't gentle. Her bra went somewhere and his teeth were at her breast and her panties went next, shredded and tossed. His hand was between her legs, forcing entry, demanding a response, and she couldn't stop it any more than she could stop the sun rising or the rain falling, she arched up into his caress with an involuntary groan.

He laughed once, low in his throat, his hand moving. "Yeah," he said. He could feel the heat rising up off her body in a scorching wave, and he reached for his fly, only to find her hands there before him. A second was too long to wait, and then he was there and sliding home, and she moaned, a long, drawn-out sound compounded of pleasure, relief, and fury, arching up in demand. He didn't bother with preliminaries, he started moving, long, slow, hard strokes, in and out, in and out. "Jesus," he said, breathless, "babe," he said, "Kate," he said, "oh Kate oh holy shit Kate, Kate, Kate!"

His eyes went dim but he felt her body tense like a strung bow and he heard her shout something, what he never knew and she couldn't remember. A blinding flood of pleasure and release started at the base of his spine and flooded up over his body like lava, burning out every living nerve end he had, leaving a wasteland of scorched earth and gray ash behind.

SEVENTEEN

He was gone when she woke up the next morning. On the whole, Kate was relieved. She rolled to the edge of the bed and to her dismay her legs wouldn't support her at first. When she felt confident enough to get to her feet, she staggered a little before she found her balance, and though she hated to admit it she was walking a little splay-legged on her way into the bathroom, where she ran a tub of water as hot as she could stand it. She let herself down into the tub with gingerly care and soaked until the water went tepid, by which time she was marginally mobile again and grateful for it.

The clothes she had been wearing the day before were beyond repair, even the jeans, the fly torn open and one of the buttons missing. She hunted for it but it was not to be found. With a sigh she bundled up T-shirt, jeans, bra, and panties and went downstairs. From her place in front of the long-dead fire, Mutt looked up and gave her a long yellow stare, eyebrows pointedly raised.

"You just shut up," Kate said, and went into the kitchen to find that Jim had left her a fresh pot of coffee. She thought about pouring it out and making her own, one untainted by Chopin hands.

Wasteful, though, and hypocritical. All her anger at him had been seared away over the long and tumultuous night. She winced into a seat at the table, and sipped coffee and watched the sky lighten in the east. Mostly cloudy, and the thermometer mounted outside the window showed the temperature at ten above. She'd miss the sun of the past week but she would welcome the warmer weather. They all would.

There was a tendency to dwell on the events of the previous evening. She forced those memories into a corner of her mind and shut the door on them, for now, turning her focus to the startling revelation Jim had made, that had knocked her so sideways she couldn't even— No, Kate, she thought fiercely. Focus.

All right. First, she had to consider the source. Howie was a congenital liar. Truth was such an alien concept to Howie that it might as well have a green card. Anything that came out of Howie's mouth had to be evaluated in the context of Howie's life, known associates, current misdemeanors, and planned felonies. There ought, in fact, to be a frequent felony plan for Howie. So many felonies and he got so many free days in jail. Oh wait, they already had one of those.

On the other hand, Howie was also capable of recognizing the truth as a commodity, with market value, which value might be exchanged for protective custody in the event Howie felt his life threatened.

Kate got up and poured herself some more coffee. She noted that half the coffee cake was gone, as well as a loaf of the white bread, most of the fried liver, leaving the rest congealed on the bottom of the frying pan, and all of the mashed potatoes. Jim had been hungry this morning.

She stood still, staring down at the empty and half-empty dishes.

If he could be believed, he hadn't slept with Talia Macleod.

One of the reasons she had a hard time believing it was that she couldn't understand why not. It was what Jim did, it was who he was.

He was a dog. He admitted it. For a long time, he had positively glo-
ried in it. The Father of the Park might be only an honorific, but it
was certainly true in spirit. Kate would need double the fingers and
toes to count the names of the women he'd been involved with over
the years.

So, why wouldn't he sleep with Talia Macleod? The question
was baffling, and unanswerable.

The cinnamon in the streusel topping teased at her nostrils, and
her stomach growled in response. She started to cut a wedge and
then put down the knife and got out a fork. She carried the cake tin
to the table with the fresh cup of coffee and waded in.

Howie could have made it up. It wouldn't have been the first
time he had indulged in creative fiction to divert attention from his
own indiscretions.

She shoved the coffee cake away. Then why did she feel so sick?
So apprehensive? So terrified?

She donned boots, parka, hat, and gloves and poured coffee into
an insulated mug, dosing it with enough half-and-half to make café
au lait. Mutt trotted over and Kate let them out the door, snagging a
blue plastic boat cushion from the bench on the deck on the way.

Around the back of the house she postholed through the snow to
the little bluff that overlooked the creek running in back of her
house. Frozen solid, the resulting chasm looked like a lightning bolt
imprisoned in the earth. Bare birch and aspen branches bent beneath the weight of frost, spruce trees slowly dying from the spruce
bark beetle infestation were transformed into fairy-tale homes for
elves and wizards. An arctic hare peeped out from a blueberry thicket,
nose quivering, and freezing into immobility when it felt the weight
of Mutt's interested eye. On the eastern horizon the Quilaks
loomed large and menacing, mercenaries in arms to the gathering
clouds overhead. Another battle for winter in the Park's near future
was imminent, or the portents lied.

"Why do I think he's telling the truth?" Kate said out loud. "I'm not even fighting it."

For some reason, she remembered the trip down the river, talking to the Kaltaks, the Jeffersons, the Rileys. As sure as she was sitting here, they were to the last man, woman, and child convinced that the Johansens were responsible for the attacks. And to the last man, woman, and child they were equally convinced that the Johansens had been brought to account for their crimes.

Kate was afraid that they were right. Someone had decided on their own to take care of the problem.

"Like the aunties," she said out loud, feeling sick again. She swallowed hard. "Like the aunties might have taken care of Louis Deem."

Kate thought back to her visit to Vidar Johansen, that cranky, lonely old man, the village built by his family emptying out two and three at a time around him. The school was gone. The post office was gone, mail delivered now to Niniltna. She could see the Johansen boys of Tikani, descendants of some of the oldest blood in the Park, getting hungrier and hungrier, too proud and too contrary to ask for help, until the only option seemed to be to forage for food and fuel wherever they could find it. From whomever they had to take it, even their neighbors.

And even if they hadn't, which she didn't know for a fact, she could see how they would be the obvious suspects.

If it was the Johansens, it would make sense that all the attacks occurred south of Niniltna, none of them north. Efficient predators know enough not to hunt too close to home. It frightens the game.

An eagle soared overhead on outspread wings, a soft presence on the minimal winter thermals generated by the rising sun. He spotted the hare and dipped his right wing, banking down into a swooping, tightening spiral. The hare vanished, snow falling from the trembling branches of the blueberry bush. The eagle straightened out and beat his wings to regain his original altitude, moving on. There would be another hare, or a squirrel, or a fox. There always was. Eagles, card-carrying carnivores, scavengers, opportunists, weren't picky about their food.

If someone had in fact constituted themselves judge, jury, and executioner in the matter of the snow machine attacks on the Kanuyaq River, that someone would have to be identified and warned against such action in future. She remembered Jim's complaints about Park rats taking justice into their own hands. Demetri attacking Smith for blading his beaver line. Bonnie Jeppsen keying the truck of the kid who as a prank put a dead salmon into the drop box. Arliss Kalifonsky putting a (probably well deserved, Kate thought) bullet into Mickey the next time he raised his hand to her. Dan O'Brien kicking a poacher's ass for trying to sell him a bear bladder.

They were all classic examples of Newton's third law, and a hundred years ago these equal and opposite reactions would have earned nothing more than an approving nod from passersby, even if those passersby were territorial policemen. In their time the TPs were even more thin on the ground than their descendants, the state troopers, and welcomed all the help they got so long as it didn't make them more work.

Today, there was a trooper post in the Park, with a trooper assigned to it full time, and the Bill of Rights was more than just a paper under glass in the National Archives in Washington, D.C. Jim was right. He should be the first call people made, and for a while he had been, or so it seemed to Kate. What had changed?

A fat, glossy raven spoke from a nearby treetop. He had a lot to say in croaks and clicks and chuckles, slipping effortlessly from one raven dialect to another. Mutt's ears twitched and she gave the raven a hard look. The raven chattered on regardless, not unaware but not afraid, either. Even Mutt couldn't climb a tree.

"Maybe Talia turned him down," Kate said. That was it, it had to be. Jim had made his move, and Talia had declined with thanks.

Kate remembered Macleod's manner with the men on the board that morning. She'd definitely had a thing with Demetri at some point, and she'd been flirting with Old Sam, probably fifty years her senior. She remembered with painful clarity the intimacy between Jim and Macleod she'd seen at Bobby's house.

No, Kate didn't think Talia Macleod would have turned down Jim Chopin. She would have tripped Jim and beat him to the ground first.

And then another thought struck her, almost blinding in its force. "Oh, god," she said. "Oh, god."

Mutt looked at her in concern. It wasn't a tone of voice she was accustomed to hearing. She nudged Kate with her head and gave a soft, anxious whine.

"I believe Howie? And I don't believe Jim?"

She had to close her eyes while the world righted itself around her, and when she opened them again she was determined to banish thoughts of Jim Chopin from her mind, at least for the present. She reacquired her train of thought and held on grimly, determined not to be thrown off track this time.

Park rats were a self-sufficient bunch, no question, but Kate would never have described them as lawless. In fact, out here on what was still pretty much a frontier, people had more of a tendency to abide by the rules than not. When your nearest neighbor lives five miles away, the golden rule in particular became not just a nice adage but a way of life. There was no phone to pick up and call 911, even if there were a firehouse or a hospital within driving distance, which there wasn't, and even if there was a road between the firehouse or the hospital and your house, which there also wasn't. When you got into trouble you were going to need help. You wouldn't get it if you had a reputation for breaking the rules, for helping yourself to a neighbor's vegetable patch when she was out fishing, say, or making off with a cord of wood when they were on a Costco run, or cleaning out the cache when they were in Anchorage getting their eyes checked. Or draining their fuel tanks when they were on vacation.

So where was this coming from?

Her butt was starting to go numb and Kate was rising to her feet to return to the house when another thought stopped her in her tracks.

Louis Deem. Shot on a deserted stretch of Park road by a still unknown assassin. Louis Deem, embezzler, confidence man, thief, triple wife murderer. Louis Deem, who had lost no opportunity to abuse and victimize any Park rat unfortunate enough to cross his path.

Was Louis Deem's murder where all this began?

She turned with decision and made for the garage.

Kate let herself in Auntie Vi's front door, only to be confronted by a stranger. "Oh," she said. "Hello. I'm looking for Auntie Vi."

The stranger—stocky, medium height, dark hair and eyes—had a broad grin that came too easily. "Don't shoot," he said genially, holding his hands up. "I'm a paying guest."

Kate smiled politely. "No problem."

The smile, set in an oval face with almond-shaped hazel eyes set on high flat cheekbones and a wide, expressive mouth, all of it framed with a short cap of black silk, the husky rasp of her voice, the whole package made him straighten up and step in for a closer look. "I'm Dick Gallagher. Hey, cool dog." He stretched out a hand and snapped his fingers. "Here, boy."

Mutt looked at him, a long, steady, considering gaze.

"Heh," Gallagher said, and dropped his hand. "He doesn't take kindly to strangers, I guess."

"She's a girl, for starters," Kate said. "I recognize your name, I think. You're working for Talia Macleod out at Suulutaq, aren't you?"

"That's right," he said. "Good job, too. Pays well."

"Congratulations," Kate said, looking around for Auntie Vi.

He hooked a thumb at the kitchen. "I could even afford to buy you breakfast. Interested?"

"I've eaten, thanks. Is Auntie Vi here?"

"I haven't seen her since breakfast. Come on, a cup of coffee can't hurt."

It had been a bitter cold ride in and she could use a warm-up, so she followed him down the passageway to the kitchen and sat down at the table opposite him.

"So what's your name?" he said, getting a plate of French toast and bacon from the oven.

"Kate," she said. "Kate Shugak."

His fork stopped halfway to his mouth. "Kate Shugak," he said.

"Yeah. Where you from?"

He shrugged, and the fork continued its upward motion. "Outside." He grinned again, although this time it seemed to lack its previous warmth. "I understand that's what I'm supposed to say."

She registered a slight tingling of her Spidey sense. She shrugged, watching his face. "It's what you can say."

He cocked his head a little. "Meaning if I do, I must be hiding something?"

She surprised both of them by laughing, a rough husk of amusement that by the appreciative gleam in his eye he found as attractive as the rest of her. "If you aren't, you'd be the only cheechako in the Park who isn't." She added, "And maybe the only one in Alaska." She looked at him, her face a genial mask. "How long you been here?"

"Couple months now."

"You like it?"

He mopped up the last of the syrup with the last piece of French toast and pointed it at her. "I'll tell you, Kate," he said, "I fucking love it. I've never seen a place with more opportunities to make a buck. Like I'm headed out on a snow machine trip today, up and down the river with my boss going to the villages to talk to the people about the mine, and I get overtime for that. Man." He laughed. "I like it all right. I got a warm place to sleep, plenty to eat, and"—he winked at her—"I'm making new friends every day. A man can get ahead here. Yeah," he said, regarding his forkful of food with a satisfaction that verged on complacency, "I fucking love it here. I'm going to stay forever."

Or at least long enough to make enough money so he could spend the rest of his life deep-sea fishing in Manzanillo, Kate thought. "You're what we call a boomer," she said.

He looked quizzical. "Baby boomer, you mean?"

"No. Just a boomer. Somebody who comes to Alaska to make good, and who does very well."

His smile hardened momentarily, only to return at double wattage. "Nothing wrong with a man making a good living."

"Nothing at all," she said cordially.

She agreed with him too easily and he didn't trust her response, which proved he wasn't entirely stupid. Still, he was incapable of stopping his eyes from drifting down over her. They lingered on her chest for a moment, and then jerked back up, to the thin, white scar that bisected her throat. He looked at her face, and back at the scar. He opened his mouth to say something else when Auntie Vi slammed in the kitchen door. She saw Kate and stopped in her tracks. "Katya."

"Auntie." Kate rose. "Something we need to talk about, Auntie."

Auntie Vi snorted. "You talk. I work." She filled the thermos she carried full of hot coffee.

"Great breakfast, Vi," Gallagher said heartily. "I don't know when I've eaten a better one."

Auntie Vi looked at him and snorted again. "You pay for what you get here." She slammed out again. Kate didn't move fast enough and almost got her nose caught in the door. She heard Gallagher chuckle behind her.

Kate found Auntie Vi mending gear in the net loft, a room over her garage that was insulated and Sheetrocked but unpainted. Heat came from a small Toyo stove, and the radio was on and currently tuned in to Park Air. Bobby's voice was transmuted by digital wizardry from its usual sonic boom to a more intimate and somehow sexier rumble, a velvet rasp of sound that made you listen whether you wanted to or not. NPR had missed out when they hadn't re-cruited Bobby Clark to replace Bob Edwards on *Morning Edition*. Of course, Bobby could be just a trifle more incendiary than Bob. "Okay, all you tree-hugging, bunny-loving, granola-eating, Birkenstock-wearing Naderites, this one's for you," he said, "the only song worth a greenie shit," followed by the seductive opening licks of Three Dog Night's "Out in the Country." Bobby, Kate thought, was the living embodiment of Emerson's dictum that a foolish consistency was the hobgoblin of little minds.

Drift nets were heaped in orderly piles all over the floor, the one currently undergoing repair draped over a couple of sawhorses. Auntie Vi sat on a straight-backed wooden chair, head bent over hands wielding a hand-carved bone needle with unerring dexterity, translucent green monofilament almost magically assembling itself into a curtain of mesh whose individual cells were the exact size to snare a red salmon right behind the gills. "I'm busy," she said without looking up. "What you want?"

Okay, no point in not being equally blunt. "Howie Katelnikof told Jim Chopin that you and the other aunties hired someone to kill Louis Deem."

Auntie Vi didn't answer. The silence stretched out. Kate looked hard at the top of Auntie Vi's unresponsive head. "Auntie, did you hear me?"

"Nothing wrong with my ears."

Kate began to feel a slow burn. "Anything you'd like to say about it?" Mutt, standing next to her, moved a pace forward, putting a firm shoulder in between the two women.

"What to say?"

"Oh, I don't know," Kate said. "How about, Howie's full of shit? How about, Howie's trying to buy his way out of getting caught with a commercial load of caribou taken out of season? How about, Howie's a little weasel who'd sell out his own mother to stay out of jail? I'm wide open for suggestions here."

"Howie got no mother."

Kate looked at Auntie Vi's bent head with a dawning horror. "Jesus Christ, Auntie. Is it true?"

"Howie say who we suppose to hired?"

There was a short, charged silence. "No," Kate said. "Not yet."

Auntie Vi finished mending one hole and put down the needle to shake the cramp out of her fingers. "Tell something to me, Katya." She looked up for the first time, and Kate almost fell back a step from the anger she saw there.

"What you do, Katya? Tell me what you do. Louis Deem monster. Monster," she said again, with emphasis, making it clear. "Liar. Thief. Murderer. Murder three wives. Three. Jessie. Ruthie. Mary. All dead, by his hand. Everybody know this, Katya. And nobody do nothing."

"Not nothing, Auntie," Kate said. "Not nothing. He was brought to trial twice."

Auntie Vi dismissed this with a contemptuous wave of her hand.

Her button black eyes burned and her face was flushed. "What that matter? They let him go. You always let him go, Katya." She looked straight at Kate. "You always let him go."

"Auntie, I—"

"Then he hurt those two girls. Those two babies. That one she comes to me crying her eyes out. She beg me for help. What do we do, Katya? You tell me. What do we do?"

Kate tried to say something and failed.

"What you do, Katya?" Auntie Vi said, and the resentment in her voice was as unmistakable as it was flaying. "What do you do?"

She took up the needle again and reached for the next hole in the gear.

Kate stood there, shocked, speechless.

"Working here," Auntie Vi said. "You bother me. Go."

Kate went.

Outside, she was just in time to see Gallagher and Macleod loading up their snow machines.

Macleod looked up and gave her a warm smile. "Kate," she said.

Kate made a heroic effort and managed a civil reply. "I hear you're making a trip downriver."

Macleod nodded. "Down first, one day in each village, back and overnight here, and then up to Ahtna, same."

"Spreading the gospel according to Global Harvest Resources Inc.," Kate said.

Macleod shrugged, unfazed by Kate's less than enthusiastic tone. "I told Global Harvest that if they wanted a successful operation they'd better get to know the neighbors."

"The 'Burbs know you're coming?"

"Oh yeah," Macleod said. "We've got town meetings set up everywhere we're stopping, and someplace warm to lay our heads every night. People have been pretty welcoming."

"So far," Kate said.

"So far," Macleod said agreeably.

Kate nodded at the rifle in the scabbard on Macleod's snow machine. "Keep that handy. There have been a couple of attacks on the river lately."

"Yeah, Jim told me."

In spite of herself Kate stiffened. "Did he."

"Yeah, I checked in with him before coming down here to pick up Dick. He wasn't happy when I told him what we were up to. He told me about the attacks and to be careful." Her ravishing smile flashed out again. "Good guy, Jim. For a trooper. Not to mention hot as a pistol."

Dick Gallagher's head whipped around at that, and his expression wasn't pretty, but Macleod didn't see. She pressed the starter and the engine roared into life. "See you, Kate!"

Kate stepped back as Macleod accelerated down the road, followed, at first tentatively and then with more assurance, by Gallagher.

Kate watched them until they were out of sight. "Yeah," she said, her lips tight. "See you."

EIGHTEEN

Y ou knew," she said to Jim. "You knew and you didn't tell me."

"You knew I was Bernie's alibi," he said.

"I sure as hell didn't know Bernie'd dragged the aunties into it," she said hotly.

"Neither did I."

She glared at him.

He leaned forward and stared back, his chin out. "Neither did I, Kate," he said again, slowly and with great deliberation, "and I'd appreciate it if you'd take my word for that, too."

A sudden rush of color scorched her face. She tried to ignore it. "Have you asked Howie who this alleged assassin was?"

"Have you asked the aunties who they hired?"

They glared some more.

"Howie's just down the hall," Jim said. "Shall we?"

"Let's," Kate said.

Oh man," Howie said when he saw Kate. "Come on, Jim, buddy, there's no need for this." He scrambled up on his bunk, pressing himself into a corner. "Don't you come near me, Kate," he said, his voice rising. "Don't you do it."

Jim opened the door to the cell and Kate sauntered in like a small but very deadly tiger, and, very much like a big cat, curled up at the end of Howie's bed. She crossed one leg over the other and linked her hands on her knee. She looked as if she felt quite at home, with no plans to leave anytime soon. She even smiled at him.

He might have whimpered. His eyes looked wild and he was definitely sweating. He gave Jim a pleading look. "Jim, come on, man."

Jim leaned against the door and crossed his arms. "You're not under arrest, Howie. You can walk out of here any time you want. You want?"

Howie licked his lips.

Howie Katelnikof was a guy who never looked as tall as he was. He had a hard time standing up straight and an even harder one looking anyone straight in the eye. No matter how often he showered his hair was always greasy, and no matter how often he changed his clothes they always smelled of sweat, cigarette smoke, and beer. He might have been a good-looking guy, he possessed the requisites, height and weight proportional, thick hair, regular features, but his character had forced his eyes a little too close together, had pushed his chin just a fraction too far back. His character oozed out of his pores and stained him for what he was, a wannabe crook who'd watched *Ocean's Eleven* so many times he thought he was George Clooney when, as Bobby said, "Who he really is is Steve Buscemi in *Fargo*."

"Let's talk, Howie," Kate said.

"I doanwanna," Howie said.

"Relax, Howie," Kate said, and reached over to pat his knee. He cringed. "I don't want to talk about the time you took a shot at me and my kid and damn near killed my dog. I'm not ready for that

226

conversation yet. Someday. I promise you." She patted his knee again. "But not today."

A bead of sweat drooped from his nose. He kept his face turned away. He might have been trembling. He looked like he felt the jaws of the snake closing around him after he'd been dropped into the glass cage.

Still in that light, good-humored, terrifying voice, Kate said, "What's this Jim tells me about the aunties hiring somebody to kill Louis?"

"I didn't do it," Howie said.

"What didn't you do?" Kate said. " 'Cause, forgive me, Howie, but the list is getting kind of long. You didn't shoot at my truck? You didn't kill Mac Devlin? You didn't hire out to the aunties to kill your best bud Louis Deem?"

"I didn't kill Louis!" He came out of the corner, realized how close that put him to Kate, and shrank back in again. "I didn't do it," he said.

"But you're saying somebody did."

He nodded sullenly.

"So the aunties hired somebody to kill Louis Deem that wasn't you."

He nodded, then shook his head, then nodded again.

"Then how do you know about it? Excuse me, but it doesn't sound like the kind of thing they're going to drop casually into the conversation, Howie. Especially into a conversation with you."

"How come you're always so mean?" It was almost a wail.

"Because you don't deserve anything better, you little weasel," Kate said.

Jim cleared his throat. She turned to look at him. He shook his head. She almost flipped him off, but he was right. In this instance, insulting Howie probably wasn't the method of interrogation most productive of results.

"Howie," she said, turning back to him, "come on. You know you're gonna tell me, one way or another. Either in here, where you've got Jim and the Fifth Amendment on your side." She smiled again, and again he cowered from it. "Or out there somewhere, with just you, and me, and none of those messy Miranda warnings to confuse either one of us."

She waited. Jim waited. Howie sniveled. It was disgusting. Kate clicked her tongue impatiently and got up to grab Howie a bunch of toilet paper. She shoved it into his hands. "Here. Blow your nose."

He did, smearing snot on his cheeks.

"Jesus Christ, Howie," Kate said, disgusted, "can't you even blow your own nose right? Come on. What did you mean when you said that the aunties hired someone to kill Louis Deem?"

He looked at the crumpled ball of tissue. "I dint do it. I dint kill Louis."

"Okay," Kate said. "Say for the sake of argument I believe you. Who did?"

"I don't know." He looked up. "By the time I found him, he was dead."

Back in Jim's office, he said, "How much of that do you believe?"

Kate dropped into a chair and rubbed her face with both hands, and then scrubbed at her scalp for good measure, ruffling the short cap of thick black hair until she looked like an angry panther. She shook her head and it obediently ordered itself again. Was there anything, he thought, that didn't do exactly and precisely what Kate Shugak told it to?

"I don't know," she said. "I talked to Auntie Vi this morning."

"And?"

"Oh, god," she said miserably.

"Did she say they did?" he asked, disbelieving.

She looked up. "She didn't say they didn't. And she gave me to understand that if they did have him killed, it was my fault for not doing it first."

"Christ." He went behind his desk and sat down with a thump. "It's the fucking Sopranos in the fucking Park."

"Okay," Kate said, clinging to sanity, "say they did hire him. Do you believe him when he says he didn't do it?"

"There was that tire track at the scene that matched Howie's Suburban. But you know as well as I do that a tire track all by itself isn't conclusive. Hell, Louis could have taken Howie's ride to go up to the Step to see Dan when I sprung him that day."

"Why wouldn't he take his own vehicle?"

"It was at home, fifty miles from here. Howie picked him up. Or he was supposed to."

Kate thought about it. "Howie sure had opportunity, Jim," she said. "And if the aunties paid him to do it, he had motive. And there must be a dozen guns out at Louis's house. He had means."

He looked at her. "Do you think he did it?"

Mutt, as was not her custom, had not gone straight to Jim and slobbered all over him when they'd arrived at the post. Instead, she had remained at Kate's side. Now she looked up at Kate with a steady yellow gaze. Solidarity, sister. "I don't know," she said. "He's just— He's such a little weasel, Jim. This is Howie Katelnikof we're talking about here, the Park rat most famous for achieving mobility while lacking a vertebral column. It's kind of hard for me to imagine him setting out to kill in cold blood."

"He took a shot at you," Jim said.

"From one moving truck, at another," she said. "He got lucky. Or maybe even unlucky."

"How so?"

"You know how hard it is to shoot a stationary target. Shooting and hitting a moving target is almost impossible, even for an expert, and he's no expert. Much as I loathe acquitting Howie of malice, he could have meant it like a shot across the bows. Throw a scare into us and then go home and tell Louis he did it. Doesn't mean he won't pay for it one day," she added.

"Never for one moment imagined otherwise," he said.

"And though Louis sure as hell wasn't anyone's nominee for humanitarian of the year, he was the closest thing Howie had to a brother. He fed him, he housed him. What little social structure Howie had, Louis gave him."

"He's still got the house," Jim said. "Him and Willard, still living on what Louis inherited from his second wife following her untimely death."

"You think Louis could have threatened to kick them out for some reason? And Howie killed him before he did?" Kate considered this. "Possible, I guess." She shook her head. "I don't know. If the aunties admit they did hire him, you can charge him."

"And if I charged him, I'd have to charge them with conspiracy to commit."

She straightened and looked at him, a sick expression on her face. "Oh. Of course. I . . . I didn't think of that."

"It's all I have been thinking about," he said grimly, "ever since Howie made me believe it might be true." He paused. "Well. Mostly all I've been thinking about."

Again she blushed, another scorcher. "There is no way," she said steadily, ignoring his last words. "There is no way you're going to march my aunties into a jail cell on the say-so of a loser like Howie Katelnikof."

"I've already winked at the law once in the murder of Louis Deem," he said. "I won't do it again, Kate."

"You'll do it for Bernie but you won't do it for Auntie Vi?" she said angrily.

He got up, came around the desk, and yanked her to her feet. She shoved her hands against his chest but he wasn't trying to kiss her. He shook her once, hard enough to rock her head back on her shoulders. "This is not about that, Kate. What happens there"—a stab of a finger in the general direction of the homestead—"stays there. What happens here is something else. Know the difference."

This time she took the bait. "How could you do that, Jim?"

"I didn't do it alone, Kate."

"I said no!" Kate said. She made an effort and said more calmly, "I said no. Lots of times."

"You turned off the stove," he said.

"I— What?"

"When I started coming for you," he said. "You turned off the stove."

She opened her mouth and nothing came out.

"Plus you came three times." He walked to the door and opened it. "We were both angry, Kate, but don't try to turn it into something it wasn't."

She found herself on the other side of his office door without knowing quite how she got there. The door shut in her face.

Maggie gave her a quizzical look.

"I hate men," Kate said.

Maggie shook her head. "I hear you, honey," she said mournfully. "Oh, how I hear you."

NINETEEN

Over the next three days Kate went in turn to all the aunties, Balasha, Edna, Joy, and even Auntie Vi again. To a woman, they stonewalled her.

"They're stonewalling me," she said with incredulity that evening. "It's like they've rehearsed or something."

"They probably have," Jim said without looking up from George R. R. Martin's *A Feast for Crows,* which he was rereading because Martin was taking an excruciatingly long time to get the fifth book out, at which time Jim might finally learn what had happened to Jon and Arya. It was a good book and a great series and he felt that rereading it was a lot more productive and infinitely more enjoyable than entering into a conversation that he felt in his bones was only going to go in circles until it started biting its own tail.

"They're stonewalling me," she said again, this time emphasizing the last word. "Me!"

"Uh-huh," Jim said.

"You should care more about this," she said, glaring down at his bent head.

There had been a lot of glaring going on lately, Johnny thought. He was keeping his own head down over his books at the dining table, praying that this night at least they'd get to eat dinner before the fight started. Place reminded him of an armed camp lately. "Place reminds me of an armed camp lately," he said out loud.

"Shut up," Kate and Jim said together.

"Okay," Johnny said, and went back to Robert Frost.

"Is Howie still at the post?"

"Yup."

Frost was a cranky old fart with a forked tongue, and you were never really confident that he was saying what you thought he was, Johnny thought. They were each supposed to memorize one Frost poem, recite it in class, and then lead a discussion on it for their lit final. His turn was fast approaching and it was crunch time for picking the poem.

"He's still afraid someone is going to kill him?"

"That's what he says."

He'd been considering one of the shorter poems, like "Fire and Ice" because of the whole kaboom thing, or "Once, by the Pacific" because he liked the monster image, or maybe "Design," because the fat white spider would freak out all the girls except Van, and that would be fun.

"Because somebody shot at Mac? And because he thinks they thought they were shooting at him?"

"Something's burning."

Kate charged back into the kitchen and yanked the moose roast out of the oven. She'd been cooking a lot lately, taking both his and Jim's turn in the rotation. The food had been really good, too, and there had been a lot of it.

He liked "Two Tramps in Mud Time" best but it was too long. Maybe "In a Glass of Cider." He read through it again. It was short enough. Maybe too short. Was there enough there to discuss? It had that whole "seize the day" thing going on. Seize the bubble thing, anyway.

"I can think offhand of a hundred people who'd like to take a punch at Howie. But shoot him? Have you investigated the possibility that whoever was shooting at Mac actually meant to? Shoot at Mac?"

"I'm looking. I'm not finding. He was a pretty solitary guy, no wife, no kids, no girlfriend. His social life seemed to center around the Roadhouse and nobody there says any different."

He hadn't seen Dick Gallagher around lately. He wondered if he was out at the Suulutaq trailer. Creepy, hanging out where a guy had got shot. He'd only seen Dick a couple of times since he'd gone out to the Roadhouse. He was secretly relieved that he hadn't been required to bring the guy home, and at the same time he was puzzled at Dick's refusals to his invitations. Polite but definite, he'd excused himself on the grounds of work. "Gotta make a good impression," he'd said, winking.

He winked a lot, Doyle did. Dick did.

"Howie can't think for one moment that the aunties would shoot at him, can he?"

"Don't know."

"I mean, why would they? If they did—"

There was sudden silence in the kitchen. It lasted long enough for both men to look up.

Kate was standing with a cast-iron lid in one hand and a large spoon in the other and an arrested expression on her face.

"What?" Jim and Johnny said together. Jim even looked over his shoulder to make sure no one had driven into the clearing. "What's wrong, Kate?"

Kate put the spoon down and the lid back on the pot. "I know why he's scared."

"Howie? Why?"

"Of course," she said, unheeding. "Of course, that explains every-thing. Not who did it, no, but all the rest of it." She smacked her fore-head. "How could I have been so stupid not to see it before? It's Howie all over!"

She went for the door, stamped on her boots, donned parka and hat, and grabbed her gloves. "Go ahead and eat, guys, it's all ready. I've got to go somewhere."

She opened the door and Old Sam Dementieff was standing there in his ragged Carhartt bibs, Sorels picked and pocked and nipped from so many years of use that they were perilously close to being ventilated, and a sheepskin flap cap with the chin strap hang-ing loose. He didn't look happy.

"Sam," Kate said, startled. "I didn't hear you drive up."

He looked past her at Jim. "Talia Macleod has been murdered."

Talia Macleod and Dick Gallagher had spent the last three days on the river, traveling from village to village by snow machine. They'd gone south first, Double Eagle, Chulyin, Potlatch, and Red Run, retracing Kate's recent journey, after which the plan was to overnight in Niniltna and head back north. The tour would end in Ahtna, where a town meeting had been scheduled and the chief op-erating officer of Global Harvest was scheduled to appear personally to answer questions and address the concerns of the Park rats about the mine.

It had been a good plan. Apart from the fact that in the middle of a cold, dark winter Bush Alaskans were glad to see anybody, Park rats also liked it when people who wanted something came to them. Bush Alaskans spent half their lives four-wheeling, snowmachining, boating, driving, and flying to Fairbanks and Anchorage and Juneau when the legislature was in session, to buy food and supplies, to go to school, to go to the hospital, to attend Native corporation shareholder meetings and the Alaska Federation of Natives' annual convention, and to bang a shoe on their legislative representative's desk. Park rats traveled from home so often not because they wanted to but because they had to.

Now someone wanted to dig a big-ass hole in their backyard, and that someone came to them, one village at a time. They could have rented the Egan Convention Center in Anchorage and left it up to the villagers to get there, and to pay to get there, stay there, and eat there. This willingness to show up in person in even the tiniest village predisposed even the most cautious, conservative and conservation-minded Park rat in their favor. Global Harvest, Kate thought, did indeed know what they were doing.

The villages south of Niniltna were bigger than the villages north, each of them on or near the mouth of a creek with a substantial salmon run, each built on what had been a traditional fish camp, summer home for the tribe before it packed up in the fall and headed into the mountains after the caribou. The villages were permanent fixtures now, each with a school, an airstrip, and a post office, even if that post office was in someone's living room. For the most part they practiced a subsistence lifestyle, but that lifestyle wouldn't have been possible without the quarterly Association dividend, the annual state permanent fund dividend, and heavy federal subsidies for health, education, and fuel. Some residents, like Ike Jefferson, had to make ends meet by moving to Anchorage for the winter. Some eked out a living trapping and tanning hides and selling them at the fur auction during Fur Rendezvous. Most of them fished salmon during the summer and halibut and crab in the fall, either on their own boats or pulling down a crew share on someone else's, and if they didn't get their moose that fall, they didn't eat meat that winter.

None of the villages were over 200 in population, Red Run the largest at 197, Tikani the smallest, the last official count showing 29, although Kate thought the next census might show one, if Vidar lived that long. Macleod and Gallagher had gone to the southern-most village first, Red Run, and spent the night. They'd spent the next day at Potlatch and Chulyin, overnighting in Chulyin. The third day they'd spent in Double Eagle, and since the weather, while overcast, was still relatively mild and since it was only a little over thirty miles, they had decided to come on into Niniltna and spend the night there.

The scheduled town meeting in Double Eagle had taken place in the school gymnasium, as all such events in the smaller villages did, the gym being the only place big enough to hold all the villagers at once. People had stayed so long and asked so many questions that some had started to bring in food, and the event had turned into a potluck dinner. Someone had brought in a boom box, and somebody else had gotten out the basketballs, and there was dancing at one end of the court and a nonstop game of horse at the other.

"It was about nine, maybe nine thirty when things broke up," Dick Gallagher told them. He looked strained, his face washed-out and clammy. "Talia told me she was going to go on ahead, and for me to stay behind and make sure any stragglers got the handout and the raffle ticket for the two nights in Anchorage, and then follow her into Niniltna."

"There's a raffle?" Old Sam said, perking up.

They were at the post. Dick Gallagher was the one who had brought the news to Bernie's. Old Sam had been there, had brought Dick Gallagher to the post and called Maggie in to babysit him, and had come for Jim. Kate and Mutt had accompanied the two of them back to town.

Gallagher nodded wearily. "Yeah. For two nights in Anchorage. Well. There was supposed to be. I don't know now."

"You were comfortable with traveling from Double Eagle to Niniltna on your own?" Jim said. "I thought this was your first time on the river. Not to mention on a snow machine."

237

"I was a little nervous about that," Gallagher said, "but Talia said that I'd be okay so long as I remembered to turn right and stuck to the river." He gave a ghost of a smile. "It's kinda hard to miss."

"The raffle's for two nights in Anchorage?" Old Sam said.

"Yeah, plus airfare, plus a rental car, plus a thousand dollars in cash. I don't know, we sold the tickets up and down the river. I guess it's still on. I'll have to get hold of Mr. O'Malley to find out. I imagine he'll want me to step in, at least for now."

Kate, standing in a corner with her arms crossed, trying to keep out of Jim's line of sight, thought that in spite of the horror of the situation Gallagher sounded just a little bit complacent about his step up in the world. She also thought he was seriously jumping the gun. Global Harvest had thus far displayed a savvy that Kate had never seen equaled by any Outside organization bent on development in the Bush, and she didn't think their management was going to endow a cheechako like Gallagher with higher powers. For one thing, he didn't have the face time or the street cred that Talia Macleod had had in Alaska. For another, he didn't have the time served in the Park.

"What time did you leave the gym?" Jim said. He was typing Gallagher's words into a statement form on his computer as they spoke.

"About ten thirty, I think. I don't have a watch. Everyone was gone, and I packed up the leftover handouts. Talia was always very anal about not leaving trash behind. I went outside and packed everything in the sled and took off."

"Which way did you go?"

"Well, the school's kind of back from the river."

"We know," Old Sam said.

"Of course. Sorry. I didn't go through the village, I took the creek and went around."

"Why not go through the village?"

Gallagher hesitated. "Well, to tell you the truth, Sergeant Chopin, I'm not real good with driving the snow machine yet. I'd just as soon not turn myself loose where there's people everywhere. You know?"

Either because Gallagher was afraid he'd hurt someone, or because he was afraid he'd make himself look bad in front of the villagers, Kate thought.

"So you took the creek to the river," Jim said. "Then what?"

"Well, it's only a couple hundred feet to the river, and it was real dark, the trees and the bushes hanging over everything and all. I didn't see her on the way down."

"What did you see?"

"Her snow machine. Of course at first I didn't know it was hers, so far all of them look alike to me. It's like women and cars, you know? Show me a female who can tell the difference between a Chevy Silverado and a Ford Ranger and I'll marry her." He smiled. "I'm like that with snow machines."

No one smiled back, and his own vanished. "But you recognized Talia's," Jim said. "How'd that happen?"

"Well, it was just sitting there, stuck in a snowbank, idling, with nobody on it and nobody around. I pulled up next to it and I saw her stuff in the trailer. I shouted for her a couple of times and there was no answer. So then I got to thinking that maybe she hit a bump and fell off and the snow machine kept going. So I went back up the creek, slow like, you know, looking for her." He paused, and swallowed.

"And?"

"And I found her," Gallagher said. "Both parts."

There was a momentary silence. "Both parts?" Jim said.

"Yeah." His face was pale and damp with perspiration, and his clasped hands were grinding against each other. "Her body was lying over to my left, kind of close to the bank, in the shadows, you know? So it was no wonder I didn't see her on the way down." He swallowed again.

"Want some water or something?"

"No, no, I'm okay, it's just, it's so godawful, Sergeant Chopin."

"What was, Mr. Gallagher?"

Gallagher looked up and said, "Her head was missing."

"What?" Jim said.

Gallagher nodded. "I found it about twenty feet up the creek."

Kate felt Old Sam look at her and turned her head to meet his eyes. It was the first time she'd ever seen that expression on his face.

"I went and got someone from the village to stay with her, and then I came back. I know you hang out a lot at that bar out the end of the road, Sergeant Chopin, so I figured I had a good chance of finding you there. You weren't but Sam was, and he brought me here."

He spread his hands. "The rest you know."

TWENTY

They left at first light, Jim on one snow machine, Kate on another, Matt Grosdidier on a third hauling an empty sled. Dick Gallagher was still asleep at Auntie Vi's, and Jim said there was no reason to get him up. They were in Double Eagle well before noon. Ken Kaltak came out to greet them, looking as if he hadn't had a lot of sleep. "Thank christ you're here so I can be done with this freak show."

"Did anybody touch anything?"

"Not after I got there," Ken said flatly. "I can't answer for before. It doesn't look like it, but I'm not a cop. Kate, Matt."

"Hey, Ken. How was she . . ." Kate's voice failed her. "How was it done?"

Ken shook his head. "This you gotta see for yourself."

He led the way to the creek, a narrow, winding affair between low banks, those banks thick with willow, alder, and spruce, all of them drooping beneath the weight of a heavy layer of snow. They turned the path of the creek into a low, cold tunnel into which even the noontime sun could not reach. Jim's head brushed a branch and snow fell silently down his neck. He stooped a little and walked on.

"Stay," Kate told Mutt, and followed him.

Talia's head was where Gallagher had said it was, about twenty feet away from her body. The face was turned away but the open portion of the neck revealed frozen blood and tissue and the bony beginnings of a brain stem. It was not a pretty sight. Kate heard Matt, just behind her, take a sharp breath.

Her body lay on its back, arms and legs splayed wide. Her snow machine was nosefirst in the snowbank on the right-hand side of the creek. The trailer had jackknifed, probably when the snow machine had run into the bank, but it hadn't overturned.

Jim bent over the windshield and ran his flashlight over every inch of the clear plastic. He stepped back and walked back up the creek. "Kate, you take the right side. I'll take the left."

"Got it."

Ken and Matt watched, Ken with his attention firmly fixed on the overhanging trees, Matt looking a little green around the gills, a color that matched one of the colors in his Cinemascope black eye. About halfway between the snow machine and the body, Kate said, "Here."

She tried not to mess up the snow next to it, but it was a futile effort. It probably didn't matter, as with the warming weather there had been intermittent snow showers over the past two days and there wasn't much to see.

She heard Jim's breath at her shoulder and pointed with a gloved finger, slightly trembling. "See it?"

His breath exhaled on a long sigh. "Yeah. Line for mending gear, right?"

"Yes."

They regarded it in silence. "You can get this stuff anywhere," he said.

She nodded. "Yes," she said again, a little mournfully. "Everybody has a spool lying around. I've got some in the garage. I think I even saw some spools at the Bingleys' store, in that corner in the back where she's got all the nonedible stuff."

"So no possible chance of tracking down which spool this came from."

"Probably not, but that's for the crime lab to say. You never know, Jim, they can do some pretty amazing stuff."

"Let me get the camera."

He was back a moment later, and took a series of photos. It took longer than it usually did because of the cold—he had to keep tucking the camera inside his parka to warm it up so the shutter would work.

They found a corresponding length wrapped around the base of a tree opposite the first one. Jim took more photos.

"About the right height," he said, measuring the top of the creek bank against his height. "Three feet, maybe?"

"The windshield," she said.

"Yeah, but it's swept, it doesn't go straight up, it slants. It hits the mono hard enough, the mono slides right up the windshield and snaps back. She must have been kneeling on the seat for it to catch her right on the neck like that."

"If she'd been sitting," Kate said, "the mono could have caught her forehead. Same result, but then maybe it would have just broken her neck."

"Would have left a mark."

Neither one of them moved to check if such a mark was on Macleod's forehead. If that was what had happened, Macleod's head would still have been attached to her body.

Kate couldn't believe she was putting those words together in a sentence. She had another thought. "That may have been more in line with what the murderer was planning, Jim. When the filament broke the two ends snapped back around the base of both trees. If she hadn't been decapitated, if we'd just found her with her neck broke, would we even have thought murder?"

He considered. "Maybe not."

"He might not have been expecting this. Who would?"

"And an accidental death doesn't come under the same magnifying glass a murder does," Jim said, nodding. "He wouldn't think he had to be that careful. Gotcha."

"Maybe not hard evidence," Kate said, "but there'll be something."

They both hoped she was right.

Nothing else was found at the scene, however. They brought the snow machine back up the creek and Jim took more photos with it positioned between the two trees. He strung crime scene tape between them, pulling it taut, and pushed the snow machine forward. The tape caught the windshield about midway. Kate climbed on, straddling the seat, and at Jim's request Ken and Matt pushed it slowly forward while Jim took photos. As the windshield pressed against the tape it rode up, until it snapped off the windshield and whipped over the top of Kate's head, ruffling her hair.

"She was practically twelve inches taller than me," Kate said, a little pale.

"Let's do it again," Jim said, tight-lipped. "This time kneel on the seat."

Ken and Matt pushed the snow machine back, Kate braced her left foot on the running board and her right knee on the seat, leaning forward on the handlebars, and they did it all over again. This time the yellow tape slid up the windshield and caught Kate across the forehead. It stung. She didn't complain.

Jim took photos of that, too, and more of the body and the head. He handed Kate a pad and pencil. "Take some notes for me?"

He got out a tape measure and measured the distance between everything, snow machine, body, head, trees, monofilament ends. Kate jotted down numbers with increasingly numb fingers.

He opened his Leatherman and reached up to cut the almost invisible length of pale green monofilament that had been wrapped multiple times around the base of the tree, taking care to preserve the knots, although the filament was so fine it would take a microscope to tell if they were granny knots or double sheet bends. He bagged it carefully, and did the same with the remnants of line on the opposite tree. "Okay," he said. "Let's bag the body and get out of here before we all freeze solid."

Kate shook out a body bag, Jim picked up the head, and Matt turned, walked two steps away, and threw up. Mutt whined once, softly.

They loaded Macleod's body on the trailer Matt was towing. Jim hooked her snow machine to his and Kate took her trailer. They hauled everything to Ken Kaltak's house and took his statement, which varied very little from Gallagher's. At Jim's request, Ken fetched half a dozen of the other villagers, and for the most part everyone's statements agreed. Everyone in the village had turned out for GHRI's dog and pony show. With that many people present, it was inevitable that there were moments when Macleod and Gallagher's time was unaccounted for, but not so often or for so very long that Jim thought he had to run down more witnesses.

"Anybody in Double Eagle seriously pissed about the mine?" Jim said.

"Not this pissed," Ken said definitely.

Jim persisted. "Macleod have any arguments forced on her? Anybody try to pick a fight?"

"Not that I saw." Ken reflected, and added, a little reluctantly, "She flirted with anything in pants. Even me, with Janice standing right next to me. But Jesus, Jim, you don't decapitate somebody for flirting. I mean, if Genghis Khan isn't around."

"She flirt with Gallagher?"

Ken thought. "He was always there, a step behind, but she kept it pretty businesslike, at least in public."

"She order him around?"

"More like he was anticipating her every need. She didn't even have to ask, and he had it ready for her."

"The perfect assistant, in fact."

"Pretty much." Ken looked at Jim. "Why, you think he did it? Stringing that line would have taken some time. I don't recollect he went missing from the gym that long. And she was his meal ticket. He looked pretty happy in his work to me."

Jim gave a noncommittal grunt, and they left soon after. The trip back to Niniltna was necessarily slower than the trip out had been, and it was almost four o'clock before they pulled up in front of the post. "I'll get George to take her into Anchorage in the morning. Help me put her in the walk-in?"

The post had a free-standing walk-in cold locker out back, lined with plywood shelves, and there they placed Macleod's body.

In Jim's office, he didn't bother to shed his parka before he called Fairbanks to let them know. Kate waited while he typed up a preliminary statement and sent it off. "I heart the Internet," he said. "Let's go home."

"Should we—"

"Tomorrow's going to be a nightmare," he said. "She was a celebrity in Alaska, and she had a pretty high profile Outside, too. Plus she was a babe, and if that wasn't enough she was a blonde. I'm guessing local media, big-time, and didn't she have a stint on one of the networks as a commentator?"

Kate didn't know.

"It's going to be about as bad as it can be," Jim said gloomily. "I hate a celebrity murder. Let's just go home, okay?"

They went home and went to bed, and Kate wasn't alone in spending the better part of the night staring at the ceiling.

Jim was gone before eight the next morning, Johnny to school shortly thereafter, declaiming something about New Hampshire in iambic pentameter, and Kate soothed the savage breast by some intensive housecleaning. When she was done the fireplace was spotless, so were all the dishes and towels, and both beds were freshly made with clean sheets, although negotiating the flotsam and jetsam of Johnny's room was as always a challenge. They could have eaten off the floor under the stove and the refrigerator, too, always supposing anyone would ever want to do that.

She made salmon salad for a late lunch—canned salmon, chopped onions, sweet pickles, and mayo—and didn't have enough energy left over to slice bread so she ate it out of the bowl with a fork, curled up on the couch and feeding herself blindly as she looked out the window. It was a gray day, which matched her mood. The previous day's gruesome sights lingered unpleasantly before her mind's eye.

She had disliked Talia Macleod on sight but she wouldn't wish something like this on her, or on anyone. Except maybe Louis Deem, and he was already dead, and to be perfectly honest she would have been wishful of rather more dismemberment about his person than Macleod had suffered.

She checked herself guiltily. This was no subject for humor, no matter how backhanded. She put bowl and fork into the sink, donned gear, said "Let's take a ride" to Mutt, and headed for town.

Her first stop was Bingley Mercantile, where she loaded up on three hundred dollars' worth of staples: flour, sugar, coffee, tea, eggs, pilot bread, Velveeta, peanut butter, grape jelly, canned milk, canned vegetables, a case of Spam, another of canned corned beef, a mixed case of Campbell's soup, salt, pepper, garlic powder, toilet paper, Ivory soap, dish soap, clothes soap, a packet of disposable razors, Tylenol, Neosporin, some Band-Aids, a box of assorted candy bars, a bag of peppermints; and at the last minute she tossed in half a dozen magazines, including a new *Playboy* and a new *Penthouse*, on the theory that foldout company was better than no company at all.

"Point of order," Cindy said when she rang up Kate's purchases. Kate ignored the reference—et tu, Cindy?—and offered a bland stare and no explanation of her purchases as punishment.

She left the store secure in the knowledge that in approximately four minutes and twenty-three seconds the rumor that Kate Shugak had turned lesbian would be circulating the Park on the Bush telegraph. It might even have gone out on Park Air, but for the fact that Bobby Clark had the best of all possible reasons to know that it wasn't true. Not that that would stop him laughing like a hyena about it, also on the air.

Be worth something to see Jim Chopin's expression when he heard it.

She loaded the small mountain of purchases in the trailer of her snow machine and headed out for Tikani. She made good time up the river beneath gray clouds heavy with moisture, presaging a big dump of snow. When she got close to the village she slowed down and approached with caution, but it was as deserted as it had been three days before. She nosed the machine up over the bank and stopped in front of Vidar's house. A wisp of smoke trailed from the chimney. The woodpile didn't look any taller than it had the last time she was there. She unloaded the trailer, piling everything against the door as quickly and as quietly as she could.

She turned the snow machine around, banged on Vidar's door with a heavy fist, hopped on, and hit the throttle, Mutt loping easily beside her. As slow as Vidar moved, they'd be out of sight by the time he got to the door. He'd have a pretty good idea who'd left him the supplies but she didn't want to put him in the position of having to thank her. It'd just make them both cranky.

She spent the rest of the daylight hours stopping at individual cabins scattered along the river between Tikani and Niniltna. Perhaps a dozen in all, some that had been there since the Ark, these occupied by crusty old farts and less frequently crusty old fartettes with a taste for wilderness and solitude, not necessarily in that order and not always both. Most were homes that had begun life as log cabins, and some of them were beginning to sag beneath the weight of accumulated decades, but for the most part they were snug, tight little dwellings, and certainly none of them were as threadbare as Vidar's. Other cabins had been built more recently of materials brought upriver by barge or down the road by semi and patiently ferried across the river by skiff one two-by-four at a time, their interiors lightened by Sheetrock and paint and their asphalt-shingled roofs a substantial contrast to tar-papered slabs weighted with sod.

They were similar in size, usually one room with a loft, a floor plan that reminded Kate with a pang of her cabin. The smaller the cabin, the less fuel it took to keep warm and the cheaper the winter fuel bill, and since heat rose, the sleeping loft would stay warm longer than anywhere else in the house. A tried-and-true Bush floor plan.

Everyone who lived on the river practiced subsistence in some form. They hunted for their own meat, they caught their own salmon, and most of them grew their own potatoes, turnips and carrots and cabbage, and tomatoes if they had a greenhouse, and broccoli and cauliflower if they were willing to fight off the moose.

There were so few of them because the properties they had been built on were some of the very few pieces of private property in the Park, grandfathered in when the Park had been created around them. The Park Service wasn't happy that they were there, and lost no opportunity to harass the owners on any pretext, improper land use, overstepping or ignoring hunting regulations, driving a snow machine through a designated snow-machine-free area. Every Park rat had been guilty of all of these transgressions at one time or another in their lives. The river rats were the ones who got the most attention, though, probably because they were the easiest to get to.

These citizens of the river were a varied lot, and some of them had extraordinary hobbies. Take Olaf Christiansen, a retired seiner from Cordova who had stumbled on an entire salmon-canning line in an abandoned cannery near Alaganik. He had disassembled it, brought it upriver by barge, and reassembled it in a lean-to next to his cabin, where he set it to run at one-tenth its normal speed. He was happy to show it to anyone who offered him five bucks, and they'd have a can of air to take home with them as a souvenir.

Thor Moonin, originally from Port Graham, was an ivory carver of world renown. He made his living on jewelry, earrings, necklaces, bracelets, but he was also a world-class sculptor, with the ability to render anything life-size into an exquisite miniature replica—human heads, castles, and once a miniature Yupik village, complete with dogsleds and mushers. In a shed he had a pile of walrus and mammoth tusks that was taller than he was, and he didn't mind the kids playing in there, either, although he did draw the line at dogs, because they had a tendency to mistake the tusks for bones.

Betty Cavanaugh was a retired librarian from Anchorage and a bibliophile who collected Alaskana. She had three separate sets of Captain Cook's logs in three different editions, and if Kate had been very good and had drunk all her coffee and had eaten all her bread and jam she was allowed to page through one of the precious volumes during a visit after she washed her hands.

They liked their privacy, the main reason they lived on the Kanuyaq River, but to a man and a woman they greeted Kate cordially, and without exception they tried to feed her. They did feed Mutt, whose sides tightened up like a drum. Nor were they backward in answering Kate's questions.

Yes, they knew the Johansen brothers. There wasn't anyone on the river who didn't, and not just by reputation, either. Bad actors, all three of them, couldn't think where Vidar had gone so wrong. Maybe if Juanita had stayed around, might have been a different story, but probably not, the bad was likely born into them and there was no getting it out. Surprised they hadn't wound up in jail permanently. Probably only a matter of time.

Yes, people had been moving out of Tikani, there had been a virtual exodus over the past year, year and a half, people streaming downriver like they were fleeing the bubonic plague. Sure, that could be put down to the Johansen brothers, who had no concept of private property. The older they got, the less neighborly they became, and besides, Kate surely knew they had lost their school as well as their post office. There was only a rudimentary airstrip, barely long enough to let a Super Cub take off, empty, and it had been allowed to go to hell with devil's club and alders. No reason for anyone to stay.

Old Vidar was still up there? You don't say. Well, I'll be. Ought to drop in on the old goat once in a while. He wasn't the friendliest person in the world but shouldn't ought nobody to be left completely alone year in and year out, wasn't healthy to have only your own self for company, start talking to yourself, worse, start telling yourself jokes, worse still, start laughing at them. Sure, they'd check on him, they'd set up a schedule. Somebody'd be dropping in on him once a week, or maybe every other week'd be all they could manage, but Vidar'd probably go nuts if he had visitors more often than that anyway. In the dictionary where it said *hermit*, there was a picture of Vidar Johansen.

Pity his boys were so useless they couldn't be trusted to look after him themselves.

Yes, they'd heard of the snow machine attacks. No, no one had tried anything like that with them. 'Course their river running days were over, and they had plenty to do to keep them safe to home. Failing that, they all had their 12-gauge, or their .30-30, or their .357.

Could they put a name to whoever was most likely to be the perpetrators of said attacks? Well now, there weren't no flies on Kate Shugak that they'd ever seen. What did she think?

Had they heard of Talia Macleod? Why, of course, the mine

woman, used to be some kind of famous athlete, wasn't it? She'd written them a letter saying she'd be stopping by, and then her man had come upriver and dropped off an information packet, along with a raffle ticket, winner got an all-expenses-paid weekend in Anchorage. Geiger, wasn't it? No, Gallagher, that was it, Gallagher. Eager beaver kinda guy, boomer, seen that type too many times before. Reckoned Macleod wanted their support for the mine, and they were all looking forward to seeing what she was willing to offer in exchange.

They were genuinely shocked when Kate told them of Macleod's death, and not a few of them were more worried when she left them than when she had arrived, for which she was sorry. It was better to put them on the alert than to leave them in ignorance of the event, though, and she promised that when the killer was identified and arrested she would let them know.

She headed for Niniltna after dark with the uneasy feeling that Park rats who lived on the river were getting out the gun oil and the ammunition all the way back to the Lost Chance Creek Bridge.

She pulled up at the post at eight that evening, noting evidence of a great many tracks in the snow in front. Only Jim's snow machine remained. She turned off the engine and got off, a little weary. Mutt took this opportunity to stretch her legs and vanished in the direction of the airstrip. There was a colony of rabbits denned up in a clearing in back of George's hangar.

Kate went inside. Maggie had already left for the day. "Jim?"

"Yeah," he said, and she went into his office.

He was stretched out almost horizontally in his chair, his feet up on the desk and his head on the windowsill. He had his eyes closed and his hands folded on his chest and he looked like he was about to be carried out of the office feetfirst to have prayers sung over him for the repose of his eternal soul. "Hey," Kate said.

He opened one eye, and closed it again. "Hey."

She sat down. "How awful was it?"

His chest rose and fell. "Could have been worse. Larry King could have shown up."

Kate winced. "Really?"

"Really." He opened the eye again. "Where you been?"

She told him. When she finished they sat there, silent, for a while. Eventually he uncrossed his feet and set them down on the floor, regaining the vertical with a mumble and a groan. His eyes looked red, as if he'd been rubbing them a lot. "You?" she said.

He gave his scalp a vigorous scrub with his fingertips and then tried to smooth down the resulting haystack. "I got the body off to the lab. I just talked to Brillo, and while he's going to do the usual, he says what we saw is pretty likely what we got."

"Was she the intended victim, though?" Kate said.

Jim raised one shoulder. "Maybe, maybe not. Everybody uses the creek after it freezes up to get back and forth to the school. If the killer really was aiming for Talia, he was taking a hell of a risk that he'd get somebody else."

"Mine related, you think?"

Again the shoulder. "Lot of people not loving the idea of that mine, Kate."

"I know," she said. "But to the point of murder?"

"Mac Devlin," he said. "At the trailer out at Suulutaq, from a distance that argues they might maybe have been shooting at anyone working for Global Harvest who happened to be there. And now Talia Macleod, Global Harvest's mouthpiece in the Park, lately to have been seen pretty near everywhere in it, promoting said mine."

"Same guy, then."

He nodded. "That's my thought. Too much propinquity not to be."

"I'm taking your Word of the Day calendar away."

He gave a tired smile. "How the river rats taking it?"

"In the immortal words of Brendan McCord, I left everyone mobilizing for Iwo Jima."

"Great," he said. "We need more bodies, 'cause it's not looking enough like the last scene in *Hamlet* already."

"They have a right to protect themselves, Jim," she said quietly.

"I know." After a brief pause, he said, "So. The Johansen brothers?"

She didn't say anything for a moment. "I don't know," she said finally.

He looked at her. "You figured them for the attacks."

"Since Louis Deem's dead, yeah," she said. "But . . ."

"What?" he said as she didn't continue. "I like that scenario. On any other day, so would you."

"Murder?" she said, and shook her head. "It's convenient, the mine as a motive, Park rats with a grudge, but I'm just not feeling it."

"I'm taking your DVDs of *The Wire* away," he said, and sat up. "That's not all, though, is it. What haven't you told me that I don't want to hear?"

Kate sighed. "I'm a little worried about the Johansens."

He raised an eyebrow. "That's a first. For pretty much anyone within a five-hundred-mile radius."

"You know I went down the river the day after you found out about the attacks. I talked to Ken and Janice, Ike, and the Rileys. On my way down, Ken and Ike were foaming at the mouth and threatening to shoot on sight."

"Who?"

"Anybody," Kate said. "I'm probably lucky they didn't take a shot at me."

"Were the Johansens mentioned?"

"Of course they were," Kate said. "They're nowhere near the caliber of natural disaster that Louis Deem was, but you don't live on the river for a year without learning who you don't want to be your new best friends. So I kept on keeping on, down to Red Run to talk to the Rileys. And here's the thing, Jim. They aren't foaming at the mouth. They aren't even mildly disturbed. They're not worried about catching the guys who attacked them, they have perfect confidence that Trooper Jim will get the job done, and they're willing to put their faith in him."

"I appreciate the confidence."

"Yeah, well, don't pin that medal on yourself just yet. I go back up the river and drop in again on Ike and Ken, and guess what? They're all calm now, butter wouldn't melt in their mouths, and what do you know, they know the law will catch up to the bad people who did this to them and that justice will be served."

She looked at Jim expectantly, and he did not disappoint. "You think the Park rats have taken care of this problem themselves."

"I'm terrified they did," she said. "I even went up and down the river looking in all the likely places to stuff three bodies."

He laughed out loud.

"Yeah, yuck it up," she said with asperity, "but then I went up to Tikani to see if maybe they were dumb enough to go home. They weren't there, and they hadn't been in a while. Vidar hasn't even heard their engines coming and going. And Jim, I just spent all day on the river, north of Niniltna, true, but nobody jumped out at me and said boo. I didn't see much traffic at all, come to think of it."

"That's not a surprise, given that two people have been murdered in the Park in the past two weeks. Not to mention it's freeze-your-ass cold outside. I'd stay home, too, if I could."

There was a peremptory bark outside and Kate got up to admit the lupine member of the constabulary. Mutt bounded over to Jim and offered an exuberant greeting. She returned to Kate's side and plunked down to begin a thorough grooming of her already magnificent self.

"I like to close a case as much as any cop," Kate said, "but murder? The Johansens?" She shook her head. "That's a hell of a step up for them."

"I've got people looking into Talia's background, see if there is anything there," Jim said. "But the Johansens attacked Johnny, Ruthe, and Van with a two-by-four, let's not forget. Not to mention Ken and Janice, Ike and Laverne, and Chris and Art and Grandma Riley."

"We think they did," she said. "Let's find them first."

He raised an eyebrow. "You got any thoughts on that score?"

"Where to find them, you mean?" Her turn to frown. "According to Vidar, they haven't been back home in maybe as long as two weeks. Out that long, they'll need shelter, and food." She got up and walked to the map of the Park on the wall, and ran her finger down the line that represented the Kanuyaq River. "I'm guessing, if they're still alive, that they've squirreled themselves away in the hills somewhere."

"That narrows it down."

"Yeah, actually it does." Her finger left the river and traced the line of foothills between it and the Quilak Mountains. "There are a lot of old mines back there, a lot of old gold dredges, too."

"Yeah," he said, "probably fifty, a hundred? You able to narrow it down any more?"

"Dan could help us do that." She looked around in time to see the expression on his face. "He's got the most up-to-date records and maps about mines and equipment in the Park. He's always on the lookout for squatters. He'll know if there is anything out there in good enough shape to be used for more than an overnight shelter."

He didn't say anything, and she said persuasively, "Come on, Jim. I don't know what's going on with the two of you, but you have to talk to him sometime."

He scowled. She waited. Mutt groomed.

"When he found Deem's body?" Jim said.

"Yeah?" Kate said.

"He tampered with the crime scene."

She waited.

He sighed. "Deem had the deed to the Smiths' forty acres in his pocket. He and Smith were co-owners. It retains subsurface rights."

"Oh," Kate said. "Like if they found gold on the creek."

"Dan's pretty sure it was all about the gold. He thinks Louis bankrolled Smith, and it was why he was going to marry Abigail and why Smith was going to let him. I think it's why Louis was headed up to the Step that day, to establish their mining rights."

"Why did Dan take the deed?"

"Ah, jesus, who knows. He was half in the bag for one thing. Moron. Nobody knows better than him, unless maybe it's you, that you don't remove evidence from a crime scene."

"You didn't charge him."

"No," he said glumly, "I didn't charge him. I should have, but I didn't."

Considering what he himself had done or not done in the matter of the murder of Louis Deem and the Koslowski murders, he was as at fault as Dan was of withholding evidence. Maybe, he thought now, that might be why he'd stayed mad at Dan for so long. It was hard to forgive someone for behavior of which you yourself were guilty. You knew only too well how much in the wrong you were.

She was silent for a moment, and then she repeated herself. "You have to talk to him sometime, Jim. If nothing else, you have to work with him."

"Fine," he said without enthusiasm. "You go on home. I'll detour up to the Step."

"No need," she said. "I passed him on the way here. Looked like he was headed for Bernie's."

He brightened a little.

They got up. Kate paused in the doorway. "Howie still in the back?"

"Yup."

"Good."

"Well, he won't leave until I catch whoever shot Mac, and when he heard about Talia I thought he was going to wet his pants. As long as I don't need the room and he buys his own food, I'm okay with it." He hesitated. "I did talk to Judge Singh, and she says that lacking anything more than a tire print we don't have a case against him for Louis."

"Did you tell her about the aunties?"

"Yes," he said, a little apprehensively. When she didn't go off on him he relaxed again. "She says she's disinclined to issue a warrant for a dog on the say-so of Howie Katelnikof."

"The aunties still not talking?"

"Haven't seen them today, I've been otherwise engaged. And Howie of course is now reneging his—quote—nonconfession confession—end quote—right, left, and center. He says he must have been drunk, and I hadn't Mirandized him, and I was threatening him anyway and he got scared and confused and he would have said anything to get me to leave him alone, and—"

"I get the picture. Still, good that he's here where we can keep an eye on him."

She preceded him out the door and she didn't see the curious look he gave her.

TWENTY-ONE

No belly dancers or church socials this evening, just the regular crowd, a group of old farts playing pinochle at the round table beneath the blare of the basketball game on the television hanging over their heads, and a mosh of couples on the handkerchief-sized dance floor barely moving to the competing blare of Linda Ronstadt's "Blue Bayou." About half the tables were filled, the amount of empties per tabletop indicating the seriousness of the drinkers seated there, although nobody seemed especially drunk. No one seemed especially happy, either, except of course for the four Grosdidier brothers, although when Kate took a closer look she could see that Matt seemed a little strained.

"Damn," Jim said, looking at the Grosdidiers, "I hadn't realized the extent of the damage. I wonder what the other guys look like."

Nick and Eve Waterbury sat at one table. Eve had one timidly restraining hand on Nick's arm and radiated anxiety. She was saying something in a low voice. Nick had his face turned away. At first glance he looked sullen, at second angry, at third despairing. Kate made a mental note of distance and elevation. Nick wasn't much of a drinker but he had a temper, and it looked like Eve was testing it.

Jim gave her a gentle nudge with his elbow. The four aunties were sitting in the corner at their regular table. There was no greeting called to Kate and Jim, just four heads studiously bent over the current quilt, a bright, geometric splash of primary colors.

Bernie was behind the bar, a tall, thin presence with a calm face and what hair he had left bound back into a ponytail that reached to his belt.

Strike that, Kate thought, looking at Bernie, not thin, gaunt. Bernie looked as if he hadn't had a good meal since his wife died. His cheeks were hollowed out, his eyes sunken, the tendons of his hands stood out like whipcord. The past year had aged him ten. "Hey, Kate," he said. "Mutt."

Instead of rearing up to place both front feet on the bar as was her invariable habit, Mutt trotted around it to butt Bernie's hand with her head. She looked up at him with what could only be described as a kind, loving gaze, if anything coming out of predatory yellow eyes could be called kind. For a moment Bernie seemed to stop breathing. Then he cuffed Mutt gently, pulled down a package of beef jerky, and said, albeit a little shakily, "Get out from behind the bar before I make you buy a round for the house."

Her tail swept a graceful arc. She nudged him again and then trotted back around the bar to Kate.

"Jim," Bernie said, looking over Kate's shoulder.

"Bernie," Jim said, looking at the bottles lined up in back of the bar.

"What'll you have?"

"Coffee," Kate said, taking a stool, "and heavy on the cream."

"Same," Jim said, sitting next to her.

On Jim's other side was Dan O'Brien, his back to them as he continued his ongoing attempts to romance Bernie's newest barmaid, one Laura Delgado, a Latina import from California who had followed a Bristol Bay fisherman north a year before. He had not proved to be as attractive in his natural habitat as he had been on a free-spending spree through the clubs of her native Los Angeles, and she had left him to start hitchhiking home the previous fall. In Ahtna she'd stopped to replenish the treasury by waiting tables at the Lodge, where she'd met and fallen madly in love with Martin Shugak.

That she'd fallen in love with Martin Shugak was a nine-day wonder in the Park, but, Kate thought, perhaps not so difficult, because no matter what Auntie Edna said the only person who could fall in love with Martin would be someone who didn't live in the Park and therefore did not know him well. At any rate little Laura Delgado had followed Martin home to Niniltna, and at the end of the road Bernie gave her a job. She was short and plump with polished golden brown cheeks, a perpetually wide smile, a perfect set of large white teeth, and a flirtatious look in her bright brown eyes that was going to get her into trouble before breakup. It didn't hurt that she sounded like Jennifer Lopez, and had considerably more cleavage.

"Bernie," Kate said in a quiet voice, "how often has Nick Waterbury been in here lately?"

Bernie followed her gaze and said with a noticeable lack of interest, "He's in here four nights out of five anymore."

"Eve always with him?"

"Sometimes yes, sometimes no."

"He drinking a lot?"

Bernie shook his head. "Not a lot. Steady, though."

"Yet another charge to put on Louis Deem's tab," Kate said.

Little Mary Waterbury, daughter and only child of Nick and Eve, had been Louis's third wife and last victim. She half rose to her feet. "Maybe I should—"

"No." Bernie held up a cautionary hand. "Leave them alone." His mouth twisted. "It's all we can do for them now, but we can do that much."

She looked at Jim. "Bernie's right," he said. "You can't fix this. If it's gonna get fixed, Nick and Eve have to do it."

What he didn't say but what they both knew was that most marriages did not survive the death of a child.

"Hey, Laura," Bernie said. "Thirsty people waiting."

She giggled, a dimple flashing in her left cheek, and with a toss of long black hair she grabbed up her tray, winked at Dan, and sashayed off, giving him a roguish look over her shoulder as she went. The impact was kind of lessened when she collided with a chair but Dan sighed anyway, a lovelorn, wistful sound. Usually it was breakup before Park rats started falling in love with anything that didn't move out of the way first.

"Hey, Dan," Jim said.

Dan's back stiffened. He turned, very slowly, his eyes wary, a thickset redhead with fair skin that flushed easily. He wore bibs over a plaid shirt and high, thick-soled leather boots. "Hey, Jim. Kate. Didn't see you come in."

"Yeah, we noticed," Jim said. "Looking for you, actually."

"Really." Dan took a long deliberate pull at his beer and sat contemplating the bottle for a moment. "What can I do for you?"

"You heard about the snow machine attacks on the river?"

The tension in Dan's shoulders eased slightly but his eyes were still wary. "It's all anybody's been talking about, and my ears work fine."

"Yeah, figures. I was thinking I'd talk to the Johansen boys about them."

Dan raised his eyebrows. "Couldn't hurt. What's that got to do with me?"

"They appear to have changed location. Haven't been home in a couple of weeks, according to their dad."

"And?"

"And I don't think they'd leave the Park. So if they're still in the

Park, and they've changed addresses, I got to thinking about where they'd go. And while I was thinking I remembered all those abandoned mines along the foothills south of the Step. Lot of old timber they could use to build a shelter inside one of them, put in a woodstove, pack in some grub, melt snow for water, you'd make it through as long as you wanted to. I was thinking, too, that you'd have the best knowledge of those mines, and maybe even a map."

Dan shook his head. "No."

"You don't?"

"No, I do, but we've been closing those old mines, caving in the entrances. They're an invitation to squatters, and they're dangerous to hikers and backpackers. Every time I hear about a new one I close it up."

Jim shrugged. "Could be one of them was dug out."

"It'd be a major excavation, requiring at minimum one of Mac Devlin's Cats," Dan said dryly. "You can bring a lot of rock down with a stick of dynamite."

"That you can," Jim said with respect. "Any other ideas you might have as to where the Johansens might be holing up?"

Dan scratched his head. "Hell, Jim, place is twenty million acres."

"I know," Jim said with equal gloom.

They shook their heads, and Kate could see that all would eventually be right in the world of their friendship.

She, on the other hand, was growing more and more worried about the whereabouts of the Johansen brothers. They weren't home. According to Dan there was no place for them to go to ground among the old mines. Kenny Hazen would have called Jim if they'd shown up in Ahtna. Where the hell were they?

It was no joke to be out in the Park without shelter at this time of year. Where could they go, especially if they were hurt? There'd have to be trees for fuel, they had to stay warm, and—

She sat up, staring straight ahead. "Hey," she said.

Before she could say any more, the door to the Roadhouse slammed open. Everyone looked around and two men stood in the doorway, one with blood frozen on his face, the other supporting him. "Somebody else got jumped on the river!"

"Fuck," Matt Grosdidier was heard to say clearly.

There was a general movement toward the two men. Jim nodded at the Grosdidiers and made a hole through the crowd, Kate bringing up the rear. The bleeding man started to slip and Luke Grosdidier slid a chair under his butt before he fell all the way to the floor. The Grosdidiers did triage surrounded by a supervisory buzz of commentary, Peter fetching a first-aid kit the size of a hospital crash cart.

Jim let them get on with it for fifteen minutes before he said, "How bad?"

"Not too," Mark said, his usually cheerful face serious as he concentrated on the task at hand. "He's got a goose egg on the back of his head and it bled a little, but he says he woke up on his own. We'll keep him awake, in case of concussion, and he should probably go into Ahtna for an x-ray, but I think he'll be okay."

"Ask him some questions?"

Mark shrugged. "If he's up to it."

Jim shouldered forward and hunkered down in front of the victim. "What's your name, sir?"

The man's eyes seemed to be wandering a little, and he made a visible effort to bring them back under control. "Oh," he said, zeroing in on Jim. "The Niniltna trooper, right?"

"That's me. What's your name, and where do you live?"

"Gene Daly. I live in Anchorage. I've got a cabin on the river the other side of Double Eagle. I was headed there on my snow machine."

"What happened?"

"Wish to hell I knew," Daly said, wincing when Matt pressed a little too hard on his head wound. Matt muttered an apology, and Kate gave him a thoughtful look.

"I was coasting down the river, smooth as you please, making for the cabin with a bunch of supplies, going to spend a week there." He put a tentative hand to his head and winced again. "Everything inside my head just sort of exploded." He looked up. "I woke up and the trailer was gone and I was bleeding and I couldn't get my snow machine started. Woulda froze to death if this guy hadn't come along. Saved my life. Thanks, man."

His rescuer looked anything but pleased at the accolade. Indeed, he was trying to worm through the crowd, on a heading for the door. Jim took three steps and grabbed him by his collar. "Hold on, there, Martin. Been looking for you. Need a word."

Jim frog-marched Martin to the bar, sat him on a stool, and said to Kate, "Watch him for me?"

Kate said to Mutt, "Watch him for me?"

Mutt looked at Martin and gave a single, authoritative bark that established a perimeter of not more than a foot in every direction that was perfectly understood by everyone concerned.

Kate followed Jim back to the victim, who was struggling to remember something, anything else. "No," he said. "I'm sorry, I just don't remember. Wait, maybe, there might have been another snow machine?" He closed his eyes and shook his head, and then stopped, grimacing, as if trying to think hurt his head. "I don't know."

"If you remember something else, be sure to contact me," Jim said, and stood, nodding at the Grosdidiers, who escorted their patient out in an EMT guard of honor. There was nothing the four Grosdidiers loved more than having a patient to minister to. They'd fixed up what was essentially a two-bed ward in their house, and Daly would be well looked after until George took him to Ahtna the following day.

Jim turned to Kate. "Well, you can stop worrying. It would appear the Johansens are alive and well and still in business."

"Not for much longer," Kate said. "Mutt!"

Mutt gave Martin a threatening glare, just to keep in practice, and shot after Kate as she headed for the door. They were both showing a considerable amount of teeth.

"Kate," Jim said.

"Later," she said. The door to the Roadhouse opened and Harvey Meganack stepped inside. He saw what was coming his way and he stepped back hastily, overbalanced on the top step, and stumbled backward. Kate and Mutt didn't so much as break stride, brushing by him as his arms windmilled and he tap-danced backward down the stairs.

"Kate!"

This time she didn't bother answering.

TWENTY-TWO

She loaded a fifty-gallon drum onto the trailer of her snow machine, lashing it down. It held gas for the snow machine, not
stove oil, but the Johansen brothers wouldn't know that and
they probably wouldn't care anyway. Around the drum on the sled,
she packed food, stove, and tent.

As angry as she was, she was glad to have a focus, a goal with a
tangible end in sight. Someone was hijacking innocent Park rats
and hapless Park visitors on the Kanuyaq River. She was going to
find them and stop them, and—she patted the rifle—if she had to
hurt someone in the process, fine by her. She might even be looking
forward to it.

She kept her thoughts firmly focused on her preparations, but
somewhere, tucked in a corner of her mind, she knew what was really pushing her down the river.

Life had taken some strange turns of late, and all of those turns
had left her on an unfamiliar path, each with a destination shrouded
in darkness and uncertainty. Kate didn't care for uncertainty. If it
came to that, she wasn't big with the darkness, either.

If that little weasel, Howie Katelnikof, were to be believed, the aunties had conspired to have Louis Deem murdered. The aunties, of all people, the fixed foot around which the rest of the Park revolved. The aunties were the first and last stop when you needed a job, a bed, a meal, or just some ordinary, everyday comfort, ladled out with cocoa and fry bread and an attentive and sympathetic ear.

She'd always known the aunties were judge and jury. She just hadn't known that they saw themselves as executioner, too.

The aunties. Conspiracy to commit murder. She couldn't believe it, and her mind refused to deal with the thought of them being tried and jailed for it.

Or of a Park without aunties in it.

The snow machine was fueled, oil checked, the rifle loaded and snug in its scabbard.

Then there was her seat on the Association board, definitely not a consummation devoutly to be wished, if she wanted to keep quoting poetry to herself, which she could if she wanted to. Not only a seat, she was chair of the board. How the hell had that happened? There followed of course her less than stellar debut at her first board meeting, as she fumbled and farted her way through an unfamiliar agenda she hadn't written, and responded—or not—to topics about which she knew little or—be honest, now—nothing.

Kate had always regarded herself as a responsible shareholder. Well, she would have if she'd thought about it. She voted in all the elections and where she felt it was necessary she spoke her mind at those—be honest again, admittedly few—shareholder meetings she'd managed to attend, work permitting. Her work took her all over the state, from Prudhoe Bay to Dutch Harbor, often at a moment's notice. The number of meetings she'd missed far outweighed the number of meetings she'd attended.

If she were being brutally honest, her shares in the Niniltna Native Association didn't mean tribal pride or self-determination or land ownership. No, what the Niniltna Native Association meant most to her was the quarterly dividend that landed in her mailbox four times a year. That dividend meant food, fuel, new jeans when the knees on the old ones ripped out, money for taxes and vehicle registration and insurance. She owned her house and her land outright, but all those things cost money to support and maintain. Her job paid well, sometimes very well indeed, but she only had on average half a dozen jobs a year, and the amount of the Association quarterly dividend was often an essential cushion between paychecks.

She went back inside and donned long johns, cotton, wool, and felt socks, down bibs, down jacket, parka, and Sorels.

Speaking of money, now she had Johnny to provide for.

Look out for Johnny for me, okay? It was very nearly the last thing Jack had said to her. Johnny was all she had left to her of Jack Morgan. And hell—tell the truth again—she loved the boy for himself, and she wanted the best for him. He had to have an education. Since he'd been with her, her quarterly dividends had been going directly into his college fund.

Johnny was another black hole, sucking in every worry and fear she had. Adolescence was the worst time in anyone's life, when the body betrayed the comparatively stable twelve previous years and erupted suddenly in every direction, things popping out, things dropping down, voices changing, hair changing, hormones launching an all-out attack, no mercy, no quarter, no prisoners. It was quite literally an outrage, physically, mentally, and emotionally, and it went on for years, during which life existed at either the zenith or the nadir, occupying no middle ground and offering no peace. It was exhausting just to think about it. All too well did Kate remember being at the mercy of a body that would not leave her alone. It was good that she and Ekaterina had come to an understanding about Kate living on her own at the homestead, because otherwise they might have killed each other.

So far, Johnny seemed reasonably sane, although there had been something worrying at him lately, leading to long, abstracted silences. She made every effort to give him as much space and privacy as he needed, in hopes that he would voluntarily tell her what it was. In the meantime, she stewed over the cause. Vanessa, maybe? Girlfriends were tough.

Not as tough as boyfriends, though. Not near as.

In the pantry she loaded the pockets of her parka with dried dates, dried apricots, tamari almonds, and roasted pecans. She didn't know how long this was going to take and she might need fuel herself before she found them.

She went back outside and rechecked the lines on the drum, Mutt trotting behind her, ears pricked, tail wagging, as always ready to go anywhere, anytime. A scattered overcast allowed some stars to peer down at her. Her breath was a white cloud in the cold air.

"I did turn off the stove," she said.

Mutt looked up at her, tail slowing.

"I did," Kate said. "I did turn off that goddamn stove."

Jim had started coming for her, and she had known what was going to happen, every cell in her body sounding the alarm.

Not just the alarm. If she had really fought him, he would have stopped. If she had said no and meant it, he would have stopped. If she had raised so much as a wooden spoon in his direction, he would have stopped in his tracks. No, it wasn't only alarm she had been feeling, as events upstairs had demonstrated very shortly thereafter. Damn him, anyway.

"I just didn't see it lasting this long," she said to Mutt.

Mutt, realizing that departure had been delayed indefinitely, sat down with a martyred air.

Kate sat down on the seat of the snow machine. "He was supposed to be long gone by now, history, conspicuous by his absence. But he's still here."

Mutt gave her a bored look. Obviously.

"Why? Is it just the sex?"

Which was a considerable factor, given the intensity of their latest encounter, and which led to a whole other worry. Passion, according to conventional wisdom and *Cosmopolitan*, was supposed to wane as the relationship aged. They had gone at each other like minks that first year, but while subsequently the frequency had decreased the intensity had remained, whether Jim took her by storm at night or she launched a surprise seduction before he had his eyes open in the morning.

"You know what the problem is?" she said to Mutt. "I like him. I really like him. He's smart, he's funny, he's good at his job." She thought for a moment and added, a little doubtfully, "Everybody tells me he's gorgeous. I guess he is. But you know eye candy's never been enough for me." She thought of Jack, whose blunt, irregular features had looked like something chipped off the cornice at Notre Dame, and smiled a little. No, she could accuse herself of many things, but falling for a pretty face wasn't one of them.

Mutt, impatient, thumped Kate's leg with her head.

"You're right," Kate said, and welcomed the rush of anticipation that washed out all misgivings and indecision. Action was what was needed to shake the cobwebs out, hard, fast action, a fight for the right, without question or pause. "Let's get a move on, girlfriend."

She mounted the snowgo, pressed the starter, waited for Mutt to jump up on the seat behind, and lit out of the clearing as if Raven himself was on her tail.

It took three days to smoke them out.

On the way through town she stopped for a late-night coffee at the Riverside Café in Niniltna, telling Laurel Meganack where she was going and what she was doing in a full, carrying voice, her words falling on a dozen pairs of eager and, she hoped, fertile ears.

Her next stop was the store, where Cindy was just closing. She bought a package of Oreos and told her all about it, too.

At the Roadhouse, Jim had left, and Kate marched back up to the bar and ordered the usual. Conversation ensued, in the course of which Kate let it be known, again in a carrying voice, that she was delivering fuel over the next week to some of the shut-ins along the river. Bernie continued noncommittal and subdued. In the corner, the aunties sewed industriously without looking her way. Old Sam, attention fixed on the slamming and dunking going on on the big screen overhead, nevertheless spared her a sharp glance. His shrewd eye lingered as the door closed behind her, before looking over at the aunties' table. None of them would meet his eye, either. He nodded as if their inaction had confirmed a profoundly unpleasant inner thought, and returned his attention to the screen.

That first night she camped on the bank of the river a mile north of Double Eagle, almost exactly at the spot where the attack on the Kaltaks had taken place. She and Mutt passed an unfortunately peaceful evening in the tent, a wood fire a safe distance in front of the flap built high enough to illuminate the loaded sled, the barrel casting a long and come-hither shadow.

The next day they trolled the river with the drum as bait, up and down the frozen expanse between Tikani and Red Run, stopping at every cabin and village on the way south. Some of them were surprised to see her again this soon but they all made her welcome.

That night they camped in a willow thicket at the mouth of the Gruening River. The next morning Kate watched the light come up on the tent wall, thinking. Mutt, a warm, solid presence next to her, stretched, groaned, and pressed a cold nose to Kate's cheek, indicating a pressing need to be on the other side of the tent flap.

Oatmeal with raisins and a couple of too-slow parky squirrels for breakfast, and they broke camp and repeated the previous day's route, north again to Niniltna and on to Tikani and almost to Louis Deem's homestead, where she could have stopped in to check on Willard, but she didn't.

Another disappointingly unmolested day with minimal traffic on the frozen length of the Kanuyaq. "Okay," Kate said at dusk. "Inland it is."

Mutt agreed, and they moved off the river.

Kate had spent the hours before dawn that morning running down the various options, snug and warm in a down sleeping bag rated to forty below placed on top of a thick foam pad, watching the vapor of her breath form a layer of frost on the inside of the tent. She'd slept deep and dreamlessly the night before. The best soporific was always a cold nose. The memory of last night's meal, moose steak, biscuits and gravy, followed by stewed rhubarb, lingered pleasantly on palate and belly, and a delicate odor of wood smoke told her that the campfire she had banked the night before was ready to be blown into flame at a moment's notice. There was nothing quite as life-affirming as a successful winter's camping trip. If she hadn't been on a mission, she would have been enjoying herself.

If, as she suspected, the Johansens had been, ah, temporarily discouraged from further attacks, her last trip to Tikani had confirmed that they had not gone home to lick their wounds. But, like Jim, neither did she believe that they would have left the Park. There was no need. To the uninitiated, the Park might appear to be twenty million acres of frozen wasteland, devoid of sustenance or shelter, but those who lived there knew better.

No. She had known however bloody and bowed the Johansen brothers might have been, they were still in the Park, providing they were still alive. The attack on Daly proved that they were both. And she finally had a pretty good idea where they'd gone to ground. She couldn't believe it had taken her this long to figure it out.

Ranger Dan's Park headquarters were on what the Park rats

called the Step, a long bluff about four thousand feet high that meandered south along the western edge of the Quilak Mountains. Where the bluff finally disappeared, the foothills got higher and more rugged and far less passable, even to snow machines. But there were ways in, especially if you'd been raised by a crotchety Alaskan old fart who'd spent Prohibition on the back of first a dogsled and later one of the first snow machines imported into the Park finding a route through the Quilak Mountains into Canada for the purposes of stocking the liquor cabinet. From a few remarks the aunties had let drop over the years, Kate believed that Abel might well have been the Park's first bootlegger.

South of where the Step ended and deep into the foothills but not quite into the Quilaks themselves, hidden in a narrow canyon with an entrance at right angles to itself that from a distance gave the illusion of an impenetrable wall, a geothermal spring bubbled up out of the ground. The water was a pleasant ninety degrees and never froze, not even in winter. Its flow formed a chain of small ponds, one emptying into another down the little canyon, the last pond draining into some invisible underground fissure, not to surface again, or not in the Park.

Very few people knew about these hot springs, and even the ones who did didn't get there often because it was so far from anywhere and it was so difficult to find. Poking around the Quilaks in winter was not a formula for longevity.

At the head of the canyon, next to the first pool, someone had knocked together a cabin from rough-cut logs. It had been pretty tumbledown the last time Kate had seen it, but if the roof hadn't fallen in it would provide adequate shelter, and the springs would be good for any aches and pains the Johansens might or might not be suffering. If they had enough food, they could hole up there indefinitely.

It was a long, cold drive into the foothills, and she lost her way twice and had to retrace their steps, first out of a box canyon that dead-ended on the west-facing and nearly vertical slope of one of the Quilaks, and second off of a narrow, twisting creek whose ice boomed ominously beneath the tread of her snow machine every five feet. Mutt got off and trotted a good ten feet away after the second boom. "Et tu, Mutt?" Kate said, and Mutt gave her a look that said plainly, *You'll be happy when you go in that I'm right here, ready to pull you out.*

Kate didn't go in, though, and once on the bank again, Mutt remounted without any further backseat commentary and they were off again.

It had been a long time since she'd been to the springs, and snow and ice were adept at disguising even the most distinctive landmark. The wind had swept the snow smooth of tracks, and Kate was working on by guess or by god when she stumbled onto the correct trail pretty much by accident. It was well past dark by then, and Kate stopped before she went around the last dogleg into the canyon itself.

She looked up at the sky. No stars. She pulled back the hood of her parka and tested the air on her face. Her weather sense, while by no means infallible, was usually pretty good. It didn't feel like it was going to snow, not quite yet. She refueled the snow machine by means of a hand pump, estimated the contents of the barrel, and recalculated a point of no return, when she would have to start heading for Niniltna so she could get there without running out of gas. She was cutting it close, she decided, but not by too much, and bagged and stowed the pump.

She pointed the snow machine toward the canyon's entrance and unhitched the sled. She didn't expect to be chased out of the canyon—in fact, she was determined not to be—but there was no sense in not being careful. In that same spirit, she tarped both sled and machine, lashing the tarps down loosely, using running loops that would give with a yank if she had to leave in a hurry. Just because it didn't feel like snow didn't mean it wouldn't.

She buckled her snowshoes on over her boots and said to Mutt in a quiet, firm voice, pointing, "By me."

She gave Mutt a hard look and said it again. "By me, Mutt." Mutt's yellow eyes narrowed and she gave a hard look back, but she did not stray from Kate's side as Kate set out.

The last dogleg in the canyon was an abrupt, narrow vee, where in one spot erosion or maybe an earthquake had knocked down part of the canyon wall. In summer, it was a tumble of sharp-edged and unexpectedly and treacherously mobile boulders, impassable by anyone who wasn't wearing steel plate armor and chain mail gloves. In winter, beneath a continually replenished layer of snow that was steadily being packed down, it was by comparison an interstate highway, albeit with one hell of a grade. Kate took her time, stopping often to breathe before her heart burst out of her chest. She also took a moment to be proud of her foresight in purchasing a new pair of lightweight snowshoes, rectangular ovals of hollow metal with a continuous strap that zigzagged across her foot from toe to instep to heel, fastened with three quick-release plastic buckles. They certainly weighed less than the old wooden ones, and were narrow enough that she didn't waddle like a penguin when she wore them. When she wasn't climbing a mountain in them, they even gave her a fairly good turn of speed.

While she was thus congratulating herself the boulder slope flattened into a tiny saddle, the other side of which looked down on the steaming ponds of the hot springs, small, dark, lustrous pools nestled in perfect snowy settings, joined one to the other like a string of black pearls displayed on a rich rumple of white velvet. At the head of the canyon she was mildly surprised to see the log cabin still standing, and was further heartened when she saw smoke wisping from the rudimentary rock chimney.

There was no one stirring outside the cabin but she lay down on her stomach anyway and wriggled forward until she had a panoramic view. She fished out the binoculars residing in one of the parka's inside pockets, where they would stay warm for use. They were anti-frost, anti-fog, digital day and night vision, and effective over three hundred yards, which view had cost her almost two dollars a yard. Not one penny of which did she grudge when through the lenses and the inexorable onset of the dark Arctic night the individual logs of the cabin sprang into view, revealing that much of the moss and mud chinking between the logs had dried up and fallen out. She could actually see inside the cabin from here, at least in places. It reminded her of Vidar's ramshackle cabin in Tikani, and she was pissed off all over again.

It was only marginally lighter inside the cabin than it was outside, a sullen glow coming from what appeared to be a stove crafted from the black curve of what was probably a fifty-five-gallon drum. A shadow moved and she jerked involuntarily. Mutt started, too, and then whuffed out a breath and gave her a reproachful look.

"Sorry," Kate said, her voice barely above a whisper, and looked through the binoculars again.

The shadow was a dark, bulky figure, which moved out of sight after a moment. What might have been a pair of legs were stuffed into a sleeping bag, whose owner might be leaning into a corner. That's where she'd be, too, given how well ventilated the cabin was, her back tucked into a corner she'd padded with her sleeping bag and probably anything else she had on hand.

She didn't see a third man. She scanned the area outside, and identified various mounds of new-fallen snow that might be hiding snow machines and sleds. There appeared to be a well-trodden path around the back, where she dimly remembered there was an outhouse.

To pee, all men had to do was hang it out the front door and shake afterward. Women required at minimum a bush and, best-case scenario, toilet paper. But sooner or later, everyone had to take a dump, and there nature had leveled the playing field. It was one of the reasons the passing of the Sears catalog had occasioned more mourning across all genders in Alaska than anywhere else in the world.

An hour later she'd worked her way around behind the cabin, mostly on her belly, leaving her snowshoes on the saddle. For once she damned the silence of the great unknown, sure that every acci-dental crunch of snow, every rasp of spruce bough over her parka was resounding off the walls of the cabin like the gong of a temple bell. But no one called out in alarm or came to the door, and she hunkered down against the back wall of the outhouse to wait. It had developed an ominous tilt to starboard and Mutt wrinkled her nose at the smell, a sentiment Kate heartily if silently endorsed. At least at this time of year there were no flies. She only hoped the damn thing didn't fall over before someone came out to use it.

There were fewer chinks in this more sheltered wall of the cabin, so she couldn't see inside as well when she peeped around the corner of the outhouse. She heard the occasional murmur of voices, and eventually sorted them into three distinct identities. It was enough to keep her there, muscles slowly atrophying from inac-tion and cold. She was grateful for the warm weight of Mutt, leaning against her, impervious to the snow and the cold.

Finally, after an hour or so, there was the sound of a heavy tread from inside the cabin, a corresponding protesting groan from the floor, a toe hitting something and kicking it across the room, a stum-ble and a curse, and then a creak and a thump as the dilapidated door was wrenched open. The crunch of footsteps in the snow came around the cabin and directly for the outhouse Kate and Mutt were crouched behind.

The door to the outhouse creaked open and slammed shut again, bouncing a couple of times on a door spring that sounded as if it were on its last legs. There followed a rustle of clothing, the sound of flesh smacking down on wood, and a "Jeeeeesus Key-rist, that's cold." The outhouse as a whole gave an ominous creak.

Mutt looked at Kate with eyes that shone bright even in the dark. Kate opened her mouth and leaned her head back, took a deep breath, and at the top of her lungs let out with an "Oooooh ooooh oooooooh!"

Mutt didn't think much of this imitation wolf howl, and she leaped to her feet and raised her muzzle to the sky to show Kate how it was really done. "OuououOUOOOOOOOOOH!"

Wolves howling miles away were scary enough. It wasn't fun when you were right next to one putting her all into it, even when you were expecting it. Kate couldn't imagine what it sounded like on the other side of the aging and insubstantial wall of an outhouse in the middle of nowhere where you were sitting with your pants down around your ankles, very probably, or so Kate hoped, unarmed.

"Holy SHIT!" the man in the outhouse cried. There was sudden movement from inside, punctuated by a thud when he leaped to his feet. The outhouse shuddered and protested again. "Ouch! Fuck! Ick! Ick, do you hear that! Ick, there's a wolf out here!"

There were more thuds and then the door slammed back with a crash. Something fell off the outhouse with a loud thud. Against her back Kate felt it lean over a little more.

"Ick, get the rifle, get the fucking rifle!"

From the cabin came a series of startled shouts and thuds and bumps and crashes. Kate motioned to Mutt and crept around to the front of the outhouse.

"Ou-ou-ouoooWOOOOOOO!" Mutt said.

"Get that fucking rifle out here, Ick! Gus! Help!"

The door to the outhouse crashed back and Daedalus Johansen stood in the opening.

"Hey, Dead," Kate said. "Your fly's open."

He gaped at her and she dropped to the snow, catching herself on her right hand, and hooked a foot behind one of his ankles and rolled, catching both his ankles in both of hers. Off guard, off balance, and tender parts well on their way to being frostbitten, he toppled backward, one wildly floundering arm catching the door frame to arrest his fall only partially. When he hit the rim of the toilet seat the outhouse groaned another protest and teetered another couple of inches to starboard.

Kate was instantly on her feet. She grabbed both his hands and slipped a plastic tie over his wrists with the end already thoughtfully threaded through the clasp. She yanked on the free end and it tightened up instantly and very nicely indeed.

It was great when a plan worked out.

Dead stared at his bound hands in stupefaction. "What the fuck?"

The door to the cabin crashed open. Kate looked at Mutt and signaled. "Go."

Mutt went around one side of the cabin and Kate went around the other, just in time to see Gus and Icarus Johansen emerge, jostling each other in the doorway to be first to their brother's aid. Both were holding rifles. Ick was facing Kate, Gus behind him, and behind Gus Mutt let loose with another chilling howl. "Ou-ou-ouoooooooooo!"

"Fuck!" Ick said, or maybe he screamed. "Shoot it, Gus, shoot it!"

And then he saw Kate. After one incredulous second, his shoulders slumped. "Oh, fuck me," he said.

Mutt jumped Gus and his rifle went flying. Gus fell backward on Ick, who stumbled and fell to one knee. Kate took one step forward, got a toe beneath the stock of his rifle, kicked it out of his hands and into the air, and caught it neatly before it hit the ground. She raised it smoothly to her shoulder, looking down the sights at Ick's face, lit reasonably well from the sullen glow of the fire streaming out the open door of the cabin. Some part of her noticed that Ick had a shiner to rival Matt Grosdidier's, two of them, in fact.

"Kate?" Ick said. "Kate Shugak?"

"Ou-ou—ouOOOOOOOOO!" Mutt said, standing with her paws on Gus's shoulders and sharp, gleaming teeth right down in Gus's face. Gus seemed incapable of either speech or movement. A moment later the acrid smell of urine filled the air.

"And that'd be Mutt," Ick said.

Dead came shuffling around the corner of the cabin, wrists still bound in front of him, pants down around his ankles, weenie wagging in the wind and accompanied by a strong smell of excrement. "Ick? Gus? Are you okay? What the hell's going on?"

From behind the cabin came a long, descendiary groan, followed by an even louder, splintering crash.

Ick Johansen started to laugh.

Kate raised her right foot. "Do you like your teeth where they are, Ick?"

Ick stopped laughing and started to whine. "Ah, c'mon, Kate. It's funny."

"You know what isn't funny?" Kate said. "Your dad, starving to death in his own cabin because his asshole brats can't be bothered to feed him." She could feel her hands tightening on the stock of the rifle, and the smile faded from Ick's face.

Mutt's head raised from Gus's throat, ears pricking. From the next mountain over came the lonesome, faraway cry of a wolf. There was another, and then another, until the pack was in full chorus. It also sounded like it was coming in their direction.

Kate looked back down at Ick, and even in the faint light cast through the cabin door she could see him start to sweat. Like all Park rats, he'd heard the story about Kate Shugak and the bootlegger. "Jesus, Kate, you wouldn't. C'mon."

She had zip-strips for Ick and Gus, too, and she used them. She picked up Gus's rifle and tossed it into the nearest pool, where it made a muted splash. Ick's rifle followed. "Mutt," she said. "Guard."

Mutt returned her attention to Gus and snapped agreement, canines gleaming. Gus whimpered.

Kate turned and headed down the little canyon.

Ick's voice followed her out of the clearing. "Kate? C'mon, Kate! Come back here! Jesus, you can't leave us like this, Kate! At least leave us a rifle! *Kate!* KATE!"

TWENTY-THREE

Jim was standing in the doorway of the trooper post when she drove up at noon the next day with the Johansen brothers in tow. Literally in tow, as she had packed the three of them into their sleeping bags and tied them into their individual snow machine sleds and hitched the sleds on behind her own in a train. The combined weight was a strain on the engine of her machine, which had not been built to pull that many pounds at once. Although the slow uphill slogs were more than made up for in the exhilarating downhill runs, when she had to go as fast as possible so the sleds didn't overtake her and the whole shebang didn't jackknife and kill them all.

Ick, Dead, and Gus, funnily enough, didn't appreciate the need for speed, instead having somehow gained the impression that she was hoping to kill the three of them before they could be put safely under arrest. They screamed a lot at first, and when that didn't do any good they closed their eyes and waited for death.

A fifth sled hitched last carried evidence, items of interest found in the hot springs cabin that Kate felt might be identified by the Rileys and the Kaltaks and the Jeffersons and Gene Daly as having been stolen from them during the attacks. Since several boxes, now mostly empty, had been clearly marked in black Sharpie RILEY—RED RUN and KEN KALTAK—DOUBLE EAGLE—WAIT FOR PICKUP, she felt fairly confident they would be.

They acquired something of a parade as they came through Niniltna, and Ick didn't think anything was funny anymore. He was swearing a blue streak by the time Jim got him out of his sled, although that turned out partly to be because he'd had to pee for the last twenty miles and bouncing up and down on the sled over bumps and berms was not kind to the kidneys. Gus and Ick, of course, were already past praying for in that direction, and Jim recoiled when he unpeeled them from their sleeping bags. "Jesus, Kate," he said.

"I know," she said, "sorry, Jim."

She didn't sound very sorry. She didn't look it, either. He finished extricating the Johansens and at arm's length marched them one at a time through a cheering crowd of Park rats. They had all heard the story of the attacks on the river and had correctly deduced the reason for this morning's perp walk.

"I could cuss you out myself," Jim said to Kate inside. "They're going to smell up my post something fierce."

Kate, feeling much calmer now that she'd taken some direct action against somebody deserving, yawned widely, jaw cracking, and said with a lazy stretch, "Quit whining. I got your guys for you."

"Holy shit," Howie Katelnikof said, wide-eyed as Jim hustled the boys into the facing cell. "It's a three-Johansen salute." When he got a better look at them his eyes went even wider. "Jesus. What'd they do to piss you off, Kate?"

Kate didn't deign to answer. Howie got a whiff of the brothers then and took a step backward, nose wrinkling. "Jeeeeeesuz, I can feel my lungs melting down. Come on, Jim, you can't lock me up with that smell."

In fairness, Kate couldn't blame him. Weeks spent holing up at the hot springs without soap or running water had left the Johansen brothers smelling pretty ripe before Kate got there, and from what she'd seen in Tikani, she had some question as to their fidelity to personal hygiene anyway. Their subsequent reaction to apprehension hadn't helped.

"Where'd you find them?" Jim said, closing the door to his office.

"The hot springs."

"Really. Heard about them. Never been there. Kinda thought they were a myth."

"No," Kate said, pulling first one arm past the opposite shoulder, and then the other. Her joints popped in protest. "They're real all right." She jumped up to grab the trim over the office door, and hung there, letting her spine unkink, while she counted to thirty. "Hard to find, is all, and you can pretty much only get there in winter, unless you want to spend a month bushwhacking through the undergrowth with a machete. I'll take you up there sometime if you want to see it."

"Sure." He sat down. "They confess?"

She relaxed into the chair opposite him. "To what?"

"To anything," he said dryly. "They look pretty beat up, Kate."

"I know," Kate said. "I didn't do that."

"What did you do?"

She told him. When he stopped laughing he said, "Okay. You didn't whale on them. Who did?"

She gave him a look.

"Yeah," he said, "we don't have to talk about that right now. Or maybe ever. So did they confess to anything?"

She shook her head. "Ick shut up Gus and Dead. You should probably separate them."

"I've only got two cells."

"Not my problem," she said. "My work here is done."

285

"Need a statement." He opened a document on his computer and gave her an expectant look. She sighed and started talking. Half an hour and some questions later he printed it out and she signed it. By way of payback she made him type up an invoice from Kate Shugak to the Department of Public Safety for services rendered and made him sign it in front of her. "Okay," she said, rising to her feet, "absent any further objection, I'm headed for the barn and a hot shower and a hot meal, and then I'm going to bed."

"Kate."

She turned, hand on the doorknob. "What?"

"Nice job." He smiled.

She smiled back, smug. "I know."

Outside, enough of the crowd remained to offer up another round of applause, approving comments, and pats on the back. Mutt stalked next to her, tongue lolling out in a canine grin, receiving her share of adulation with less than appropriate humility. George Perry was there, laughing out loud, Demetri Totemoff with one of his rare smiles creasing his dark face, Laurel Meganack and her father, who looked less than thrilled, Old Sam, Keith Gette, and Oscar Jimenez. Kate realized that they must have hit town the same time as the mail plane. At the edge of the crowd she saw the four aunties, huddled together, chirping away at each other in whispers. Auntie Joy saw her looking at them and the usual radiant smile faltered at Kate's expression. She said something and the other three aunties turned to look at Kate.

She returned their gaze for a long moment, her eyes traveling from one face to another. Auntie Edna, the bully, strong, unyielding, always right, always willing to say so, always with that anger simmering away beneath the surface. Auntie Balasha, the sentimentalist, soft, tender, a heart made for unconditional love. Auntie Joy, the idealist, who saw good in everything, impervious to evil.

And Auntie Vi, the independent businesswoman, the entrepreneur, the capitalist, the hard-eyed realist who knew stability, accountability, and transparency were essential to increase business to, from, and within the Park and who knew they would come only with a steady hand on the Park's tiller, and so much the better if it was the hand of her choice.

All four pairs of eyes bored into her back as she mounted her snow machine, called to Mutt, and left.

She didn't go as advertised, though, instead cutting through the village and following the track about a quarter of a mile downriver. She pulled up in front of a two-story house with blue vinyl siding, black shingles, and a deck the width of the house that faced the river. Safely above its frozen surface, a handsome drift netter called the *Audra Sue* sat in dry dock.

There were four snow machines in the shed at the side of the house, along with some other interesting items. Kate climbed the stairs to the deck and banged on the door. She had to repeat the action a second and a third time before Matt Grosdidier, his shiner somewhat less spectacular now, poked his head outside. "Kate?" he said, sounding dazed. "What the hell time is it?"

"Late enough to come calling," she said, shouldering her way inside. "Get your brothers up." He stared at her, his hair flattened on one side and a pillow crease on his cheek. "Go on," she said, "go get them. This won't take long."

She gave him a hard look that propelled him upstairs, and a moment later she heard him thumping doors and calling his brothers' names. In the meantime, she looked around her at the chaos that was the Grosdidier en famille. Their front room looked like a larger version of Johnny's room. She shuddered.

In short order they were assembled before her, wary at this home invasion and assuming an early morning grouchiness to cover it up.

Without preamble she said, "Whose idea was it to go after the Johansens?"

Luke, Peter, and Mark looked at Matt, who grinned. "Don't know what you're talking about, Kate."

"I'm not looking to jam you up here," she said. "I'm just looking to fit in another piece of the puzzle. You four are looking like ten rounds with Muhammad Ali. The Johansens are looking like fifteen with Mike Tyson. Seems reasonable to suppose the two groups might have encountered each other recently."

Luke, Peter, and Mark looked at Matt again. It wasn't that they couldn't all speak, it was just that Matt was oldest. It was habit, mostly. He'd been the only one of legal age when their father's boat had gone down off Gore Point with their mother on board, and he'd raised the other three, seeing them safely through puberty and high school, working as a deckhand until he'd saved enough money to buy a boat so he could work his father's drift permit with his brothers as deckhands.

She looked them over dispassionately. They were an attractive bunch, medium height inherited from their French father, black hair inherited from their Aleut mom, ruddy outdoor skin and dark, merry eyes. They were loud and boisterous and good-humored, and they fought each other with enthusiasm, until one was attacked by some clueless other, and then the four of them united to annihilate him with even more enthusiasm. They were fair about it, they cheerfully patched up whoever they beat the snot out of, but Jim Chopin had been known to observe that these occasional contretemps appeared to be more a matter of drumming up EMT business than of wreaking vengeance.

They seemed to have adopted the Park as a fifth sibling since they'd all four graduated from the EMT class, however. Kate, looking past Matt, saw a framed copy of the Hippocratic oath hanging crookedly on the wall, surrounded by a bunch of family pictures.

She sighed. "Did you bait them out? I saw the sled with the supplies packed into it in the garage. I also noticed that all the boxes
were empty."

"You're a snoop, Kate Shugak," Matt said without heat.

"Yes, I am, Matt Grosdidier," Kate said. "Did one of you bait
them out and the rest of you jump them when they bit?"

He looked at his brothers. "If we did, so what? Boys needed a
whupping." He looked back at her. "And at the time it didn't look
like anyone else was going to give them one."

Kate ignored the unspoken implication. "So you stepped up."

He shrugged. "Even if we did, and I'm not saying that, it didn't
do a whole lot of good, now, did it? They jumped that guy from Anchorage."

"So it doesn't count if it didn't work?"

He didn't answer.

"Will you tell me one thing?" she said. "Was it your idea?"

His eyes shifted. "I don't know what you mean, Kate."

The Johansen brothers emphatically, categorically, and compre-
hensively deny killing Talia Macleod," Jim said that evening.

"Of course they do," Kate said.

"They say they didn't kill Mac Devlin, either."

"Of course they do," Kate said again. She was stretched out on
the couch with a copy of Christopher Hitchens's latest polemic
against all gods, all faiths, and all those who sailed in them. Since she
agreed with every word he said, naturally she considered it a work of
genius, and she wanted to get back to it. Besides, she had a feeling
that this conversation was going to do nothing but go around and
around, like a snake chasing its own tail and eventually eating itself.
Serene in her ignorance of Jim thinking the same thing about a previous conversation, she said with as much disinterest as she could in-
fuse into the words, "What else would you expect them to say?"

He hung coat and cap and toed off his Sorels. "Nothing," he said, staring at his feet with dissatisfaction.

"They cop to the river attacks?"

"Yes."

"The last guy, whatshisname, too?"

"Gene Daly. Yeah, him, too. All of them, no problem there." Mutt extricated herself from the quilt in front of the fire and bounded over for reassurance that she still occupied the first and largest place in his heart.

"I can imagine," Kate said, very dry. All Jim would have had to do was tell the Johansen brothers they were going down for murder one and they would have confessed to anything else going on anywhere else in order to get out from under. "Ick do most of the talking?"

"Ick did all of the talking. Doesn't he always?" Jim gave Mutt a final scratch between the ears and stood up. "Kid home?"

"Studying in his room."

"Am I cooking tonight?"

She went back to her book. The Old Testament was a scary place, although the New Testament might be even scarier. "Did you know that hell and damnation aren't mentioned by any of the Old Testament prophets?"

"Really?"

"Nope. Oh, they'd sell their daughters to angry mobs in exchange for their own safety and they'd slaughter opposing tribes by the thousand, but after that they were pretty much done. It's only Jesus who preaches hell and damnation in the afterlife if you don't believe in him."

By this time Jim had deduced that if he wanted to eat, he was, in fact, cooking dinner that evening. Unperturbed, he went to the kitchen and as he expected, found a package of caribou steaks thawing in the sink and bread rising in a bowl. He opened the refrigerator and with great contentment found a six-pack of Alaskan

Amber. Kate wouldn't bring home beer for just anyone. He un-capped a bottle and took a long swallow. "I made a bunch of calls the last couple of days. It turns out, our Talia got around."

Kate peered at him over the top of her book. "Do tell."

He nodded, put down the beer, and started chopping onions. "We all know there were enough Park rats around who wanted to take her down because of the mine," he said, pouring olive oil into a cast-iron frying pan and turning the heat on beneath it. "And let's face it, you didn't help."

That brought her upright, book discarded. "I beg your pardon?"

He shrugged. "You straddled the fence on the mine at the last NNA board meeting. Because you didn't vote to throw the bastards out, some people could get the impression that Talia was a serious threat to the Park and to their way of life." He looked up and met her eyes. "You could have helped make her a target, Kate."

She didn't go immediately on offense, which surprised and re-lieved him. He needed her as a sounding board and it wouldn't help the discussion along if she got too mad to listen.

She sat in frowning silence for a moment. He tilted the cutting board over the frying pan and used the knife to push the onions into the oil. They sizzled. He stirred them with a wooden spoon.

"Okay, say that's true," she said. "Let's leave that for the mo-ment, and you tell me about these calls you made."

He flattened some cloves of garlic, peeled them, and minced them. "Talia was a busy girl."

"Busy how?" Kate said, alert to the change in his tone.

"Busy between the sheets."

"Takes one to know one."

He looked at her, a steady, unflinching gaze.

She could feel the color rising into her cheeks. She looked down, picking up her book and smoothing the cover unnecessarily, mum-bling something that might have been "Sorry."

The onions were beginning to brown and he added the garlic, stirring it in and leaving it over the heat just long enough to perfume the oil. "Understand that all I've been doing is gathering information," he said, using a slotted spoon to move them to a saucer. "Can't dignify much of it as more than gossip." There might have been an added bite to that last sentence. Mutt, having resumed her position in front of the fire, flicked her ears.

Kate's lips pressed together but she didn't say anything.

"The word is she was sleeping with both the mayor of Cordova and the manager of the Costco store in Ahtna. Plus I think she gave Gallagher a tumble, too."

"The mayor of Cordova is married," Kate said, making an effort to keep her voice neutral.

"Yeah," Jim said, "I don't think that mattered much to Talia." He took a deep breath and said, "She hit on me, too. When I was in Cordova, putting Margaret Kvasnikof and Hally Smith on the plane for Hiland Mountain."

"Oh," Kate said inadequately.

The hard part out of the way, he took another deep breath and let it out. "I also got Brendan to find out who was her attorney. I called him, and after he swore me to secrecy he told me that she had a chunk of nonvoting stock in Global Harvest."

"Part of the paycheck," Kate said. She felt a little light-headed, and forced herself to focus.

"Yeah, but. There's a weirdness."

"Which is?"

"These particular shares are held by a limited group of Global Harvest stockholders. They own their shares for the period of their lifetimes in joint rights of survivorship, accruing all dividends generated by those shares to themselves. But they can't sell them or trade them or leave them to anyone else. Once they die, the shares revert to the other partners."

Kate digested this in silence for a moment. "So her relatives don't inherit, beyond what she'd already earned?"

"Nope."

"Which puts any of them out of the running."

"Normally I'd say not unless they knew, but it turns out they did know. Part of the deal that employees at that level make when they sign on with Global Harvest is they also have to sign an affidavit saying they so informed their nearest and dearest, with registered copies going out to and signed for by all of same."

Kate said admiringly, "So Global Harvest pays you well—"

Jim put his head back and gave forth with a long, loud wolf whistle.

"—okay, extremely well, so long as you're alive, but they don't have to worry about the shareholders getting uppity and voting the board out of office during that time, and they don't have to worry about who the stock goes to once you're dead, averting an unfriendly takeover. All the shareholders get is the money, no voice."

"You got it."

"Is that legal?"

"Brendan says it's a contract, and everyone who signed off on it was of legal age. He says if you had a cranky enough heir it could be tested in court, but . . ."

"Man. I wonder how the shareholders of the Niniltna Native Association would like that. All the money and no voice."

"Everyone in this particular group of shareholders is also doing a job of work for the company," Jim said. "Talia was drawing a hefty salary. The shares were just a bonus."

Kate detected a possible hitch. "Do they keep the stock even if they quit the company?"

"They keep it and any dividends the stock pays until they die," Jim said, "whether they're working for Global Harvest or not. The stock reverts to the company. The earnings to date then go to their heirs."

Kate stood up, her book sliding to the floor. Her eyes were bright and she had the beginnings of a smile on her face. "It's a tontine."

Jim dredged the steaks in flour and salt and pepper and put them in the frying pan. The smell was instant and intoxicating and his mouth watered. He wrested his attention back from his appetite. "It's a what?"

"I read about it in a novel once." Kate got up and walked over to the kitchen, her nose almost twitching with interest. He hid a grin. Kate the detective in action. It was always fun to watch. Not to mention which, anything that diverted her from his little bombshell was bound to be a good thing.

"A tontine is a kind of contest," she said, "where a bunch of people pay into a kitty and whoever lives longest gets the dough."

"Whoa," he said, browning the steaks for a couple of minutes on either side.

"Yeah," she said, a smile spreading across her face. "Did you get the names of the other shareholders?"

"Why," he said, dragging the word out, "I just might have done that little thing."

He moved the steaks from pan to warming plate with care and deliberation.

"So?" she said. "Anybody we know on it?"

"One name kinda jumped out at me," he said. He poured a cup of chicken broth into the pan. "Is that leftover bottle of white wine still knocking around anywhere?"

TWENTY-FOUR

L ike I keep telling you, I was at the Roadhouse that night with my wife," Harvey Meganack said. "You can check. Must have been a hundred other people there. After that, we came right home. Didn't we, honey?"

The four of them were sitting in Harvey's front room, in the largest and newest house in Niniltna, the first one you saw when you drove in from Ahtna. The frozen surface of the Kanuyaq River was just on the other side of the dock that began down the stairs from the house and extended twenty-five feet out from the bank. It looked nowhere near as well used as the Grosdidiers' dock did, although the *Laurel M.* was in dry dock next to it, looking very fine in new white paint with blue trim.

Inside, everything was equally brand spanking new, and it all matched. The bright floral couch matched the bright floral love seat and the bright floral easy chair. The faux mahogany coffee table with the identically turned spiral legs matched the three end tables. Four matching brass lamps with white pleated shades and swing arms stood on either side of the couch and at exactly the same distance from the right arm of both the love seat and the easy chair, and everything in the room was placed at precise angles and a precise distance from everything else on the twelve-foot-square area rug, with colors that picked up the flowers on the couch, love seat, and easy chair.

Kate thought about the chaos of her own front room, the lone couch, the aunties' quilt crumpled on the floor before the fireplace, the mismatched bookshelves that lined one wall, the throw pillows of various sizes and ages and colors and patterns that lay where they fell, until someone came along and pulled them into a pile large enough to flop down on. Mutt didn't shed a lot but there was definite evidence of dog everywhere.

She wondered if she were suffering from house envy. She looked around the room again, and then back at Harvey, sitting on the extreme edge of the floral couch, sweating bullets. Next to him sat Iris, a pillar of rectitude, presently inflamed by Kate and Jim's presence in her hitherto pristine and perfect home.

Nope.

Everyone looked at her and she realized she'd said it out loud. She looked at Iris. "You sure you want to back him up on this, Iris?"

"Why wouldn't I? It's the truth." She looked at Kate, not bothering to hide her resentment. She had wanted Harvey to be chair of the Niniltna Native Association board, primarily so she could be the wife of the chair of the board. If there could be said to be even one Park rat with a social agenda, that rat would be Iris Meganack. Kate realized for the first time that it was far more likely Iris who had spread the stories of Kate's first board meeting, not Harvey. Iris, motivated by malice and envy, would have no internal editor. Harvey, motivated by greed and ambition, would not want to be shoved out of the loop and therefore might think twice about pissing off the however temporary current board chair.

The door opened and Laurel Meganack walked in. Her eye lit upon Jim first and a smile spread across her face. "Jim, hey. What're you doing here?" She fluttered her eyelashes. "Asking Dad for my hand in marriage?"

She saw Kate. Her smile faded. "Oh. Hey, Kate."

"Hey, Laurel."

Laurel looked from Kate to Jim and to her parents as realization dawned. "Dad. What's going on here?"

"None of your business, Laurel," her mother said sharply. "What are you doing here?"

"I came to pick up some more of my stuff," Laurel said, still looking at Harvey. "Dad, is everything all right?"

"Of course everything's all right," Iris said. "Go get your stuff."

"Go ahead, honey," Harvey said, passing his sleeve across his forehead and managing a smile. "Everything's fine."

Laurel looked at Kate, no trace of smile present now, and her thoughts were transparent. *If you think you're going to hurt my dad, think again.* It made Kate think better of both of them.

Laurel left the room. Kate waited until she heard a door open and close, and said in a lowered voice, "You see how it looks, Harvey. Talia Macleod has stock in Global Harvest that reverts to the chunk of stock held by the other shareholders in her particular group. It bumps up everyone's portion, increases everyone's income. You're one of the shareholders, so far as we know the only one who is also a Park rat. So you have motive."

"I was at the Roadhouse the night she was killed," Harvey said. "Ask Bernie if you don't believe Iris. Ask Old Sam."

"You know how to drive a snow machine," Kate said as if she didn't hear him. "You know the way to Double Eagle. I'm sure you must have a few spools of monofilament lying around here somewhere."

"Ask the aunties," he said, "they were there. There's no way I could have left the Roadhouse and killed her and gotten back in time to come home with Iris."

297

"And he didn't leave," Iris said fiercely. "Instead of wasting your time harassing us why don't you go find the real killer?"

Kate looked at Jim and raised an eyebrow. Jim got to his feet. "All right, Harvey. We'll check your alibi. Don't leave the Park until you hear from me, okay?"

"How dare you—," Iris started to say, and Harvey grabbed her knee. "Don't, Iris." He looked up at Jim and nodded. "Okay."

Kate stood up and looked at Harvey's bent head until he felt it and looked up. "I want to know what Global Harvest hired you for, Harvey. The board's going to want to know, too. And when they hear about it, so are the shareholders."

"We can own stock in them if we want to!" Iris said shrilly. "It's none of your business! Who are you, Kate Shugak, to be asking? You live halfway to Ahtna in a house you didn't even pay for! You get a job you don't even know how to do, and instead of learning how you run around poking your nose into other people's business! Poking and prying, that's all you know how to do!"

"Nice seeing you again, Iris," Kate said, and followed Jim to the door. "Harvey, could you step outside for a minute? Board business, Iris. You understand."

Kate pulled the door shut firmly in the face of Iris's spluttering, and said bluntly, "You and Macleod were awful friendly at the board meeting in October, Harvey. Anything you want to tell us about that?"

He tried to bluster his way out of it. "I don't know what you're talking about, Kate. I'm a married man."

She looked at him. Jim stayed quiet.

Harvey's face reddened, and he cast an apprehensive look over his shoulder at the closed door. "Okay, maybe, once. It was just— It just happened one time when I was in Ahtna meeting with—" Too late he caught himself.

"Meeting with Macleod?" Kate said. "And maybe somebody else from Global Harvest?"

He stared at her, trapped.

She looked at Jim, who shrugged. "Think Iris is going to change her story?"

"She might if she knew Harvey'd been screwing Macleod. Iris can get a little proprietary."

Jim didn't doubt it for a moment.

"Jesus!" Harvey said in a whisper, casting another agonized glance over his shoulder. "You can't do that, Kate! Besides, I keep telling you, I didn't do it! And besides," he said, a sudden flash of intelligence piercing his panic, "why would I kill her if I was sleeping with her?"

Good question," Kate said back at the post.

"It's too good an alibi not to be true," Jim said.

"But you'll check anyway."

He nodded. "I'll check. In the meantime, you've got work to do."

"Really. Work for which I will be paid?"

She went directly to the airstrip, where she commandeered George and his Cessna, and flew to Cordova, where she tracked the mayor down at a Chamber of Commerce luncheon at the Elks Club. He paled when he saw her but he didn't object when she beckoned him out of the room. Lacking a better option, she barred them in the men's room and said point-blank, "Were you sleeping with Talia Macleod?"

He gulped and lost color but said baldly, "Yes."

She appreciated the no-frills reply. She appreciated further that he made no apologies and no explanations, and dealt with him more gently than she might have otherwise.

The affair had been short-lived, beginning the day of Talia's first visit to Cordova as the local rep for Global Harvest. The mayor, a tall fair man with blue eyes and a pink complexion, attractive but not overwhelmingly so, said that it amounted to half a dozen encounters over a couple of months, and faded out mostly from lack of opportunity and, Kate suspected, his own fear of discovery.

He'd been in Cordova at a basketball game the night Talia was killed in Double Eagle, accompanied by his wife and two youngest children. His oldest child, a son, was the star point guard for the Wolverines' varsity team.

"Thank you, Mr. Mayor," Kate said, and opened the door to the very irritated man who had been thumping on it for the past five minutes.

She went directly to the high school and spoke to a large, fair woman with flyaway blond hair and china blue eyes with the thickest, longest lashes Kate had ever seen. Chris confirmed that there had indeed been a varsity home game that night and that the mayor—and his wife—had been in the audience. Indeed she, Chris, had been in the same section of the bleachers, one row up, and had said hello to the mayor's family as they had come in.

Kate went to the Club Bar, where she found George simultaneously wolfing down a serving of fish and chips and hitting on the waitress. She interrupted this budding romance without compunction, and heard about it all the way to Ahtna, landing there as the last light leached from the sky.

They spent the night at the Lodge—any excuse for one of Stan's steak sandwiches—and were at the door of Costco when it opened the next morning. They sought out the manager, a short, square man with a twinkle in his brown eyes that complemented a broad smile, and a bushy crop of wayward hair that was graying at the temples.

Yes, he had heard of Talia's death, a shame, a young woman of so much talent and promise. Yes, he said, they had had a relationship, brief, mutually enjoyable, nothing serious. He'd been in Ahtna at work the night she had died. Kate checked with the staff at the store, who corroborated his statement. He was unmarried, he told her three or four times, and let her go with regret and a complimentary wedge of Cambozola cheese and a box of Bosc pears, enjoining her to drop by when she was next in town.

"I like the way you interrogate a suspect," George said when she loaded the loot in the back of the Cessna, but then he'd been doing some shopping of his own and the back of the Cessna was full.

They touched down on the airstrip in Niniltna at two o'clock that afternoon. Kate drove directly to the post, where Mutt, who hated being left behind, got up from her spot on the floor next to Jim's chair just so she could flounce around in a circle and thump down again with her back pointedly to Kate. And then she farted.

Jim reached behind him and opened a window. It must have been ten degrees outside, but it was necessary. "Anything?"

"Nothing," Kate said. "Mayor and manager both had affairs with Macleod. Mayor and wife have the same rock-solid alibi, son's basketball game, confirmed. Manager, single, was working that night, also confirmed."

Jim nodded. "It figures. They know if she was sleeping with anyone else?"

"I asked. The mayor said probably, the manager said maybe. It doesn't sound to me like anyone in pants was safe from Talia Macleod, married, single, old, young. Anything here?"

"Nothing new," he said.

He was a little tight-lipped. Kate could choose to believe it was because of her tone in speaking of Talia Macleod, who'd at least had the good taste to hit on him, too. She didn't say anything though, because she'd been where he was. The longer a murder went unsolved, the less likely it was ever to be solved. Practicing police officers hated mysteries. They especially hated mysteries that involved public figures.

"I'm for home," she said. "Don't be late, something special for dinner tonight."

TWENTY-FIVE

When he walked in the door there was a large plate with a wedge of some gooey blue cheese and a mound of toasted, salted walnuts, accompanied by a bowl of pears. There were napkins and paring knives at each place setting.

"No meat?" Jim said.

"Trust me," Kate said, and raised her voice. "Dinner!"

Johnny ambled down the hall and flopped into his chair. "What's this?"

"Cheese and fruit and nuts," Kate said. "Trust me."

Both of her men behaved as men will do and grumbled and whined and wrinkled their noses and shuffled their feet and implored the gods to explain why she was trying to starve them to death, but in the end plate and bowl were both empty.

"Okay, nice appetizer," Jim said, "what's for dinner?" He ducked out of the way of the thrown napkin as Johnny snickered.

"Oh well, if you insist," Kate said, and went into the kitchen and pulled a moose burger meatloaf and roast potatoes out of the oven, loftily ignoring the cheering section.

"You know," Jim said, sitting back from the table after the second course had likewise been cleared away, "this case is lousy with mo-tive. What it lacks is evidence. Well, except for the body."

Johnny watched and listened, his eyes following the conversa-tion from one face to the other and back again.

Kate nodded. "Talia could have had other lovers." He gave her his patented shark's grin, and unreasonably reassured, she said, "And much as I hate to say it, I think our killer is a Park rat. There are no strangers in town unaccounted for in the witness statements."

Johnny looked at Kate and opened his mouth, and then closed it again.

"My question is, do we still think the same person killed Mac as killed Talia?"

"Been thinking about that," Jim said. "What did they have in common? Global Harvest. Mac hated Global Harvest for ripping him off. But Talia was Global Harvest's point man in the Park. I don't know, Kate, if Talia had died before Mac, Mac would have had the hell of a motive for killing her."

"I don't see that," Kate said, frowning slightly. "Anyone could have told you that Mac was always a guy with an eye to the main chance. He was hoping to get more money out of Global Harvest for the Nabesna. Why would he kill the goose he was hoping would lay him a golden egg?"

"By the way, I heard from the crime lab as I was leaving the post today. Howie's rifle didn't fire the bullet that killed Mac Devlin."

"Really. What a shame."

"Yeah, that's what I said. Or something like it." He paused. "What I'd like to do is charge him with the murder of Louis Deem."

Kate looked at him. "Are you going to?"

"I said what I'd like to do. Louis was killed with a shotgun, and I didn't get enough evidence at the scene even to guess at how tall the perp was. Let alone who he was."

"There's the tire print at the scene. You matched it to Howie's truck."

"Yeah, but as Howie, the little weasel, points out, there isn't a Park rat who doesn't leave his keys in the truck when he gets out. Doesn't matter if it's at the store, the post office, the café, the Roadhouse, the school, home."

Kate remembered taking the key of her snow machine with her when she'd stopped to see Vidar. One time in how many years? Maybe her lifetime?

"Anyone could have driven off in his truck. And the tire track alone won't make a conviction, as Judge Singh was pleased to tell me."

"She wasn't pleased," Kate said.

Jim, a little ashamed of himself, said, "I know. I'm just—"

"I know," Kate said.

"Kate?" Johnny said.

"And I told you, Howie's reneging his confession all over the place anyway."

"And the aunties? What was the story they told you?"

"Pretty much the same one they told you," Jim said, unsmiling. "To a woman, they are shocked, shocked at the very idea of such a thing. Auntie Balasha says Howie must be mistaken, and she bawls when she says so." He shuddered. "Auntie Edna says he's full of shit. Auntie Joy says he was such a handsome little boy, she can hardly look at him without smiling at the memory."

"And Auntie Vi?"

"Auntie Vi told me to tend to my business and the aunties would tend to theirs."

"Ouch."

"Yeah."

"Was it just a story, then? Howie made it up?"

Jim thought of Bernie. "I don't know, Kate. I wish I did."

"Kate!"

They both looked at Johnny in mild surprise. "There's no need to shout, kid," Kate said. "Something on your mind?"

Now that he finally had the floor, Johnny seemed reluctant to talk.

"Spit it out," Kate said. "Van's not pregnant, is she?"

Johnny blushed beet red. "No! No, it's nothing like that. Jeez, Kate."

"Sorry," Kate said, sounding less than repentant. "What's up?"

"There's something I've been wanting to tell you for a long time," Johnny said, and again seemed incapable of saying more.

"You're flunking physics," Kate said.

"No, Kate, stop it! It's that guy."

"What guy?"

"That guy, Gallagher."

This was so far removed from the topic at hand that Kate was at first wholly at sea. "Huh? Who?"

"The new guy?" Jim said.

"Yeah, or he was last fall, anyway," Johnny said. "He showed up in September. Van and I ran into him in Ahtna."

Kate sat up. "When did you and Van run into him in Ahtna?"

He looked at her, caught off guard. "I . . . I . . . it was after we brought the truck home." He could see the thunderheads darkening and he cringed.

"You skipped school," she said in a level voice.

His own voice was very small in reply. "Yes."

"And you went to Ahtna without permission."

"Yes."

"And you took Van with you."

"Yes."

"Your name is Johnny Morgan, prepare to die," Jim said in a fake Spanish accent.

Johnny swallowed hard and risked another look at Kate. "I know you're mad, Kate, but we need to talk about that later. The thing is, I know this guy."

"We all know him now, Johnny," Kate said. "Well, it's not like he's a fixture, but we've all met him by now. He didn't run screaming at the first snow, so I'm willing to give him the benefit of the doubt. Let's see if he makes it through the whole winter."

"Kate!"

"Sorry, sorry." Kate bent her head but Jim could see the corners of her mouth indent. Johnny would pay for skipping school, but that would be later, and she did so love giving the kid a ride.

"I know him," Johnny said again. "I rode with him."

That brought Kate's head up again, all traces of the smile erased. "What do you mean?"

"On the way here. I rode with him."

"From Phoenix? When you hitched home?"

"Yeah."

Kate stared at him out of narrow eyes, long enough to make him want to squirm some more. He didn't, but it was a near thing. "Did he threaten you? Harm you in any way?"

"No! No, nothing like that, Kate, I promise."

Jim saw Kate's breast rise and fall on a long, silent sigh. "So you know him. He gave you a ride. He didn't hurt you. He also didn't turn you over to the nearest cop shop, which he should have. Although I can't say, when all's said and done, that I'm sorry he didn't."

"Me, neither," Johnny said, with emphasis.

"So what?" Kate said. "Other than the fact that I should look this guy up and thank him for taking you from—outside Phoenix?—to where?"

"All the way to Seattle."

At that Kate did look impressed. "Wow. Okay, that was a nice big chunk of the journey out of the way." And a long way out of his mother's reach. "We owe him, no question. What, you want us to give him some moose? I could make him fry bread. Does he need a job? Or no, wait, he's got one."

"That's not all there is to it," Johnny said miserably. "There's something else. Something I should have told you when he first came to the Park."

They left Kate's snow machine in front of the trooper post and walked the rest of the way to Auntie Vi's. It was full dark and cold with it, and their breath frosted on the air and their boots squeaked on the road no matter how stealthy they tried to be. By contrast Mutt skimmed soundlessly over the snow, drifting in and out of the shadows like a ghost.

Auntie Vi's house was on the uphill road between the village and the airstrip, just up from Bingley's store and just down from the trooper post. It was a sturdy, practical, two-story home that Auntie Vi, a sturdy, practical, and entrepreneurial woman, had built specifically for a bed and breakfast. It was, so far, the only place to rent a room in Niniltna proper, but to be fair, Auntie Vi didn't short her customers just because they had no choice in the matter. Her mattresses were new, her sheets clean, her pillows soft, and her meals as good or better than what you got at the Riverside Café. There was a common room with squashy couches and chairs, a television and a DVD player with an extensive library of films, a bookshelf full of books, a pile of board games, and a desk.

"How many people has she got staying there at present?" Kate said, her voice a whisper of sound.

"I don't know," Jim said. "I'm hardly ever here. Have you met Gallagher?"

"Yeah."

"What did you think?"

"I could feel my Spidey sense tingling. You?"

"I thought he was bent. No more or less bent than anyone else who comes into the Park, you understand. You know how it is, Kate. Lots of people come to Alaska on the run from something. Wives, cops, job. Traffic. You heard the story Gallagher—do we call him Greenbaugh now?—you heard the story he spun Johnny. Could be true."

"You didn't check him out?"

Again with the shrug. "No reason to so long as he kept his nose clean in the Park. I'm not one for borrowing trouble. There's plenty of it already on offer."

"Grim but true," Kate said. "Why didn't you do a wants and warrants on him before we came?"

"I'd rather talk to him first, get a feel. If I think he'll bolt, I'll grab him up for twenty-four. Be easier to run a search with prints anyway."

"But I notice we're whispering," she said. "Also tiptoeing."

"Girls tiptoe. Guys sneak."

They came to Auntie Vi's driveway, overgrown with spruce and alder and birch and fireweed and way too much devil's club. Unless it was edible, Auntie Vi didn't care enough about landscaping other than to keep the driveway clear enough to drive on.

There was a light on in the living room. The front door was unlocked, as usual, and Jim led the way in. "Stay," Kate said to Mutt, and followed.

The living room was empty. So was the kitchen. So was Auntie Vi's little suite in back of the kitchen.

They went upstairs. "Which one is his?" Kate said.

Jim nodded at a door and Kate tried the handle. "Locked."

They stood side by side looking at the door with, had they but known it, identical speculative looks on their faces. "I know where the keys to the rooms are," Kate said.

"So do I." He looked at her. "I'm a practicing professional police officer. I need a warrant."

She made a face and went downstairs, returning a few moments later with a key. She inserted it into the lock and the door opened smoothly, as any door installed beneath Auntie Vi's auspices would have if it knew what was good for it.

The room held a full-size bed with a nightstand and a lamp next to it, a dresser with four drawers, and an easy chair grouped with a floor lamp and an end table. A tiny bathroom with a toilet, a sink, and a shower was tucked behind a door between dresser and chair. Outside the window spruce branches brushed the glass with scratchy fingers.

"Not a neatnik," Jim said from the doorway.

"Looks like Johnny's room," Kate said. "Or the Grosdidiers' house."

"Huh?"

"Never mind."

The bed was a jumble of blankets and sheets, socks and underwear spilled out of an open drawer, dirty clothes were tossed in a corner. Crumpled beer cans had missed the wastebasket.

Kate made a quick circuit. "No letters, bills, mail of any kind. Stack of these, big surprise." She held up a fistful of copies of the latest Global Harvest flyer.

"When did Johnny say Gallagher showed up?"

"September."

"Four months. Long time to go without paying a bill."

"Auntie Vi would have kicked him out if he hadn't been paying his here." Jim looked over his shoulder. "What?"

"Thought I heard something."

"Mutt's outside."

"Right. Gallagher own a vehicle?"

"A pickup, Johnny said."

"Global Harvest would have given him a company snow machine for the river trip."

"Yeah, he had his own when I saw them leaving for the trip on the river. Wasn't any snow machine outside."

Kate looked under the bed, and pulled out a large duffel bag, black and red and worn at the seams. "Padlocked." She slung the bag over to the door. Jim got out his key ring, selected a slender tool, and bent over the lock. It took about two seconds. "Pitiful. No wonder it's TSA approved." He shoved the bag back at her.

She unzipped the bag and looked inside. She looked inside for so long that he said, "What?"

"Who's dealing coke in the Park these days?"

She dragged the bag back over to him and they both looked down at the Ziploc with the white powder inside it.

"Open it up," Jim said.

Kate did, and Jim licked his little finger, dipped, and tasted. "Yeah. Coke."

"Isn't full, either."

"I noticed."

"That's a lot for personal consumption."

"I noticed that, too."

"Maybe my question is, who's using in the Park these days, and who's supplying?" She looked at Jim.

"I haven't heard anything. Even Howie seems to have stopped dealing lately." He thought. "Actually, I haven't heard of him dealing anything since before Louis died."

"Me, either." She nodded at the Ziploc. "But one of us would have heard if Gallagher was dealing."

Too late, they both remembered that Kate had been left out of the loop on the assaults on the river. "You'd think so," he said, voice carefully neutral.

"Shit." Kate rested her elbows on her knees. "Would you like me to investigate further, officer?"

"Can't use any of it as evidence."

"Fruit of the poisoned tree," she said. "Still." She reached in the bag and moved the Ziploc to one side. "Well, well."

"What?"

She pulled out a wad of bills fastened together with a rubber band.

There were a dozen more. All the bills looked well-used. Like maybe Gallagher had been taking payments in cash for something he was selling.

Kate repacked the bag, relocked the lock, and restowed the duffel beneath the bed. She rose to her feet, dusting her hands and knees. "Now what?"

"Well," Jim said, "we know more than we did before. We know Gallagher's running under an assumed name, and we know he is or was dealing coke."

"Doesn't mean he killed Mac or Macleod."

"No. Does Auntie Vi ever make her guests fill out any kind of form?"

She looked at him. "Did she make you fill out one?"

"No." He smiled down at her. "But that's me."

She rolled her eyes. "As long as their check or Visa card clears the bank, she doesn't care who they are or where they come from."

They closed the door and locked it and put the key back on the hook in the kitchen. Kate, unable to help herself, made a beeline for the flying pig cookie jar on the counter. No-bake cookies today. Kate took one, put the lid back, and then took the lid off again and took one more.

Auntie Vi's counters, while scrupulously clean, were barely visible beneath the detritus of her life, of which the flying pig was only one manifestation. There was a stack of unread *Alaska Fisherman's Journals*, another of legislative circulars that had been heavily notated and highlighted in yellow. She had three sets of canisters, one brass, one bright blue enamel, the third Lucite. A knife block bristled with knife handles, there was a beer box full of bright squares of fabric, a copy of *The Fannie Farmer Cookbook* on a stand, open to a scone recipe.

Kate sorted idly through a large shallow wicker basket that held a jumble of those tools essential to everyday civilized life. Pens, pencils, a Frosty the Snowman notepad, a handful of Hershey's Nuggets, a tape measure, an oven mitt, pushpins, safety pins, paper clips. There was a *Camelot* CD (original cast, Auntie Vi was a known Robert Goulet enthusiast). There were twist ties, a roll of duct tape, a roll of electrician's tape, a roll of Scotch tape, a spool of string.

Under the roll of duct tape she found a small untidy ball of green monofilament. "Hey," she said.

"Wait a minute." Jim was looking at the calendar hanging on Auntie Vi's wall. It was a big one, featuring gorgeous photographs of the Hawaiian Islands. The month pages featured large squares for the dates. There was something written in almost all of them, bake sales, basketball games, due dates for Park rat soon-to-be moms.

"Look at this." He turned his head and she held up the monofil-ament. "He eats breakfast in this kitchen every morning."

"Uh-huh," he said. "Look at this." He pointed at that day's date.

She followed his forefinger to the entry. "GH mtg, RC, 7pm." She looked up at him. "Global Harvest, Riverside Café?"

"Let's go see."

They parked in the store's parking lot and walked but they needn't have bothered. There was almost no one parked out front of the café. Kate sighed.

"What?"

"If Global Harvest stays on this mission of all information, all the time, people are bound to get bored and wander off."

"Think that's their plan?"

"It'd be mine, if I wanted to put in a strip mine in Iqaluk and I knew it was going to piss off a lot of people in the Park."

Jim held the door for her. "Stay," she said to Mutt, and went in.

Inside, Laurel Meganack was drying glasses behind the counter. She gave Jim a flat, inimical stare. She wouldn't even look at Kate. Maybe a dozen people were gathered around the corner table. Gallagher was on his feet, talking animatedly as he pointed to a map of the Park he'd taped to the wall. He looked up and his voice faltered when he saw Kate and Jim. Heads turned.

"Hey, Dick," Jim said.

"Sergeant Chopin," Gallagher said.

"Or should I say Doyle," Jim said.

"Who?" Gallagher said, but he waited a beat too long.

"Got a few questions for you," Jim said. "If you could come on down to the post, I'd appreciate it."

Gallagher looked past Jim at Kate, and whatever he saw in her face made the rest of the color drain from his own. "Sure," he said, "no problem. Just let me get my coat."

He turned and reached for the coat lying over the back of a chair. As he did so Kate hit Jim with a low tackle behind the knees and the bullet from the Sig Sauer P220 Compact only knocked the ball cap from his head and shattered the window in the door. From the other side of the door Mutt uttered a series of outraged barks.

There were screams and shouts and chairs scraping and bodies hitting the floor, and then another loud crash when a second window went. Kate and Jim were on their feet and looking at the broken window at the end of the counter Gallagher had evidently dived through. Jim started forward and Kate turned and hit the front door. "Mutt!"

Mutt was quivering with rage, teeth bared in a vulpine snarl. She snapped and growled, dancing around Kate. She didn't like people shooting at her. "Come on!"

Kate ran around the back of the café just in time to see Jim finish knocking the rest of the glass out of the frame and jump outside. "Which way?" Something sang by her ear, followed by the distinctive crack of the Sig. "Fuck!

Jim had his 9mm out. "Stay back!"

"Like hell!"

"Goddammit, Kate, you're not armed!"

"Like hell!"

There was the sound of rapidly receding footsteps and Kate went after them, Mutt shooting past her, a gray streak with her head lowered between her shoulders, long legs eating up the ground, and a feral and terrifying growl issuing from her throat.

They all heard the snow machine start, and rounded a corner in time to see Gallagher start off on somebody's dark blue Polaris.

"Kate!"

"Mutt! Take!"

The gray streak that was Mutt seemed to flatten out and gather speed. The snow machine had to slow for a second to take the corner of the Kvasnikof home and as it did Mutt launched herself in mid-lope and hit Gallagher in the back with all of her not inconsiderable weight. Gallagher rolled from the seat and went tumbling head over heels. Mutt did a kind of mid-air jackknife to make a four-point landing, falling over Gallagher like a net, teeth bared and snapping inches from his face. He froze in place, and then the hand that was still somehow holding the Sig raised it and squeezed.

"Goddammit!" Jim said, and dived, landing on his belly with an ungraceful flop and skidding three feet farther on the snow and ice. Ahead of him, Kate had dodged behind the Kvasnikof house. The bullet hit the house next to her with a deafening bang and startled cries issued forth from all around them.

Mutt went ballistic. She snarled and bit Gallagher on the face, tearing skin and drawing blood, and then she went for his gun hand. Thirty feet away Jim could hear the crunch of bones breaking.

Gallagher shrieked and dropped the Sig. Kate ran out from behind the Kvasnikofs' and scooped up the Sig on the fly, and by the time she slowed forward momentum Mutt had her teeth on Gallagher's throat, that slow, steady, emasculating growl issuing from her own. He made one feeble effort to shove her away. Her jaws closed tighter and she shook her head. He screamed, or tried to. The result was a garbled, gargling sound.

Jim got to his feet. "Kate. Call her off."

"Why?" Kate said, torn between fright and fury. She didn't like getting shot at, either.

"Kate."

"Oh, all right. Mutt, release. Mutt! Mutt, release! Come on, girl, it's okay. Get off him. Off, Mutt, now!"

Mutt looked up at Kate, her jaws bloody from Gallagher's face, wrist, and throat, still that steady rumble, like tank tracks, issuing forth.

Kate grabbed Mutt's ears and shoved her down to the ground, her face right in Mutt's, her own bared teeth inches from Mutt's throat. "No! No! Release, I said! Release!"

"Jesus, Kate," Jim said, shaken.

Inexplicably, Mutt went motionless. Jim wasn't even sure she was still breathing.

For a long moment the three of them remained frozen in place, to the accompaniment of Gallagher crying and whimpering in the background. Jim couldn't say he blamed him much.

A soft, conciliatory whine sounded. Mutt stuck out a long pink tongue and washed Kate's cheek.

"All right then." Kate released her. They both got to their feet. Mutt shook herself and gave another ingratiating whine, touching her nose to Kate's hand. Kate cuffed her and Mutt cringed and whined again. "Oh shut up, you big baby," Kate said, and gave her a rough caress. Mutt bounced in place, yipped, and wagged an ingratiating tail.

"Holy shit," Jim said.

"No big," Kate said. She shook her hair out of her eyes, feeling suddenly, debilitatingly weary. "Once in a while I have to remind her who's still the alpha dog in the pack. She is half wolf, you know."

Nevertheless, Jim made a big circle around the both of them when he went to peel Gallagher off the ground.

TWENTY-SIX

The cells at the post were getting crowded. "It's time for you to go home, Howie," Jim said. "I've sent word for Willard to come get you."

Howie looked torn between being booted out and scared that his life might still be at risk. "You don't think I killed Mac Devlin anymore," he said, a little crestfallen.

"Sorry, no," Jim said, pushing Howie in front of him. "Ballistics say you didn't. Not with your own rifle, at any rate."

"Well, I didn't kill him. I didn't kill Louis, either, Jim."

Jim looked down at him. It was hard to detect truth from bullshit with Howie Katelnikof. The shifty eyes, the sly face, the involuntary instinct to lie his way out of every situation, all these were Howie to the bone and none of them inspired confidence. "You told me the aunties hired you to kill him. Was that true?"

Howie sent an uneasy glance down the hall to where the three Johansens were still smelling up the jail and the cell across the hall where Gallagher had taken Howie's place. He was stretched out on the bunk and was attended by all four Grosdidier brothers, who were in hog heaven at the amount of bandages that were going to be required. "We might even need a Life Flight!" Luke said, ecstatic.

In the other direction Maggie was visible through the doorway, sitting at her desk and pretending her boss wasn't having a whispered conversation with Howie Katelnikof. "Off the record, Jim?"

Jim looked at the ceiling and thought about it. If the aunties had hired Howie to kill Louis and he had, Howie would be guilty of murder and the aunties of conspiracy to commit. If the aunties had hired Howie to kill Louis and he hadn't, all four would still be guilty of conspiracy to commit.

Of course, any charges would be contingent upon Jim's ability to prove said charges in a court of law. With the aunties' unparalleled ability to stonewall so amply demonstrated of late, see Kate Shugak here, he didn't look forward to any conversation upon that topic with Judge Singh. On the other hand, Howie's understanding of "off the record," like his understanding of "immunity," came more from television than hands-on experience. "Okay," he said mendaciously. "Off the record."

Howie leaned in and said in a voice just above a whisper, "They did hire me to kill him. The aunties. I told you the truth about that."

"Uh-huh," Jim said. "And did you? Kill Louis?"

Howie shook his head vigorously. "No, Jim. No, I told you, I didn't. For one thing, I didn't have a shotgun with me that day."

"How did you know he was killed with a shotgun?" Jim said. "Very few people know that, Howie."

Howie's voice dropped even lower. "Like I told you before. Because I saw him."

Jim looked down at him, considering. "I remember. You said you found Louis dead on the road to the Step."

"Yeah." Howie swallowed and looked a little sick. "Yeah. I was driving out the road and he was just lying there. I pulled over and I got out and he was just . . . lying there, with his chest all blown open. Gut shot." He shuddered.

"Uh-huh," Jim said again. "What were you doing on the road to the Step that day, Howie?"

"I was supposed to pick up Louis when you let him out of jail," Howie said. "He was already gone when I got here. I knew he'd be mad I wasn't here on time, and he told me he had to talk to Ranger Dan, so I figured I'd find him on the road." He swallowed again. "And I did."

Jim took down Howie's statement, for what it was worth, and, after an internal debate that lasted a good five minutes, went ahead and released Howie into Willard's tearful arms. Willard probably hadn't eaten a decent meal since Howie went inside.

"Hey, Howie," Jim said, as they were leaving. "Who was that poaching caribou with you up Gruening River way?"

Howie hesitated, and then shrugged. Loyalty was never one of Howie's strong suits. "Martin Shugak."

"You already told me that, Howie. There was someone else, though, wasn't there? I saw a third rig under the trees."

"Fuck," Howie said, disgusted. "Al Sheldon."

Not one of the usual suspects, but the name nevertheless sounded familiar to Jim. He tried to track it down in his memory and came up empty.

There were two reasons he let Howie go. For one thing, he needed the cell. For another, if Howie hadn't fled the Park before this, chances were he wasn't going anywhere now. Still, Jim called Kenny Hazen and asked him to keep an eye out for Howie and Willard in Ahtna, just in case.

At some point he was going to have to talk to the aunties again. By rights, as a practicing policeman, he should bring them all in for questioning. He was already guilty of dereliction of duty by leaving it this long.

Although he had been busy, no denying that. Gallagher's prints had gone out before midnight, and before eight the next morning there was a match. Dick Gallagher was Doyle Greenbaugh, all right, and he was wanted for questioning for a double homicide at a truck stop outside of Boise, Idaho.

Johnny stopped by on the way to school and on Google Earth identified the truck stop as one of the stops Gallagher had made on their way north. "Here's the newspaper story about it," Jim said, handing him a printout.

BOISE, ID (AP): Two bodies were found in the parking lot of the Riders of the Purple Sage Truck Stop on Franklin Road, Caldwell, a suburb of Boise, early this morning. The first victim was a white male in his early forties, the second a white male in his teens; they have been identified as Dennis McMillian, a local businessman, and his fourteen-year-old son, Mark, both on a routine early morning walk with their dog, Rusty. Police say both appeared to have been shot by a large-caliber handgun, the elder victim in the chest and the younger in the back some distance away. Rusty was crouched next to the younger victim when the bodies were found.

"The incidence of violent crime has only been increasing on I-84 over the last ten years," said Representative Cole Blanchette (R-Boise) in an impromptu press conference near the scene yesterday morning. "It's what I've been trying to hammer home on the floor of the House every session, that we need an automatic death sentence for anyone convicted of committing a crime with a firearm."

An anonymous source in the police department said that traces of cocaine found near the bodies indicated that the two

victims may have interrupted a drug deal. The same anonymous source reported that police have long suspected a net-
work of drug dealers working truck stops across the nation.
"It's natural," the source said. "Interstates go everywhere,
and those big rigs go everywhere on them. It would make for a
very efficient operation. They'd be mostly anonymous to the
locals, so they'd never show up on the local cops' radar. They
get here, they do their deal, they move on. And they've got a
cover story that isn't even a cover story, it's a real job, they
have a reason for passing through."

Police are canvassing the area for witnesses to the crime. A
high-placed source in the police department who wishes to
remain anonymous says that special attention is being paid to
traffic in and out of the truck stop between the hours of midnight and six A.M.

"He bought me breakfast there," Johnny said, handing it back.
He looked sick. "I was starving. I thought it was so nice of him. He
left me at the counter, said he had to see a man about a horse."

"How long was he gone?"

"Twenty minutes, maybe? Half an hour?" Johnny shook his
head. "I don't remember exactly. I thought—"

"What?"

Johnny ducked his head and studied the floor intently. "I
thought maybe a woman. I saw them, the ones who hang around the
truck stops. They were everywhere we pulled in." He glanced up
fleetingly. "I'm sorry, Jim. If I'd told you when he got here—"

"It's okay," Jim said.

"No, it isn't. Maybe Ms. Macleod would be alive if I had."

"You didn't kill her, Johnny. And Gallagher hasn't confessed."

"Yet. But you got him. Kate told me about the monofilament."

"Yeah," Jim said, not without a certain satisfaction. Besides the little bundle in the kitchen catch-all, there was enough mending twine in Auntie Vi's net loft to stock a marine supply store. Jim didn't know if the geeks at the crime lab could match batches of the stuff, but even if they couldn't it put the means of Macleod's murder very close to Gallagher's hand.

They'd recovered the bullets in the Boise homicides, too, and Gallagher's weapon was already on its way to the crime lab in Anchorage. "Yeah," he said, "we got him."

Kate came in as Johnny was leaving. "You okay?" she said.

"Jim says I didn't kill her."

"Jim Chopin, while a man and by definition foolish and fallible, is in this case absolutely and miraculously right."

Johnny watched his hands as they tried to tie his knit cap into a knot. "I shouldn't have told him where I was from, Kate. He wouldn't have shown up here." He looked up. "Maybe if I hadn't, Ms. Macleod would still be alive."

"Maybe. Maybe not. He'd already killed two people, don't forget. And you were with him. You could have seen something."

He paled a little. "You think he would have tried to kill me."

"I don't know. Fortunately, not an issue now."

Johnny's expression lightened. "I guess so. Yeah."

"Go on," she said, opening the door to the post. "You're going to be late for school. Just make damn sure that's where you're going."

"Yes, Kate," he said, and bolted out the door.

I saw Howie and Willard, headed for home," she said in Jim's office. "You still think he might be making it up about the aunties hiring him to do Louis Deem?"

"You asked them again?"

"Haven't had time."

He snorted. "Yeah, you're as petrified as I am that it's true. And then what?"

Kate had other issues with the aunties as well, but he couldn't help her with those. "You're sure he didn't kill Mac Devlin?"

He nodded. "Yeah. He was out there all right, with your cousin Martin and some guy named Sheldon, poaching caribou for resale. And Howie's rifle doesn't match the bullet the ME dug out of Mac's back." She was silent, frowning at the floor. "Kate?"

She looked up. "Want me to talk to Martin and Sheldon?"

"Sure. Probably even pay you for it. I'm going to take Greenbaugh into Anchorage personally as soon as it gets light."

"He okay to travel?"

"They got doctors in Anchorage can take care of him just fine. The sooner he's safely inside Cook Inlet Pre-Trial, the better I'll feel."

"Has Greenbaugh said he killed Talia yet?"

"He's not talking. After Mutt's emergency tracheotomy last night"—Mutt's ears perked up at mention of her name—"I'm not sure he can. But I called Global Harvest. The day Macleod died, he called them and told them he wanted her job."

"They give it to him?"

"Are you kidding? Guy hasn't even been in the state a year. Hasn't even made it through his first winter. No time served, no name recognition. Global Harvest didn't get to be the world's largest gold mining company because they were stupid."

It was almost word for word what she'd thought herself. Spooky. "So who's the new Talia, did they say?"

"They don't know yet. The guy said they'd made a job offer and were waiting to hear back. You get a call you didn't tell me about?"

Kate smiled, a little distracted.

"You okay, Kate?"

"Yeah, I'm fine. I'll go talk to Martin and Sheldon today."

She didn't bother looking for Martin. Instead, she went straight out to the Sheldons' place. It was about five miles downriver from

Niniltna on the road to Bernie's, a couple miles after the turnoff to
Bobby's place on Squaw Candy Creek and a couple of miles before
the turnoff to the Nabesna Mine. The Sheldons had been Mac Devlin's nearest neighbors.

The snow machine nosed down the narrow track, which went in
about a mile before ending in a large clearing. There was a small,
neat house, a cache on stilts, and a couple of outbuildings. Next to
one of these was a D6 Caterpillar tractor, yellow body and ten-foot
steel blade. Kate recognized it immediately, as some years back
she'd had occasion to employ it as a means of resolving a chronic
property dispute between the Jeppsens and the Kreugers. It would
have wrung Mac's heart to see it sitting out in the weather. He'd always taken good care of his equipment. It was one of his few dis-
cernible virtues.

She pulled up to the house and killed the engine. Mutt hopped
down and Kate dismounted as the door opened. A man stood in the
doorway squinting out at the morning light, tall, balding, sus-
penders holding up his Carhartts, T-shirt stained with coffee and
what looked like egg, worn leather mocs on his feet.

"Mr. Sheldon?" Kate said, without moving, because he was also
holding a bolt-action .30-06. He wasn't aiming it anywhere in particular and she wasn't going to give him cause to do so. She hoped.

"Yeah?"

"I'm Kate Shugak, Mr. Sheldon. I'm a Park rat like yourself, live
about thirty miles the other direction, off the road to Ahtna."

"I've heard of you." The rifle remained held loosely in front of
him. "What do you want?"

"I need to talk to you. Okay if I come in?"

He seemed about to refuse, and then Mutt trotted up and
looked at him with wide eyes and alert ears. "Nice-looking dog. Got
some wolf in her."

"Some. May I please come in and talk to you, Mr. Sheldon?"

He shrugged and stepped back. "Sure, I guess. If you want."

She waited until he set the rifle in a corner before stepping into the kitchen, where unwashed dishes were piled high in the sink and more were spread on table and countertop, along with silverware, cutlery, and pots and pans. There was the sour smell of moldering food in the air, probably emanating from the gnawed-looking haunch of caribou sitting on the table, and dirt crunched underfoot.

"Sorry about the mess," Sheldon said. "My wife's away."

There was a propane cooker and a woodstove with a kettle on top. He moved the kettle to the cooker and turned the burner underneath on high, produced a jar of Sanka and another of creamer and a bowl of sugar crusted around the rim from countless wet spoons dipping into it. The kettle boiled almost immediately and Sheldon used his arm in a sweeping movement to shove everything on the table to one side and set out heavy white mugs and Fig Newtons in a tattered plastic sleeve. Kate doctored her coffee, sipped it, and took a bite of a cookie. She fed the rest to a bright-eyed Mutt sitting alertly at her side.

Hospitality satisfied, Sheldon said, "What's this about?" His face looked hollowed out, his eyes bruised. His thinning hair looked as if it hadn't been combed in a week or washed in a month. He hadn't shaved in a while, either, and his fingernails were grimed with dirt. He spoke in a monotone, without life or hope.

"I think you know, sir."

"Do I?"

Kate made her voice as gentle as possible. "I understand your son was killed this fall."

His head snapped up and he stared at her. His eyes reddened and filled with tears. "Shit," he said, rubbing them with the back of his hand. "Shit. You'd think after all this time . . ." He dropped his hand and glared at her. "What's that got to do with you?"

"I understand it was an accident," Kate said. "The Cat turned over on him."

"Accident my ass," Sheldon said, firing up, "that fucker Devlin sold me that Cat when he knew the track was about to fall apart. My boy took it out to work on the creek out back, been showing some color. He thought he might pick up a few nuggets, maybe pay for his tuition, price of gold what it is . . ." His voice trailed away as the energy drained out of him again. "Killed him, that piece of shit Cat did." He looked at Kate again but the glare was gone. "Devlin sold me a defective piece of equipment. Should have known when he let it go so cheap. Should have looked it over more careful." His head drooped. "Should never have let Roger drive it."

"Is that why you killed him, Mr. Sheldon? Is that why you shot Mac Devlin in the back?"

His head came up again and they stared at each other, the silence stretching out between them, pulling tighter and tighter, until he seemed to realize that he'd left his answer too long.

"You were hunting caribou up back of Suulutaq with Howie Katelnikof and Martin Shugak," Kate said. "Mac went out to the Global Harvest trailer, probably to steal what he could and trash the rest. You saw him on your way out. Followed him. Shot him in the back as he was going inside. That the way it happened?"

He was still staring at her. "Was Roger your only son, Mr. Sheldon?"

He blinked, and looked down at the table, his eye lighting on something. He stretched out a hand possessed of a fine trembling and pulled it out of the mess. "Yes," he said, looking at it. "He was our only child."

He handed it to her. It was a photograph of three people, a man barely recognizable as the one sitting in front of her now, not much younger but healthy and happy. The woman was attractively plump, and they were both looking adoringly at the third person in the photo, a gangly young man with a large Adam's apple and silver-rimmed glasses perched on a hawk beak of a nose identical to the one on the face before her.

"I'm very sorry," she said, handing the photograph back.

"Me, too," he said.

"You didn't go out there meaning to kill Mac Devlin, did you, Mr. Sheldon?"

"I didn't even know he was going to be there." Sheldon spoke in a dreary tone. "Martin told me they could use an extra hand with the caribou, and I'm a good butcher. They were going to pay me in meat, so I said I would. He told me to come out a day after them, so they'd have some shot and gutted and ready for me to work on. So I did." He turned blind eyes toward the window, the only source of light in the room. "It was like you said. I saw that bastard Devlin at the trailer." He shrugged. "I had my rifle with me." He picked up the photograph again. "Seemed the right thing to do at the time."

She sat in silence with him for some minutes, before getting to her feet. "I'll have to take your rifle in, Mr. Sheldon," she said. "Give it to the trooper in Niniltna. I expect he'll be out here in the next day or so."

He nodded. "Good. Give me a chance to clean up the place." He looked around. "Although I don't know what for. Nobody going to be living here now."

It about killed her to drive off and leave him there, alone with his ghosts.

TWENTY-SEVEN

It snowed for Christmas, dry, fluffy flakes that piled up fast, twenty-eight inches in eighteen hours. Christmas Day dawned clear and cold, a beautiful morning. "Let's ski over to Mandy's after dinner," Kate said.

"Deal," Johnny said.

They even had a tree, small enough for one string of lights and a few bright ornaments, and topped with a tiny Eskimo doll in an exquisitely hand-worked sealskin kuspuk and mukluks that Annie Mike had given all the board members for Christmas. They'd agreed on the rules beforehand. There would be no singing of carols, no recitation of the Christmas story, and each of them was allowed to give the other only one gift. Kate gave Johnny a leather-bound atlas of Middle-earth, elaborately illustrated and annotated, and Jim the four-book memoir by Gerald Durrell about growing up on Corfu between the World Wars, first editions Rachel had found for her on the Internet. Johnny gave Jim a Leatherman, the new Skeletool model. He gave Kate one, too. Jim gave Johnny a small telescope, an Astro-Venture 90mm, with its own spotting scope. "Your math better be up to this," he told him, "because mine isn't."

While Johnny stuttered in vain for something to say that might come close to expressing his surprise, his wonder, and his gratitude, Jim turned to Kate and handed her a small, flat package wrapped clumsily in gold foil. A red peel-and-stick ribbon was stuck to one corner. "Merry Christmas," he said, the corner of his mouth kicking up in a half smile.

It was a copy of *Robert's Rules of Order (Newly Revised, In Brief)*. She opened it and read out loud, her voice breaking on the words, "'So You're Going to a Meeting.'" She closed the book and looked at him through misty eyes. "Oh, Jim."

He leaned over and kissed her. "Tear 'em up, babe."

Later they ate ham roasted with pineapple rings and cloves in a brown-sugar sauce, and after that they strapped on skis and went over the river and through the woods to see Mandy, who heard their laughter long before they arrived and was waiting for them at the door. "Hey, guys! Come on in, I've got pumpkin pie fresh out of the oven."

Chick was home, sober again and cheerful about it. The five of them sat down and tucked into pie and lingered over coffee, catching up on Park gossip and lying about their New Year's resolutions.

Chick gave Mandy a meaningful glance, and Mandy stirred in her chair. "Yeah," she said. "I've got some news of my own."

"Serve it up," Kate said, absorbed in picking up crust crumbs with a licked forefinger.

Mandy looked at Kate's bent head. "I'm the new Talia Macleod."

Kate went very still, one finger halfway between plate and mouth.

Into the silence Mandy said, "Global Harvest asked me a week or so after she died. I told them I had to think about it. Chick and I talked it over, and last week I said I would. I wanted you to hear before they made the announcement, or before Bobby finds out and puts it out on goddamn Park Air."

No one laughed.

"Anyway," Mandy said. "There'll be a press release after the first of the year."

There was a brief silence. As if they were propelled by marionette strings, everyone turned to look at Kate.

Kate licked the last of the crumbs from her finger and sat back. "Are you sure you want to do this, Mandy?"

Mandy shrugged. "No. But it's a big paycheck. And a chunk of stock."

"We heard about the stock," Jim said in a carefully neutral voice. "Hard to turn down something like that."

"You need money?" Kate said.

Mandy shrugged. "This place takes a lot to keep it going. Like I told you in October, my trust fund never covers all of it. Whatever prize money I got for a race always helped." She put her hand over Chick's. "We don't want to live anywhere else. And besides." Mandy spread her hands. "They keep canceling the races, Kate, or delaying them. There's never enough snow anymore, or it all melts too soon and the trail just beats you to death. It was fifty-two degrees when we went through Cripple last year, did I tell you? Jesus. You can't run dogs at those temperatures."

She smiled at Mutt, sitting next to Kate, ears up, eyes inquiring. "And the competition gets stiffer every year. Publicity's about ruined the Iditarod. Outsiders from Montana, Norwegians, for god's sake, even a blind musher. What the hell's that about?" She sat back in her chair. "It's just not as much fun as it used to be."

And you aren't winning the way you used to, Kate thought, but she would have cut out her tongue before she said it out loud. "I told you I got shanghaied to be chair of the NNA board."

"You did," Mandy said, nodding.

"Lot of talk about that mine."

330

Mandy's smile had faded, too. "I know."

"Lot of people against it."

"Are you against it?" Mandy said.

Everyone looked at Kate again. "Not the point," Kate said. "What I'm saying, Mandy, is a lot of Park rats won't be happy you're the new mouthpiece for Global Harvest."

Mandy set her jaw. It was a good jaw, square and firm. "They'll get used to it."

We'll have to, Kate thought.

JANUARY

"Auntie Joy," Kate said, "please sit here, on my right. Old Sam, on my left, please. Harvey, Demetri, there and there."

Auntie Joy looked startled but took the seat Kate indicated. Old Sam gave Kate one of his patented, narrow-eyed looks, waited long enough to establish that it was his own idea, and sat. Harvey looked mutinous but short of summarily dislodging two venerable elders there was nothing for him to do but sit where he was told to. Demetri took the last seat without comment.

"You'll find copies of an agenda on the table in front of you."

She gave them a few minutes to run their eyes over it, and then rapped the table once with a small gavel made of fossilized ivory, its creamy surface swirling with golds and browns. She'd commissioned Thor Moonin to carve it for her after the holidays. "The meeting will come to order."

It came out a little more authoritarian than she had meant it to and the table sat up with a collective jerk. Auntie Joy turned a shocked eye on Kate. Old Sam relaxed again, with the beginnings of a smile indenting the corners of his mouth. "You all had copies of the last meeting's minutes hand-delivered to your doorstep two weeks ago. I'm going on the assumption you've read them. Are there any additions or corrections you would like to propose to the minutes at this time?"

Harvey opened his mouth, encountered Kate's level gaze, and shut it again.

"If there are no corrections or emendations, the minutes are approved. May we have the treasurer's report?"

Annie Mike gave a brisk rundown of the numbers. Kate moved that they be approved and accepted, Auntie Joy seconded the motion, it passed.

"Membership report," Kate said.

This was new, and Harvey said, "What's this?"

"Point of order," Kate said coolly. "The chair has not recognized Mr. Meganack."

"Oh, come on, what's this bullshit?"

"This bullshit is Robert's Rules of Order," Kate said. "You must be recognized by the chair before you are allowed to speak. And you have to stand up before I can recognize you."

Harvey sat there with his mouth half open.

"On your feet, Harvey," Old Sam said, smirking.

Harvey, red with anger, nevertheless stood up. "Madam Chair."

Kate gave a curt nod. "The chair recognizes Mr. Meganack."

"What's this membership report? We've never done this before."

"It's a tally of shareholders," Kate said, "which the board will update at every meeting. I think it's important we keep track of the number of shareholders we have on a regular basis. It helps remind us to whom we are responsible when we take action at these meetings."

There had been eleven children born over the past year who qualified under the Association's one-thirty-secondth rule, specifically that after adding up their Native heritage on both sides each shareholder had a minimum of one-thirty-secondth of Native blood.

Assimilation and intermarriage over the last three hundred years meant a lot of shareholders just barely squeaked in under that rule, and it also meant that many of the next generation of babies wouldn't qualify at all. In the back of her mind Kate noted that some action should be taken to ensure that the tribe increased rather than decreased in size as the years went by. They might have to go to one-sixty-fourth. "Total shareholders, Ms. Mike?" she said.

"Madam Chair, as of January first, the Niniltna Native Association had two hundred and thirty-seven shareholders," Annie said. "Approximately one hundred of them live in Anchorage, Fairbanks, Juneau, and Outside."

"Thank you, Ms. Mike."

Harvey sat down slowly.

Kate tried not to let her relief show. In truth, she was a little surprised at herself. She hadn't planned to address everyone by their surnames, it had just come out, but the formality felt right. "Any further reports, Ms. Mike?"

"Not at present, Madam Chair," Annie said, her brisk manner rivaling Kate's own. Imitation, in this case, was the sincerest form of approval.

"Thank you, Ms. Mike. Moving on. Old business." She looked up. "I move that we table old business today. There is nothing left over that is pressing and we've got the general shareholders meeting to get to."

"Second," Old Sam said.

"It is moved and seconded that the board carry any old business forward to the next regularly scheduled board meeting. Debate?" There was none. "Those in favor, say aye."

Auntie Joy, Old Sam, and Kate said aye. Harvey was back to looking furious. "The ayes have it, and the motion is adopted. Next item. New business."

Kate sat back in her chair and fixed Harvey with a cold and

unflinching eye. "I have three items I wish to bring to the board's attention this morning."

Harvey stiffened, and she knew he was thinking that she was about to bring up his job with GHRI, whatever it might be.

"All three items," Kate said, "will by Association rules be put to the vote before the general shareholders meeting."

"Along with the election of the board members," Harvey said, rallying.

"Out of order, Mr. Meganack, but so noted. First on our agenda is the creation of an advisory committee consisting of qualified volunteers drawn from Association shareholders to advise and consent to every single step Global Harvest Resources takes in developing and producing the Suulutaq Mine. Further, I propose that we approach Global Harvest Resources to fund said committee. At this time, I so move."

"Second," Old Sam said promptly.

"The motion to create an advisory committee for the Suulutaq Mine and to make Global Harvest pay for it is moved and seconded," Kate said. "Debate? The chair recognizes Mr. Meganack."

Harvey had shot to his feet but he'd also had the sense to wait this time until he was recognized. "You want to put our people on Global Harvest's payroll? Won't that make them more rather than less inclined to sign off on anything GH wants to do?"

The irony inherent in his protest seemed not to occur to Harvey. "Not if we choose the committee members carefully," Kate said, and added softly, "and watch them."

He reddened. "Who'd you have in mind for this committee?"

She looked at him. "You, for a start."

It was hard to say who was more surprised by this blunt statement, Auntie Joy or Harvey. Old Sam, of course, gave out with his braying laugh. Demetri remained his taciturn silent self.

"I seem to recall you have a degree in civil engineering from the

University of Alaska Anchorage," Kate said. "You've got the education required, you're a shareholder, and you're even a member of the board, duly elected, which means you're trusted by the shareholders to run things right. Who better?"

Harvey sat down as if his legs had suddenly given out from under him.

Kate figured she couldn't beat Global Harvest in a race for Harvey's mercenary heart, but she could damn well give them some competition. She wasn't going to out Harvey, not yet anyway. Either Harvey would realize how inappropriate—and how impossible—it was to try to serve two masters, or he'd eventually have enough rope to hang himself with.

"Any further discussion?" she said. There wasn't. "All in favor?" Unanimous. "The board moves that the creation of a Suulutaq Advisory Committee be brought before the general membership at today's meeting. Second item on the agenda. I move that we ask the general membership to increase the Niniltna Native Association board from five members to nine."

"What! Katya!"

"Out of order, Ms. Shugak," Kate said, ignoring the stricken expression on Auntie Joy's face, albeit not without a twinge of conscience.

"Second," Old Sam said, although not quite as promptly as he had before. He looked at Kate with a quizzical eye, as if to say he'd go along, but only until and unless she proved her case.

"Moved and seconded," Kate said. "Discussion."

"Madam Chair!" Harvey said, on his feet.

"Madam Chair!" Auntie Joy said, on hers.

"The chair recognizes herself," she said, and got to her own feet. Auntie Joy subsided, hurt. Harvey subsided, pissed off at being steamrollered.

"I went back and checked the records of previous meetings,"

Kate said. "On average, we have to cancel one a year due to lack of a quorum." Quoting from what she was beginning to refer to as the Book, at least to herself, she said, " 'Any substantive action taken in the absence of a quorum is invalid.' Lacking a quorum, the Association board can't get its business done. Four more members on the board means four more paychecks, true enough. But if we establish five members—the same number we have now—as the minimum number required to constitute a quorum, with a nine-member board we can be four members short and still get the job done." She paused, looking around at each board member for effect. "And there's going to be a lot to get done, shortly."

She sat down and recognized Auntie Joy, who beat Harvey to his feet by a hair second. Auntie Joy spoke forcefully if incoherently on the value of tradition, of institutions created out of necessity and the importance of inclusion, the responsibility of the governing body to run a frugal business, and of the virtue inherent in running such a business. After a while she ran out of steam, looked confused, and sat down without offering an amendment to the motion. Kate didn't remind her, either.

In the meantime, Harvey, looking unusually thoughtful, had thought better of speaking and waved a dismissive hand when Kate looked at him. "The chair moves that the motion to increase the Niniltna Native Association board from five members to nine should be brought before the general membership for approval. All in favor say aye."

Kate, Old Sam, Demetri, and Harvey voted aye. Auntie Joy said nay and looked as if she might burst into tears.

Kate hardened her heart. "Last item. I move we commission a new NNA logo."

"Second," Demetri said, and everyone looked at him in surprise.

"Moved and seconded," Kate said, with a nod to Demetri. "Debate?" No one said anything so she held up the NNA mug with the ink blot logo. "This logo sucks. It's not instantly recognizable, it doesn't say Park or NNA or anything at all, really. Plus it's poorly drawn and it's ugly. Symbols are important. Take Global Harvest's logo, for one example. Sunrise over the Quilaks. They're practically branding the Park with it. I move that at today's general meeting we tell the membership that the board is starting a contest, beginning today and running, what, six months? Mr. Totemoff?"

"Make it nine months," Demetri said, standing. "Give momentum time to build, word of mouth to spread, get people excited. The more entries we get the more choice we'll have. Choose the winner at the October board meeting and unveil the new logo at the general meeting next January. Besides, be good not to do any of this before, during, or after fishing season."

"No kidding," Old Sam said, and flashed his evil grin when Kate gave him the evil eye for speaking out of turn.

"The motion is to have a contest for NNA shareholders to create a new Association logo. All in favor?"

Unanimous.

Really, Kate thought, there was nothing to running a board meeting.

Not when you'd spent the last month memorizing the first ninety-five pages of *Robert's Rules of Order (Newly Revised, In Brief)*, there wasn't.

TWENTY-EIGHT

Y ou can't stop the Suulutaq Mine," Kate said, "and I'll tell
you why.

"A thousand dollars an ounce."

Most of the Niniltna Native Association's 237 shareholders were
in the Niniltna School gymnasium that afternoon, sitting on gray
metal folding chairs. There was a continual susurration of whispering, an occasional baby's cry, the clink of dishes as aunties Vi, Edna,
and Balasha set out a potluck lunch on a row of tables at the back of
the room.

Kate was front and center on the little stage, speaking into a microphone, not liking the sound of her voice as it reverberated off the
high ceiling, not liking being the cynosure of all eyes, hating the position of responsibility and leadership into which she had been
thrust this day. Oh Emaa, if you could see me now, wouldn't you be
pleased.

In a line of folding chairs on the stage sat the other members of
the board, Auntie Joy still hurt, Old Sam sardonic, Demetri taciturn,
Harvey pugnacious, but they were there, lined up at her right hand

like the good soldiers they were. At a card table on her left, Annie Mike took industrious notes and recorded votes. Solidarity forever.

Right.

"We can't demonize the people who want to build it, either," Kate said, "because at a thousand dollars an ounce they'll build it anyway. And then here we'll be, the mine a going concern and the people running it with no reason to do us any favors." She paused, and added, "Or hire any Park rats."

A lot of them didn't like what they were hearing. Fine, they could fire her in the vote to follow.

"I'll tell you what we can do," she said. "We can get in bed with Global Harvest, all the way under the covers, and make sure we're watching over their shoulders every step of the way. That is what this proposed advisory committee is for. You don't like the idea of earthen dams? Fine, tell Global Harvest to come up with something better. At a thousand dollars an ounce, they can afford it.

"You're worried the arsenic they use in the extraction process will pollute the groundwater? At a thousand dollars an ounce they can come up with a process that leaves a friendlier environmental footprint.

"You're worried about what the influx of increased population will do to the nature and character of the Park? Okay, we set some guidelines, starting with they can't build a road from the Nabesna Mine to Suulutaq, they have to build their own airstrip. We set more guidelines about the use of the road to Ahtna, too, like maybe they can access it only on a limited, supervised, case-by-case basis. At a thousand dollars an ounce, they can afford it."

Auntie Vi had paused, plate in hand, to listen. On either side, aunties Balasha and Edna were listening, too.

"You're worried that Global Harvest is going to hire all Outsiders for the good jobs?" Kate said. "Then our first order of business is to ask Global Harvest, 'What do you need in the way of employees?' and get them to help us create—and fund—an educational program for the kids of the Park. At a thousand dollars an ounce"—she was startled when almost everyone in the room said it with her—"they can afford it!"

There was a ripple of laughter, and a couple of people even exchanged high fives.

On stage, the board members gave each other covert looks. No one had stirred up a shareholders meeting like this since Ekaterina Shugak had been chair, and Ekaterina, a woman who personified dignity, had not encouraged public displays of either approval or dissent.

"Is there any further discussion? No. Okay. I'll ask you now to vote on the expansion of the board of directors, the creation of the mine advisory committee and the contest for a new association logo. Voice vote first. If there is no clear majority on voice vote, Ms. Mike will distribute ballots. Then, a voice vote on the election of myself to the board of directors, followed by a shareholders' confirmation vote on the board's selection of chair."

She looked at Annie. Annie nodded.

"The motion before the Niniltna Native Association is to increase the membership of its board of directors from five to nine members, with all the rights and responsibilities accruing thereto. All in favor?"

When it was over she touched Auntie Joy on the arm before she could leave the stage. "Come with me, please, Auntie."

Out of the crowd she picked out Auntie Vi, Auntie Balasha, and Auntie Edna. Avoiding all the glad-handing and congratulations pointed her way, she led them into the kitchen, where she threw everyone else out and closed and locked the door.

"We have to serve food, Katya," Auntie Vi said, bridling.

"They can serve themselves for a few minutes," Kate said. She folded her arms and looked them over with a bleak eye. "I'm only going to ask you this once. If you lie to me and I find out later that you lied, I will never trust you, any of you, individually or together, ever again."

Auntie Vi ruffled up like an irritated cockatoo, but before she could say anything Kate said baldly, "Did you hire Howie Katelnikof to kill Louis Deem?"

A ghastly silence fell over the room. It was an incongruous setting for this discussion, stainless steel cupboards, counters, sinks, and appliances, with here and there evidence of hasty meal prep, a few elbows of macaroni, a lone potato chip, a brilliant purple spill of grape Kool-Aid mix.

The four aunties exchanged sidelong glances and by some secret signal agreed to maintain a wary silence. Kate hadn't really expected anything else. This confrontation was about the future, not the past.

"If you did, you took the law into your own hands," she said. "You set yourselves up as judge, jury, and executioner." She paused, giving Auntie Vi a chance to break into her standard accusation about Kate not doing her job and the aunties having to step in. Auntie Vi glared but did not speak.

"Have you noticed what's happened since?" she said. "It's spreading, this vigilantism of yours. It's like an infection, spreading across the Park like some kind of disease. You settle the score with Louis, then Mary Bingley decides she can handle Willard's shoplifting on her own, Demetri beats the crap out of Father Smith for blading his trapline, Bonnie keys the truck of the kid who put a salmon in the mailbox, Arliss shoots Mickey before he hits her again."

Kate shook her head. "And then you do it again."

She waited, watching as they exchanged sidelong glances.

"Yeah, you get the Grosdidier boys to track down the Johansens and beat on them."

Their heads snapped around at that, all right. "Don't bother denying it. You did, I know you did, we'll leave it at that."

She frowned at the floor for a moment, and looked up again. "Don't you see, Aunties? You're the center. If you don't hold, it's almost like you give permission for things to fall apart."

"We tell no one," Auntie Joy said, and then at a fiery glance from Auntie Vi her mouth shut again with an audible snap.

"Auntie," Kate said with admirable patience, "this is the Park. You sneeze on one side of it, five minutes later on the other side of it you're dying of pneumonia. Did you really think you could keep it a secret? Any of it?"

Again she looked at Auntie Vi, and again Auntie Vi remained silent, although it was pretty obvious the top would blow off the bottle in the not-too-distant future.

"Okay," Kate said. "Best we say nothing more about this, to anyone. For the record, Howie ratted you out, and then reneged on his confession. Now he's saying he didn't kill Louis at all, and Jim and I halfway believe him. He and Willard only have one shotgun out at their place, and we checked. The shot in the shells they've got doesn't match the shot that was found in Louis's body."

The expressions that crossed their faces were interesting, to say the least. Shock, surprise, then anger. "He's been blackmailing you, hasn't he?" Kate said. It was what she'd realized that evening, moments before Old Sam came in the door to tell them about Macleod's murder. "Saying he'll tell if you don't give him money?"

Again, she read her answer on their faces. "Well, now that you know we know, you don't have to pay him any more."

She looked at them, at these four doughty, indomitable forces of nature, Balasha in her seventies the youngest, the rest of them over the eighty mark. They'd been a power in Kate's life from her birth.

She could count on one hand the times she'd gone up against them, and never without guilt or remorse. It grieved her now to have to lay down the law to them, but someone had to.

"Insofar as what happened out there today," she said, and they looked up at the grim note in her voice. She nodded at the door. "They confirmed me in office, Aunties. You got what you wanted. And you'll get it for two more years."

"Katya—," Auntie Vi said.

"Two more years," Kate said again, her voice not rising but her tone inflexible, "the time remaining in Billy Mike's term of office. Then I step down." She surveyed their consternation with no little satisfaction, and maybe just a hint of a tremor that she might be wrong about this. Only now was she beginning to wonder about Eka-terina's choices when she had been named to the board. Was it, after all, what she had really wanted? Or had it been forced on her, too?

She banished the niggling doubts and said firmly, "Two years is long enough to find and groom the next chair, and bring them up to speed. Two years is long enough to build a policy to ensure that Global Harvest treats fairly with us over the Suulutaq Mine."

"That mine not a done deal, Katya," Auntie Vi said sternly.

"No," Kate said, "and I imagine you and a bunch of other people are going to have a lot to say about that over the next fifty years."

"Somebody strong needed to guide the people during that time," Auntie Vi said.

"A lot of strong people will be necessary," Kate said. "I'm not Emaa, Aunties." She said it again just to be sure they heard her, whether they believed it or not. "I'm not Emaa. She was Associa-tion chair for twenty years, and after a while she got so she thought she'd been anointed rather than elected."

This was heresy. There were shocked and reproachful looks. Okay, fine. "You remember Mark Miller, Aunties? The park ranger who went missing seven years ago? Yes, I can see that you do. She was willing to have an innocent man convicted of that crime rather than see one of her own go down for it."

They didn't say anything, and prudently, she didn't ask them if they had approved of Emaa's actions. "I'm not Emaa," Kate said again. "I won't ever be Emaa. I'll do what I can for the shareholders, for the Association, for the Park during the next two years, and I'll do my best to handpick a competent successor. But you should also know one of the first things I'm going to do is propose an amendment to the bylaws for term limits for board and chair. Two terms, max, and then they're out. George Washington was right about that."

"What!"

"Katya, this lousy idea, you—"

"Ekaterina would roll in her grave!"

"Then she rolls," Kate said. "No one should be in power for that long, Aunties. After too long, the people holding office start to feel invincible, arrogant, as if the power is theirs by right and not by the consent of the governed. One shareholder, one vote. One board member, two terms."

"Won't pass," Auntie Vi said.

"Yes, it will, Auntie," Kate said. "If I have to convince every shareholder one at a time, baby to elder, including every one of you, yes, it will."

They looked to a woman spitting mad, even Auntie Joy. Kate grinned at them, although it was an expression lacking any real amusement. "You wanted me to be on the board. You wanted me to be chair. Be careful what you wish for, Aunties. You might just get it."

She went to the door and paused for her parting shot. "Oh, and on a personal note."

She looked at Auntie Balasha. "I'm not moving into town, Auntie. I like my homestead, and I've got all the company I want or need. I don't want to be any closer to family. I don't want to be any closer to the other shareholders, or to the Association office. I'm right where I want to be, and I'm going to stay there."

She looked at Auntie Edna and her eyes hardened. "My personal life is my own affair, Auntie. Don't you tell me who I can or can't have a relationship with ever again."

The other three aunties looked at Auntie Edna in surprise. Kate looked at Auntie Vi. "I'm not going to be the next Association chair for life, Auntie. In case, you know, you didn't hear me the first sixteen times."

Lastly, she looked at Auntie Joy. "And thanks for being the only auntie who didn't try to rearrange my life, Auntie Joy. I appreciate it."

She left.

As she was leaving the gym she felt someone touch her sleeve, and turned to see Harvey Meganack. "It wasn't a landslide, Kate," he said. "You only won by four votes. Next time it'll be different."

"Yeah," she said, "next time I won't be running."

He snorted his disbelief and walked away.

Why was it so difficult for anyone to believe that she didn't want it, any of it, not the power, not the glory, not the responsibility, none of it?

She thought again of Tikani vanishing slowly down the years, its patriarch starving to death, its youth wasted from a lack of occupation, sinking into a life of poverty and despair. Too many villages were going the same way. If something didn't change, if someone didn't bring in more jobs to the Park, they would vanish, too.

Niniltna could be on that list one day.

She turned and looked at the crowded room, the chairs shoved against the walls, filled with people gossiping with neighbors over plates of fry bread and smoked fish and mac and cheese, exchanging family news at the laden tables when they went back for seconds. Elly Aguilar, Auntie Edna's granddaughter, was sitting next to Martin

345

Shugak, her belly pushing out almost to her knees. She smiled shyly in answer to a question Martin asked, and took his hand and put it on her belly. A second later he jumped, and they both laughed.

Kate shook her head. Every now and then Martin made her think that there might be more than a loser residing in that body after all.

The basketballs were out, a line of kids from eight to eighty doing layups, jumping, hooking them in, bouncing them off the backboard, and then by some unspoken osmosis the layup line re-formed in the key and it was free throws. Free throws win ball games. One of Coach Bernie Koslowski's immutable laws.

A little girl in a pink kuspuk skittered out of the crowd and careened into Kate's legs with such force that she bounced back and landed on her fanny on the floor. She looked up, eyes wide, too surprised to cry. Kate laughed and tossed the girl up into her arms. "Hey," she said, softly chiding. "Watch where you're going, you could hurt somebody."

The little girl stared at her wide-eyed, one finger in her mouth, a little snot leaking out of her nose, before wriggling free and careening off in a different direction.

Kate opened the door and went outside.

Not on her watch.

TWENTY-NINE

That night the Roadhouse was packed to the rafters. Everyone was back in their accustomed places, Old Sam with the other old farts at the table beneath the television, the aunties working on the new quilt at the round table in the corner, Bernie behind the bar. "I hear you kicked Association ass today, Kate," he said with a faint approximation of his old self.

"Not kicked ass, Bernie," she said, and gave it some thought. "Gently but firmly encouraged the shareholders to walk in the proper direction. Me and Robert's Rules of Order."

Next to her, Jim grinned.

"What'll it be?" Bernie said, and they ordered all around. After a bit a couple of guys got out the beater guitars Bernie kept in the back and started singing from the Beatles' songbook, and a while later the belly dancers showed up, and from the jukebox Jimmy Buffett started threatening to go to Mexico again. Demetri stepped up next to Kate, gave her his reserved smile, and ordered a beer. Harvey Meganack was sitting at a table with Mandy and Chick, and from the nauseous expression Mandy had to repress from time to time Kate gathered that he was holding forth with his usual know-it-all swagger to GHRI's new representative to the Park. Be careful what you wish for, indeed.

"True what I heard?" Jim said, following her gaze. "You're going to make him boss of that mine advisory panel you're putting together?"

Kate toasted Harvey with her Diet 7UP. Taken aback, he was a beat late in returning the salute, but return it he did. "Keep your friends close," she said, "and your enemies closer."

"You'll have to watch him."

"I always do. What do we hear about Gallagher?"

"Greenbaugh."

"Whatever."

"He's lawyered up."

"Who?"

"Frank Rickard."

Kate winced. "Is Rickard the biggest asshole magnet in the state, or what?"

Jim shrugged. "If Alaska fails to convict on the Macleod murder, Idaho's drooling at the prospect of indicting him on the truck stop homicides."

"Will Johnny have to testify?"

"Maybe." Jim raised his beer. "Here's hoping nobody else shows up from his hitch north, okay?"

"I heard that." They clinked glasses.

At the end of the bar Nick Waterbury sat hunched over his beer, a full one waiting to one side, no Eve in sight. "Poor bastard," she said.

She looked past him at the aunties, receiving obeisances from a train of Park rats on their way home or to Ahtna from that day's meeting. "Howie isn't here tonight," she said. "He wasn't at the shareholders meeting today, either."

"Even Howie's smart enough to figure it'd be a good idea to stay out of the aunties' way for a while," Jim said dryly.

She looked back at Nick. At that same moment he raised his head and met her eyes, and she was struck by the similarity she saw between him and Al Sheldon. They were nothing alike physically, one tall, the other short, one dark, the other fair, one white, the other Native. They reminded her of Bernie, come to think of it. The loss of a child told the same story on all three faces in sunken eyes, drawn complexion, the agony of loss, the absence of hope.

She gasped. "Jesus Christ," she said.

"What?" Jim said. He looked from Kate to Nick and back to Kate. "Kate?"

They borrowed one of Bernie's cabins out back. Nick followed them there without protest. When asked the direct question, he confessed without surprise, in a flat monotone that had all the life leached out of it, a monotone that reminded Kate only too painfully of the interview with Al Sheldon.

Yes, he'd been at the post office that morning. Along with everyone else waiting for their mail he'd heard that Louis Deem was going to go free.

He'd sat in his pickup down the street from the trooper post, and when Louis Deem walked out and started up the road to the Step on foot, Nick had taken his shotgun and followed.

"I stayed far enough behind so he wouldn't hear me," Nick said. "When we were a couple of miles out of town, I caught up with him. And I shot him."

He didn't look at either of them as he sat there, big, gnarled hands hanging between his knees. He got up and followed Jim obediently out to Nick's truck and watched silently as Jim took his shotgun from the rack in the back window.

Later, at the post, he repeated his words and signed the statement and shuffled into the cell vacated when Greenbaugh was moved to Anchorage. He lay down on the bunk, clasped his hands on his chest, and closed his eyes. He looked ready to be placed in a coffin.

Kate and Jim gaped at him for some moments before Jim recalled himself and closed and locked the door. Back in his office he repeated Kate's totally inadequate words with force and feeling. "Jesus Christ. I feel like I ought to be fired. Hell, I feel like I ought to resign in protest of my own total and complete incompetence and malfeasance and just all around general stupidity."

He dropped his head into his hands. His voice sounded tinny and far away. "This is what comes of crossing the line, Kate. You think the right reason trumps doing the wrong thing, and then you never get to the truth, when the truth is mostly a good thing and almost always the best thing to get to."

"I can't believe I missed it," Kate said, still dazed.

"I will never do something like that again." Jim said it like he was taking a vow. "I don't care what the provocation is. I don't care if the perp is Satan himself. Never ever again."

"He was sitting right there in the courtroom when the verdict came down," Kate said.

"I was so sure I knew how Louis Deem died. I was so sure I knew who did it, and why, and I worked so hard to prove otherwise that I couldn't even see who had the biggest motive of all."

"We all saw how angry Nick was," Kate said. "It's Morgan's First Law. 'The nearest and the dearest got the motive with the mostest.' And I was so blinded by my hatred of Louis Deem that I didn't even think of it."

They sat in silence, trying to move beyond stunned disbelief to acceptance.

Kate looked up and said, "We have to tell Bernie."

He felt his expression change.

"What?" she said.

"Nothing," he said. "You're right. We have to tell Bernie, and the aunties. And Howie, the little weasel."

Later that night he lay in bed next to Kate and wondered why he hadn't told her about Willard right then and there. It had been the perfect moment.

There were lots of reasons.

It would hurt her.

It would hurt the aunties, because she would surely tell them.

It would hurt Willard, who would very likely wind up in long-term, court-mandated psychiatric care somewhere that wasn't the Park and might not even be Alaska, which would very probably kill him. He was cared for where he was, more or less, and absent the fell influence of Louis Deem was unlikely to be incited to burglary and murder a second time. His trigger was dead and buried.

And telling wouldn't change anything. Enid and Fitz would still be dead.

All telling Kate about Willard would do was make him feel better. Carrying around a secret this big was a blight and a burden. It weighed on him, preyed on his mind, made him feel guilty, which made him feel cranky and snappish. Confession was good for the soul, and all that crap.

Still, he was a big, strong man. He'd taken an oath to serve and to protect.

But what it all came down to, really, was that telling Kate about Willard would hurt her.

It wasn't that he hadn't wanted to sleep with Talia Macleod. Attractive and willing and every bit the dog he was, how could he resist her? More to the point, why on earth would he? No doubt that it would have been a very enjoyable evening. Who would it have hurt? Not Talia. Not Jim. Not Park society, or he'd have been stoned to death by now.

Hard questions. Easy answer, though.

Kate. He hadn't slept with Talia because Kate would have been hurt.

Funny how more and more often the focus of serving and protecting, for him, came down to serving and protecting Kate Shugak.

He rolled over and slid an arm around her waist, pulling her into the curve of his body, tucking his knees into the backs of hers. He nuzzled the nape of her neck, and she made a sound somewhere between a grunt and a purr.

He slept.

A MONTH LATER

ANCHORAGE, AK (AP): Global Harvest Resources Inc. (GHRI), the world's second largest gold producer, announced today the results of supplementary exploratory drilling in the Suulutaq Mine during last summer's drilling season.

A clearly euphoric Bruce O'Malley, GHRI's chief executive officer, said that core samples taken by the five rigs working 17 new holes had still not discovered the limits of the Suulutaq deposits. O'Malley said that GHRI would be mobilizing two more drill rigs next year. "It's now the second largest mine of this type in the world," O'Malley said. "If we keep drilling, we might get to be the largest."

GHRI currently estimates that the Suulutaq ore deposit contains 42.6 billion pounds of copper, 39.6 million ounces of gold, and 2.7 billion pounds of molybdenum. The gold alone at current prices is estimated to be worth over $35 billion. GHRI is estimating that it will take $3 billion to $5 billion to develop the mine, and hundreds of millions of dollars to operate it.

"Global Harvest is in this for the long term," O'Malley said. "We'll see in the next five generations of Alaskans."

Suulutaq is located on state lands near the Iqaluk Wildlife Refuge and the headwaters of the Gruening River, one of the major tributaries of the Kanuyaq River, home of the world-renowned run of Kanuyaq River red salmon. The confluence of the two rivers is the calving grounds of the Gruening River caribou herd.

Significant opposition is developing among local residents, including fishermen, hunters, trappers, and some Alaska Natives who are concerned that by-products of the toxins used in the mining process will pollute the groundwaters that are the source of the Kanuyaq and irreparably harm salmon and other wildlife.

The Kanuyaq salmon fishery is currently valued at $110 million.